It's been twenty years since Nathen and Authia left Africa to live their lives and raise their son, Joshawa, in the mountains of British Columbia. Tammy, Hansen, and their daughter, Becca, join Nathen and his family. Together they build a home for their families and live in peace. However, their tranquil lives are threatened when they discover that the Ancestors of the Jelani Tribe are not finished with them. A battle for dominance over the Jelani people has woven its way into Nathen and Authia's world. Nathen and Authia stand to lose what they cherish most, and even their unique gifts cannot help them.

Legacy of the Lion People 1
Copyright © 2022 Christine Frances
ISBN: 978-1-4874-3554-7
Cover art by Martine Jardin

Published by eXtasy Books Inc

# Extasy
## BOOKS

Look for us online at:
www.eXtasybooks.com

# LEGACY OF THE LION PEOPLE 1
# LORD OF HIS PEOPLE 4

## BY

## CHRISTINE FRANCES

# DEDICATION

*I started writing one book, Lord of His People, with no aspirations that it would be anything more than one book. I had started this book years earlier but put it to one side to raise my children and run my business. I decided to bring the book out of mothballs and started working on it for no other reason than to prove to myself that I still possessed the talent and creativity to breathe life into my characters, to tell a story that would captivate my readers and leave them wanting one more chapter. Now, Lord of his People is a series, and four books later, I have accomplished so much more than what I set out to do.*

*My sister, Patrice, has played an integral part in the writing of my books. Her unwavering support and encouragement have given me the confidence to do what I love to do. Writing is my passion, and I wouldn't be where I am now without Patrice.*

*I also owe my success to Jay, my publisher's EIC of Devine Destinies. She believed in me and gave me the opportunity and the tools I needed to flourish. My editor, Laura McNellis, has taught me so much. Laura has played an essential part in my writing, and I can't thank her enough for spending the time to teach me how to become a better writer.*

# CHAPTER ONE

Burwood, British Columbia, Canada, September 2010

The giant redwood stood majestically before him. The evergreens and other redwoods paled in comparison next to one of the oldest redwoods in the forest. This was his sanctuary, a sanctuary he named Grot—fer lot, which, in the language of a people he would never meet, simply meant cavern. His father, Nathen, had his own sanctuary in a cavern chiseled deep inside a mountain that rose high above Burwood. However, that wasn't for Joshawa. He wanted nothing to do with his father and his safe places. Naming his sanctuary in the language of his people was Joshawa's way of tormenting his father.

Joshawa smiled as he gazed up at the substantial canopy of Grot. The branches of the tree swayed gently in the wind as if they were welcoming him. It was fall, and the leaves on the trees had changed their colors from greens to vibrant reds, oranges, and yellows. Grot was located north of his home and further up the mountain range. The air was much cooler here, but Joshawa took no notice. He had purposely left his jacket at home, confident in the knowledge that the arduous trek to Grot would keep him warm, and to be honest, he welcomed the cool air.

Joshawa's tree stood over two hundred and fifty feet high, and its girth at the base was at least twenty feet. The thick bark that encompassed his tree was scarred with long claw marks. At first glance, you would think they were made by a grizzly

1

marking his territory. But as you looked closer, you would find that the marks continued up the tree as far as you could see, too tall for even the largest of the grizzlies that made these mountains their home. Joshawa knew what caused these marks, and as he held his hands in front of him, all he could think of was that he was his father's son. Joshawa had wished many times that he would've inherited his mother's traits and that he would appear normal. He had her dark hair that fell in gentle waves to his shoulders and her deep brown eyes, but the rest of him was all Nathen.

Amy had been hiding behind a redwood tree for what seemed like hours. The tree's girth was not as wide as the stranger's tree, but still wide enough to conceal her. She was sitting on the ground, her back resting against her tree. She'd wrapped her arms around her bare legs and pulled them tight against her chest in an attempt to ward off the morning chill. She rested the right side of her head on her knees, which caused her long hair to fall across her face. That annoyed her, and with her right hand, she tucked her hair behind her ear, hoping that it would stay in place.

Amy closed her eyes and listened, patiently waiting for her stranger to arrive. She knew that he would come as he did most every morning, and she was prepared to suffer the chilled air for a chance to see him. Her reasoning was simple. Amy didn't understand what he was, and something deep inside her told her she needed to know. Her curiosity brought her to this place every morning.

As she waited for him to appear, she would always ask herself — *is he like me, or is he more like the animals that roam these woods?* Amy had barely pondered her question for a moment when she heard a noise coming from the direction of his tree.

She sat up straight, and her back pressed firmly against her tree with her knees still bent toward her chest. Then ever so carefully, she peered around her tree.

He stood at the base of his tree, staring up into the branches. From Amy's vantage point, she could see him clearly. He appeared so much taller than she was. His body was very muscular, with biceps and thighs that were more developed than any other animal she'd ever seen. He wore a white shirt that was completely open, revealing his broad chest and narrow waist. Amy marveled at the muscles on his stomach that were incredibly pronounced. She sat back against her tree and lifted her shirt to reveal her stomach, which was flat and smooth. Amy lowered her shirt and peered back around the tree.

She continued to watch the stranger that had crept into her dreams and into almost all her thoughts. His shirt sleeves were missing, and the pants he wore were so tight that she wondered if he could actually get them off. That was where the similarities to her ended.

The rest of his appearance caused her to question his lineage. His face was slightly longer than hers, his cheekbones were more prominent, the bridge of his nose was wide, and there was a cleft in the middle of his upper lip. His hands were covered in a fine layer of hair, his fingernails were long, and after what she had witnessed so many times, she could only guess that they were very strong.

Amy sat as quiet as a mouse as she watched and wondered.


Joshawa scanned the woods that surrounded him. He wondered if Africa was as beautiful as his woods and if it smelled as clean and crisp. He thought of the animals that roamed the jungle, and he was jealous that those animals could call Africa their home. He knew that he appeared very much like the majestic lion, just like his father, just like the people that lived in the village that his mother and father left behind. It was a decision his father had made, and it was a decision that Joshawa would never forgive him for.

Joshawa gave his head a shake, then using his claw-like fingernails, he scaled the tree to the very top.


Nathen sat on the swing that hung from the front porch of the log cabin that he and his family called home. He wore his jeans and a long-sleeve shirt to ward off the morning chill. As he gently rocked the swing, he allowed his gaze to wander, taking in all that surrounded him. The front porch was open and ran the entire width of the nine hundred and fifty square foot cabin. The area around the cabin was very well kept, with dozens of wildflowers and flowering bushes carefully arranged in among small rock gardens.

For decades, their cabin had stood alone and mostly uninhabited until late 1990, when Nathen and Authia moved in. However, when they returned from their trip to Africa, they built a second log cabin so their friends could remain close. Hansen and Tammy's cabin was built at the edge of the yard directly across from Nathen and Authia's cabin. Tammy had initially wanted the cabin to face south, but that entailed taking down an extremely old redwood tree. The tree held special memories for both Nathen and Authia. The tree would remain standing, and the cabin was built far enough away so that it wouldn't endanger the tree in any way.

Nathen continued to scan his yard until his focus fell on that very redwood tree. At that point, he just stared off into the forest as if he were looking at a blank canvas. His eyes may have been unresponsive. However, his mind was filled with thoughts of his son and their relationship.

In Nathen's point of view, it was a relationship hanging by a thread. Joshawa had turned nineteen only a couple of months earlier. Even though it should have been a joyous occasion, Joshawa was unhappy. Not that Nathen could blame him, because he'd felt the same way at his age—the fear of never knowing love or never hearing the cries of his own children, that no woman would ever look upon him as anything but a freak.

"You always overthink." Nathen glanced over as Authia sat next to him, handing him a mug of steaming coffee. To Nathen, Authia was the personification of beauty. Even after all these years, she could still excite him with a simple smile. Her dark brown hair was just beginning to show signs of gray, and her brown eyes sparkled as she spoke. Her tanned complexion was flawless, and she had the most enticing figure. She was wearing an oversized gray sweater, a pair of blue jeans that complimented her figure, and her favorite dark blue sneakers. "He'll be fine. He's just going through a phase like any other boy who finds himself turning into a man."

Nathen returned his gaze to the forest. "He's not *like* any other boy, or man for that matter." He took a sip of his coffee then turned to face Authia. "I know exactly what he's going through. I lived it myself. I'm beginning to believe that we shouldn't have told him about Africa, about the Jelani Tribe."

Authia's expression was that of disbelief. "How can you say that? You spent the first twenty-nine years of your life wondering who you were, wondering what you were. How can you deny your son that knowledge?"

Nathen closed his eyes as he rested his head against the back of the swing. At least he'd had the opportunity to live in both worlds. When he decided to return to Burwood, he'd known firsthand what both worlds had to offer. His decision was sound, and he didn't regret it. His only hope was to convince Joshawa to open his heart to Burwood. Only then would Joshawa know why his home was at Burwood and not with the Jelani Tribe.

Joshawa sat on the highest branch of Grot. The branch was so wide that he could barely straddle it. He surveyed his domain — a place untouched by civilization. The redwoods were rich in color, and the morning dew that blanketed the evergreens sparkled in the sun. Other than himself, only the creatures of the forest roamed these grounds. It was located so far north that even the inhabitants of Burwood didn't venture here — a fact that Joshawa was incredibly pleased with. This place was his and his alone. The animals of the forest didn't judge him. They didn't whisper behind his back. Joshawa's smile turned to sadness. Was his mother right? Was it only his imagination that Burwood judged him? He was aware that they watched him, even to the point of staring at him.

Deep down, Joshawa believed they were laughing at him. That they considered him to be a freak of nature. As far as Joshawa was concerned, his mother honestly didn't understand. Her features were normal, and she didn't have to suffer the scrutiny of others.

Joshawa stood and was about to climb down when something caught his attention. He was over two hundred feet off the ground, but still, he could see the floor of the forest as clearly as if he were only five feet away. He wasn't sure of what he was witnessing. It moved like an animal hiding from whatever it was being hunted by. But it didn't appear to be an animal itself. It stood on its hind legs as it moved with the agility of a monkey.

Curiosity got the better of Joshawa, and he descended down the tree as he'd done a hundred times before.

After reaching the ground, he knelt on one knee and examined the ground before him. The moss grew thick and lush, the pine needles and pinecones littered the ground, and the leaves from the trees had started to fall. All these conditions made it perfect for him to track whatever it was he saw.

But what Joshawa found were not the tracks of a forest animal, but rather that of a human. They were small, child-like bare footprints leading further up the mountain range that towered high above the forest. He followed the tracks for only a few minutes, and then they disappeared as if the person had just vanished. He slowly turned as he studied the forest around him. However, there were no obvious signs that he was not alone.

Then something deep inside of him told him to look up. There, in the trees, he could have sworn he saw movement. He started to head toward one of the trees, not taking his focus off the canopy, but then thought better of it. No, if he was going to discover who or what this was, he would have to be smarter than his prey.

He turned and started to head home, knowing that he would come back tomorrow, sit in his tree, and wait. Then he intended to follow whatever it was he'd seen, only this time he would keep to the trees, out of sight. Joshawa smiled at the prospect of playing a hide-and-go-seek game. He ran toward his home, and with his powerful legs, he'd made the distance in less than half the time it would have taken an ordinary man.

Hansen stood on the porch of his cabin observing Nathen and Authia. He'd seen Joshawa leave earlier in the morning, and judging from Nathen's expression, Joshawa hadn't returned. Hansen felt for his friend because he was sure that loving a child who blamed you for his very existence wasn't easy. Hansen and Nathen had become good friends on the first night they'd met. Nathen was over six feet tall, and he had golden-red hair that fell in waves to his shoulders. His facial features and hands were identical to that of his son. He was an imposing man with massive biceps and thighs similar to tree trunks. But Nathen, the man, was kind, compassionate, caring, and the best friend a person could ask for.

As Hansen stood watching his friend, he compared himself to Nathen. He felt small next to Nathen, being a good four inches shorter and possibly fifty pounds lighter. However, even at one hundred and eighty pounds, Hansen knew every ounce was pure muscle, and he could handle himself in most physical altercations. He was proud of the fact that at fifty years old, he was in amazingly great shape.

His black hair showed no signs of gray, and his brown eyes were sharp and clear. His wardrobe was simple, consisting of only jeans and t-shirts.

Hansen reached down and picked up the ax that was resting against the cabin wall. He swung it onto his right shoulder, then walked down the porch steps and into the yard. He smiled as he approached Nathen. "That winter firewood isn't going to cut itself. You helping, or not?"

Hansen didn't wait for a response. He just laughed as he headed to the back of the cabin where the stockpile of wood was waiting for them.

A few minutes later, Nathen joined Hansen. Leaning against the woodpile were two axes — one for him and one for his son. As he retrieved his ax, he glanced over to Joshawa's. A profound sense of sadness washed over him. He loved his son dearly, and he was afraid of losing him. He turned to face Hansen, who was placing a log on one of the three chopping blocks. "Joshawa should be here with us, not gallivanting in the forest."

"No worries. I'll just let you work twice as hard." Hansen laughed as he imbedded the blade of his ax into the log, effectively splitting it in half.

"Seriously, Hansen, he should be here helping."

Hansen embedded the ax into another log then turned to face Nathen. "Look, Nathen. He's a good boy. He's just going through a lot of shit right now. He's got a lot to come to terms with. Give him time."

Nathen sighed. "That's what Authia keeps telling me. I'm just afraid that with each passing day, we grow further apart." Nathen wasn't expecting, or for that matter, wanting, a response. He just placed a log on the chopping block, and not another word was said as he and Hansen worked at creating a dent in the massive pile of wood.

Joshawa slowed his pace from a full-out run to a controlled walk as he entered the yard to his home. He stopped next to a redwood tree and gazed at Hansen's cabin. In the background, he could hear the chopping sounds of wood being split, but that wasn't what captured his attention.

The sweet aroma of freshly baked pies filled the air, which meant that Becca was sure to be home. Becca was Hansen and Tammy's only child, and she held a special place in Joshawa's heart. She was only a year younger than he was, and to Joshawa, she was the most beautiful girl that he'd ever met. Becca was five and a half feet tall and had an hourglass figure. She had honey-blonde hair and the most dazzling smile. But the best part was that she looked upon him as if he were normal. She cared about him, and deep down, Joshawa hoped that just maybe she even loved him.

He snickered to himself. *I'm such a love-sick fool.* But it didn't matter how high the odds were against her ever truly loving him. All he could think about was her, and he would continue to court her, in his own way, until she told him to stop.

As Joshawa headed toward her cabin, he drew a deep breath then slowly let it out. He hadn't taken three steps when his mother's thoughts filled his mind. She and his father could meld minds just like he could. His father possessed the ability to feel other people's emotions, a gift that he passed on to Joshawa. However, his mother was so much more. She could see the past and future of a person with just a simple touch. She could hold an item in her hand and tell you who it belonged to, and that just scratched the surface of her gifts — gifts that Joshawa was in complete awe of. Unfortunately, the melding could prove to be a bit of a nuisance.

*And where do you think you're going?*

Joshawa turned to face his cabin. *Just going to see Becca.*

*I don't think so, young man. She's most likely doing her chores as you should be. Your father and your uncle are chopping wood. I'm sure they would appreciate your help.*

Joshawa rolled his eyes as he sighed. *Really? I wanted to go see Becca.*

*It wasn't a suggestion.*

Joshawa looked back over his shoulder at Becca's cabin, then returned his gaze toward his own cabin. The tone of his response was that of defeat. *All right, I'll go.*

*Joshawa, you should want to. Your father has done a lot for you. He loves you. Can't you see that?*

*I'll go chop wood, but only because you've asked me to. All my father has done for me is to imprison me in a world that I don't belong in.* The conversation was over, and Joshawa went to help chop wood.

There would be a fall celebration in Burwood today, and everybody contributed to the evening feast. Becca's family contribution would be freshly baked pies. The scent of the freshly baked fruit wafted throughout the small cabin and into the yard. Becca's hands were covered in flour as she helped her mother prepare the pie crusts. Becca's hair was tied back into a ponytail, and she was wearing a bib-apron that covered her from the neckline of her t-shirt to just above her knees. She managed to keep the bottom half of her jeans free of flour. However, the short sleeves of her light blue t-shirt and her bare arms revealed traces of the white powder.

As Becca placed a pie on the windowsill to cool, she noticed Joshawa heading toward her cabin. She smiled and was about to call out to him when he suddenly turned. He stopped for just a moment, glanced back in her direction, then headed back toward his cabin. Becca was disappointed as she watched Joshawa until he disappeared behind his cabin.

She turned and went to retrieve another pie. "I just saw Joshawa. He started to head here, but then changed his mind."

Using the back of her right hand, Tammy wiped the flour that had sprayed up, covering the right side of her face. "He has wood to chop. Something I'm sure your aunt reminded him of."

Becca just shrugged her shoulders, then placed another pie on the windowsill. As she turned to face her mother, she laughed. "How do you manage to have more flour on you than you do the pie dough?"

Tammy's blonde hair was also tied up into a ponytail, and she also wore a bib-apron which covered her black tank top and blue jeans. However, unlike Becca, she was covered head to toe in flour. Tammy looked up from her pie crust, giving her a sarcastic look. "It's not my fault if the flour has a mind of its own. But now that you mentioned it, you can finish. I'm going to go clean up." Tammy rubbed her hands over the table in what appeared to be a futile attempt to remove the flour that caked both hands. Then she removed her bibbed apron and headed toward the bathroom.

Authia brought a chocolate cheesecake to Tammy and

Hansen's cabin. She'd spent the previous day baking apple, pumpkin, and chocolate cheesecakes. When Authia entered, she observed Becca placing two pies in the wood-fueled oven. "Good morning, Becca. I thought we would do a little taste testing." She placed the cheesecake on the kitchen table then looked around the cabin. "Where's your mom?"

"She's cleaning up. It's going to take a while. She has more flour on her than the pies do."

Authia smiled at Becca. "You have the same sense of humor as your mom. You're so much like her." Authia walked over to Becca and wrapped her arms around her. However, it wasn't the hug she expected. A series of visions bombarded her.

She could feel the dampness of the cave. She could smell the mustiness that hung in the air. As a figure approached her, his laughter resonated off the cave walls. The sound of his laughter sent shivers down her spine. She tried to concentrate, to see the face of the man that taunted her, but her vision wouldn't allow it. He came closer, his words echoing in her mind.

*You freak, I will have you mounted on my wall!*

His pace quickened, and when he reached Authia, he passed right through her. In her vision, Authia spun around only to find that the man was gone. Another voice filled her mind, pleading with her to save him. Her vision faded from view, but not before she witnessed her son lying on the cold dirt floor of the cave, contorting in pain.

# CHAPTER TWO

Dameon shifted his weight ever so slightly. Even though he was perched sixty feet off the ground, concealed in the canopy of a young redwood tree, he didn't want to take the chance of spooking his prey. He was sitting on a large branch with his legs dangling over the sides while he rested his back against the trunk of the tree. He chose this branch because he knew it would easily support his five-foot eleven-inch, one-hundred-and-ninety-pound frame.

Before he left his camp, he'd dressed entirely in the same style of camouflage that hunters would wear. He'd painted his face in browns and greens and wore a black skull cap that completely covered his blond hair. He was aware of the fact that his deep blue eyes stood out against his painted skin, and he would usually wear dark contacts to conceal himself further. But that wasn't necessary for this particular hunt.

His weapon of choice was a compound bow with arrows, and they were secured to the branch directly in front of him. Once again, he raised his binoculars, increasing the magnification until the large Kodiak grizzly came into view. His partner Jax and he had been following this bear since late June. They'd found their prize north of their current location, higher up in the mountains. They knew this was the bear their client wanted, so they tagged it with an electronic tracker paired to their GPS.

The bear was incredibly territorial and wasn't venturing far from its comfort zone. So Dameon and Jax settled in, waiting while the bear gorged itself for its long winter hibernation.

The bear fed for most of the morning, and it had found a secluded place to sleep for the afternoon. The bear would wake up late in the afternoon and feed until he went to sleep for the night.

Dameon smiled to himself as he lowered the binoculars, placing them carefully on the branch in front of him. The bear was worth its weight in gold to him, which meant that this would be his last hunt. He could retire with the money they would make on this bear, combined with the previous few hunts. Not bad for someone who was only forty-five years old.

Dameon rested his head against the tree trunk, closed his eyes, and thought of the events that had led him to this last hunt. He and his partner, Jax, were hunters for hire. They grew up together in southern Manitoba, and at an early age, they started to hunt together. First it was deer, caribou, bear, and moose. They hunted for food, and they hunted legally. But as they got older, the hunt no longer challenged them, and they sought out larger, more dangerous prey. The high they experienced as they killed their prey was not unlike that of a drug addict shooting up a syringe of cocaine. Like an addict, they continued to take on more dangerous prey to experience that high over and over again.

Dameon and Jax traveled the world hunting any animal they were legally allowed to hunt. Their reputation grew worldwide, and soon the wealthy and privileged sought them out. They were offered large sums of money to hunt animals that were endangered or protected by law. And they accepted, hunting everything and anything, legal or not, as long as the price was right. Their current client had his own private zoo on an island he owned somewhere in the vicinity of Fiji. They didn't know with any certainty the actual location, and that suited them just fine.

Dameon and Jax were responsible for supplying the bulk

of their client's collection. And not one animal that they were hired to deliver was legal. This bear was going to be the client's crowning glory. The client was a fanatic about bears and had every bear imaginable. Now he wanted one last bear to complete his collection. He wanted a grizzly, and not just any grizzly. He wanted a Kodiak, male and big. He was offering a bonus of fifty thousand dollars for every hundred pounds over the promised eight hundred. Another smile graced Dameon's lips, for this bear was easily pushing a thousand pounds.

Nathen swung his ax and sliced the large log in two as if he were breaking a twig in one fluid motion. He placed another log on the splitting block and glanced over to his son. Joshawa stopped his swing in midair then turned his attention to his father. He continued to stare at Nathen with a look of contempt while he embedded his ax into the log.

"What?"

Nathen placed his ax against the splitting log and walked over to Joshawa. "I don't want to fight."

"Then leave me alone and let me . . ." Joshawa's voice trailed off, and both he and Nathen stared at each other.

Nathen could feel Authia's anguish, and by the look on Joshawa's face, so could he. They could feel her pain as if it were their own. Without saying a word, Nathen bolted for Hansen and Tammy's cabin, with Joshawa close behind.

Becca smiled, eyeing the cheesecake as she placed her arms around her aunt. But just as she was about to hug her, Authia started shaking. Becca pulled her away and gazed upon her aunt in shock at what was transpiring in front of her. Her aunt's eyes were open as wide as they possibly could be, tears were streaming down her cheeks, and she appeared as if she'd witnessed something horrific.

"Aunty, what's wrong?" Becca continued to hold Authia as she slowly crumpled to the floor. Becca sat next to her, holding Authia tightly against her chest as she yelled out to her mom. "Mom! Mom! I need you!"

Tammy came running out of the bathroom, wrapping her pink knee-length housecoat around her. "What's wrong?"

Becca, full of concern, didn't take her focus off Authia. "I don't know. She hugged me, then she became really upset and would have dropped to the floor if I weren't holding her."

Tammy sat on the floor next to Authia. "Give her to me, Becca. You go get your Uncle Nathen." In the time it took Tammy to wrap her arms around Authia, the cabin door burst open, and Nathen rushed to Authia's side.

Authia could feel Nathen as he wrapped his arms around her. She couldn't stop trembling, and the fear that resonated from her very core was more terrifying than anything she'd felt before. She gazed up at Nathen, who looked upon her in anguish.

"What happened, my love?"

Authia watched as Joshawa joined his father, kneeling close to her. He gently placed his hand on her shoulder. "Mother, what's wrong? What happened?"

Authia pulled herself away from Nathen's embrace and wrapped her arms around her son's neck. She drew him close, not wanting to let go. She held on so tight that Joshawa had to place his hands on her arms and gently pull her away.

"Mother, you're choking me."

Authia removed her arms and placed her hands on either side of Joshawa's face. "Were you in a cave this morning?"

Joshawa appeared puzzled at his mother's question. "A

cave? No. Why do you ask?"

"Have you ever been in a cave that your father or I don't know about?"

"No. I've never been in a cave. What's going on?"

"You must never enter a cave of any kind." Authia glanced over to Nathen. "That includes your cavern as well." She focused her attention on Joshawa and looked upon him scared and concerned. "Promise me that you will never enter a cave."

Joshawa's expression was that of complete bewilderment. "Of course. Are you going to tell me why?"

Authia lowered her hands, taking Joshawa's hands in hers. How much should she tell him? How much should she reveal to either Joshawa or Nathen? She glanced over to Nathen, then back to Joshawa. Authia knew she had no options. She needed to protect her son.

"I had a vision. When I hugged Becca, I was given a vision of the future. Your future, Joshawa." Authia paused as she thought of what she'd just said. Slowly she turned to face Becca, letting go of Joshawa's hands as she did.

Authia suddenly realized that she received the vision of Joshawa's future through Becca and not Joshawa himself. How could that happen? She glanced over to Nathen, and by the look on his face, she knew he was thinking the same thing. She returned her gaze to Becca. "Have you been in any caves?"

"No. Never. Why are caves so important?"

"The question should be, why did I receive the vision by hugging you? To be a conduit, you would've been present when the vision occurred. But I didn't see you or feel your presence."

Nathen tenderly took Authia's right hand in his, which caused Authia to turn her attention to him.

"What exactly did you see?"

Authia took a deep breath. "A man who I didn't know, though something about him seemed familiar. The sound of his voice and what he was saying gave me shivers. But that wasn't what scared me." She turned to face Joshawa, her tears running freely down her cheeks. "I saw you lying on the cave floor. You were in pain, and you were pleading with me to save you."

Dameon had been perched in the tree for hours. The rumbling of his stomach told him that it was getting close to lunchtime. The bear hadn't budged and wouldn't for another couple of hours. He raised his arms above his head in an attempt to stretch out his back and neck. As he linked his fingers together and stretched his arms in front of him, he felt something hit his left leg. He glanced down to find Jax standing at the base of the tree.

Dameon nodded at Jax, then unfastened his bow and arrows from the branch. He secured them to a rope that he'd tied to the branch when he first arrived. He then proceeded to lower the bow and arrows to Jax slowly. As soon as Jax had them, Dameon placed the binoculars in the pouch attached at his waist and headed down the tree.

"You move like an old lady."

Dameon jumped the last five feet to the ground, landing directly in front of Jax. Jax was also dressed in camouflage with his face painted. However, his hair was as dark as night, so he had no reason to cover it. Jax stood three inches taller than Dameon and outweighed him by twenty pounds. Jax offered Dameon a canteen of water which he gladly accepted. As he handed it back, he smiled at Jax. "You sit in the tree for hours on end and see how you move."

"Would be better than you. How's our prize?"

"He's pretty much settled in for the afternoon. His den has

to be close."

"I agree. For the entire time we've been watching him, he hasn't ventured very far." Jax glanced back in the direction of the bear. "I know we're pretty much isolated up here, but I still want to keep a close watch on him." He returned his gaze to Dameon. "He's worth too much, and we have too much invested to take any chances."

"How long do you want to keep watching him?"

"He could easily put on another hundred pounds before he's ready to hibernate. That's another fifty thousand in our pocket."

Dameon knew Jax was right. But he also knew that with them being so high up in the mountains, the weather could change from one hour to the next. "We don't have any cold-weather gear, and I don't want to be caught up here in tents when it dips below freezing. Let's bag him now, collect our bounty and call it a day."

Jax's humorous expression turned to that of disapproval. "You losing your edge? Since when do you walk away from fifty thousand dollars? We're staying. Besides, we may not have to be confined to a tent."

"What are you talking about?"

"I was scouting to the south and came across an old homestead. Looks like it's been abandoned for years. There's two buildings and an outhouse. Haven't checked out the buildings yet, but they might be able to provide the shelter we need. So no more talk about ending this hunt. The hunt ends when I say it ends. Get your gear, and we'll scope this place out."

Dameon walked over to a patch of low-lying shrubs and retrieved his backpack from underneath. He placed it on his back, then turned to face Jax. Jax's persona was changing and had been ever since the rhino hunt in Java three years earlier.

A ranger had the misfortune of running into them while

they were crating the rhino. Jax didn't even hesitate. He calmly walked up to the ranger and plunged his hunting knife into the ranger's belly. Then he dumped the ranger's body in an estuary to be eaten by the crocodiles that lived there. That was the beginning, and ever since that first human kill, Jax did everything in his power to have an opportunity to kill again. He purposely put their hunt in an area where they had a good chance of being discovered. Thankfully, the opportunity hadn't presented itself since Jax killed the ranger. Killing animals did nothing for him anymore. Dameon feared that Jax would soon hunt people in his desperate search for the ultimate high.

Amy sat cross-legged in her cave, warming herself in front of the small fire she'd made. She held her soiled hands close to the flames finding comfort in the warmth. Her earlier romp in the forest had chilled her to her very core. It didn't help that she only wore shorts that were too small for her, barely covering her buttocks. The tank top she wore was made of satin and resembled a camisole. It had been a lovely shade of peach at one time, but now it was soiled and stained. Unlike the shorts, the camisole was too big for her tiny frame. Her hair fell to her slim waist, and she knew her eyes revealed the emptiness that she felt. She hadn't spoken to another person since she'd been left alone in the cave she now called home. All she knew, all she could remember, was that she was to be as quiet as a mouse. That there was an evil waiting for her in the forest—an evil that would hurt her. She was to remain in the cave and wait for the return of the man who'd left her there.

Nathen sat at the edge of his bed, watching as Authia slept. She was on her side with her back facing Nathen. Authia seemed so peaceful, as if she was unaware of the events that transpired not two hours earlier. Gently, he ran his hand along her face, then pulled the duvet over her bare shoulder. Authia had decided to change before she went to bed and was now wearing a white tank top and a pair of black sweats.

Ever since Authia had been a part of Nathen's life, she'd experienced many visions. Still, none had affected her as significantly as this one. Nathen harbored no doubt that his son was in danger. But would protecting him be as simple as keeping him from entering a cave? Nathen was distracted from his thoughts as Joshawa entered the room. He'd changed his shirt and now wore a dark blue hoodie. Nathen watched as his son made his way over to the bed and gazed down at his mother.

"Is she okay? What was that all about?"

"She's fine. She just needs her rest." Nathen glanced over to Joshawa. "Your secret place. Are you sure there are no caves?"

Joshawa glared at Nathen. "There are no caves. How many times do I have to say it?"

"Why don't you take me there? Maybe there's a cave that you don't know about. Together we could find it."

Joshawa shook his head in disbelief. "I'm not a child. That is my place, and I don't want you anywhere near it." Joshawa turned to leave but seemed to change his mind as he put his hand on the doorknob. Keeping his back to Nathen, he made one last parting comment. "There's no together for us. There's no forgiveness for what you did to me."

"Joshawa, what I did, the decision I made, was for the best. I wish you could see that."

Slowly Joshawa turned to face Nathen. "You've sentenced me to a life of loneliness." He raised his right hand, gesturing to his face. "This will never be accepted. You know that. You lived it. And after everything you went through, you still brought me here. I belong in Africa. I belong with my people."

Before Nathen could respond, the temperature of the room dropped drastically. Nathen could see his breath as it hung in the air. Joshawa stood shivering before him. Nathen stood from the bed, and both men scrutinized the room, not knowing what they were looking for. Nathen glanced down at Authia and discovered that she was no longer lying on her side but instead was now on her back. Her eyes were wide open, the duvet had been pulled down to her hips, and she was covered in a layer of frost. Her face was pale, and her lips were blue.

Slowly Authia moved her head to the side, staring at Nathen and Joshawa. In a female voice that was not hers, Authia spoke. "My Lord, it is time."

Nathen cautiously approached the side of the bed. There was something about the voice. Something familiar. "Time for what?"

"Time to meet your destiny. Time to learn who you are."

"I know who I am. I have met my destiny."

"I am not speaking to you, my Lord Nathen." Authia closed her eyes, her head fell limp against the bed, and as Nathen approached her, the smell of incense filled the room.

# CHAPTER THREE

Jax and Dameon made their way into the clearing of the small homestead. The forest was doing its best to reclaim the land, as trees and evergreens of varying sizes grew among the tall grass. It was apparent that nobody had been at the homestead for an exceedingly long time. There were two log cabins and a small outhouse situated in an area that had not yet surrendered to the forest. For reasons he didn't understand, Jax was drawn to the smaller of the two cabins. There was only one door in the center of the wall facing him, and after a quick check of the rest of the walls, he discovered that there were no windows.

The cabin was built on the ground, and surprisingly the bottom logs were still intact. Moss and vines grew on the sides of the cabin and continued up onto the roof. Jax put his backpack on the ground a few feet from the door and retrieved his flashlight. When he approached the door, he realized that there wasn't a doorknob. Instead, there was a small hole bored into the door approximately twelve inches higher than where you'd expect a doorknob to be. Sticking ten inches out of the hole was a thick rope with a knot tied at the end.

Jax glanced over his shoulder at Dameon, who was staring into the forest at the edge of the property. He called out to Dameon, raising his voice so he could be heard. "You see something?"

Dameon slowly shook his head as he turned to face Jax. "You won't believe this, but there's a dugout filled with bones not ten feet from the property."

"Bones? Animal bones?"

Dameon approached Jax, placing his backpack next to Jax's. "God, I hope so." He retrieved his flashlight and motioned toward the door. "Shall we?"

Jax pulled on the rope, and the door swung outward, creaking on its hinges. Jax and Dameon entered the cabin, and the first thing that hit them was the powerful odor of mustiness and death. Using their flashlights, they surveyed the fourteen by fourteen-foot room. The floor of the cabin was comprised entirely of dirt. Mushrooms and moss grew wherever they could take root. There was a crudely built wooden table in the middle of the room. It stood waist high and was approximately three feet wide and five feet long. The skeleton remains of two, possibly three, small animals were on the table.

The odor that emanated from the table was vile. Jax shone his flashlight on the walls of the cabin. The wall to his left was covered entirely with dozens of animal traps, all hanging from large nails protruding from the wall. The traps appeared to be homemade and were of varying sizes. Judging from the degree of rust that coated the traps, no one had used them for decades.

An old wooden cabinet stood four feet high and three feet wide and was placed against the wall directly across from him. It also appeared homemade and contained four drawers that were the length of the cabinet. Stacked on either side of the cabinet were live trap cages of varying sizes. They completely covered the seven-foot-high wall, floor to ceiling.

Jax walked over to the cabinet and cautiously opened the top drawer. What he discovered sent chills down his spine, however, not in a bad way. "Dameon, you got to see this."

Dameon joined Jax shining his flashlight on the tools contained in the drawer. "What the hell? These are surgical tools." Dameon shone his flashlight on the wall covered in animal traps, then returned his attention to the open drawer. "What would a trapper be doing with surgical tools?"

Jax didn't answer. Instead, he opened the remaining drawers one by one only to find some very intricate handmade tools that only had one purpose. "He was dissecting, possibly even torturing the animals he caught." The prospect of torturing an animal excited Jax, not that he would share his excitement with Dameon.

"Are you sure? Maybe he was a taxidermist?"

Jax looked over at Dameon with an *are you crazy* look on his face. "Really? Look at these traps. They're all made to either maim or capture their victims alive. These aren't the tools of a taxidermist. They're the tools of one sick individual. And he wasn't a trapper in the true sense of the word. He didn't trap animals to make a living. I bet you anything that he was trapping to feed himself and to do whatever he was doing in this room. Judging from the traps hanging on that wall, he was going after animals as small as squirrels up to friggin bears."

"What do you think happened to him?"

Jax slowly closed the drawers as he scanned the room. "Mother Nature's a bitch. And so is payback. He's probably dead somewhere in the forest. Attacked by one of the animals he hunted. One thing's for sure. He hasn't been here for a while."

"I agree, and thank God for that. He's one asshole that I wouldn't want to run into. Enough of this place. Let's go check out the other cabin. Hopefully, it's more inviting cause I sure in hell ain't staying in this one."

Jax thought he'd tease Dameon and see what reaction he would get. "Or just maybe Mother Nature has nothing to do with it, and we'll find our trapper in the larger cabin."

Dameon whirled around and shone his flashlight in Jax's face. Jax raised his right hand in front of his eyes to deflect the light, and at the same time, he laughed. The look on Dameon's face was priceless. "I was only kidding. You need to relax a little more."

"Not in this place, I don't." Dameon turned and headed for the door.

As Jax was about to leave, he shone his flashlight on the last wall of the room. It was plastered with black and white photographs, the kind that you would take with a polaroid camera. They were graphic photographs of slaughtered animals in varying stages of dissection. In some of them, he could easily tell that the animals were still alive while being cut open. Jax smiled as he scanned one picture after the next. There were times when he wanted to watch as an animal suffered in pain before it succumbed to death. But Dameon would always put the animal out of its misery, depriving Jax of his fun.

He continued to scan the pictures, and on the far right of the wall was a section of photographs that were not of an animal but rather a woman. They were all headshots from her shoulders up. And even though the pictures were in black and white, you could still see the bruises. You could see the anguish in her eyes. Jax smiled because, at that very moment, he understood the person who took the pictures. Animals weren't enough. No matter what he did to them, no matter how challenging the hunt or kill was, it was nothing compared to the thrill that came from taking the life of a human being. Jax tapped his flashlight against one of the pictures of the woman. This was his destiny. He was meant to find this place. Cautiously he checked the room to make sure Dameon had left. Then he quickly ripped down the dozen or so pictures of the woman and shoved them into his vest pocket.

Authia sat at the kitchen table wrapped in a blanket in the hope of warming her body. She was ice cold right down to her bones. Joshawa had made her some hot tea, which she was so grateful for. Eagerly, she wrapped her hands around the mug to warm them. Nathen and Joshawa sat quietly at the table and waited for Authia to start the conversation. Her thoughts were chaotic, and she wasn't particularly in the mood for conversation. Instead, Authia focused her thoughts on the memories of when she and her mother first moved here. She and Nathen had lived under this roof for over eighteen years, and now it was all starting again.

A small smile graced her lips as she allowed her gaze to roam the room. It hadn't changed in over twenty years. There was only one large room that served as the living area and the kitchen and eating area. Three doors were located on the east wall that led to two bedrooms and a bathroom. The kitchen counter ran the entire length of the north wall except for a doorway on the far right. There was a small wood stove, fridge, and sink along the same wall.

Authia smirked to herself as she remembered the first time she tried to cook on the woodstove. Not a complete disaster, but it was challenging. She loved the pine cabinets mainly because they were designed with no doors, which gave the cabin the appearance of being larger than it was.

In the middle of the kitchen was the old wooden table that she was sitting at. However, her favorite spot was an old oversized armchair that she spent countless hours curled up in. She would either read or spend her time enjoying the fire that burned freely in the massive stone fireplace.

Authia glanced back over to Nathen and Joshawa. It was time for a reality check. Something very wrong happened, and they would have to discover who or what was behind it. She directed her question to Nathen. "What happened? Why am I freezing?"

"What do you remember?"

"Other than being very cold, I don't remember anything. I

went to sleep. I could feel the cold, but I couldn't wake up. It was as if I didn't have control of my own body."

"Do you remember speaking?"

Authia shot Nathen and Joshawa a puzzled look. "I was speaking? What was I saying?" Without realizing what she was doing, Authia placed her right hand on her chest just over her left breast. Gently she pressed on it, grimacing in pain as she did.

Nathen was quick to react. "What are you doing, Authia?"

"Oh, nothing. It hurts." Authia saw Nathen's eyes go wide. "No, not a heart attack hurt. More of a burning pain."

Nathen reached over and gently pushed the blanket off Authia's left shoulder. The strap of Authia's tank top covered most of her blue tattoo, so Nathen maneuvered the strap of her tank top down the side of her left arm so they could see the entire tattoo. The tattoo's outline was raised as if it had just been done, and the blue was much more prominent. Authia glanced down at it, then back up at Nathen. "It's never done that before. Not even when I first got it."

"Why did you get the tattoo, Mother?"

"That's a story for another time."

"You've been saying that for years. Are you ever going to tell me?"

"Maybe when I'm ready. So, Nathen, what did I say?"

"You looked at Joshawa and me and said, My Lord, it is time."

"Time? Time for what?"

"That's what I said. And you replied that it was time to meet my destiny, time to learn who I was."

"Why would I say that? We've already gone down that road."

"Actually, Mother, I think you were referring to me. At least you said you weren't speaking to Father. And I was the only other person in the room."

Nathen interjected. "There's something else. Before you fainted, I could *definitely* smell *incense*."

Authia's eyes went wide, and her mouth gaped open. She couldn't believe what she was hearing. "That's impossible. She's dead. Not to mention that when she was alive, she was a world away."

"She's not really dead, my love. Her spirit lives on with the Ancestors that watch over the tribe. And in the beginning, when she was a spirit determined to see me die, she wreaked havoc here, under this very roof."

"But she's not that person anymore. I don't understand."

"You're referring to Serena, right, Mother?"

"Yes, I am. And if she's here, then there has to be something terribly wrong."


Becca was sitting at the kitchen table with her mother and father. She'd removed her bib-apron and put on a clean tee-shirt and jeans. A slice of her aunt's cheesecake was sitting on a plate in front of her. She had no appetite and just stared at the cake as she poked at it with her fork.

All Becca could think about was her aunt and the look her aunt gave her when she inquired about the cave. It was as if she blamed her for what had happened to Joshawa. As if she had something to do with Joshawa's pain.

She glanced back up at her mother and father. Becca could clearly tell that they were anxious, especially her mother. She pushed her plate away and rested her arms on the table. "It's been a while. Can I go over now?"

Tammy sighed as she reached over and placed her hands over Becca's. "I'm sure either Nathen or Joshawa will come to get us when your aunt is ready for company."

Becca glanced up at the clock situated on the wall behind the couch. "It's after one. Are we still taking the pies to

Burwood?"

Tammy nodded her head in agreement. "Yes, we should."
She glanced over to Hansen. "I'm going to go see if Authia
needs any medical attention. You take Becca to Burwood with
the pies and let Charles know what's going on."

Charles was Authia's father, the founder of Burwood, and
the man who'd saved Tammy from herself. When she was
young and a nurse living in Vancouver, she was heavily ad-
dicted to alcohol and drugs. Charles welcomed her into Burwood, and between him and Nathen, she was able to heal her
emotional wounds, which gave her the strength to put down
the bottle and the needle. She learned to love life again and
had been Burwood's resident nurse ever since.

Tammy was still in her housecoat, so she quickly changed
into jeans and a red sweatshirt. Then she retrieved her medical bag from a cabinet in the kitchen and headed over to see
Authia.

When she entered the cabin, she found Authia sitting at the
kitchen table. She was pale, her lips and cheeks drained of
color, her eyes dull. And when she glanced up at Tammy, she
seemed so lost. When Nathen took Authia back to their own
cabin, she was in bad shape, but nowhere near as severe as
she was now.

Tammy went over to Authia and placed her medical bag
on the table. Then she moved one of the kitchen chairs so that
she could sit next to her. Tammy tenderly placed her hands
on either side of Authia's face, only to discover that she was
ice cold to the touch. Tammy reached into her bag, pulled out
a thermometer, and placed it under Authia's tongue. "Okay.
What did I miss? You look terrible."

Nathen went to stand next to Tammy. "She had an episode.
We were in the bedroom, and suddenly the room went frigid,

and she was covered in frost. She spoke to us, then passed out."

Tammy removed the thermometer and was astonished to discover that Authia's temperature was normal even though her body was an icicle. She placed her fingers on Authia's wrist and realized that her pulse was slow, barely discernable. "How do you feel?"

"Cold, tired, confused."

Nathen reached over and gently pulled the blanket aside so Tammy could see Authia's tattoo. "Take a look at this."

Tammy reached up and ran her fingers along the edges of the tattoo, and as she did, Authia grimaced in pain. The tattoo was raised and red hot as if it had just been burned into her skin.

"What the hell?" Tammy looked over at Nathen, who just shrugged his shoulders to say he had no idea. She glanced back over to Authia. "We have to warm you up. Joshawa, can you start a fire, please." Tammy stood up and helped Authia to her feet, keeping the blanket wrapped around her shoulders. "Let's put you in your chair."

Tammy helped Authia to her chair. Then she stood to one side. Nathen placed another blanket over Authia's legs and tucked it around her waist. He leaned over and kissed her on her forehead. "You're going to be fine, my love. We're going to figure this out."

Tammy watched as Joshawa placed kindling in the fireplace in the shape of a tepee. He set the tepee on fire then placed larger logs over the kindling. When the larger logs caught fire, Joshawa went over to his mother and knelt by her side. He placed his hands over hers. "I'm going to take care of you, Mother. I'm going to stay by your side. I'm never going to leave you."

Tammy watched on in disbelief. It was as if Authia was transforming right in front of her. The color returned to her lips and cheeks. Her eyes brightened, and she appeared refreshed as if she'd just woken up from a long nap. Tammy walked over to Authia and repositioned the blanket to one side so she could see the tattoo. Seconds ago, it had been inflamed, hot to the touch, and painful. Now, it was simply an old tattoo.

Joshawa could feel the warmth returning to his mother's hands. He glanced over to his father, expecting an explanation, but even his father appeared confused. He returned his gaze to his mother as he smiled up at her. "Are you feeling better, Mother? Can I get you something?"

"Yes. Much better. And no, thank you, I'm fine." Authia glanced over to Nathen while Joshawa watched her every move. He couldn't tell if she was scared or utterly perplexed by what she was experiencing. He let go of her hands and sat on the floor beside her chair.

"Nathen, what's going on? What's happening to me?"

Nathen knelt in front of Authia and took her hands in his. Slowly he shook his head from side to side. "I can't tell you, but we're going to figure this out. There's an explanation, and I think we need to start with Serena."

Authia closed her eyes and sighed. Slowly she opened them and gently shrugged her shoulders. "And how are we going to do that?"

"As I said, she's one of the Ancestors tasked with the responsibility of watching over the Jelani Tribe. We're still part of that tribe."

Joshawa snorted at his father. He looked up at him, his tone nothing short of combative. "How in any way are we part of that tribe?"

Joshawa was hoping to get a rise out of his father. Instead, Nathen just stared him down, letting Joshawa know that he couldn't intimidate him. "Leaving Africa doesn't take away our birthright." Nathen returned his gaze to Authia. "She will come to us."

The sun beat down on the entrance to the cave. Amy sat in the open, basking in its warmth. It was safe in the sun, safe to leave her cave. The animals that hunted at night were in their homes, waiting for darkness. To Amy, they were the evil that she had to hide from. Only the gentle animals of the forest ventured near her during the day. But they would only visit her, and they never stayed for very long. Amy's one constant companion was her bear, and he was the closest thing she had to a friend.

They discovered each other the first winter she stayed in the cave. He was small, like her, and he was alone. For that entire winter, Amy kept warm curled up next to him while he slept. Then, when the snow was gone, and she was barely alive, Amy ventured into the forest.

It was against everything she was told to do, but somehow, deep inside, she knew that she had to leave the safety of the cave to survive. But Amy didn't have to do it alone. Her bear stayed by her side and protected her, and with his help, Amy learned how to prevail. She lived in harmony with the animals and her bear, believing that she was alone. Then after a long cold winter, Amy discovered just how wrong she was.

As Amy sat in front of her cave, she recalled the first time she caught a glimpse of something in the forest, something strange. It was shortly after the snow melted, and on that day, she'd ventured far from her cave. Further than she had ever gone before. And there he was, just standing by a large tree. Amy was confused by him. He looked like her, but at the same time, he didn't. She continued to watch him as the trees bloomed and the animals had their babies.

Amy marveled at how he could climb his tree so quickly. She learned how to climb trees and hide in their branches, but not like him. And then today, she'd gone too close, and he almost caught her. She pulled her knees tight against her chest, then wrapped her arms around her legs. She trembled in fear at the thought of being discovered. She didn't understand why she should fear being found, only that she should.

# CHAPTER FOUR

Jax and Dameon walked up to the second cabin. It was similar to the smaller cabin in that there were no windows and only one door situated in the middle of the wall facing them. This door also only had a rope for a doorknob. Jax went up to the door, pulled on the rope, then pulled the door outward. They walked into what was obviously the living quarters of whoever had built these cabins.

They shone their flashlights around the room as they tried to see in the pitch darkness. Jax surmised that the cabin was approximately seven hundred square feet. Unlike the other cabin, the floor was made of wooden planks. In the middle of the room was a small wooden table with four chairs. Hanging from the ceiling were four kerosene lanterns.

To his right, pushed into the corner of the wall, was a set of crudely made wooden bunk beds. It would be tight, but two people could sleep on each of the bunks. The top bunk was far enough from the ceiling so that an adult could sit up with just an inch or two to spare.

Attached to the wall at the end of the bunks were six large wooden pegs situated five feet off the floor. Jackets and rain gear hung from the pegs. Two large, old steamer trunks were placed side-by-side on the floor underneath the jackets. Against the wall, next to the head of the bunk beds, was another steamer trunk. It was considerably smaller than the other two. A lantern was placed on top of it, along with an old coffee mug made of tin.

The cooking area that was situated across from the door

was comprised of a six-foot, very narrow, wooden table secured to the wall. A shelf underneath the tabletop contained pots for cooking, eating utensils, plates, and mugs. Everything was made of either metal or tin. Jax shone his flashlight along the wall but couldn't find any indication of running water or refrigeration.

On the wall opposite the bunk beds was a large stone fireplace. The stone hearth was twelve inches high and protruded into the room a good three feet. In the fireplace was a metal frame from which a large kettle hung. There was also a metal coffee perc and a large frying pan. It was apparent that whoever lived here did all their cooking in the fireplace. Two wooden rocking chairs faced the fireplace, and that was all they had for furniture.

Jax turned to face Dameon. "What do you think? Home sweet home?"

"Well, it's a hell of a lot better than the other cabin. I suppose we could stay here." Dameon shone his flashlight in the direction of the makeshift kitchen. "There doesn't seem to be any source of water. I'm going back outside and see if there's a well or a stream nearby. How about you look around and see if there is any kerosene lying about? It would be good if we could get these lanterns lit."

"Sure. Then we should check up on our bear and move our camp here before it gets dark."


"Sounds good." Dameon walked out into the yard, shoved his flashlight back into his backpack, then searched the yard for some sign of a well. When he walked around to the back of the cabin, he noticed what appeared to be an old path leading into the forest. It was so overgrown with vegetation that he couldn't see how far it went. He thought about getting Jax, but really, was there any threat? It wasn't as if the previous owner would jump out of the woods brandishing an ax. Dameon thought about it for just a second, then drew his *Glock 40* from its holster. He kept it down at his side with the muzzle facing the ground and his finger on the trigger.

Dameon took a deep breath and started making his way down the path. He hadn't gone far when the trail opened into a small clearing. On one side of the clearing were a dozen fifty-five-gallon metal drums. On the other side was an old-fashioned water pump. The path continued past the water pump and farther into the forest. With his *Glock* still at his side, Dameon continued down the path. Within a couple of minutes, he could hear the sound of water rushing over rocks. To his delight, the trail ended at a beautiful stream that was about fifteen feet wide. The water was so clear that he could see the fish swimming among the rocks. Dameon smiled as he holstered his *Glock*. Fresh fish would be a welcome respite from what he'd been eating for the past couple of weeks.

Dameon made his way back to the water pump and started pumping the handle. It took several minutes, but his patience was rewarded as water started spewing from the pump. At first, the water was cloudy and had a strong odor, but after five minutes of pumping, the water was crystal-clear and odorless.

Next, he checked out the drums. He grabbed the rim of one of the drums and tried to move it. It was extremely heavy, and he could hear a sloshing sound coming from inside the drum. Each barrel had a sizable screw-on cap located on the top of the lid close to the rim. Dameon unscrewed one of the caps and was immediately assaulted with the powerful odor of kerosene. He'd just replaced the cap when Jax came into the clearing.

"I was wondering where you got to."

"Well, we have kerosene." Dameon motioned toward the drums. "Bet you some of those, if not all, are filled with it."

Jax appeared astonished at what he was looking at. "How in the hell did he get them here?"

Dameon shrugged his shoulders, then motioned toward the pump. "And we have water, and there's a stream further back, filled with fish." Dameon noticed that Jax wasn't paying attention to the pump—he was focused on something else. Dameon followed his gaze to a large redwood tree. Nailed to the tree were a pair of rusted, iron shackles.

As promised, Joshawa remained at Authia's side until he was sure she was okay. While he sat there, he listened to the conversation about Serena. His parents had told him about the Priestess years ago. But after listening to their conversation, he realized that there was much more to the story.

He'd always blamed his father for keeping things from him, from not allowing him to know his people. But as he listened, he realized that his father was not the only one keeping secrets. Finally, he stood up and interrupted the conversation. "Now that Mother is feeling better, are we still going to Burwood?"

Authia looked over at Nathen. "I'm not up to it. But you guys go ahead." She glanced over to Tammy. "Has Becca and Hansen left yet?"

"I don't think so." Tammy got up and looked out the window. "Nope. The cart's still in front of the cabin."

"Good. Joshawa, would you please pack the cheesecakes into the cart? Then you can go to the party with Becca. It'll be fun for you."

"I don't want to leave you alone, Mother."

"She won't be." Nathen walked over to the fireplace and placed another log onto the fire. "I'm staying. You two go. Have a good time."

Joshawa just shook his head. His parents had a bond that

he could never understand — a bond that he would never have an opportunity to share with anyone. He went over to the kitchen counter, grabbed a couple of cheesecakes, and headed outside. As Joshawa approached the cart, Becca came out of her cabin carrying a plaid jacket. Her face lit up when she saw Joshawa.

"Joshawa!" Becca walked over to him and placed her hand on his arm. "How's your mom?"

"Better. Something happened to her after we went back to our cabin."

Becca appeared totally confused. "What are you talking about?"

"I don't know, and my parents aren't sharing." Joshawa went over to the cart and placed the cheesecakes next to the pies. "Nothing changes."

"Joshawa, don't feel that way. I'm sure they just think they're protecting you." Becca put her jacket on, then walked over to Joshawa and took his hands in hers. "You really have to lose that chip on your shoulder. Maybe start trusting your parents."

The second Becca took his hands, Joshawa's heart started beating faster. It felt like it was going to explode from his chest. He smiled at Becca. "Trust goes both ways. There's so much that I know they're hiding from me."

"And they'll tell you when the time is right. In the meantime, you have me."

Joshawa wanted to ask her what she meant by the comment. But the truth was that he was too afraid that he wouldn't like the answer. "And I appreciate that, Becca, I really do."

"Good." Becca leaned up and tenderly kissed Joshawa on his cheek. "Let's go get the rest of those cheesecakes."

Joshawa just stood there watching Becca as she headed toward his cabin. She'd kissed him. She actually kissed him. A smile graced his lips as he slowly reached his hand up to touch his cheek. Everything around him vanished, and all he could see was Becca.

Nathen watched out the window at the interaction between Joshawa and Becca, though he really didn't need to. Joshawa's emotions were alive inside of Nathen, and he knew his son was head over heels in love with Becca, and he had been for some time. The question was, did Becca feel the same way? He kept watching as Becca and Tammy loaded the last of the cheesecakes into the cart.

He glanced over his shoulder at Authia. She was still wrapped in her blankets and curled up in her chair. He walked over to her and tenderly kissed the top of her head. "I'll be right back."

Authia smiled as she glanced up to Nathen. "No worries, sweetheart. I'm not going anywhere."

Nathen left the cabin and headed toward Joshawa, who was securing a tarp over the cart. As he approached, Hansen came out of his cabin. "Hey, Nathen. You coming with us?"

"No. Authia's not up to a party, so I'm going to stay with her. But Joshawa is going to go with the three of you."

"Any excuse to have the cabin to yourself." Hansen grinned and winked at Nathen. Then he went over to the cart and started helping Joshawa finish with the tarp. "Since you're coming with us, guess who's pushing the cart?"

Nathen laughed. "Yeah, good idea. You're getting too old to push carts."

"Watch it!" Hansen smiled as he walked over to Nathen. "Tammy told me what happened in the cabin. I'll fill Charles in. He'll probably want to come to see Authia."

"Thanks. I appreciate that. But tell Charles he can wait until tomorrow. Authia won't want him to miss the party." Nathen turned to face Joshawa. "Have a good time, son. I'll see you when you get home." Nathen wanted *nothing* more than to hug his son, but from Joshawa's stance, he knew that it was not what Joshawa wanted. So, Nathen just turned around and headed back to his cabin.


Authia sat curled up in her chair, staring into the fire. Now that her body temperature had returned to normal, she no longer needed the blankets, which were folded and lying on the love seat. However, the fire was a different matter. She found comfort in watching the brilliant yellows and oranges of the flames as they danced around the logs. They distracted her from what was rattling around in her brain. She was so mesmerized, so lost in the beauty of the fire, that she didn't hear Nathen return. He'd startled her when he came up behind her and placed his hands on her shoulders.

"Oh my God, Nathen. I didn't hear you come in."

"Sorry. I didn't mean to frighten you." Nathen moved the blankets off the love seat and onto the floor. He sat down then patted the cushion next to him. "Come sit with me."

Authia moved over to the love seat and sat facing Nathen with her legs crossed in front of her. "So, Serena. Nathen, do you honestly believe that Serena is with us?"

"Yes, I do. And I believe that your tattoo is the connection."

"My tattoo?" Authia placed her right hand over her tattoo. "I don't understand. Serena gave this to me when she gave her life for mine. She told me that she was going to leave a little of herself behind."

"Exactly. Maybe she left more than just a tattoo. She was, and still is, an extremely powerful Priestess."

"But why? And if she did, why wait till now to contact us?"

"There's only one way to find out. We need to meld with her."

"How? We've melded with her before when she was a spirit, but only because she was a part of us." Authia stopped in mid-conversation as she realized what she'd just said. "You think that because of the tattoo, she's a part of me and has been since Africa."

"There's no other explanation." Nathen reached over and took Authia's hands in his. "It's been a while, but I think it's time for us to try to meld with Serena. I'll meld with you. I'll be your strength so you can meld with Serena."

Authia took a deep breath. She hadn't melded with anyone other than Nathen and Joshawa since Africa. Melding took a lot of discipline, inner strength, and the ability to project one's thoughts clearly to another mind. Deep down, Authia highly doubted that she still possessed the talent to perform such a deep meld. "Nathen, I don't know about this. I don't know if I'm strong enough."

Nathen smiled at her, and in his eyes, she could see the compassion he had for her. "I understand. But she's using you to communicate with our son. We need to know why."

"You're right." Authia gently squeezed Nathen's hands. "Just like old times." Authia let go of Nathen's hands and placed her hands on her knees. She took a deep breath, and as she slowly released it, she focused her eyes on Nathen's. "Lose yourself to me, Nathen. Look deep into my eyes. Become one with my mind. We will be as one." Authia could feel Nathen. He was with her, hiding in the shadows of her mind. It was time for her to seek out Serena.

Authia closed her eyes and concentrated her thoughts, projecting them outwards in search of Serena.

*I know you're there, Serena. I need to speak with you.*

Authia slowly opened her eyes.

She was surrounded by jungle. She could smell the dampness, and she could feel the jungle floor beneath her feet.

*Serena? Speak to me, Serena.*

Authia could feel the cold building up inside of her. She

could feel her tattoo burning into her chest.

*Yes, I am here. I am sorry, my Mistress, that I must do this to you. But it is the only way I can communicate.*

*What are you doing to me? And why can't I see you?*

*You cannot see me because your meld is weak. You are my passage to my Lord. Unfortunately, in order for me to speak through you, I must become you.*

*Try speaking to me instead.*

*But it is not you that I need to speak with.*

*I don't understand, Serena. What's going on?*

*It is time for my Lord to learn our ways.*

*Nathen already knows your ways. And why do you need to speak to him through me?*

*My Mistress, has it been so long? You are not as clever as you used to be.*

*What do you mean? No games, Serena! Tell me what you want.*

*It is not what I want but rather what the Jelani Tribe needs.*


Serena sat on the lush green grass that covered the grounds in the Realm of the Ancestors. This was her new home, and it wasn't much different from the home she came from. The jungle was vibrant in color and always smelled of sweet honey. It was a fragrance produced from the flowers that populated the Valley of the Lion People and the Realm of the Ancestors.

There were no huts or shelters of any kind in her new home. The Ancestors didn't require to sleep or seek shelter from Mother Nature. Serena learned that the Realm of the Ancestors was strictly for the three Ancestors chosen to watch over the Jelani Tribe. The Realm would allow the Ancestors passage to the world of the living. It would enable the Ancestors to observe, listen, and be in a better position to protect or punish the Jelani Tribe. The Land of the Spirits was where her people went after death. If she was successful in her task, then she would be allowed to join her people in the Land of the

Spirits.

Serena had no idea how vast the Realm of the Ancestors was. She was not permitted to leave her post, and since her arrival, she had only seen Lord Chike. Serena assumed the remaining two Ancestors, Lord Adeeowale and Imani, were occupied watching over the Jelani Tribe. As Serena listened to Authia, she sensed that she was not alone. She ended her connection with her Mistress, stood up, then turned to greet her Lord. "It has begun, Lord Chike."

"You have done well, High Priestess Serena. But time is not our friend. A great evil has entwined itself with our Lord's future. You must retrieve him before evil finds him."

"But, my Lord, by your own edict, I can only retrieve him if he is willing."

"Then you must convince him. That is your task. It is what you owe me for your existence here, in the Realm of the Ancestors."

Serena slowly shook her head from side to side. Lord Chike was an imposing man, standing over six feet tall and weighing two hundred and fifty pounds of solid muscle. He wore an animal skin vest that barely covered his chest. It was adorned with pictographs of symbols that were as old as time itself. His animal skin loincloth fell to just above his knees. Serena's halter top and skirt were also made of animal skin, though a lot plainer than Lord Chike's.

He seldom smiled, and when he looked at her, it was as if he could see inside of her, as if he could threaten her very existence. His facial appearance was harsh. He bore a scar that started beneath the right side of his chin and continued upward to his left temple. It was a good inch wide and left a permanent indent for the entire length of the scar. The knife that had given him that scar also removed a small section of his right upper lip. It just missed his left eye as the blade traveled to his temple. Serena had no idea how or why he was injured. What she did know was that when he looked at her, it would send shivers up and down her spine. Serena wasn't easily intimidated, but when it came to Lord Chike, she was cautious in how she approached him.

"No disrespect, but it is not only our Lord I have to convince. You know that just as well as I do." Serena bowed to Lord Chike, effectively ending the conversation.


Lord Chike observed Serena as she turned and headed toward the Realm's edge. She would not have been his first choice for pulling off this coup. Her tenacity and her penchant for misbehaving were well known and could be his downfall. But on the other hand, what Serena valued most was her existence. He would use that fact and hold her existence ransom until the rightful Lord of the Jelani Tribe was where he should be. The anger and hatred he felt for the outsider that dared to call himself Lord of the Jelani Tribe welled up inside of him. He clenched his teeth, and his eyes narrowed as he stared off into the distance. No son of an outsider would be Lord—he would see to that.

Lord Chike turned and headed toward the other two Ancestors. They did not share his hatred for the outsider, which meant he had to hide his animosity from them. He had to make them believe that he would protect the outsider and his bastard child. However, when his plan was fulfilled, he would no longer hide behind a veil of deception. He would protect the heritage of the Jelani Tribe and kill all those who dared try to protect the outsider.


Authia slowly opened her eyes. She was back in her cabin, sitting on the love seat with Nathen staring back at her. His facial expression revealed how concerned he was. "Did you hear my conversation with Serena?"

"Yes. She's trying to tell us something."

"I agree, but why doesn't she just say what she has to say?"

"I don't know. Serena's acting no different than she did when she was trying to fulfill the curse she placed on me."

"Yes, you're right. We're going to have to pay closer attention to what she says."

Authia stood up and began to pace back and forth in front of the fireplace. Nathen was right. Serena was up to something. She had an agenda that she apparently couldn't share. Authia stopped her pacing and gazed back at Nathen. "She told me that I wasn't as clever as I used to be. She said that after I inferred that it was you she was speaking about."

"When she was speaking through you, I made the same mistake, and she corrected me. She's referring to Joshawa. If we had stayed in Africa, he would be next in line to become the Lord of the Jelani Tribe."

Authia was exasperated, because she'd played these mind games with Serena years ago. She hated them back then, and now that they involved her son, she hated them even more. "Okay, let's say it's Joshawa that she's referring to. How is he going to learn the ways of the Jelani Tribe while he's here? I mean, you could teach him, but it wouldn't be the same as living it. And if it *is* Joshawa that the Jelani Tribe needs, he's got no way of getting there. The entrance to the valley is sealed."

Nathen walked over to Authia and wrapped his arms around her. When she gazed upon his face, he tenderly smiled at her. Authia knew he was just softening the blow of what he had to say. "There's no question that Serena is after Joshawa. The why and the how we're going to have to figure that out. But as difficult as it may be, we have to acknowledge that there's one way for Joshawa to find the Jelani Tribe."

Authia's heart skipped a beat. She felt as though her legs

were going to buckle under her. "You mean as a spirit, don't you?"

Nathen nodded his head then gently pulled Authia against his body.

She held on to him as tight as she could. *No, Serena, you can't! You can't take my son from me.* No matter how hard or how loud she pleaded, no answer came, and the reality of what her vision could mean became abundantly clear.

The sun was hiding behind the treetops, casting a shadow over Amy's cave. The days were becoming shorter, and the air no longer warmed her. She retrieved a brown linen jacket that was lying on top of an old, tattered trunk. The jacket, which fell to just above her knees, was several sizes too big for her. She put it on, then overlapped the front of it and tied it off with a belt she'd found in the trunk. Amy had no idea where the trunk had come from. All she knew was that it had been there as long as she had, and for that, she was grateful.

Amy made her way through the forest to a stream that originated high in the mountains, far beyond what she considered as her safe place. The water was so cold that it would numb her feet when she waded in. It was so clear that she could see the fish that would become her meal, darting in among the rocks and vegetation. She stood at the edge of the stream, waiting for her friend. He didn't disappoint, and twenty minutes later, he ambled toward her.

He'd grown so much this season, and Amy felt tiny when she stood next to him. The first winter they spent together, she'd named him Alex. It was a name, a word, that she felt safe with. And since she felt safe with him, it only made sense to call him Alex. She ran her hand over the large hump between his shoulder blades and down his back. Then she stood in front of him, placing her right hand on his snout. "Are you hungry, Alex? I am. Can you feed me?" She placed her hands on the sides of his face, smiling at him. "Then we can play." She stood aside and watched as her grizzly waded into the stream. Then using his massive paws, he started catching their dinner.

# CHAPTER FIVE

Joshawa pushed the cart up to the large wooden gates that served as the entrance to Burwood.

Each of the two gates was six feet wide and eight feet high. Usually, the gates would be closed, but one gate had remained open for the few people who were a part of Burwood but didn't reside within its walls.

For decades, Burwood had existed in the forest, protected and hidden by nature herself. It was a home, a sanctuary, for those who were abandoned by society, secluded from the people who might harm its inhabitants. There was no electricity or running water, and everyone lived in small log cabins with enough room for their beds and a small sitting and eating area.

The cabins were heated with wood fireplaces, and they used candles and kerosene lanterns for light. A crystal-clear stream ran through Burwood, giving its inhabitants all the fresh water that they needed. There were two large cabins in among all the small ones. One was for their medical needs, and the other was their main meeting hall. They would share all their meals in the meeting hall and hold social events.

The only luxury that the inhabitants of Burwood were allowed were three generators, one for the medical building and two for the main hall. The generators were used for refrigeration and to power the radio they used for communicating with the outside world.

The festivities for the fall dinner were in full swing, and Burwood was alive with excitement. Joshawa pushed the cart past the gates and into the courtyard, where he stopped to watch a group of children participating in a sack race. In different areas of the courtyard, adults were competing in games that involved ax throwing, archery, and feats of balance and strength. Colorful handmade quilts were being displayed as well as homemade soaps, candles, and wreaths. Joshawa glanced over to Becca, who appeared to be enthralled by everything that was going on. "Looks like they started without us." He smiled at Becca as she linked her arms around his massive bicep.

"As if they'd wait." Becca giggled as she turned to face Joshawa. "Come on. Let's take the cart to the hall and then join in."

Joshawa went to grab the cart's handles when Hansen placed his hand on Joshawa's shoulder. "Never mind. We'll take the cart. You two go and join in with the festivities."

"Are you sure? I don't mind. It won't take us long."

Hansen just shook his head. "No. Go. Have fun." Hansen grabbed the handles to the cart, then he and Tammy headed toward the hall.

Becca grabbed Joshawa's hand and pulled him toward the area where the men were competing in an ax-throwing competition. Joshawa learned long ago not to compete with the boys his own age. No matter what the competition involved, he would always win, each and every time. And for that, he earned their resentment and their jealousy.

As they approached the crowd gathered to watch the competition, Joshawa was distinctly aware that he was being watched. He scanned the crowd until his gaze came upon Adrian. Adrian was one of three boys Joshawa's age, and at twenty years old, the oldest of the boys. He stood just over six feet tall, had blond hair, blue eyes, and an impressive physique. He was the alpha in his small pack, and the other two boys followed him everywhere he went, taking everything that he had to say as gospel truth.

Adrian was standing at the edge of the crowd facing Joshawa, not the competition. His arms were folded across his chest, and he glared at Joshawa as if he were taunting him to make a move. The black t-shirt he wore was so tight that it accented his muscular build, which intimidated the younger residents, and in truth, some of the adults. However, it didn't threaten Joshawa, and he stared Adrian down until Becca gently squeezed his hand.

"He's not worth it." Becca glanced over to Adrian, then back to Joshawa. "He's just trying to get a rise out of you."

Joshawa averted his gaze from Adrian to Becca. She had a stern look on her face, which told Joshawa that she was serious. "All right, but can we leave?"

"Sure." Becca smiled at Joshawa. "I need a new quilt. Let's go check them out."

They were about to leave when Adrian, George, and Dennis blocked their path. George was a good four inches shorter than Adrian. He was plump and had shocking red hair, a round face, pale complexion, and his eyes always appeared as if he were squinting. Dennis, on the other hand, was as tall as Adrian. He had a slight build, dark hair, hazel eyes, and was notorious for causing trouble.

Adrian, who stood between the two boys, took a step closer to Joshawa. "Leaving so soon? I thought you'd want to try your luck."

Joshawa had no use for Adrian or his sadistic taunting. "Not interested. Come on, Becca."

Adrian moved over so that he completely blocked Becca's path. Becca let go of Joshawa's hand and wrapped her right arm around his left bicep.

"You look beautiful, Becca, as usual."

Becca didn't respond and showed no expression on her face.

Adrian just smirked at her. "I'm sure you're aware that there's a dance tonight."

"Yes, I know."

"Good. If you decide that you would prefer to attend with a real man instead of this sorry excuse for one, then I would be happy to escort you."

Joshawa could feel the anger building up in Becca. She let go of his arm and stood toe-to-toe with Adrian. Angrily she poked at Adrian's chest with her right index finger. "Nothing on this earth could convince me to go anywhere with you. And for your information, Joshawa is, and always will be, twice the man you could ever hope to be." Becca grabbed Joshawa's hand. "Come on, Joshawa, we're leaving." Becca nudged Adrian aside with her left shoulder as she walked past him. When they were out of Adrian's earshot, Becca stopped and glared back at him. Joshawa glanced back in Adrian's direction as well, and it was clearly evident to him how angry Adrian was.

Becca shook her head as she returned her focus to Joshawa. "He's such a pompous ass."

Joshawa smiled as he faced Becca. "Twice the man?"

"Oh, shut up." Becca blushed, rewarding Joshawa with a very sensual smile. She grabbed his hand and motioned toward the quilts. "Come on. You're buying me a quilt."

"Gladly." The smile Becca gave Joshawa caused his heart to swell with excitement, and there was no disguising the happiness he felt at that very moment.


Charles was supervising the preparation of the hall for the banquet. Half a dozen men and women were in the kitchen area preparing the meal. The serving table that separated the kitchen from the hall was decorated with pumpkins, gourds, large acorns, candles, and an array of colorful leaves from the trees that were a part of Burwood. The hall itself contained twelve long tables that seated ten people at each table. The tables were covered in white linen tablecloths and were decorated exactly as the serving table was.

On the wall that faced the kitchen was a water feature that Nathen had built for Authia as a wedding gift. It was a beautiful stone waterfall that fell from the ceiling to a pond at its base. Candles were resting on dozens of stone shelves that jutted out from the waterfall. Three large wooden chandeliers hung from the ceiling over the dining area. Each chandelier held twelve candles. When the chandeliers were lit in the evening, it gave the hall an aura of enchantment. To Charles, the hall appeared almost magical. He was about to start lighting the candles on the tables when Hansen and Tammy entered the hall.

Hansen entered the building and was immediately awestricken by the ambiance and the enticing aromas that filled the hall. As he handed his tray to one of the women from the kitchen, he noticed Charles lighting one of the many candles that adorned the dining tables. Hansen smiled to himself as he recalled the first time he'd met Charles. He was immediately impressed by the man who had given birth to Burwood. Charles was a loving, caring man who treated all the inhabitants of Burwood as if they were family.

Charles looked up from his candle and smiled at Hansen, and in that very second, Hansen saw Authia. Authia had inherited Charles's large, beautifully shaped eyes. However, hers were a dark brown and not the rich hazel of her father's. They also shared the same high cheekbones and a smile that invoked tenderness and sincerity.

Hansen had no idea exactly how old Charles was, but he assumed he was a lot older than he appeared. Charles had an incredible physique. His salt and pepper hair had more pepper than salt, his mind was sharp, and his eyes sparkled when he spoke. He was dressed in jeans and a dark brown sweatshirt that enhanced his tanned complexion.

Tammy had just handed off her tray of pies when Hansen caught her attention. "I'm going to go talk with Charles about Authia. I'll be right back to help you with the trays."

Tammy leaned up and affectionately kissed Hansen on his cheek. "Take your time."

Hansen smiled as he watched Tammy leave the building. To Hansen, she was the most amazing and the most attractive woman he'd ever seen. He was so grateful to have won her heart and to have her in his life. Once Tammy had left, Hansen focused his attention on Charles. "Looks good, Charles."


Charles beamed with pride as he scanned the hall. "Yes. Everyone's done an exceptional job." He then glanced past Hansen to the entrance of the hall. He'd seen Tammy enter but not his daughter. "Where's Nathen and Authia?"

"They stayed behind. Authia had a pretty disturbing vision this morning. Then when she went to lie down, their bedroom got very cold, and she spoke to Nathen and Joshawa without even being aware that she was speaking."

Charles felt as if his heart fell to the pit of his stomach. "Is she okay? I should go see her."

Charles started to leave, only to have Hansen place his hand tenderly on Charles's arm.

"Tammy checked her out, and Nathen stayed at the cabin with her. She's fine. She wants you to stay here and enjoy the party. You can go tomorrow. Besides, Joshawa's here, and I know he's looking forward to seeing you. That is, if you can pull him away from Becca."

Charles sincerely doubted that Authia was fine, and he

wasn't totally convinced that he shouldn't go to her. Authia hadn't had a disturbing vision for over eighteen years. Why would they be starting again? "Are you sure? Maybe I should send Edward."

"Come on, Charles. You know Edward can't make that walk anymore. She'll be fine. And you know very well that she'll be pissed at you if you miss the party on her account."

Charles knew exactly how Authia would react. So even though he was reluctant, he conceded to her wishes. "Yeah, you're right. What are Becca and Joshawa up to?"

"They were going to check out the competitions. We've got more pies to bring in. Want to give us a hand?"

"Sure. But before we do, I have a question for you."

"Okay. Shoot."

"You do know that Joshawa's in love with Becca?"

Hansen chuckled. "Everybody knows that."

"My question is, does Becca love him?"

"I believe she does. I know that she definitely cares a lot about him."

"Caring's not loving, and I'd hate to see Joshawa hurt. He's going through a lot right now."

Hansen's expression went from carefree to serious. "Becca would never hurt Joshawa. She's her mother's daughter, so believe me, if Joshawa doesn't step up and admit to her that he loves her, she will. But I know what you mean. Joshawa's so conflicted right now."

Charles sighed as he recalled Nathen when he was a young man. "He's going through the same heartache that Nathen went through at his age. He desperately wants to know who and what he is and where he belongs. I wish Joshawa could go to Africa and meet his people. At least then he could make an educated decision as to where he feels he should be."

"Well, that's not going to happen. There's no way to get to the tribe now. Joshawa's just going to have to trust in

Nathen's decision."

Once again, Charles thought back to when Nathen was conflicted and angry at the world. He'd needed Nathen to trust him, to trust his judgment. But Nathen's anger had ruled his mind and his emotions. It took Charles years of perseverance and, in the end, Authia's love to conquer the beast that lived within Nathen. "Take it from me, Hansen. That's easier said than done."

Jax and Dameon couldn't believe what they were seeing. Dameon walked over to the tree and picked up one of the shackles. He glanced over to Jax with a look of bewilderment mixed in with a healthy dose of fear. "What the hell, Jax? What was this guy up to?"

Jax had a good idea who the shackles were for. However, he wasn't prepared to share that information with Dameon. "Nothing good, that's for sure. But it doesn't really matter, because whoever lived here is long gone. Look, our bear should be awake by now. Why don't you go check on him? And I'll start tearing down our camp." Jax walked over to the drums, took hold of one, and moved it back and forth to determine its weight. "We should be able to roll one of these to the cabin. That way, we won't have to go too far to fill the lanterns. I think I remember seeing a hand pump in the smaller cabin."

Jax made sure the cap on the drum was tight, then he and Dameon gently lowered it onto its side. They had the drum set up in front of the cabin within twenty minutes with the hand pump in place. Dameon left to check on the bear while Jax filled the lanterns.

The first thing Jax did was to prop the door to the cabin open in the hope of airing it out. Then he filled the six lanterns, placed them in the cabin, and lit them. He got a good look at what he would be living in for the first time. The place was covered in dirt and dust from years of neglect. The bedding on the bunks was thin and smelled of urine and mold.

He stripped the top bunk down to the plywood base and threw the bedding along with the straw mattress outside. But when he went to strip the bottom bunk, he found another pair of shackles at the head of the bed, nailed to the cabin wall. Jax had always envisioned what it would be like to torture animals, but the guy that lived here took it one step further.

Jax gathered the bedding and mattress from the bottom bunk, and as he threw it outside, he envisioned the woman from the pictures shackled to the bed. A cruel smile graced his lips at the thought of her anguish, her pain, her suffering. He drew a deep breath then went back inside the cabin.

He started to move the table only to discover that two of the four chairs were nailed to the floor. Knowing full well what he was going to find, he crouched down to check the underside of the table. He wasn't disappointed when he discovered that another set of shackles had been secured underneath the table at one of the chairs.

Slowly Jax shook his head. What was going on in this cabin? Jax would have loved to have been a fly on the wall when all this was going down. He scanned the cabin one more time and was about to leave when something under the bunk bed caught his eye.

Jax grabbed his flashlight from inside his backpack and walked over to the bed. He knelt on both knees and shone his flashlight under the bed. What had captured his attention was the front of a metal box that had been placed just past the edge of the bed. He could see a metal handle that appeared to be riveted to the side of the box.

Jax reached under the bed, grabbed the metal handle, and then slowly inched it out until the box was free from its hiding place. It was about three feet long by two feet wide, eighteen inches high, and was severely tarnished with age. There was an additional handle on the opposite end of the box. The lid to the box had been secured with an old, rusted padlock. Jax took hold of the handles then carried the box over to the table to examine it. He looked at the padlock, and even though he knew it was a wasted measure, he grabbed hold of it with his right hand and yanked on it as hard as he could. The padlock didn't budge, which meant that he would need something a little more persuasive. Jax headed over to the smaller cabin, retrieved a hammer, and smashed the lock until it broke free.

Inside the metal box were several drawings done in pencil. They were of various animals posed in natural settings, and Jax was surprised at the quality of the illustrations. At the bottom of the box was a journal. Jax sat at the table and carefully opened the leather-bound cover.

The pages were dated starting in the late fifties. For the first two decades, the drawings were of animals and a man. The man had a strange look about him, as if he wasn't quite there. His eyes were sad, and not one picture showed him smiling. In the seventies, the drawings started to morph from beautiful and carefree into something cruel and horrific. The drawings of the man had stopped. The author was only interested in the animals and what he was doing to them.

On one page of the journal was a graphic description of an animal and the cruelties the man was inflicting. Mutilation, dissection while the animal was still alive, and finally, death. On the corresponding page were drawings depicting every cruelty that had been performed on the animal. This went on for years, each year more horrific than the last. Jax had often envisioned what it would be like to torture an animal, to watch it die a slow, painful death. But never, in any of his fantasies, did he imagine what he was reading in this journal.

Then, in 1983, the woman whose pictures were on the wall of the small cabin also appeared in the journal. What he did to her was far worse than what he did to the animals. Shortly after the woman was introduced in the journal, the author added notes about something he saw in the woods.

He described it as *very large,* and it moved unlike any animal he had ever seen. He drew an outline of an animal that walked on two legs. He became obsessed with this animal to the point that he focused only on it. No other animal appeared in his journal, and in 1989, even the drawings of the woman finally stopped.

He spoke of where he saw the animal, how he tracked it, and what he wanted to do with it. And as Jax continued to read the journal, the drawing came to life. He turned the page, and staring back at him was a beast that stood and dressed like a man. It appeared to be very tall, and its face resembled that of a lion, which didn't seem feasible to Jax. The cats in this area would be lynx, cougars, and bobcats, and none resembled what was depicted in the drawing. The last entry was how the journal's author planned to kidnap a child from where he knew the beast frequented. He would hold the child ransom in exchange for the beast. The journal entry was dated 1990, twenty years ago.

Jax's mind was racing with thoughts of the beast. *Could this beast still be alive? Did it really ever exist?* If it did, it would be worth a fortune — that was, if he decided to sell it. Part animal, part man — the perfect high. The best of both worlds. The problem was, should he tell Dameon? Dameon would disapprove of what Jax was thinking of. But if he was going to track this beast and determine if there were still any signs of it, he would need help.

His decision was made for him as Dameon returned to the cabin. "What the hell have you been doing? I thought you were tearing down the camp." He walked over to where Jax was sitting. "Where did the box come from?"

"I found it under the bunk bed. I opened it and found this

journal among some drawings. You're going to like this." Jax pushed the journal across the table toward Dameon.

Dameon looked confused as he picked up the journal and took in the drawing. "What's this supposed to be?"

"If it's still alive, the biggest game we've ever taken down."

# CHAPTER SIX

Nathen sat on the swing, his arms folded across his chest, his feet gently pushing against the deck so the swing would rock back and forth. He stared out into the forest without really seeing the beauty that lay before him. His mind was occupied with dozens of questions, and there was no room for anything else. His most important, most daunting question was why? *Why now, after so many years? Why does Serena want Joshawa? Why is she speaking to Joshawa through Authia when she could just as easily meld with him directly?* Nathen closed his eyes, leaned back, and rested his head on the back of the swing. There was only one person who could answer those questions, and that was Serena. Nathen was so lost in his thoughts that he barely noticed Authia when she sat down beside him.

"Here, I made us something to eat."

"I should be making lunch for you, not the other way around." Nathen sat up and looked over to Authia. She passed him a plate that held a delicious-looking BLT with a pickle on the side.

"I'm fine. A little troubled, but fine."

"I'm glad you're okay. What's Serena up to? Why is she communicating with us after all these years?"

"I think we're missing the bigger picture."

Nathen was puzzled by her comment. "Bigger picture?"

"Think about it. When we were in Africa, Serena did everything she could to make amends. In the end, she was on our side. Not to mention that she gave her life to save mine. So, why, after all that, would she do something that she knows very well would hurt us?"

"She wouldn't."

"Exactly. So why is she? I think that the bigger picture is not what Serena is up to, but rather who's controlling her."

Nathen thought about what Authia was saying. Could Serena be under a darker, more sinister influence? "Maybe she's once more the puppet. Like when her mother tried to control her. When her mother tried to bring back the destroyer."

"Exactly. We need to read between the lines. She's giving us clues, and we need to figure out how to interpret them."

"And what if we're wrong? What if she's the Serena we first met?"

"It's a chance we have to take. The Serena we first met was sadistic and full of hate. I didn't sense any of that in the meld. We need to trust her. That's the only way we're going to figure out what's going on."


Serena positioned herself at the very edge of the Realm of the Ancestors. From there, she could eavesdrop on Lord Nathen and his family. As a High Priestess and an Ancestor, Serena had the capability to listen and communicate with the living. The three Ancestors who watched over the Jelani Tribe were impressed with her sacrifice to save the life of one she'd once despised. They were even more impressed when she turned her back on her own mother to save the Jelani Tribe. As a reward for her courage, she was given the honor of becoming an Ancestor whose sole purpose was to watch over the Jelani Tribe. It was an honor she readily accepted. However, it came at a price. As she watched over the young Lord, her heart saddened at what this honor would cost.

The competitions were over, and the residents of Burwood joined in the meeting hall to partake in the fall dinner. The hall echoed in laughter and music as everyone found their table. Next to the water feature was a small band comprised of two men playing guitar, one man playing a fiddle, a man playing the piano, and a woman who possessed an incredible voice. Becca had made sure she sat right next to Joshawa. Her parents sat across from her, and on the other side of Joshawa was Charles. Edward, Burwood's resident doctor, sat across from Charles.

Edward was in his eighties but appeared and acted so much younger. His hair was completely gray, and he would always say that the wrinkles on his face were from a long, happy, fulfilling life. Edward always wore plaid flannel shirts and jeans. Becca had heard Edward's and her mom's stories so many times.

Edward had taken Tammy under his wing when she first arrived at Burwood. He taught her everything he knew about the medical field, and within only a few months, they developed a tight bond. Becca loved how Edward considered her mom family and treated her like his own daughter.

When Becca was sixteen, she was told the story of how Edward's wife and daughter died tragically when their house caught on fire so many years ago. It was a sad story, but one with a happy ending because now, with her Aunt Authia, her mom, and herself, they made his life complete.

Next to Edward was Billy. Becca smiled as she watched Edward tuck a linen napkin into the collar of Billy's white dress shirt. As he did, he shared with the group how important it was to Billy to dress up for the occasion. When Edward spoke of Billy, it was clearly evident how much love and compassion he had for the child trapped in a man's body.

Becca's mother had told her what she knew of Billy. He was

a mentally challenged man who came to Burwood when Joshawa's parents left for Africa. He had lived his entire life in the forest, with his brother being his only companion. When Billy's brother died, Nathen had brought Billy to Burwood so he could live his life in a safe environment.

Edward took on the responsibility of caring for Billy, and from that time forward, Billy was family. No one knew for sure how old Billy was, though they guessed that he'd been in his mid-thirties when he first came to Burwood. He was of average height, but his build was solid and square. Billy was powerful but totally unaware of his strength. It was fortunate that in his mind, he was a happy, contented child. Otherwise, his strength could have proven to be a huge problem.

Becca scanned the hall, taking in all the happiness and camaraderie that was evident among the participants of the fall dinner. She glanced over to Joshawa, who was laughing at a story Charles was telling. Joshawa's eyes sparkled, and he had the most infectious laugh. When Joshawa was happy, she couldn't help but be happy with him. When he was sad, it almost broke Becca's heart.

If anyone was to ask her when she'd fallen in love with Joshawa, she would know the answer without hesitation. As far as Becca was concerned, she'd been in love with Joshawa ever since she became aware of what love was. She knew he loved her, but what she didn't know was if he loved her more than his desire to be in Africa with his people.

Becca's mood saddened as she continued to watch Joshawa. She wanted nothing more than to wrap her arms around his neck, kiss him and tell him just how much she loved him. But that wasn't going to happen. She would be devastated if he chose Africa over her. So she would wait until he realized where he genuinely wanted to be.

Amy returned to her cave carrying five large trout in an old metal bucket. Typically, Alex would follow her, but today, he seemed to be out of sorts. He kept sniffing at the air, then finally took off deep into the forest, away from the direction of her cave. Something deep inside of Amy told her that things were not as they should be. She stood at the entrance to her cave, staring into the forest. The animals she'd passed on her way back to the cave were acting as they usually would. It was only Alex that was acting strange. She continued her vigil for several minutes, then just shrugged her shoulders and went inside. To Amy, if she didn't see the danger, if her animal friends were not afraid, then there was nothing for her to fear.

Amy started a small fire, gutted the fish, then secured two of them to a large stick. As she rotated them over the fire, she made a mental note of the supplies she would need to keep her alive over the winter months. She glanced over to the large stockpile of wood that she'd gathered since spring. Water wasn't a problem, given how much snow fell over the winter, and she'd become quite adept at snaring small animals that ventured too close to her cave. Amy returned her focus to the fish and withdrew them from the fire. Then she used another smaller stick to slide the fish onto her tin plate

While the remaining three fish cooked over the open flame, Amy devoured the sweet-tasting fillets. After her meal, she burned the carcasses and guts of the fish. When she'd first started catching fish for her meals, she would just throw the carcasses and guts into the forest. But that only attracted the animals that hunted at night. It only took one misadventure for Amy to learn her lesson. If it weren't for Alex scaring off the wolves, she wouldn't be alive.

Amy threw a couple more logs on the fire and was about to curl up next to it when Alex appeared at the mouth of the cave. He stood staring at her, then started to growl as if he were trying to tell her something.

Amy walked over to him and placed her hand gently on the top of his head. "What's wrong, Alex? You've been acting strange all day."

Alex slightly turned, which allowed him to see outside the cave. He then turned back to gaze at Amy.

"Is there something out there that I need to be afraid of? Am I in danger, Alex?"

As if to answer her, Alex gently nudged her further into the cave. Then he turned and went back to the entrance. He lay down on the ground, and Amy knew deep in her gut that he was guarding her against some evil that only he knew existed.


Holding the leather-bound journal in one hand while engrossed in the picture Jax showed him, Dameon grabbed the back of the chair in front of him and tried to pull it out. When it wouldn't budge, Dameon diverted his attention from the journal and to the chair. He glanced down at the back legs while he tried for a second time to pull the chair away from the table. That's when he noticed that the legs were nailed to the floor. He glanced over at Jax. "What the hell?"

"I know." Jax pointed to the chair across from him. "That one is nailed to the floor as well. There's also a set of shackles nailed to the underneath of the table."

Dameon placed the journal on the table then peered underneath. Sure enough, a set of shackles were hanging from the bottom. Dameon stood back up, shaking his head. "I don't know what went on here, but whatever it was, it sure in hell wasn't good."

Jax placed his boot against the seat of the chair that wasn't secured to the floor and pushed it out. "There's also a set of shackles nailed to the wall where the bottom bunk is."

Dameon sat down, taking a quick glance at the bed as he

did. He returned his gaze to Jax. "I feel like I'm in a horror movie, and some deranged man is going to jump out at us at any moment."

Jax chuckled. "You watch too many horror movies. Now, what's your opinion of the beast in the drawing?"

Dameon reached over and pulled the journal toward him. The drawing depicted a man, tall and very muscular. However, the fact that he stood upright and had two arms and two legs was where the similarities to a man ended. His face was long, with high cheekbones, cat-like eyes, and a cleft in his upper lip. His hair fell in waves to his shoulders. His hands were large, and his fingernails were long, and they tapered to a point. It was difficult to determine his age. The date on the page was twenty years ago.

"I don't get it, Jax. Are you suggesting we hunt this . . . creature?"

"Yes! Can you imagine what something like that would be worth?"

Dameon flipped the journal over on the table so it would remain open on the page he was examining. He leaned back into his chair, keeping his hands on the table. Something wasn't right. Something deep in his gut gnawed at him. "Come on, Jax. You want us to hunt bigfoot? Cause that's pretty much what we'd be doing. Not to mention that the drawing's twenty years old. Even if that thing did exist, it's probably long since dead."

"Maybe and maybe not. The journal has detailed maps of where that thing was sited. There's even a cabin that it apparently hung out at all the time. Look, our bear is tagged. It's not going anywhere, and we were going to give it a month or so to fatten up anyway. What would it hurt to check out some of these landmarks?"

Dameon leaned forward, picked up the journal, flipped it over, and stared at the drawing, trying to decide if he was looking at a man with deformities or an actual bigfoot. "I don't know, Jax. What if he's just some man hiding his deformities from the world? We don't hunt people."

"Look at the drawing. He's not people. I'll tell you what. Let's just check out some of the landmarks. See if there are any signs that it's still around. If we find it, then we'll decide if it's a man or beast."

Dameon stared at Jax. He knew Jax wanted it to be part man, part animal. He wanted to hunt it, to experience the ultimate high. Dameon also knew that Jax would pursue this person . . . animal . . . with or without him. Maybe if he went with Jax and they found their prey, he could be the voice of reason if the drawing was that of a man. "All right, we'll check it out. But under no circumstances are you to hurt or injure whatever this is until we know more about it."

Jax looked at Dameon as if he were weighing his options. "This could be the biggest catch of our lives."

"Yes, or it could be just a man hiding from the world. I need your word, Jax."

Jax sighed, glanced over at the journal, and then back up at Dameon. "Okay. You have my word. But if this is not a man, then it's fair game."

"Fine. Where do you want to start looking?"

Jax grabbed the journal from Dameon and flipped through the pages until he came across a drawing of a cabin surrounded by forest. He placed the journal on the table facing Dameon. "Here. This is where we'll start."


The crescent-shaped moon shone brightly in the clear evening sky. Nathen sat on the swing, staring up at the stars. As he took in the beauty of the night, a shooting star fell from the sky. Nathen sighed to himself. *To wish upon a shooting star.*

If he could have only one wish, it would be that his son

would love him again, that Joshawa would understand why Nathen had chosen to raise him in Burwood rather than Africa. The Jelani Tribe might have been *what* Nathen was, but they were not *who* he was. Nathen belonged to the tribe because of tradition, because he was a descendant of the Lord of the Lion People. But not because of who he was as a man. He belonged in Burwood because he was loved. He belonged because of who he was. He earned his place in Burwood by helping those in need. Tammy helped him to see that. Now, he had the daunting task of trying to get his son to see it as well.

Authia walked over to the swing and sat next to Nathen. She wrapped her oversized sweater so that it overlapped, then cuddled against Nathen as he put his right arm around her shoulders. "You know, Nathen, Joshawa will eventually see it on his own. Just as you did."

"Most likely." Nathen leaned over and kissed Authia on the top of her head. "I just hope it happens before I'm too old to enjoy the revelation."

"It will be."

"Have you heard anything more from Serena?"

"No. I've been trying. I know she can hear me. But for some reason, she's ignoring me."

"I think she's waiting. Waiting for something to happen."

Authia gazed up at Nathen. "What do you think she's waiting for?"

"Only Serena knows the answer to that." Nathen stared off into the woods. There was one fact that he did know. Serena was after his son, and his wife was Serena's gateway to the world of the living.

Lord Chike headed back toward the camp he shared with Lord Adeeowale and Imani. They'd been chosen decades ago to watch over the Jelani Tribe. Lord Chike was in the Realm of the Ancestors when Lord Joshawa dishonored his people and took an outsider as his wife. At that time, many people felt as Lord Chike did.

When Serena and her mother killed the Lord and his outsider wife, Lord Chike thought that all would be set right. Never had he been so wrong. Serena's hatred and jealousy proved to be her undoing. Moments before the wife had died, she had given birth to a son. A son that Serena allowed to live, wrapped in a curse of eternal life. Lord Chike could feel his own hatred building up inside of him as he recalled that evening so long ago. What Serena and her mother had done swayed the Ancestors, his own people, to favor the bastard son of Lord Joshawa and the outsider, Julia.

Lord Chike stopped at the edge of the camp and remained hidden in the trees. He observed the two Ancestors as they too returned to the camp. They approved of an outsider ruling the Lion People. They were traitors to the Jelani Tribe and to everything the Ancestors stood for. A wicked smile graced his lips.

*And all traitors will answer to their crime.*

Serena spent hours watching and listening to Joshawa and the people that were in his life. Becca could prove to be a problem if Joshawa realized that she loved him. And then there was Nathen and Authia. Serena knew they would put up a fight. Serena observed Joshawa as he danced the night away with Becca. To do what was expected of her, she would have to fan Joshawa's animosity for Nathen. She had already established a link to Joshawa through Authia. The tattoo that was embossed on Authia's skin was actually a conduit between Authia's world and the world where Serena resided. Now that it was activated, she could speak directly to Joshawa.

Serena was saddened as she continued to watch the young Lord. There was a time when she would have had no problem destroying Nathen and his family. But now, there was hesitation. Her entire existence rested on her being able to do as she was told. She had already given her life once before to save Authia. But that was different. She knew then that she would only be sacrificing her body. Her spirit, her essence, would live on with her Ancestors. Now, if she chose not to comply with the conditions Lord Chike had imposed on her existence, she would perish. Nothing of her would be left. Serena sighed, then focused her thoughts on those of Joshawa's.

*Why do you take up all of Becca's time? You know you have no chance with her. She is much better off without you. You belong with your own people, the people that your father deprived you of. They, the Jelani Tribe, are your family.*

# CHAPTER SEVEN

Joshawa held Becca in his arms as they danced to the waltz. He chose not to pull her tight against him, because he wanted to keep just enough distance between them so he could gaze into her eyes. Her beautiful blue eyes gazed upon him as if he were normal, as if he were a real man. Joshawa was lost in the moment, and he didn't want the dance to end.

While he held her, his hands in hers, it felt like she was his. He wanted to blurt out that he loved her so much. Three simple words were all that it was going to take. And if she loved him back, life would be wonderous. Maybe he could even experience the same love that his parents shared.

Joshawa decided that the time was right, so he maneuvered Becca to the edge of the dance floor. He was about to pull her aside when he heard something coming from the farthest recesses of his mind. It was as if someone was trying to meld with him. He strained to listen to the voice, but it was just out of his reach. Then suddenly, a wave of uncertainty crashed against his awareness. He looked away from Becca as he tried to shake off the emotions that were building up inside of him. When he glanced back, she was no longer smiling. Instead, she looked concerned and even a little worried.

Becca took Joshawa's hands in hers. "Joshawa? Are you all right?"

Joshawa didn't know what to say. The desire to tell her he loved her was no longer there. All he could think of was the Jelani Tribe. He gazed around the room, but it wasn't the people of Burwood that he saw—it was the people of the Jelani

Tribe. They were everywhere. Joshawa closed his eyes, then slowly opened them. The tribe was gone, and he found himself staring at Becca as she stood in front of him. Joshawa was so confused. His thoughts were chaotic, with one thought crashing into another. The only thing that made any sense to him was leaving and getting as far away from Burwood as possible. Joshawa glanced away from Becca, and with his voice trembling with uncertainty, he came up with an excuse. "I'm tired. I'm going to go home."

"Give me a second, and I'll come with you."

Joshawa let go of Becca's hands and just shook his head. "No. I need to be alone." He turned his back to Becca and left Burwood.

Authia could feel the turmoil that resided deep within Nathen. The conflict between him and Joshawa was tearing him apart. She hadn't seen Nathen in this state of mind since he was battling the creature that dwelled within him when she first met him. As she raised her head off his shoulder to look up at him, she felt a searing pain on her chest. She bolted upright and placed her right hand on her sweater in the area where her tattoo would be. She could feel the heat emanating from the tattoo as if nothing were covering it.

Carefully she pulled back the sweater and the strap to her tank top to expose her tattoo. Once again, the outline was raised, and it appeared as if it had just been burned onto her chest. She glanced up at Nathen, knowing that he would see and feel the fear that enveloped her.

Nathen placed his hands on the side of Authia's shoulders. He glanced down at her tattoo, then back up at her. "What's going on? Is this you Authia, or am I speaking to Serena?"

Authia pulled her sweater back over her tattoo, then searched her mind for any signs of Serena. But her mind only contained her own thoughts. "It's me. Serena's not here."

"Then what's happening to your tattoo? It only acts that way when Serena is preparing to speak to us through you."

"I know, and I don't understand it either." Authia paused while she recalled the last time her tattoo came alive. "It wasn't really us she was speaking to. It was Joshawa that she was reaching out to."

"But he's not here. So, what's she trying to do?"

Authia slowly shook her head. "I don't know, but I think my tattoo is the key to finding out."


Becca stood on the edge of the dance floor, dumbfounded by Joshawa's sudden departure. She watched as he walked away from her. And as he left the hall, her tears ran freely down her cheeks. She was so disheartened that she didn't hear Adrian walk up behind her.

"I would never treat you so badly."

Becca quickly wiped the tears from her face then turned to face Adrian. "I have no idea what you're talking about." She went to leave, but Adrian grabbed her hand. Becca glanced down at her hand, which was now firmly in Adrian's grasp, then she looked back up at Adrian. Her expression was that of annoyance. "Let go of me."

Adrian didn't comply and continued to hold her hand. "Come on, Becca. He left you standing here. I would never do that to you. Come sit with me." Adrian started to pull Becca toward his table, but she held her ground.

"Let go of me, now! I don't want to sit with you or be with you." Becca was about to pry his hand off hers when he suddenly let go, turned around, and headed back to his table. Becca was surprised by Adrian's sudden departure. However, when she looked behind her, she found her dad standing there. If looks could kill, Adrian would have been a pile of ash.

Hansen reached out and gently took Becca's hand. She watched him as he examined her hand, and she knew that he was looking for signs that Adrian had hurt her. "I'm fine, Dad. He didn't hurt me."

Hansen gently let go of Becca's hand and placed his hand tenderly on her shoulder. "If he's bothering you, I can take care of it."

Becca smiled at her dad. "He's a nuisance. That's all."

Hansen looked around the room, then returned his focus on Becca. "Where's Joshawa?"

Becca was no longer smiling. She gazed upon her dad, her feelings of sadness radiating from her. "He went home."

"Really?"

"He was happy one minute and then the next . . . well, he seemed confused. Then he left. Said he wanted to be alone."

Hansen put his right arm around her shoulders. "Joshawa is confused. He's trying to figure out where he belongs. Nathen went through the same thing. Now come on, your mom and I are about ready to leave."

Becca's heart ached, for she knew what confused Joshawa. Africa stood between her and the man she loved. As she walked with her father toward their table, she wished that Nathen had never told Joshawa about the Jelani Tribe.


Dameon opened his eyes and stared at the ceiling of the cabin. He'd spent the night on the top bunk because he had no intention of sleeping on the bottom bunk with the shackles. The aroma of coffee filled the cabin, and the door had been propped open, allowing the morning sun to stream in. Dameon sat up, nearly hitting his head on the ceiling as he did. The first thing Dameon noticed was that all the supplies from their camp were now piled next to the rocking chairs.

Dressed only in his camo pants, he threw off his sleeping bag and jumped down from the bunk.

Jax, who was dressed in his camo gear, including his jacket and boots, was at the table studying a current map of the area. He had the journal open and was obviously trying to connect something from his map to the map in the journal.

Dameon grabbed a dark green tee-shirt from his duffle bag and pulled it down over his head. Then he sat on the lower bunk, pulled his boots on, and laced them up. As he poured himself a cup of coffee, he commented on the pile of supplies. "You were busy. It looks like everything from our camp is here."

Jax glanced up and shrugged his shoulders. "I wanted to make up for not doing it yesterday."

He returned his gaze to the map and shook his head in what appeared to be pure frustration. "This guy knew the woods like the back of his hand. But his references, his land-marks, don't make any sense."

Dameon, steaming cup of coffee in hand, stood next to Jax as he watched him scrutinize the modern-day map. Jax had drawn four small circles on the map. "What do the circles represent?"

Jax pointed to each circle individually. "This one is where we are now. This one should be a water source. But according to our map, there isn't one. This one should be in a large grove of redwoods where he'd seen that creature. I know that area. It's covered in redwoods and evergreens. It's not dominantly redwoods. And this last one, that was where he built a shed to contain the creature. God only knows if it's there or not."

Dameon studied the drawing and found it to be extremely detailed. Jax was right. The guy did know the area. Dameon snickered as he sat down at the table across from Jax. He placed his mug on the table in front of him and wrapped his hands around it.

Jax glared at him. "What's so funny?"

"I can't believe you missed it."

"Care to enlighten me?"

"You remember that rhino hunt we did in the Congo?"

"Yeah. What of it?"

Dameon leaned back in his chair, trying to contain his laughter. It took a couple of minutes, but Jax finally caught on.

"Shit! I'm such an idiot!" Jax picked up the current day map and threw it on the floor. "The journal's twenty years old. It's not going to line up with our map. Mother Nature has seen to that. We're going to have to make our own map based solely on the journal."

Dameon raised his coffee mug in a salute to Jax. "Give the man a prize." Dameon took a sip of his coffee then placed the mug back on the table. He reached for the journal, placing it in front of him to read the map. "Since this is my area of expertise, you're going to have to be patient." Dameon glanced up at Jax and grinned. "Not one of your stronger suits."

"How long is it going to take you?"

"I don't know. I'll start with his map, but I'm going to have to go through the entire journal and confirm landmarks."

Jax was quiet as he observed Dameon studying the map. The last thing he wanted was for Dameon to read the entire journal. It could easily change his mind about tracking the creature. Jax had to think of something fast, and it had to be something that wouldn't offend Dameon. "Well, since we don't have a lot of time, let's work on the map together."

Dameon looked up from the map with an expression of surprise. "Since when do you want to help draw out a map?"

"I don't." Jax reached over and grabbed the journal. He checked the back of the page where the map was drawn to confirm that it was blank, then tore it from the journal. He passed the torn page to an obviously stunned Dameon. "You can start with this. I've read the journal a few times. I'll earmark any references to landmarks, and you can make your map from those pages. It will save us a lot of time."

As Dameon took the page, Jax could tell that Dameon was a little apprehensive. "What if you miss a landmark? You said yourself that you've read the journal a few times. Maybe a fresh pair of eyes will catch something you've missed?"

Jax stood from the table, picking up the journal as he did. "I haven't missed anything. You can go check on our bear. Then when you get back, you can start working on the map. By the time you've finished drawing out a larger scale map, I'll have your landmarks for you." Jax left the cabin, not waiting for a response from Dameon.


Joshawa woke up just as the sun's rays appeared over the horizon. He lay in his bed and listened for the obvious signs that his parents were up. The only sounds he could hear were the birds that sang cheerfully outside his bedroom window. Joshawa assumed his parents were still sleeping, which suited him just fine. He had no desire to be questioned about what had happened the night before.

Joshawa pulled on his jeans and hoodie and quietly left his bedroom. As he surmised, his parents were still in their bedroom. Joshawa grabbed his boots from next to the door and quietly left the cabin. After he laced his boots up, he gazed over to Becca's cabin, hoping that they, too, would be asleep. The cabin was still in darkness, but that didn't ease his nerves. He knew that he would have to face Becca and his uncle sooner than later. Joshawa headed to the back of his cabin and started chopping wood, not for the purpose of adding to the winter firewood, but rather for a release of the anger that consumed him.

As Joshawa sliced through each log of wood, he thought of how he'd walked out on Becca the night before, and for the life of him, he couldn't remember why. He raised his ax, then with all his strength, fueled with anger, he embedded the ax into the chopping block. Joshawa let go of the ax and just stood there, staring out into the forest. He remembered feeling confused. He remembered seeing nothing but the Jelani Tribe. The next thing he knew, he was halfway home and without Becca. He went to grab for the ax, but his father's thoughts filled his mind.

*I'm here for you, son. Do you want to talk about it?*

Joshawa turned around to find his father standing several feet away from him. "I'm right here. You don't have to meld with me."

"I didn't want to startle you." Nathen approached Joshawa until he was standing only a couple of feet away. "I can sense the conflict that's raging inside of you. If you would only talk to me, tell me what's bothering you."

Joshawa didn't know if he wanted to share his experience or not. He knew his parents were concerned for him and that they wanted to help. However, the question was did he want their help, "I can't explain it. In all honesty, I have no idea. One minute I was dancing with Becca, and the next, I was halfway home. What happened in between was almost like a dream."

"A dream? What happened in the dream?"

Joshawa stood very still, staring at his father. How could he possibly share something he didn't understand himself? "I don't remember. I need to go apologize to Becca."

Joshawa walked past his father and into the cabin. He would take a hot shower and then work up the courage to apologize to the girl he loved.

Serena observed the interaction between Joshawa and Nathen. He was so close to speaking to his father, and that was something she couldn't let happen.

"You had an opportunity to intervene. Why did you not take it?"

Serena turned around to find Lord Chike standing only a few feet away from her. He was scowling at her, and his body language made it very clear that he wasn't happy with what he had just witnessed.

"Lord Chike." Showing her respect, Serena bowed her head. As she looked back up at her Lord, she quickly thought of a response. "The conduit is in place. I am now speaking directly to Joshawa."

Lord Chike corrected her. "You will address him as Lord Joshawa."

"He is not a Lord, at least not in the true sense. My Lord, with all due respect, I must tread lightly. Lord Nathen and Mistress Authia suspect that something is amiss. And if I am not careful, they will discover what is happening. You chose me because I have a history with the family. You must trust me to know when to intervene and when not to."

Lord Chike remained quiet for a moment as if he were digesting what Serena had to say. "There is a lot at stake, High Priestess Serena. For both you and the Jelani Tribe. You have proven yourself a worthy addition to the Ancestors. However, I will not hesitate to take that from you if you fail. Do I make myself clear?"

"Abundantly, my Lord." Serena watched as Lord Chike turned and walked away. She gazed over her shoulder and down toward the cabin and Joshawa.

*I'm so sorry, my Mistress, please forgive me.*

Amy woke up just as the sun's rays were poking their head over the horizon. She glanced toward the entrance of her cave to find Alex still at his post. He was lying on the ground, awake, his head raised as he stared out at the forest. Amy got up and neatly folded the thin blanket she'd used to cover herself. She was still wearing her shorts and camisole from the day before, and the cool morning air caused her to shiver. Amy placed kindling and two more logs in the firepit. Then she knelt beside it and blew on the hot coals until the fire came alive and engulfed the kindling. Satisfied that the fire was well on its way, she grabbed her linen jacket that was lying on the trunk and walked over to Alex. She placed her arms around his massive neck, though they barely covered half the expanse.

"Good morning, Alex." Alex gazed over at Amy. She smiled at him as she stood back and ran her hand along the top of his head. "Let's go to the stream. I'm hungry." Amy waited while Alex stood up and ambled into the forest. She followed him, but her thoughts were focused on something else.

After she ate, she would head back to the tree where she'd seen him. A debate was going on inside her head as to whether or not she should reveal herself to the stranger. She'd been watching him for a long time, and he seemed perfectly safe. He didn't harm any of her friends. In fact, he often fed them and cared for them.

Alex stopped and looked back at her as if he could hear her thoughts. She gazed at him like a child who got caught with her hand in the cookie jar. "All right. I'll just watch." Amy walked past Alex, pouting as she made her way to the stream.

Joshawa had finished his shower and was in his bedroom getting dressed in a clean pair of jeans and a black sweatshirt. He glanced over at the image that stared back at him in the oval mirror that hung over his dresser.

*Could Becca actually love what she saw? How could she?*

Joshawa's expression saddened as he stared back at the image that he'd grown to despise. He was so close to telling her how he felt about her. But what if she rebuked him? How could he live so close to her, knowing that she didn't want him?

*Of course she does not want you. You do not belong here. You do not belong with these people. There is an entire tribe of people, your people, waiting for you, my Lord. A tribe from which you can choose a woman who will love you for who and what you are.*

Joshawa stared deep into the mirror. Once again, he saw the Jelani Tribe. They were gathered in a large hut. At the back was a platform covered in what appeared to be a tapestry. On the platform was a woman who looked just like him. She was smiling at him as she gestured for him to approach. His mind saw only the woman. He found himself standing in the hut, captivated by her beauty. He started to walk toward her, but the sound of his name being called brought him back to reality. The vision faded, and it was only his image that stared back at him.

His father's voice bellowed inside the cabin. "Joshawa!"

Joshawa gave his head a shake. "Coming." He took one last look in the mirror and then went to see what all the commotion was about.

When he came out of his bedroom, he found his mother sitting at the kitchen table. She was dressed in jeans and a long-sleeve sweatshirt. Her right hand was covering the area on her chest where her tattoo would be, and she appeared to be in pain. His father, dressed only in jeans, sat next to his mother, holding her left hand in his.

"What's going on?" Joshawa rushed to her side and knelt next to her. "Are you okay, Mother?"

Nathen answered. "No, she's not. Something's going on, and we have to figure it out."

"What do you want me to do?"

Nathen glanced over to Joshawa. "It's time you learned

everything there is to know of Serena. We're going to need your help to strengthen our meld and reach out to her." Nathen helped Authia remove her sweatshirt, then gently moved the strap to her tank top to one side. "Serena gave your mother this tattoo, and now she's using it to communicate with the three of us. But for whatever reason, your mother and I are not strong enough to reach her."

Joshawa was taken aback at the sight of the tattoo. As before, it was raised, appearing as though it had been burned into her skin. When he placed his hand close to it, he could feel the heat. He could see his mother's pain reflected in her eyes. He looked back toward his father. "Serena is doing this? How is this possible?"

"I don't know, son. But whenever she communicates with us, your mother's tattoo does that. Problem is, she didn't communicate this time."

Joshawa recalled the vision he had last night and again not minutes ago. "Mother, did your tattoo react last night while I was at Burwood?"

Authia looked at Joshawa, obviously puzzled by the question. "Yes, as a matter of fact, it did. Why?"

"Because last night someone spoke to me, and I saw a vision of the Jelani Tribe. When I was in my room not five minutes ago, the same woman spoke to me. I saw another vision of the tribe."

Authia and Nathen appeared to be in shock. They just stared at Joshawa, their eyes wide, their mouths slightly opened. Finally, Authia spoke. "What did Serena say to you? What did she want?"

"She wants me to go back to the Jelani Tribe."

# CHAPTER EIGHT

Becca woke up to the sounds of birds chirping in the redwood tree that grew next to her bedroom window. She always slept better when the window was open, allowing the cool night breeze to fill her room. In the morning, her alarm clock was the birds that sang so sweetly to her.

A family of Peregrine Falcons had made their home on one of the lower branches of the redwood tree. The nest was still quite far from the ground, but not so far away that Becca couldn't see the baby birds from her window. She lay in her bed staring at the ceiling as she recalled the events from the previous night. Joshawa had been so happy and carefree, and he appeared as though he was enjoying himself. While they danced, Becca had a distinct impression that he wanted to tell her something, but then everything changed.

Sadness washed over Becca as she recalled watching Joshawa walk away from her and leave the building. She gazed about her room, oblivious to the furnishings and to the decorations that adorned her walls. Her mind was consumed as she debated the ramifications of telling Joshawa how she felt, a debate that rattled around in her brain more times than she cared to admit.

If Becca told Joshawa that she loved him, and Joshawa admitted that he loved her, she would be ecstatic. However, if the time came and he chose Africa over her, she would be devastated. The hurt would be so deep that it would never go away, and she would never be whole again.

That being said, if she didn't tell him, then he might believe that Africa was his only choice. Becca climbed out of bed, walked over to the three—by-three-foot window, and gazed out into the forest. She wore a light pink tank top and cream-colored flannel pajama pants. The morning air had a chill to it, causing Becca to shiver. She grabbed her dark blue hooded sweatshirt lying on the bed and pulled it over her head. With determined strides, Becca left her room to seek out her mother. It was time to tell her mother how she truly felt about Joshawa.

Joshawa and his mother sat at the kitchen table in silence while his father went to the bedroom to finish dressing. When he came out of the bedroom, he was rolling up the sleeves of his gray shirt. Without saying a word, Nathen proceeded to cook bacon, eggs, and toast for breakfast. The smell of bacon wafted throughout the cabin, but Joshawa didn't notice.

He was focused on his mother's tattoo. And as the minutes ticked by, her tattoo became less and less noticeable. Joshawa glanced over at his dad, who was placing the breakfast onto plates. "So, what do you have to tell me about Serena that I don't already know?"

His father placed the three plates on the table then sat in his chair as he glanced over to Authia. Joshawa could tell that his father was waiting for approval. When his mother nodded her head, his father began their story.

"We've told you how your mother and I met. You know that Serena placed a curse on me while I was still safe in my mother's womb. At the same time, she placed a curse on my father, a curse that she believed would last an eternity. You also know what your mother and I had to go through to save my life as well as yours."

"Yes, you told me all that. You and my grandfather killed Serena. So how is she back? How can she have control over

Mother?"

"You have to understand, son. Serena was, and still is, an immensely powerful Priestess."

"What do you mean by *still is?*"

"When we killed Serena, I thought we were done with her. But our Ancestors, the ones that watch over the Jelani Tribe, had other ideas. They chose to allow her to continue to exist as a spirit. They put her in a very dark place as punishment for what she did to our family. It was a prison of solitude from which there was no escape."

"So if she's been in prison all this time, how did she get here?"

"When your mother and I were living in Africa, we were threatened by a group of men . . . outsiders, who were looking for the entrance to our valley. To help protect us, our Ancestors released Serena from her prison and sent her to us. What we didn't know was that it wasn't only the outsiders that we needed protecting from."

Joshawa looked upon his father in complete bewilderment. "Why would the Ancestors send a Priestess to protect you that had already tried to kill you? That doesn't make sense. And who else did you need protecting from?"

At that point, Authia interjected. "Our Ancestors are very cunning, and they hold the Lords and Priestesses accountable for any and all indiscretions. However, they are also bound by some extremely strict rules. The Ancestors themselves can't physically hurt a Lord or Priestess, but they could send someone or something else to do the job for them. Serena's mother, Celest, was also punished for her involvement in your grandfather's death, as well as for her tyrannical rule over the Jelani Tribe. Once Celest died and her essence was depleted, the Ancestors were able to imprison her."

"What's essence?"

"Essence is at the very core of every Priestess. With this

essence, she can create spells, incantations, see and hear things that no one else can. Every Priestess hides a portion of her original essence in order to protect her own existence. If her original essence is destroyed, then she becomes nothing more than a tribe member. She's no longer a Priestess. When this happens, the Ancestors are free to do with her as they see fit."

"So was Celest the threat to you?"

"Yes. A very real and dangerous threat."

"I thought that there was no escape from the prison. If Celest didn't have her powers, then how did she get out?"

"Celest was a High Priestess who mastered the dark side, the pure evil of all the spells and incantations that the priestesses used. Somehow, she hid a portion of her original essence from the Ancestors. Then she waited until the time was right. The Ancestors discovered that she had escaped, but they couldn't touch her. So, they sent Serena to us. They knew that she would be the only one that could defeat her mother."

"Did she?"

"Yes. If she hadn't, you, your father, and I wouldn't be here today." Authia glanced over to Nathen. "She not only protected us from her mother, but she also saved my life."

Nathen reached over and took Authia's hand in his.

Joshawa observed the interaction between his parents as his father gazed upon his mother with love. It was obvious that something about that last comment hit a nerve with his father.

"If Serena hated you so much, why would she save your life?"

It was Nathen's turn to continue the story. "Serena discovered that her mother was just using her to get what she wanted. It was that revelation that convinced Serena that we were not the enemy. At that moment, she became an exceptionally strong ally. We said that the outsiders were a threat to our village. There was one outsider in particular. His name was Obasi. He believed that our valley contained great wealth, and he wanted to plunder that wealth. We set a trap for him, but he was too smart. Joshawa, he stabbed your mother, killing her where she stood."

Joshawa's eyes widened in disbelief. "What do you mean he killed her?" Joshawa pointed toward his mother. "She's sitting right there."

"Your mother was dead. Serena forfeited her life so your mother could live. Before Serena joined our Ancestors, she told your mother that she was going to leave something of herself behind. She always wore a beautiful rather seductive blue dress."

Joshawa glanced over to the blue tattoo that was now back to normal. "So that's how you got the tattoo?"

"Yes. And now Serena is using it to communicate with us."

Joshawa corrected his mother. "You mean me. She's not speaking to us, Mother. She's speaking only to me."

Authia's face drained of color. Joshawa could see the fear in her eyes. "Yes, you're right. She's only speaking to you. And we need to find out why she wants you back in Africa. Because, as far as your father and I know, there is only one way you can get there."

Dameon sat at the kitchen table, staring straight ahead, thinking of the journal that Jax found.

The creature from the journal did pique his curiosity. Was it just the author's imagination, or had he sketched the creature from what he'd actually witnessed? Dameon knew that he should be checking on the bear, but to create a map from landmarks that were twenty years old was a challenge he couldn't wait to start.

He got up from the table and went over to his backpack,

then he opened it and removed his GPS. He turned it on, and the screen came alive with color. The screen was predominantly green, with dark circles expanding outward, each circle larger than the next. The steady red dot in the center of the screen, which was also the center of the smallest circle, was him. The yellow light was his bear. The bear hadn't moved far, only a few hundred yards from where it was yesterday at this time. Dameon decided to check on the bear later. He shut off the GPS, returned it to his backpack, then walked over to the supplies Jax had brought to the cabin.

Dameon retrieved his sketching kit and a three-foot-long roll of parchment paper. He rolled out a section of parchment that was approximately three feet by three feet on the table. Next, he removed a pencil, scissors, and ruler from his sketching kit. He penciled a line at the three-foot mark and then skillfully cut the parchment so that it was perfectly square.

Satisfied with the size of the parchment he'd chosen, he rolled up the remaining parchment and placed it aside. Then he strategically placed a scale ruler, compass, T-square, and protractor on the parchment. He started by drawing the cabin he was calling home in the center of the map. From the page Jax had torn from the journal, Dameon was able to map the stream that flowed behind the cabin. But most importantly, he was able to map out three separate sites where the creature had been seen.

The map was incredibly detailed, but what astonished Dameon was that it only spanned in three directions. There was nothing north of the homestead. It was as if the author of the journal never traveled in that direction.

Dameon tapped the pencil against the table as he studied the torn page of the journal. He was so focused on the landmarks that he didn't hear Jax enter the cabin. It wasn't until Jax dropped the journal on the table that Dameon glanced up.

"Good. I need more information to finish this map."

Dameon put the pencil down and went to reach for the journal, only to have Jax move it out of his reach.

Dameon was confused. Was it his imagination, or was Jax being a little too possessive of the journal? He watched Jax as he sat at the table with the journal firmly grasped in his left hand. To Dameon, it looked as if Jax was deciding whether or not he wanted to give it up.

"Do you expect me to use telepathy to read the journal?"

Jax placed the journal on the table. However, he didn't let go of it. "You don't have to read it. I've marked the pages that we need. I'll read them to you, and you can do your thing."

Dameon rested against the back of the chair as he scrutinized Jax. He was sure Jax was up to something he didn't want to share. "Since when do you read to me? Just give me the journal." Dameon extended his right hand toward Jax, but he wouldn't budge. "Okay, spill. What's going on with you and that journal?"


Jax's mind was going over all the scenarios that Dameon might believe. Jax needed Dameon's unique talent for creating detailed maps of places that had existed long ago. However, to accomplish that, Dameon needed the journal. The problem with that was if Jax allowed Dameon to read the journal, then there wouldn't be any chance that Dameon would help hunt down the creature. Jax knew that he would have to make a difficult decision if Dameon refused to help. "That smaller cabin freaked you out, didn't it?"

"Of course it did. Are you going to tell me it didn't freak you out?"

"Not particularly. Dameon, that cabin is tame compared to what he wrote in this journal. Believe me. You don't want to read it." Jax didn't take his gaze off Dameon, and he didn't let go of the journal. "You want this to be your last hunt. Face it,

Dameon, you've changed. The hunt no longer thrills you like it used to. We'll make a good dollar on our bear." Jax opened the journal to the drawing of the creature then held the journal so that it was facing Dameon. "Think of what we could make on this creature. You'd never have to worry about money again." Jax closed the journal and placed it in front of him. He could tell that Dameon was weighing out his options, and for that matter, so was Jax. This hunt meant everything to him, and he would do anything to make it happen.

Dameon leaned forward, resting his arms on the table. "I'm not the only one who's changed. The hunt doesn't thrill you either. It's the kill. You're like family to me, Jax. But you're going down a path that I can't follow. And you're right about our bear. He *is* my last hunt. As far as that creature goes, I honestly believe it doesn't exist. That drawing is nothing more than the imagination of the guy that used to live here. However, since we have time, I'll help you check out where the creature was sited. But . . . and this is a very big but . . . if this creature still exists and it turns out that the creature is a human being, then you'll have to go through me to capture him or kill him. Is that understood?"

"Perfectly. Now let's work on the map."

Dameon stood, pushing his chair away from the table as he did. "No, I'm going to go check on our bear. We'll work on the map later."

Jax observed Dameon as he grabbed his camo jacket from the back of his chair. He retrieved his backpack from his bunk and slung it over his right shoulder. Just as Dameon was about to leave the cabin, he turned and faced Jax. "We've been together for a long time, Jax. But don't think for one moment that our friendship will cloud my judgment. If it comes down to it, I will protect that creature."

Dameon left the cabin, closing the door behind him. Jax stared at the door for several minutes. He looked down at the journal, then back up at the door. "And I won't let anything come between me and that creature. Including you, my good friend."

Becca sat at the kitchen table, her left cheek resting in the palm of her hand as she stared down at her plate. Usually, she would devour her breakfast, but instead, she just poked at her scrambled eggs with her fork. Her hair was loose, spilling over her shoulders and almost onto her plate. Becca could sense that her parents were staring at her.

She sighed as she gazed up at them. "I need to talk to Mom, alone." She glanced over to her father. "Girl talk. Would you mind, Dad?"

Hansen, dressed only in his jeans, stood away from the table then went to grab his flannel jacket that was hanging on the wall next to the door. He put it on and then grabbed his plate and coffee from the table. Hansen smiled at Becca. "It's a nice morning. I think I'll eat outside."

Becca smiled back, though she felt bad that she wasn't including her dad in this conversation. She watched as he left the cabin then turned her attention to her mom. Tammy was dressed in a sleeveless, blue flannel nighty that fell just past her knees. She stood from the table and went to stand behind Becca. Gently she gathered Becca's hair into a ponytail then used an elastic to hold it in place.

Tenderly Tammy placed her hands on Becca's shoulders. "You know the rules." Tammy kissed the top of Becca's head then sat back down at the table. She pushed her half-finished plate away from her, folded her arms on the table, and smiled at her daughter. "Let me guess. This has something to do with Joshawa and what happened last night."

Becca tried to hold back the tears forming in the corner of her eyes. "I don't know what to do, Mom. Joshawa isn't just a friend. I love him." Unable to contain herself, Becca started crying, her tears running freely down her cheeks. "I've been wanting to tell you for a long time."

Tammy reached across the table and took Becca's hands in hers. "Oh sweetheart, we all know that you love Joshawa."

Becca was stunned. She hadn't told anyone about her feelings. "How do you know? And who's everyone?"

"Pretty much everyone but Joshawa."

"I've been that obvious?"

Tammy smiled as she gently shook her head. "You'd have to be blind not to see it. It's written all over your face every time you see him or talk about him."

"Then why hasn't he figured it out?"

"Because he's a man and the subject of your attention. You'd have to hit him over the head with a two-by-four before he'd realized that you loved him." Tammy gently squeezed Becca's hands. "You're not one to beat around the bush. Why haven't you told him? You do know he loves you?"

Becca gently pulled her hands away and leaned back against the chair. "No, I don't know that he loves me. Well, I think he loves me. Mom, I don't want to tell him because I'm scared that he's going to want to leave for Africa."

"If he knew you loved him, he probably wouldn't go."

"Exactly. You said probably. There's no guarantee that Joshawa would stay. And I can't follow him. As it stands now, it would break my heart if he left. How would it be if I told him I loved him, if I gave him my heart, and he still left?" Becca started to sob. "I couldn't handle it, Mom."

"Why can't you follow him?"

Becca wiped the tears from her face with her hands. "Mom, I couldn't leave you and dad. And I don't think I could live with the tribe being the only outsider."

"You wouldn't be the only outsider. That being said, I understand where you're coming from. I know firsthand what it's like to be so different. Actually, my stay in Africa has given me a better perception of what Joshawa must be going through."

"Do you think he should go?"

"Doesn't matter what I think or what you think. It matters what Joshawa thinks."

Becca's emotions blanketed her as if they were a dark cloud with no silver lining to escape to. "I don't know how to figure that out. I want to scream to the heavens that I love him. But what if that's not what he wants? I don't know what to do, Mom."

"Well, then there's only one thing we can do." Tammy stood up and started clearing the table.

"What are you doing?"

"You and I are going to get dressed, and then we're going to pay your aunt a visit."

"You want me to tell Aunt Authia how I feel about her son?"

Tammy placed the dishes in the sink then turned to face her daughter. By the smirk on her face, Becca knew her mom was up to something. "No, we're going to let her tell us."

"I don't understand."

"You will. Now go get dressed." Tammy went to her bedroom, closing the door behind her leaving Becca completely confused.


Dameon headed into the forest in the direction he last saw his bear. The forest was alive with the animals that called these woods their home. Their voices harmoniously echoed throughout the treetops. Dameon always found comfort in the sounds of the birds, squirrels, and coyotes, but unfortunately, peace was not afforded to him as he trekked through the woods. His mind was occupied with Jax and his unsettling behavior.

Dameon was confident in the knowledge that the bear's existence was safe. He was worth nothing if Jax killed him. Even though the bear wouldn't be free to roam the great Rockies, he would be well cared for. It was the creature that Dameon had issues with. That journal was over twenty years old, and if that smaller cabin was any indication, then the journal was the writings of a mad man. Was this creature something from his imagination? And if it wasn't, what were the odds that it would still be alive?

Dameon was so preoccupied with his thoughts that when a snowshoe hare jumped out of the bush and onto his path, he nearly tripped over it. A small smile graced Dameon's lips as he stood perfectly still. He observed the hare and was fascinated that it didn't appear to be frightened. It just sat on the path, staring right back at Dameon. At that moment, his uncertainty of the journal and of Jax and the creature became abundantly clear. Dameon knelt on his haunches, not taking his focus off the hare. The hare remained still, his nose slightly twitching as it continued to stare back at Dameon. However, when Dameon reached out to the hare, it took off, disappearing into the forest. Dameon stood up, staring off after the animal.

Jax was not one to chase after ghosts or creatures that their clients would dream up. He turned down extremely lucrative hunts for bigfoot and the Loch Ness monster. But this time, Jax was adamant that not only did this creature exist, but it was still alive. Something in the journal convinced Jax of the creature's authenticity. Dameon needed to get his hands on that journal without Jax knowing. And if the journal was right, and this creature did exist, then Dameon knew it would be as trusting as the hare. It wouldn't recognize the danger that stood right in front of it. And that was reason enough for Dameon to protect it from Jax.

# CHAPTER NINE

Joshawa had finished his breakfast in silence. His parents were debating why Serena wanted to speak to him and why she needed Authia as a conduit. He used his toast to mop up the last of the egg from his plate, washed it down with the last of his milk, then loudly cleared his throat. Both Authia and Nathen turned their attention to him.

"You two aren't focused on the real issue."

Nathen spoke up. "And what is the real issue?"

"Me, of course. Granted, I believe that we need to know why Serena has to speak to me through Mother. But what we really need to find out is what she wants with me. Why she's so insistent that the Jelani Tribe needs me, that I belong there. Once we know that, then the rest should just fall into place."

Joshawa pushed his chair back, picked up his plate and empty glass, then placed them in the kitchen sink. He stood for a couple of seconds just staring at the wall above the sink. His mind was consumed with Serena and the visions she afforded him.

He needed to think, and there was only one place where he could do that in peace. He turned to face his parents. "I'm going to go out for a bit." Joshawa walked over to Authia, tenderly kissed her on the top of her head, then headed toward the door. He was reaching for his fleece-lined jean jacket that was hanging on the wall next to the door when Nathen interrupted him.

"Where are you going?"

"For a walk. I need to put everything Serena has shown me

96

into perspective."

"Don't you think you need our help to do that?"

"No disrespect, Father, but no, I don't. I need to understand what Serena is showing me. When I figure that out, then we can work on the why." Joshawa slipped his jacket on and left the cabin.


Amy was sitting next to the stream, watching Alex as he caught their breakfast. He always caught her fish first. Then he would stand in the middle of the stream and gorge himself with the succulent fish. Usually Amy would sit for hours watching him play in the water. Sometimes she would even wade into the stream and play with him. But with the change in seasons, the water was now too cold for Amy. Besides, she had other things on her mind. Amy ate her fish raw, threw the carcasses in the stream, then knelt by the edge of the water and washed her hands and face. As she stood, shaking her hands dry, she gazed over at Alex.

"Alex, I'm going now. I'll see you later." She turned to leave, only to have Alex approach her from behind and give her a gentle nudge. Amy turned to face him, then placed her hands on her hips and frowned at him. "What do you think you're doing? You're not coming with me." Amy stood staring at Alex as if she expected a verbal response. He remained motionless, staring right back at her. Amy sighed as she placed her hands on either side of his snout. "Go back to the cave. I'll be back soon. I promise."

Amy turned to leave, but Alex was persistent, much to her dismay. Once again, he gently nudged her, only this time he walked in front of her, effectively blocking her path. Amy knew he was only trying to protect her. Once again, she sighed. "All right, you can come. But stay out of sight." She rolled her eyes as she walked around him. "As if you could."

Amy headed into the forest, followed closely by nine hundred pounds of grizzly.

Dameon found the spot where he'd last seen his bear. He stood scrutinizing the area for any sign that his bear was nearby, but there was nothing. The site was full of shrubs that were weighed down with fresh berries. With the amount of food available in such a small area, his bear should have returned.

Dameon took off his backpack, placing it on the ground next to him. From inside the backpack, he removed his GPS and turned it on. The GPS immediately picked up the signal showing that the bear was a good half-hour north of his current location. He appeared to be next to a water source, which could explain why he hadn't returned Dameon picked up his backpack, slung it over his left shoulder, and with the GPS in his right hand, he started to follow the signal.

Joshawa was conflicted about whether or not he should speak to Becca before leaving for Grot. When he walked down the steps of his porch, he saw his uncle sitting in one of the four sizable high-back wicker chairs that were situated on the right side of his porch. He had his feet propped up on the railing and appeared to be eating his breakfast.

The decision was made for Joshawa when he made eye contact with Hansen. Joshawa took a deep breath then headed toward Becca's cabin. He was nervous, not knowing how his uncle would receive him, especially after he'd walked out on Becca the night before. However, as he got closer, he could see that his uncle was smiling at him, which made him feel a little more at ease.

Joshawa climbed up the stairs of the porch and stood

before his uncle. "Is Becca up?"

Hansen took his feet off the railing, placed his plate on the small wicker table that was next to his chair, and motioned for Joshawa to sit down. "Take a load off. I think you and I need to talk."

Joshawa sat in the chair next to Hansen's. His uncle didn't appear to be upset with him. However, it was his daughter that Joshawa walked out on. "You probably want to talk about last night."

"Yeah, I do. What happened, Joshawa? Why did you walk out on Becca?"

"Look, I'm really sorry. I shouldn't have done that. And to be honest, I don't know what came over me. It was almost as though I blacked out. One minute I'm dancing with Becca, and the next, I'm halfway home."

Hansen moved his chair so that he was directly facing Joshawa. "What's going on with you? And before you start, I think it's a lot more than just trying to discover who and what you are."

Joshawa covered his face with his hands and leaned back against the chair. Slowly he removed his hands and rested them on the arms of the chair. Joshawa wasn't comfortable looking directly at Hansen, so he focused his gaze on his own cabin. "I guess it's safe to tell you. You know who Serena is?"

"Yeah, I do."

"Well, she's been communicating with me. She's trying to convince me to go to Africa. Sometimes she gives me visions, and when she does, I lose myself in these visions. I'm totally unaware of what's going on around me."

"What kind of visions?"

Joshawa glanced over to Hansen. "They are all pretty much visions of Africa and the Jelani Tribe. I think she's trying to show me what I'm missing out on."

Hansen and Joshawa remained quiet for several minutes.

The silence hung in the air like a thick fog that refused to dissipate. Joshawa felt apprehensive and wished he could just get up and leave. However, he knew that wasn't an option. He was in the wrong, and he would sit and wait until his uncle had said his piece.

Finally, Hansen broke the uncomfortable silence. "Where does Becca play in all of this?"

Joshawa had no idea how to answer that question. Should he tell his uncle the truth? He hadn't even mustered enough courage to tell his parents, or Becca, for that matter. "Becca is very special to me."

"Cut the crap, Joshawa. Level with me. Do you love her or not?"

Joshawa closed his eyes as he drew a deep breath. When he opened his eyes, he gazed upon his uncle with trepidation. Someone once said *the truth can set you free.* Joshawa just sighed. *Or it can kick you in the ass.* "Yes. With all my heart. But I'd rather that stay between us."

"Why? Why not tell her?"

"Really? Come on, uncle. Look at me. I know Becca cares for me. But do you honestly believe she could love this?" Joshawa circled his face with his right hand. "Do you honestly believe that she would want to spend the rest of her life chained to me?" Joshawa stood and started to walk down the porch steps. He stopped and turned when he reached the bottom. "She could do so much better than me. And please, keep this conversation between the two of us." Joshawa turned and headed into the forest.

Amy was close to her destination. Cautiously she scanned the area searching for the strange man she was so obsessed with. Off in the distance, she could see the redwood tree that he would climb day after day. He never climbed any other tree, just that one. As far as Amy could tell, he didn't appear to be in the area. However, she couldn't see into the canopy of his tree from where she stood.

Amy glanced over her shoulder at Alex and slowly shook her head. "This isn't going to work, Alex. He's going to see you."

She glanced back in the direction of the redwood, then turned to face Alex. "You see that tree next to the big one he hides in?" Amy was pointing behind her in the direction of the redwood. "I'm going to have to climb it to the very top if I'm going to see him and stay hidden." Amy placed her hands on her hips and gave Alex a stern look. "You can't follow me. If you stay here, he's going to see you. You're huge!" Keeping her left hand on her hip, she pointed her right index finger in the direction of the cave. "Go back to the cave."

Amy stood her ground, folding her arms across her chest as she waited for Alex to leave. However, Alex wasn't playing her game. He just ambled past her in the direction of the tree she wanted to climb. Amy threw her arms in the air.

"Really . . . stupid bear." She stomped past him reaching her tree before him. Once again, she stared him down. "Fine. Stay. But if you scare him off, I'm going to be very mad at you." Amy watched as Alex headed toward some tall shrubs growing in front of a large evergreen tree. The lower branches of the evergreen were about three feet off the ground.

Alex maneuvered behind the shrubs and lay on the ground underneath the tree. Amy smiled as she shook her head. He managed to blend in with the shrubs and the dark earth beneath the tree. She knew he was there, but the man she was looking for might not.

Amy turned around and gazed up at the large branch that was a couple of feet above her head. She could have easily climbed the tree, but not while wearing the jacket. It was too cumbersome, and she would have to take it off. The downside was that the morning air was chilly, and Amy had no idea how long it would be before he arrived. Her shorts and tank top would not keep her warm, so leaving the jacket behind was not an option.

Amy glanced down at her jacket, undid her belt, grabbed the hem of the jacket, and brought it up to her waist. She folded it one more time so that the jacket only reached her hips. Then, as tight as she could, she tied the belt around her waist, hoping it would keep the jacket in place.

Amy glanced up at the branch that she needed to reach. She stepped back a few feet then ran up to the tree, jumping at the last moment. Her hands firmly grasped the branch, and then with ease, Amy pulled herself up until her hips were resting against the branch. She threw her left leg over and then straddled it. Amy gazed up to the canopy of her tree. The rest of her climb would be easy.

She took one last glance in Alex's direction, then using the tree's branches as if they were rungs in a ladder, she started her ascent.

Dameon continued to head north, following the signal on his GPS. At one point, he stopped to get his bearings. His bear was much further north than he had been before. Dameon was confident that the bear's den was more to the south. But if that was the case, then why had he headed so far north? Since Jax and he had tagged the bear, they hadn't used the GPS.

He was ridiculously easy to follow. Now, it was as if the bear knew he was being followed and decided to make them work for their bounty. Dameon glanced back down at the GPS. His bear was on the move heading slightly northwest. Checking up on his bear was going to take longer than he anticipated.

Should he continue and catch up with the bear or head back to the cabin and work on the map?

*Screw it! The bear is real. That creature isn't.*

Dameon repositioned his backpack and headed in the direction that the GPS indicated.

Joshawa made good time heading to Grot. The entire time he thought of nothing but Becca. His stomach was in knots, thinking of what might happen if his uncle chose to tell Becca about how he felt. But then part of him hoped he would. That way, he wouldn't have to face her rejection in person. He'd just have to hear about it.

Joshawa kept a steady pace until he was about a mile away from Grot. He slowed his pace down and stared off into the distance. He had hoped to arrive at Grot as early as possible, but that didn't quite work out for him. Now he ran the risk that whoever was out there was already near his tree.

Joshawa scanned the canopy of the trees that soared high above him. His best chance was to get as close as he could, then make his way to Grot using the upper branches of the surrounding trees. With a plan firmly set in his mind, Joshawa carefully made his way closer to Grot.

Amy worked her way high up into the tree until she found a branch wide enough to sit on, and also one that was concealed by the beautiful fall-colored leaves that adorned the tree. She sat cross-legged on the branch, gazing through the smaller branches and leaves that wove their way through the canopy of the tree.

Even though the stranger's tree was much higher than hers, Amy felt confident that he wasn't there. She didn't see any fresh signs that he was around, and if he had been here when she first arrived, she was sure that Alex wouldn't have hidden so willingly.

Amy glanced down toward the evergreen Alex was hiding under. From her vantage point, she could see the tree but not Alex. She shrugged her shoulders, then continued to watch the redwood tree for any signs that would indicate he was there. Time dragged on, and Amy was getting restless. She had just decided to leave when she heard a noise coming up from the forest floor. It was the sound of a branch being broken.

She gazed down, trying to see what was at the base of her tree. Unfortunately, she was too high up. She glanced over to the massive redwood tree. After seeing nothing, she returned her gaze back down at the ground. Unconsciously, Amy nibbled at her lower lip as she tried to decide if she should check out the noise or just wait and see if she heard it again. It could very well just be an animal, or it could be him.

Amy sat quietly, straining to hear any noise. Her patience was rewarded but not with a noise that she was familiar with. It was a beeping sound that started softly then got louder and louder. Then it just stopped, and everything went quiet. Curiosity got the better of Amy, and she began to make her way down the tree as quietly as possible.

Dameon followed the GPS as it took him deeper into the forest — deeper than he had ever been before. His bear was now stationary, possibly asleep for the afternoon. Dameon continued to push his way through the forest, ever mindful of the animals that made this area their home. According to his GPS, he was getting close.

A half-hour later, he was standing on the very spot his bear was supposed to be. Dameon cautiously looked around but saw nothing. Confused, he glanced back down at the GPS, which indicated that his bear was right where Dameon stood.

Again, he scrutinized his surroundings. How could he not see a nine-hundred-pound bear? Before he headed out, he'd silenced his GPS, mostly because he didn't want to make any unnecessary noises. However, either his GPS wasn't working, or his bear was right in front of him in plain sight.

Dameon trusted the GPS over his own eyes, so he turned it on. It started to softly beep, and as Dameon ever so slightly turned his body to the left, the beeping got louder. When he pointed it toward an evergreen tree, the GPS went nuts. Dameon turned it off, placed his backpack on the ground, and then put the GPS inside.

He slowly drew his *Glock* from its holster with his right hand, positioning it an arm's length away from his body at chest level. He held the exposed portion of the gun's grip with his left hand to steady his shot. Cautiously Dameon crept toward the evergreen, focused on where his bear was supposed to be. His heart was racing, and his palms were sweaty, which was something he'd never experienced before. He had never been on his own when confronting a dangerous animal. Dameon knew that if the bear was there and he decided to charge, the only thing Dameon's *Glock* would do would be to piss it off.

Dameon approached the shrub that was directly in front of the evergreen tree. Aiming his *Glock* toward the shrub, he used his left hand to pull some of the shrubs to one side. Dameon stood perfectly still. His heart was racing inside his chest—staring right back at him was his bear. The bear was lying on the ground, his head raised, his piercing black eyes looking right through Dameon.

He was so close to the bear that he could feel its breath. Dameon stared at the bear, his mind reeling as to what to do. He knew he couldn't make any sudden movements, so he slowly let go of the shrub. His left hand immediately went back to holding the grip of the *Glock* as he cautiously backed up. He didn't take his eyes off the shrub for one second.

After he'd backed up a dozen steps, his foot hit his back-pack. He reached down with his left hand, feeling for the backpack's strap while he still watched the shrubs. When Dameon found it, he didn't put it over his shoulder—he just held onto it as he continued to slowly back up. His bear made no attempt to follow him, and after a few minutes, Dameon felt safe to stop. He placed his backpack down and retrieved the GPS. However, he didn't holster his *Glock* until the GPS proved that his bear hadn't moved.

Amy cautiously climbed down the tree until she reached a branch with enough girth that she could lie on it and remain concealed. She also wanted to be close enough to hear and see what was happening. Amy lay down on her stomach with her head facing toward the tree's trunk. She then leaned over ever so slightly so she could see who was on the ground.

There was someone there, but it wasn't who she was ex-pecting. This person was different. He was strangely dressed, and he held some sort of box in his hand. It glowed with a green light, and it made that beeping sound she heard.

The man moved ever so slightly, and as he did, the beeping sound came faster. Amy gasped when the man pointed the box in Alex's direction and then didn't move. The box was beeping as fast as her heart was thumping in her chest. Amy watched as the man put the box away, and then he took some-thing off his belt. He pointed it in Alex's direction as he started to walk toward him. Amy held her breath as the man pulled the branches away and revealed Alex's hiding spot.

All Amy could think of was that she had to save Alex. She sat up on the branch and was about to start climbing down when the man started backing away. Amy hesitated as she watched the man back up, almost to her tree. Then he removed the box from the bag he was carrying. The box came alive with the green light, but the beeping was very faint. The man replaced the box, put something into his belt, and then slung the bag onto his back.

Amy thought he would leave, but he didn't—he just stood very still for several minutes. From Amy's vantage point, it appeared as if he was checking the area out. Amy was now sitting cross-legged on her branch. She placed her hands in front of herself so she could maintain her balance as she leaned over to get a better look at the stranger. At that exact moment, the man looked up. Amy jolted upright, closed her eyes as tight as she could, and listened for any sound that indicated the man had seen her.

Dameon's heart was pounding with so much force that he thought it would burst from his chest. Once he was confident that his bear wouldn't come after him, he holstered his *Glock* and then started to survey the area.

As far as he could see, there were only mature evergreens and redwood trees. There wasn't enough food in the area to sustain his bear, so why was he here? Dameon's gaze fell on the evergreen his bear was hiding under, and he wondered why the bear didn't come after him. The bear was cornered, yet he never moved a muscle. He didn't even make a sound. The bear's reaction made absolutely no sense to Dameon.

He picked up his backpack, slung it over his shoulder, and was about to leave when he got the uneasy feeling he was being watched. Dameon gazed upwards and thought he saw movement in the branches of the tree that stood a foot away from him. He had stepped back to get a clearer line of sight when he heard the shrubs behind him rustling. Slowly he turned around with his right hand on the grip of his *Glock*.

His bear was no longer hiding. He was standing in front of

the shrubs moving his body ever so slightly from side to side. Dameon knew he was warning him and could charge at any moment. Dameon didn't take his eyes off the bear as he slowly maneuvered his way backward. He had only backed up a few feet when the bear turned and made his way back under the evergreen. Dameon closed his eyes, said a silent prayer, then started to make his way back to the cabin, constantly checking over his shoulder the entire time.

# Chapter Ten

A uthia had finished the breakfast dishes and then decided to relax in her favorite chair. Joshawa had left for his walk, and Nathen was splitting wood, leaving her alone with her thoughts.

Authia had removed her sweatshirt but left her tank top on. She placed a blanket around her shoulders, and as she curled up in her chair, she wrapped the blanket around herself. Authia felt safe in her home, in her favorite chair, but she knew only too well that it was a false sense of security. She and her family would not be safe until they figured out what Serena was up to.

Authia's mind was consumed by only one thought, and that was Serena. She closed her eyes and reached far within her mind. Authia needed to block her thoughts and emotions from Nathen and Joshawa, something she hadn't done for quite some time. She needed to think, and she needed to do it alone. If either one thought she was distressed or unsettled, they would be at her side within minutes.

Authia sighed as she stared blankly at the cold, lifeless fireplace. It took her a little longer than usual, but in the end, she was successful in blocking them from her thoughts and emotions. Now she had the daunting task of reaching out to Serena. It felt like an eternity since she'd tried such an in-depth meld, and if the truth was known, she had little confidence that it would work. Authia focused her thoughts and tried to reach out to Serena, but no matter how hard she concentrated, Serena didn't respond.

Unconsciously, Authia placed her right hand directly onto her tattoo. She tenderly guided her fingertips as they traced the outline of the tattoo. She continued to run her fingertips along the edges, and within seconds the tattoo grew hotter to the touch. The sudden heat startled Authia, and she immediately pulled her hand away and moved the edge of her tank top to see her tattoo. The edges had raised ever so slightly, and the blue coloring was more prominent. She was about to call out to Nathen when an idea came to her.

She placed her fingertips back on the tattoo, and even though it was painful, she allowed her fingertips to delicately trace the edges. She could feel the heat building within the skin and felt the tattoo raise beneath her fingertips. She closed her eyes and sought out Serena.

*I knew my Mistress was clever. You have figured out how to communicate with me.*

*What's going on, Serena? What do you want with my son? Can he hear our conversation?*

*You are always so full of questions.*

The pain from the tattoo was becoming unbearable, so Authia withdrew her hand. The minute her fingertips left the tattoo, the connection with Serena was broken. At that moment, Authia realized that in order to communicate with Serena, it would come at a price. Would she endure the pain to connect with Serena? If it meant saving her son, then there was only one answer. Authia sat straight up in the chair, squared her shoulders, and once again placed her fingertips on the tattoo. The pain and heat came much faster this time. Authia ignored the agony and once again reached out to Serena.

*So, this is the way we can communicate?*

*This is the only way. It affords us privacy.*

*Then no one else can hear our conversation?*

*That would be the meaning of privacy.*

*I'm not in the mood to play games, Serena! Tell me what's going on!*

*I am sorry, my Mistress, but this conversation must wait for another time.*

*I'm still your Mistress, and you're going to tell me exactly what you want with my son!*

*Another time. You have company, and I must tend to my obligation.*

*What obligation?* Serena was gone, and Authia could feel the heat and pain diminish as her tattoo returned to normal. In that short exchange, Authia could sense that Serena was battling her own demons. What those demons were and what they had to do with Joshawa was still a mystery that needed to be revealed.


Tammy had changed into a pair of jeans, a red t-shirt, and a gray sweater that fell to just below her waist. When she walked out onto the porch, she found Becca sitting in a wicker chair. Her hands were folded in her lap, and she was staring out into the forest. She was still dressed in her pajama pants and a blue hoodie. "I thought you were going to change. And where's your dad?"

Becca answered her mom without taking her focus off the forest. "Dad went to help chop wood, and I didn't feel like changing." Becca stood and faced her mom. "Joshawa's not home, so it really doesn't matter what I wear."

Tammy looked at her daughter with trepidation. "So you're planning to stay in your p-jays all day?"

"Well, at least until Joshawa comes home."

Tammy watched her daughter as she left the porch and walked toward Joshawa's cabin. Becca had always stood up to any challenge, and she would never allow herself to be emotionally brought down. She always found the silver lining in any situation, no matter how bad it was. Her current mood told Tammy that maybe her daughter possessed an Achilles heel. It was her love for Joshawa that would be her undoing.

This revelation confirmed to Tammy that no matter the outcome, good or bad, Becca needed to speak with Authia.

Tammy had caught up to Becca and slowly opened the door. "Hey, are you decent? Becca and I are . . ." Her voice trailed off when she saw Authia's face. Her pain and anguish were clearly evident. "What the hell?" Tammy ran over and knelt down in front of Authia, taking her hands in hers. She glanced over to her daughter. "Becca, get your aunt some water." She then gazed up to Authia to see tears starting to form in the corner of her eyes. "What's going on?"

Authia closed her eyes and slowly shook her head. When she opened her eyes, the tears ran freely down her cheeks. "I was able to communicate with Serena. She's scared, and she didn't have time to tell me why. All I know is that it involves Joshawa, and that scares the hell out of me."

Tammy let go of Authia's hands as Becca handed her a glass of water. When Authia accepted the water, Tammy smiled at Becca as she motioned for her to sit on the floor next to her.

Becca followed her suggestion sitting as close to her as possible. She crossed her legs in front of her then glanced up to her aunt. "Is Joshawa going to be okay?"

"I hope so, Becca. But I honestly don't know."

Tammy glanced over at Becca then back to Authia. "I was going to ask if you wanted to play one of your mind games with Becca, but I'm thinking now that maybe she could help you in another way."

Tammy could see that Becca was perplexed. "I was going to have your aunt look into your future and see if Joshawa was part of it." She then turned her attention to Authia. "I mean, it's no secret that Joshawa loves Becca. And you and I both know that Becca loves him."

"Mom!"

Tammy glanced over to Becca. "What? I told you that it

wasn't a secret." Tammy returned her focus on Authia. "Yesterday, when you hugged Becca, you were given a snapshot of Joshawa's future. Maybe, if you try again, but you're in control this time, you'll see more."

Authia knew Tammy was right, but she didn't want to do it alone. She needed Nathen, but she had to remove the blocks that prevented Nathen and Joshawa from hearing her. It only took seconds, then Authia reached out to Nathen. *Do you have a minute, sweetheart?*

*Of course. I'll be right there.*

*Thank you. Oh, and bring Hansen with you.*

Authia quickly wiped the tears from her face, gave her cheeks a slight pinch to bring color to them, then focused on Tammy and Becca. "Nathen and Hansen are coming in. I don't want Nathen to know about my encounter with Serena."

Tammy looked confused by Authia's request. "You're not going to tell him you spoke to Serena?"

"Yes, I am. But not now. Let's focus on whatever vision is afforded me through Becca."

Nathen and Hansen entered the cabin, and they both seemed surprised to see Tammy and Becca there. Nathen hung his jean jacket up on the wooden hook next to the door, then washed his hands in the kitchen sink. He faced the group as he was drying his hands on a dishtowel. "So, what's going on?"

Authia smiled as she motioned toward Tammy. "Tammy has an idea that might help us figure out what my vision means."

Nathen grabbed a kitchen chair and placed it next to Authia while Hansen took his turn to wash up. When he was finished, Hansen sat on the love seat and motioned Tammy to join him. He then focused his attention on Authia. "You're talking about the vision you had when you hugged Becca?"

"Yes. I'm going to try to see the vision again. Only this time, I'll be prepared for it. Nathen, I want you to meld with me. I want you to see the vision as well. Maybe you'll catch something I'm missing."

Nathen stood and offered his hand to Authia. "Sounds good. Let's sit at the kitchen table."

Just as Authia was about to place her hand in Nathen's, Becca interjected. "Maybe we should just sit on the floor. Last time, aunty, you almost fell flat on your face. If we're on the floor, you won't have so far to fall."

Authia giggled as she joined Becca on the floor. "You do have a point." Authia also crossed her legs in front of her as she sat across from Becca. She patted the floor next to her as she gazed up at Nathen. "Come join me." Authia glanced over to Tammy and Hansen. "Do you two mind sitting this one out?"

Tammy smiled at Authia. "Not at all. Just watch over my daughter." Authia could tell Tammy was anxious, but then so was she.

The three sat in a circle facing each other. Authia took a deep breath, then held her left hand out to Nathen. "Watch over us. Keep me strong so I can stay in the vision longer."

Nathen took Authia's hand in his, then reached his left hand out to Becca. "I'll help strengthen your vision, but I'll also keep you safe. I'll end the vision if I feel it's getting too dangerous."

"Fair enough." Authia reached her right hand to Becca. "I want you to take my hand, close your eyes, and think of Joshawa and only Joshawa."

Becca took Authia's hand and closed her eyes. Authia also closed her eyes and focused all her thoughts on Joshawa. She could feel the energy coursing from Becca to her.

The cave started to form around her. She could smell the

dampness and feel the cold stone beneath her feet. She pressed on, delving deeper into Becca's subconscious. Now she could hear a noise, a rumbling. She strained to listen, to understand what she was hearing.

*I cannot allow you to go further. You are treading in dangerous waters, my Mistress. We both are.*

The vision was gone, and so was Serena. Authia let go of Nathen's and Becca's hands. She turned to face Nathen as she pulled the strap to her tank top away from her tattoo. She glanced down at her tattoo and then back up at Nathen. The tattoo hadn't changed, yet she heard Serena. "Did you hear her, too?"

"Yes, I did. Serena finally spoke to us. She was warning us."

"Nathen, I have a confession. I spoke to her earlier."

Nathen appeared confused. "What do you mean you spoke to her?"

"Apparently, if I rub my tattoo, I can communicate with her. She said it was the only way to keep our conversations private."

"Private from who? Me?"

"Yes, but I don't think it's just you. She's scared. And I agree, she's warning us. There's something else. I think I know where the cave is." Authia placed her fingers on her tattoo and gently started tracing the edges. The burning sensation came on quickly and Authia's mind filled with Serena's voice.

*You do not disappoint.*

*Are you responsible for the vision?*

*Yes and no.*

*Serena, I said no games. The cave you are showing me. It's the cave behind the falls that separates the two worlds, right?*

*All I can say is what you see will come to pass. Only you, my Mistress, can prevent it.*

*Why can't you tell me more? Are our conversations not private?*

Authia could hear Serena sigh, *Yes and no. We must tread lightly. There is much at stake. Remember the past, and you will know what to do.* With those parting words, Serena was gone.

Joshawa had made his way deep into the forest, and when he believed that he was a safe distance from Grot, he stopped. Cautiously he scanned the area for any sign of movement. Any indication that he was not alone. His first thoughts were to climb the tree that stood next to him and slowly make his way over to Grot through the canopies of the surrounding trees. His only concern was, could he do it quietly? Maybe, if he took his time. But unfortunately, he had already arrived later than he usually would.

Joshawa decided that the canopy wasn't an option. He didn't have the time to waste, so he decided to stay on foot and use the trees to conceal himself. As he made his way through the forest, he knew the chances were slim that whatever he'd seen would be there again today. However, his curiosity was greater than his common sense, so he forged ahead as quietly as he could.

At one point, he stopped and listened, but there was no sound. The forest was unusually quiet. It was as if it were holding its breath, waiting for something to happen. As Joshawa carefully approached Grot, he could have sworn he saw movement just beyond his tree. Then he heard a sound, a faint beeping sound. Joshawa hid behind the immense girth of Grot, pressing his back firmly against the trunk. The beeping sound intensified, piquing Joshawa's curiosity. Slowly he peered around his tree, and his eyes widened as he saw a man, dressed entirely in camouflage, holding what appeared to be a GPS device.

Joshawa watched as the man turned the GPS off, placed it in his backpack, then withdrew a gun from his belt. Joshawa turned away and pressed his back tightly against the tree. It was as if Joshawa wanted the tree to swallow him whole so he would not be discovered.

So many questions were bombarding his mind, but the priority was to get out of sight. He only had one option that would ensure a quiet retreat. He turned to face his tree, then slowly started to make his way upwards, toward the safety of the thick branches and multitude of leaves that made up the tree's canopy.

He managed to climb halfway up without being detected. Joshawa chose a branch that would be wide enough to conceal him. Then he sat down with his back against the trunk. Carefully he peered down and watched as the man pointed his gun toward an evergreen tree. Joshawa's stomach was in knots, and he felt sick at the thought of being discovered.

He'd always felt safe here, because no one had ever come this far north. He observed as the man slowly moved some shrubs aside, and then he just stood there. Joshawa couldn't see past the shrubs, but whatever was there caused the man to let go of the shrubs and slowly back up, keeping his gun aimed at the evergreen tree the entire time. He backed up so far that Joshawa couldn't see him anymore. He needed to know what this man was up to, so he started to climb down to a lower branch.

Joshawa was twenty feet off the ground before the man came into sight again. Joshawa selected a branch and positioned himself as far out on the branch as he could. He had no choice but to straddle the limb to maintain his balance. He was facing the tree, and from where he sat, he had a clear line of sight to the man. The man had his backpack slung over his shoulder, and his gun was holstered. He was scanning the area as if he were looking for something, and then suddenly, he looked up.

Joshawa sat straight up, his legs still dangling on either side of the branch, and he prayed to God that the man didn't see him. He closed his eyes, held his breath, and remained perfectly still. When he finally opened his eyes, the man was no longer looking toward him. Instead, he was staring down the biggest grizzly Joshawa had ever seen. The man slowly backed up and disappeared into the forest. When the man was out of sight, the grizzly turned and headed toward the evergreen tree.

Amy watched the man until she could no longer see him. When she was confident that he was gone, she scanned the area for Alex. Amy was relieved that he'd already returned to his hiding place. She closed her eyes and sighed as she gently shook her head back and forth. Amy had risked a lot just to see the stranger.

She opened her eyes and gazed into his tree. She couldn't see him and saw no obvious signs that he was there. Annoyed, she rolled her eyes and then climbed out of her tree. When she reached the ground, Alex came charging out of his hiding place. He ran up to the stranger's tree, growling, his teeth bared. He reached up a good eight feet slamming his massive paws repeatedly against the tree. Amy watched in horror as her stranger fell from the tree, hitting the ground so hard that she was sure she heard bones breaking. Alex dropped to the ground then stood over the stranger.

"What did you do, Alex?" Amy chewed on her lower lip as she approached the stranger. He wasn't moving, and neither was Alex. Amy gently nudged Alex's shoulder so he would move away from the stranger. She knelt by his side and placed her hand on his chest. He was still breathing, but just slightly. Amy placed her hand underneath his head to cradle it, only to discover that it felt wet and sticky.

She gently pulled her hand away and gasped at the sight of her hand covered in blood. She had to help him, but she was too afraid to do that in the open. "Alex, I need your help. Come, lie beside him." She motioned for Alex to lie alongside the stranger. Then with all her available strength, she grabbed the stranger's jacket and started to pull him onto Alex's back. She struggled with his weight, but she was determined and finally managed to get him straddled across Alex. "All right, Alex, we're taking him home."

# CHAPTER ELEVEN

Lord Chike concealed himself at the edge of the jungle behind a kapok tree. In front of him was a small clearing, lush with green grass and wildflowers. Lord Adeeowale was standing at the edge of the clearing watching over the Jelani Tribe. He was dressed in the tribe's traditional animal skin loincloth that covered him from his waist to his knees. He wore an open animal skin vest that revealed his bare chest and stomach.

Lord Adeeowale had passed into the Spirit World at the age of sixty. And now, centuries later, he hadn't aged a day. His hair was still a brilliant red, his eyes were sharp and clear, and his cheekbones were very prominent, as was the cleft in his upper lip. His physique was not only muscular, but it also portrayed strength. He had all the bearings of a true Lord. Lord Chike scowled as he stared at the Ancestor. He didn't possess the same attributes and features of a true Lord, only those of a warrior.

He shook his head in frustration. Of all the Ancestors he had to be chained to, it had to be Lord Adeeowale. But then, nobody knew the history they shared. Even Lord Adeeowale was unaware of who Lord Chike truly was, a revelation that would remain hidden until Lord Chike decided otherwise. He took a deep breath then slowly let it out.

*You will remember, old friend. But by then, it will be too late.*

Lord Chike turned then disappeared into the depths of the jungle.

Lord Adeeowale stood at the edge of the Realm of the Ancestors and observed the Jelani Tribe. They were at peace and lived in harmony with the outsider. He particularly watched the young Lord. He was seventeen and well on his way to becoming a strong and just leader. His father, Rick, was an outsider who'd earned the right to become Lord of the Lion People. His mother, Tamara, was the High Priestess of the tribe. When Rick was honored with the title of Lord, the Jelani Tribe chose a new name for him. The name they chose was Zareb, which in their language meant protector, a fitting name, for that was precisely what he did. He protected the tribe from outsiders that would have destroyed the entire valley, including the Jelani Tribe.

Lord Adeeowale continued his vigil as he watched the tribe start a new day. When they prepared their noonday meal, Lord Adeeowale concluded his surveillance and returned to join Imani and Lord Chike. He found Imani in her usual place, sitting on the ground in front of a roaring fire. She also wore her animal skin halter and skirt. He smiled at her as he sat on the ground next to her.

There was no need for warmth or much else in the Realm of the Ancestors. However, ever since she was a child, Imani had been obsessed with fire. It had always fascinated her. She loved to watch the colors and how the flames danced in among the logs. Imani smiled at Lord Adeeowale, then returned her gaze to the flames.

"Are they not wonderous?" she asked, not taking her focus off the fire.

"Yes, they are, and you are still so young at heart." Lord Adeeowale was already in the Spirit World when Imani became one with the spirits. They'd known each other when they were alive, and even though he was already mated, he always had strong feelings for her, a fact he painfully kept to himself. She was so beautiful, with her red hair cascading down her back. She was average in height, standing at five-foot-ten inches, but her physique was delicate. Lord Adeeowale would even go as far as saying graceful and elegant.

She had an innocence about her, and her smile could always melt his heart. He was saddened by her death, for she was only thirty-five, which was way too young to join the spirits. Normally, only a true Priestess was given the honor of becoming an Ancestor. But Imani had made the ultimate sacrifice, giving her life to save the life of her Lord. Because of that sacrifice, she was afforded the honor of becoming an Ancestor even though she was only a tribesman.

After Imani's death, Lord Adeeowale spent over two decades in the Valley of the Lion People. When it became his turn to join the spirits, Lord Adeeowale was at peace, because now he could spend an eternity with Imani.

Lord Adeeowale casually scanned the surrounding area and was surprised that Lord Chike was nowhere to be seen. His gaze fell back on Imani. "Is Lord Chike not here?"

Imani glanced up from her fire and slowly shook her head as she shrugged her shoulders. "I have not seen him for quite some time. I thought perhaps he was with you."

"No. I was alone."

Lord Chike had hidden behind a kapok tree and listened to his comrades. When he overheard the comments, he decided that this was a good time to make an appearance. He walked around the kapok tree and approached the fire pit. Lord Chike assessed their facial expressions to get a sense of their mood. As always, Imani was engrossed in her fire, and Lord Adeeowale was engrossed with her.

"Sorry I could not join you earlier. I was watching a warrior that left the hunting party. I was curious as to where he was going." His words were a lie that he hoped would not be detected.

Imani smiled at Lord Chike as she motioned for him to join them. "And where did your warrior go?"

Lord Chike sat across the fire from Imani and Lord Adeeowale. He returned her smile, only his was a smile of relief. "He met up with a woman. She is the sister of one of the other warriors. From their exchange, I gather that her brother does not approve of their coupling."

Lord Adeeowale chuckled. "The oldest story of our long history. One seeks out what they cannot have. A story that never ends well for either party. I spent my morning watching Lord Dava."

Lord Chike was quick to correct Lord Adeeowale. "He is not a Lord. He is only a child, the prodigy of the current Lord and Mistress."

"That is true, but he does have the makings of a great Lord. He will usher in a new age for the Jelani Tribe."

Lord Chike chose his next words carefully. Lord Adeeowale was of the mind that having an outsider as a Lord was, as he put it, a progression needed for the Jelani Tribe to move forward. "Yes, he could. Maybe it is the destiny for the Lords of the Jelani Tribe to be outsiders."

Imani gazed up from the fire and looked directly at Lord Chike.

To him, she looked as if she was trying to understand what he had just said. He offered no explanation and waited to see what she had to say about his comment.

"Dava is a child of both worlds. He may appear as his father does, but he is also very much his mother's child. He is a union of both worlds. He is proof that not all outsiders are evil. My hope is that in time, the word *outsider* will cease to exist, at least the negative meaning of the word. Going forward, our Lords will always be the children of both worlds."

Lord Chike observed Lord Adeeowale as he gazed upon Imani with such tenderness that it revealed his love for her. *What a fool. You are in love with a common tribe member. She is no more a Priestess than that child is a Lord.* But Lord Chike knew to keep his thoughts to himself. "You are so right, Imani. A child of both worlds. It is a wonderous thing."

Lord Chike stood, brushing away a hot ember from his loincloth as he did. "I will take my leave." He bowed to his companions, and as he turned his back to them, a wicked smile crossed his lips. *That child will never be Lord. That child will not live to see his next birthday.* With that thought, Lord Chike disappeared into the jungle in search of Serena.

Joshawa felt as though he was floating on his stomach but not as if he were in water. It felt different, as if he was suspended in midair. The movement was jerky, and the air around him smelled foul. He tried to focus, to open his eyes to see where he was, but his eyes would not cooperate. He tried to move, but his body was also an unwilling participant. Joshawa could feel a heaviness cloud his mind. Then there was only darkness as Joshawa once more passed out.

Nathen listened to Authia as she recounted her conversation with Serena. *Remember the past, and you will know what to do.* Serena could not be more cryptic if she tried. They had so much *past* with Serena. How were they supposed to know which part she was referring to?

Nathen stood up and helped Authia to her feet. Becca joined her mother on the love seat while Authia went to the kitchen for another glass of water. Nathen observed Authia as she filled her glass, then turned and leaned against the counter. She held the glass in her right hand at waist level while she strummed the fingers from her left hand against the glass.

"Care to share your thoughts?"

Authia gently pushed away from the counter, placed her untouched glass of water on the kitchen table, and went to sit in her favorite chair. Nathen took his chair and positioned it so that he would be facing Authia. Authia slowly shook her head as she sighed. "What part of the past are we supposed to remember? She's been a part of our life for twenty years. She's been entwined in your life for over two hundred years. Seriously, how am I supposed to be clever enough to figure this out?"

Nathen could hear the sound of defeat in Authia's voice. He leaned in, took her hands in his, and gave them a gentle squeeze. "You are clever enough. You know that. We'll figure this out just like we always do."

Tammy interjected. "I know I haven't been a part of this craziness for very long, but maybe if you went over every-thing that's happened since the curse? Make a Cliff-notes ver-sion and write down the highlights. Then maybe the answer will jump out at you."

Nathen smiled at Tammy. "You're absolutely right." He re-turned his focus to Authia. "If we write down the key points of all the events from the time I was cursed up to us leaving Africa twenty years ago, then maybe we will see a common thread."

Authia nodded her head in agreement. "Maybe if we're close to the answer, Serena will . . ."

Nathen didn't hear Authia finish her sentence. His mind was flooded with Joshawa's emotions. He stood up quickly, knocking his chair over as he did. At first, Nathen could sense that Joshawa was scared, but seconds later, Joshawa was en-veloped in pain, and then there was nothing.

Amy led Alex back to the cave. But when she tried to enter, Alex put himself and his passenger between her and the entrance. Amy stood there, completely bewildered by his actions. Once again, she tried to pass, but Alex refused to cooperate. Confused by his actions, Amy moved closer to Alex so that she could see his face. Amy tilted her head slightly as she tried to understand what Alex was trying to do.

"Do you not want me to come into the cave? It's our home. Why can't I?" Amy tried to push her way past Alex, only this time, he pushed back. "Okay, you're making me mad. Move!" Amy extended her right arm as she pointed to the cave wall. "Now!" Alex still did not move. He just stared at her. They stood there for several minutes, then Amy had an idea. "Okay, if you're not going to move, then lie down so I can take the stranger off your back." Amy gestured toward the ground as she spoke.

To her astonishment, Alex lay down. But by doing so, he'd effectively blocked the entrance to the cave. The mouth of the cave was only inches wider than he was long. Amy smiled at Alex. "Two can play this game." She climbed over Alex, then stood facing him and placed her hands on her hips. "Ha! I'm in the cave now."

Amy glanced over her left shoulder then back to Alex. She had to get the stranger over to her fire, but she didn't believe that Alex would be of any assistance. She shrugged her shoulders, grabbed the stranger's jacket, then gently began to pull him off of Alex.

She tried to avoid hitting his head on the ground, but the stranger was too heavy, and when the bulk of his weight was off Alex, he crashed to the ground. Amy gasped as she covered her face with her hands. Slowly she removed her hands to see the stranger lying contorted on the ground. She bit at her lower lip as she knelt to see if he was still breathing. To her relief, he was still alive.

However, she still had the daunting task of dragging him to the fire. She carefully rolled him onto his back, but when she grabbed his legs, Alex got up and stood over the stranger. Amy dropped the stranger's legs and just then realized what Alex was doing. "It's not me. It's him. You don't want him in our cave." Amy stepped closer to Alex and put her hands on either side of his face. "What's wrong, Alex? Are you afraid of him?" Amy glanced down at the stranger, then back up to Alex. "You're being silly. He's hurt, bad. And you're huge. I'm not afraid. I know you'll protect me. Please, Alex, I want to help him." Amy stared into Alex's eyes. She smiled at him, because she knew that he understood. Amy reached down and once again grabbed the stranger's legs, only this time Alex didn't get in her way.

Dameon couldn't get back to the cabin fast enough. He occasionally checked the GPS and watched as his bear left the area and headed further north. It wasn't until late afternoon when Dameon finally reached the cabin. He was angry, frightened, and baffled about his bear's actions.

He entered the cabin to find Jax sitting at the kitchen table, totally engrossed in his journal. Even that, which would typically upset Dameon, didn't faze him. He unceremoniously tossed his backpack onto the kitchen table as he headed straight for the kitchen counter. He retrieved a bottle of whiskey, filled a tin cup halfway, then downed it in one gulp. He put the mug on the counter and just stood there staring at the back wall.

"Having a bad day?"

Dameon turned around and went to sit at the table with Jax. He leaned back in his chair, his arms folded across his chest, and the look he gave Jax was one of pure frustration. "I should be dead. Our friggin bear should have killed me."

Jax put down the journal, his eyes wide with surprise, his mouth trying to form a sentence that wasn't there. He stood up and went to get the whiskey and two tin mugs. He placed them on the table, poured a healthy amount in each cup then slid Dameon's across the table. "Okay. What the hell are you talking about?"

Dameon sat up straight, took the mug, and once again downed the fiery liquid in one gulp. He placed the empty cup on the table and just shook his head. "I was this close to our bear." Dameon placed his right hand at eye level and extended his thumb and index finger till they almost touched. "I had him cornered. He should have charged at me. But instead, all he did was warn me off."

"Maybe he didn't consider you a threat."

"You don't get it. He was hiding under an evergreen tree, using shrubs to conceal himself. When I moved the shrubs, he should have charged."

"You're talking about him as if he were a person. He's a stupid animal. I don't think he was concealing himself. He was probably just staying cool."

"Jax, we're in the mountains. It's friggin cold out there. Winter is around the corner. He wasn't keeping himself cool." Dameon ran the events through his head, and none of them made sense. "When I discovered him under the evergreen, he never moved. He let me back up and walk away. But when I was going to leave, I could have sworn that someone was watching me. I thought that there was someone in the trees."

Jax snorted as he rolled his eyes. "Who the hell is going to be watching you way out here? Seriously, are you letting the squirrels freak you out now?"

Dameon shot Jax a look of contempt. "There was something there. I know there was. And when I started to go check it out, our bear came out of hiding and challenged me. As soon as I started to leave, he went back to his hiding place.

You have to admit, grizzlies don't act that way. He should have charged me and torn me to shreds."

"So, you're saying he was protecting something?"

"There was no food in the area. Why else would he be there?"

"Question is, what would he feel the need to protect? We've been following him for months. He has no mate, no attachments. There's nothing for him to protect."

"You and I both know everything there is to know about grizzlies. I'm telling you. He was protecting something."

"Okay, say I agree with you. Is he still there?"

"No. He left the area shortly after I did. He headed north."

"North? Toward the stream?"

"In the general area. So, what do you think a nine-hundred-pound grizzly would want to protect?"

Jax smiled at Dameon, but it appeared more sinister than friendly. "Maybe he was protecting another animal."

"What animal lives in the trees and would entice a grizzly to protect it?"

"Maybe an animal that isn't quite all animal."

Dameon chuckled, because he knew what Jax was inferring. "Tell me you're not thinking that our bear is protecting whatever that is in your journal."

"Of course. It makes sense. Maybe this creature was able to befriend our bear."

"You're trying to tell me that some man was able to make friends with a grizzly. Are you off your rocker?"

"We don't know if this creature is man or beast. Our bear hibernates in this area every year. Maybe they met and became friends. Whatever the reason, our bear didn't attack you. I think a trip to that spot is in order."

Jax pushed his chair out, placed the whiskey bottle back on the counter, then went to his bunk bed to grab his backpack. Dameon remained sitting, observing Jax, but when Jax went to grab his jacket, Dameon spoke up. "We're not going there today. It's too far, and I'm not taking chances of running into our bear in the dead of night. However, we could pass the time exploring the journal." Dameon reached in the direction of the journal, but before he could put his hands on it, Jax was already at the table. Dameon watched as Jax grabbed the journal from the table and shoved it into his backpack. "You really don't want me to read that journal."

"You couldn't handle it. Trust me. You don't want to read it." Jax sat back down at the table, placing the backpack by his chair.

"Are you at least going to let me see the map references?" Dameon could tell that Jax was weighing out his options. Dameon could press the journal issue, but that probably wouldn't go well. There was something in that journal that Jax didn't want him to see, and Dameon wasn't sure how far Jax would go to keep him from reading it.

Jax's expression of indecision morphed into a smirk that Dameon knew only too well. "You know, Dameon, we might not need the map. The landmarks are decades old. We know the general direction of the cabin. And after what happened today, I think our bear is going to be our best option for finding whatever is in the journal."

Dameon knew he had to be cautious about how he dealt with Jax. He also knew he had to read that journal. He decided he'd play along with Jax. Then when the opportunity arose, he'd take advantage and hopefully gain the upper hand. "All right, we'll head out at first light." Dameon grabbed his backpack off the table and walked over to the bunkbeds. He placed the backpack on the floor next to the beds, then turned to face Jax as he removed his jacket. "So, what's it going to be. Are we going to try to find the cabin or the bear?"

Jax smiled at Dameon. "We know where the bear is. Let's look for the cabin."

Lights were flashing inside of Joshawa's head. They flashed faster and faster until they blurred together, spinning out of control. He tried to open his eyes, but the daylight caused his head to ache with so much pain that it was unbearable. His stomach was churning so much he knew he was going to vomit. He could feel someone cradling his head, then tenderly lifting it up. He tried to speak — he tried to form a simple sentence, but nothing came out. The fog that enveloped his mind created a barrier between him and the outside world. He thought he heard a voice, a whisper, but he couldn't make out what was being said. He felt something against his lips, something metal, then realized he was being given something to drink. Joshawa had never been so scared. He had no control over his body and no control over his mind. He could feel himself drifting out of consciousness, and before his mind would succumb to the darkness, he thought of the one person who could save him. A single tear fell down his cheek. *Please, Father, help me.*

# CHAPTER TWELVE

Nathen stood by his overturned chair. His eyes were closed, his mind focused on the emotions that slammed against his own. The emotions only lasted seconds, but Nathen knew without a doubt that Joshawa was in trouble. He was aware of Authia's hand on his shoulder, and he sensed that she was speaking to him, but her words fell on deaf ears.

Nathen had to focus on Joshawa, because he couldn't risk losing the connection to his son. Joshawa's emotions were fading in and out, as if his mind was trying to shut down. At first, Joshawa was experiencing incredible fear, and then what followed was excruciating pain that encompassed his entire body. Next was darkness, and Nathen could tell that he was losing the connection.

However, he refused to give up, so he focused everything he had on what was no more than a glimmer of Joshawa's emotions. Minutes later, the darkness lifted, and he could sense that Joshawa was confused. His mind was jumbled, and Nathen had difficulty understanding what his son was feeling.

Normally he could use the emotional connection like a GPS, guiding him to where Joshawa would be. But Joshawa's mind was not strong enough, and Nathen believed that Joshawa was fading in and out of consciousness. That was the only explanation for why he couldn't pinpoint his son's location.

The connection that Nathen was so desperately hanging

onto was gone. He opened his eyes to find Authia standing in front of him. Her hands were in his, and she appeared to be as frightened as he was. She was still speaking to him, but it took a second for her words to register. "Nathen, what's going on? You're scaring me."

Nathen glanced around the room, then focused his attention on Authia. "Joshawa is in trouble. I have to find him."

Authia's eyes widened, and she looked as if she was going to burst into tears. "What do you mean he's in trouble? Where is he?"

"I don't know."

Authia let go of Nathen's hands. "What do you mean you don't know?"

"His emotions are chaotic. He's not awake long enough for me to get a fix."

Authia's right hand covered her mouth as she shook her head. Nathen might not sense Joshawa's emotions, but Authia's were so strong that they almost brought him to his knees.


Serena sat at the edge of the Realm and watched in horror as Joshawa fell to the ground. Her immediate reaction was to go to him, to save him, but Lord Chike had denied her access to the world below. She was only permitted to possess Joshawa's mind, to connect with him through his thoughts and emotions.

She continued to watch as Joshawa slipped in and out of consciousness. Serena knew that Nathen wouldn't be able to find Joshawa in his current state. Without hesitation, Serena stood and left her post to seek out Nathen. She had only taken a couple of steps when Lord Chike's voice resonated within her mind.

*Where do you think you are going?*

Serena slowly turned to discover Lord Chike standing only

a couple of feet away from her. His expression was dire, and she knew he wouldn't be impressed with her answer. *Do you wish to communicate through melding, my Lord?*

Lord Chike was livid, of that Serena was certain. He chose to speak to her directly. "I will ask again. Where do you think you are going?"

Serena squared her shoulders and tried her best to hide the contempt she felt for her Lord. "I would think that would be obvious. Joshawa is hurt, and I am going to make sure he is found."

"You seek out his father?"

"Yes." What happened next was a blur to Serena. Lord Chike's fist connected with her jaw, sending her flying to the ground. She felt his fist connect, and she felt the pain, which completely baffled her. Serena lifted herself up slightly, resting on her left elbow. With her right hand, she tenderly touched her left jaw and cheek. Lord Chike stood over her, his legs straddling her body, so even if she wanted to, she couldn't stand up.

He glared down at her, his teeth clenched, his fists ready to inflict more pain. "You try my patience. Our Lord is hurt, but time will heal his injuries. You know that as well as I do. Your job is to fan our Lord's hatred for his father. Not help that traitor find his son."

Serena didn't move a muscle. She just stared up at Lord Chike, trying desperately to remain calm. "His injuries are severe, my Lord. And yes, he will survive, but there is no guarantee that he will be himself when he heals. The mind is delicate, and he may lose everything that he is. If his father finds him, then Joshawa will have a better chance of becoming the Lord you want him to be."

Lord Chike knelt on one knee, and with his right hand, he grabbed Serena by the throat and started to squeeze. The pressure he was inflicting on her throat caused her to gasp for breath, and even though she was in pain, she wouldn't give him the satisfaction of trying to remove his hand. She just lay there, accepting the pain. And as he tightened his grip, she feared that her throat would collapse.

"You take me for a fool. I watched you play with the minds of the outsiders. I watched you convince a broken man that he was whole. You will enter Lord Joshawa's mind, and you will ensure that his thoughts and emotions are not heard by anyone, especially not his parents." Lord Chike violently let go of Serena's throat, smashing her head against the ground as he did.

Once again, he stood over her, smirking at her as if he dared her to make a move. "It does not matter what his condition is while he occupies his body. As a spirit, he will be whole again and ready to take his rightful place. Now do your job, or I will see to your destruction!" Lord Chike moved away from Serena, then disappeared into the jungle.


Amy had managed to drag the stranger to her firepit and lay him as close to the fire as she could. She wanted him close enough so he would feel the heat but not so close that he would get burned. He was still unconscious, and Amy was beginning to fear that he would never wake up.

When she'd removed his jacket, he had screamed out in pain, and for a moment, she thought he was awake. Unfortunately, after Amy had folded his jacket and placed it under his head, he had once again closed his eyes and wouldn't respond to her.

She knelt by him, staring at him as she wondered what to do. Gently she placed her hands on his chest, closed her eyes, and listened to his breathing. His breathing was shallow, and if he took too deep of a breath, he would gasp in pain. Amy removed her hands from his chest, then continued to examine the rest of his body. The elbow on his left arm was out of place, and when she tried to straighten his left leg, he would moan as if he were in agony.

From all the blood, she knew he had a serious gash to the back of his head. She had to do something to help him. Amy got up, grabbed the two metal buckets that she used to haul water, and headed for the stream.

Serena sat on the ground, legs crossed in front of her, as she watched the interaction between Joshawa and the girl from the cave. To do what Lord Chike wanted of her, it would be best if the girl wasn't present.

Serena gingerly stretched out her jaw as she tenderly rubbed the left side of her face with her right hand. Then she moved her hand down to her throat. She still had difficulty breathing, and her throat was incredibly tender.

*I wonder if spirits bruise. If we do, I am sure that my throat will be black and blue. How did he manage to inflict so much pain? We are spirits of our former selves. We should not feel pain.*

Those that lived in the Realm of the Ancestors, or the Land of Spirits, could not inflict pain onto another. Only the Council could inflict pain, and only as a punishment. She gazed over her shoulder into the jungle and wondered why she hadn't seen Lord Adeeowale or Imani. Serena was aware that they were also in the Realm of the Ancestors. She had so many questions.

And just now, there was something Lord Chike had said that troubled her. *He would see to her destruction.* Serena looked out at the emptiness that surrounded the Realm of the Ancestors. Something about the phrase, something about him really bothered her. Serena was frustrated with herself, and as she stared out into the emptiness, she gently shook her head.

She hated the fact that she couldn't figure out what was gnawing deep within herself. Serena gazed back down at Joshawa just in time to see the girl leave the cave. This was the opportunity that she needed. Serena stood, took a step into the emptiness, and immediately transformed into a tiny blue wisp.

Joshawa could feel the battle that was wreaking havoc inside his head. Part of his mind wanted to wake up, and part wanted to slip away, allowing the darkness to take over. The latter was an acceptable choice, because in the darkness, he knew there would be no pain. However, if he were lost to the darkness, his father wouldn't be able to find him. What an ironic place to be.

Because of his hatred for his father, he'd never shared where Grot was located. If he allowed the darkness to consume his body, his father wouldn't even know where to begin looking. If he fought to stay awake, his father could use their emotional bond to find him. The problem with that scenario was the pain, and Joshawa didn't know if he was strong enough to endure it. Joshawa tried to think, he tried to reason with himself as to what he wanted, and then she came to him. An image of Becca that was so vibrant, so real, that he felt like he could touch her. She spoke so softly to him.

"Joshawa. You have to fight. You have to live. Do it for us."

Serena flew straight to the cave then delicately landed on Joshawa's chest. His eyes were closed, his breathing labored, and it was so apparent that he was in a bad way. Joshawa had scarcely parted his lips as he tried to take a deeper breath.

When Joshawa grimaced in pain, Serena flew past the parted lips and deep into his subconscious. She melded with him, and what she saw, what she felt, almost made her sick. He had suffered a deep gash to the back of his head, causing a severe concussion. The gash would have to be tended to, or it would become infected, and Joshawa would surely die. He suffered three broken ribs, his left elbow was dislocated, and his left leg was broken. It was a clean break, but it would have to be set in place to heal properly.

Serena had a difficult decision to make. According to Lord Chike, she had to block Joshawa's link to and from his family. Then time would heal Joshawa's wounds. Serena had little faith that any amount of time would heal the severity of his injuries. She couldn't reach out to Nathen or Authia, but nothing was said about reaching out to anyone else. As a wisp, the Ancestors could not track her or know what she was up to. However, Serena was sure Lord Chike would be paying close attention to how long she was absent from the Realm.

Serena had to work fast if she was going to put her plan into action. Joshawa was unconscious, so Serena thought it would be best to start with the girl. She left Joshawa, flew past the bear, and followed the path she knew the girl had taken. She hadn't flown far when she came across the girl returning to the cave carrying two buckets filled to the brim with water. Serena wasted no time and forced her way into the girl's mind.

Serena became one with the girl, who she learned was called Amy. What immediately caught Serena's attention was that this little child-like girl was much older than she appeared. And even though Amy was clever to the ways of the wilderness, she knew nothing of medicine. Amy's intelligence was most likely stunted because she spent almost her entire life living alone in a cave with a bear that she called Alex.

So much information about this child, this woman, was flooding Serena's mind. However, the only information she needed was that Amy had no idea how to heal Joshawa. Serena didn't have the time to plant the necessary information into her mind. It was then that Serena decided on a more radical approach. She would share her consciousness with Amy, at least everything to do with healing, making medicines, basically being a Priestess. Serena delved deep into Amy's consciousness. She put a block in place in the hope that Amy would not question her new ability to heal Joshawa.

*Amy, hear my voice. Open your mind to the gift I offer you.*

Serena segregated the portion of her mind that knew all the incantations, all the remedies, everything a Priestess was taught from birth.

*I will share this with you so that you can save Joshawa. You will not question where this information came from. You will see it as something you have known how to do since childhood. Do you understand?*

Amy nodded her head, acknowledging that she understood.

*That is good, Amy. When I leave, your only thoughts will be to save Joshawa. Do you understand?*

Again, Amy nodded that she did.

*Through these memories, we will be connected, and we will remain connected until such time as I remove my gift. Save Joshawa, Amy. You have to save Joshawa.*


Amy stood on the path, holding a full bucket of water on either side of her. She stared off into the distance, seeing nothing. Though her eyes were open, her mind was blank. Then suddenly, as if a hood had been removed from her head, the forest appeared in front of her. She could hear the sounds of the forest, and she could feel the slight breeze as it gently caressed her skin. Slowly, she gazed at her surroundings, wondering why she had stopped. Then her gaze fell upon the path in front of her, and all she could think of was that she had to save Joshawa.


Serena left Amy and quickly flew back toward Joshawa.

When she reached the cave, she hesitated as she hovered over Alex. He lay at the entrance to the cave in an apparent attempt to protect the inhabitants. Serena was about to fly away, but Alex lifted his head and stared directly at her. Their gazes met, and Serena realized that he was no ordinary bear. She landed on his snout and reached out to the mammoth bear.

*Yes, he is special. Please help me protect him.* Serena required no response, for she already knew what was in the bear's heart.

Serena flew over to Joshawa to discover that he was still unconscious. The very thought of what he was experiencing caused her heart to ache. She didn't want to do what Lord Chike had ordered her to do. But unfortunately, at this point, she had no choice. Serena had to act fast. She couldn't risk being in the cave when Amy returned, and she definitely couldn't risk Lord Chike accusing her of taking too long.

Serena quickly took possession of Joshawa's mind. The first order of business was to create a barrier that would prevent Lord Nathen from sensing Joshawa's emotions. The barrier would also prevent Lord Nathen and Mistress Authia from receiving Joshawa's melds. The barrier appeared as a bright blue veil that completely encompassed Joshawa's mind. Serena then whispered ever so softly to Joshawa's subconscious. *Do you hear me, my Lord?*

Joshawa replied within the confines of his mind. *Yes.*

*Do you know who I am?*

*No.*

*You must think, my Lord. You know my voice. You know who I am.*

There was a brief moment of silence. Serena was becoming nervous. What she was trying to accomplish was taking too long. *Think, my Lord. It is important that you know who I am.*

*Serena?*

*That is good, my Lord. Now forgive me, but I must do this. The voices of your parents will be beyond your reach. Their voices will sound like whispers in the wind. Do you understand?*

*Whispers in the wind.*

*Good, my Lord. Their voices will be whispers in the wind.*

*Whispers in the wind.*

*However, my voice will be your tether to reality. Hear it, know it. I will protect you.*

Serena left Joshawa but remained, hovering just above his broken body. She closed her eyes and reached out, knowing that her message might never be heard by its intended recipient. *Clues. I have left you clues.*

Amy quickened her pace as she headed toward her cave. When she arrived, she ignored Alex and pushed her way past him. Amy placed the buckets of water next to the firepit, then placed a crudely made iron frame over the pit. From that, she hung a large, heavy, cast-iron pot that was rusted with age.

She filled the pot with the water from the buckets, then placed branches and logs in the firepit. She would light the fire later when she returned with what she needed to save Joshawa. Amy glanced over at Joshawa, who lay motionless on the ground, and she knew exactly what she had to do. It came to her so effortlessly.

She grabbed the handles of the two empty buckets and placed the knife she used to fillet fish in one of them. Then she retrieved a small hatchet, put it in the bucket, and headed toward the cave entrance. This time she stopped and acknowledged Alex. She smiled at him as she stroked his snout with her free hand. "Watch over him, Alex. I won't be gone long." She glanced over her shoulder at Joshawa, then looked back at Alex. "He is special, Alex, and we have to save him."

Nathen stood on the open porch and stared into the pitch darkness of the night. The cool mountain air penetrated his sweatshirt, which caused him to shiver. But that did not deter him, nor did the absence of light. The moon was concealed behind a blanket of blackness, casting the forest into complete darkness. Nathen's cat-like eyes pierced that darkness, which allowed him to see beyond the yard and into the depths of the forest.

He had spent hours searching for Joshawa to no avail. Hansen had offered to help, but Nathen could cover more ground without him, so Hansen stayed behind in case Joshawa came home. While Nathen searched, he would catch a glimmer of Joshawa's emotions, which gave him hope. But after two hours of feeling nothing from Joshawa, Nathen's hope faded away.

He returned home without his son, without any idea where Joshawa was. Nobody questioned him, including Authia. They gave him his space, and he'd remained standing on the porch ever since. The night grew colder, which caused Nathen's breath to hang in the air. And as midnight approached, Nathen came to the bitter reality that his son might be lost to him forever.

"Don't you dare give up on him!"

Nathen turned to find Authia standing next to him. She was dressed in her jeans and a light blue t-shirt. Her hair was pulled back into a ponytail, and the cool breeze caused her arms to break out into goosebumps. He gazed upon her, feeling completely defeated. "I can't feel him. I can't meld with him. I know he was seriously hurt, because I could only grasp segments of his emotions, and then his mind went blank." Tears started rolling down Nathen's cheeks. "We've lost him." The next thing Nathen felt was the pain on his left cheek as Authia slapped him with everything she had.

"He may be hurt, but he is still alive. Don't you dare speak of him in the past tense! We are going to find him, and we are going to bring him home." Authia stormed off the porch.

"Where are you going?"

Authia stopped and turned to face Nathen. "If anyone knows where Joshawa is, it will be Becca, whether she realizes it or not."

# CHAPTER THIRTEEN

A my was on a mission that was lodged deep within her. Her mission—her sole purpose—was that she had to save Joshawa. The knowledge that she was the only person that could save his life fueled her determination, no matter the consequences.

Amy headed toward the river, where the ground was moist and ideal for growing the particular moss that she was looking for. It wasn't long before she found what she desired growing in abundance at the base of trees and rocks. Amy placed the buckets on the ground, removed her knife, and started cutting away at the moss. As soon as she filled one bucket with the moist, green moss, she placed her knife in the second bucket, grabbed the handles to both buckets, and headed north. Amy continued to travel deeper into the forest. However, she made sure she kept the river in sight. Amy had never traveled this far north before, and she had no desire to lose her way, especially since it was so close to the darkness overtaking the forest.

The river was also home to the tree she sought, so she felt confident in her pursuit. It wasn't long before she came across the black barked trees that would provide the necessary ingredients that she needed to heal Joshawa.

Amy gazed up at the evening sky. Soon the sun would be gone, and without Alex at her side, she would be at the mercy of the animals that hunted at night. To save Joshawa, she needed to harvest the roots and buds from the black tree that stood before her. Amy would also need to bring back several of the tree's leafy branches. It was a lot to accomplish in so little time, but Amy had no choice. To save Joshawa's life, she needed the healing powers that the tree possessed.

Amy removed her hatchet from the bucket, knelt on the ground, and was about to start hacking at the root that lay exposed before her when she heard something moving through the forest. By the sound it was making, Amy knew it would be big. She wondered if the wolves were roaming the forest early, and with that thought in mind, she started to panic. Amy remained kneeling on the ground, motionless, just staring at the tree that stood before her. The belief that the wolves were descending on her fueled her fear, which caused her heart to beat wildly in her chest. Her mind was alive with options, but every option that saved her life would result in Joshawa's death.

Authia ignored the cold, and with determined strides, she headed for Becca's cabin. Tammy, Hansen, and Becca had left for their own cabin hours ago, and Authia wasn't sure if they'd even be awake. Not that it mattered—she was determined to meld with Becca and even more determined to find Joshawa.

When Authia reached the cabin, she didn't bother to knock. She walked in and discovered that Tammy and Hansen were still awake. They were sitting in front of a roaring fire, and when they glanced over to Authia, there was no doubt that she had startled them.

Hansen got up and rushed over to Authia. "What's wrong? Did you find Joshawa?" The words hadn't left Hansen's lips when Nathen entered the cabin. Hansen glanced over at Nathen then back to Authia. "What's going on?"

Authia searched the cabin for Becca, and when she didn't see her, Authia headed straight into Becca's bedroom. Even with all the commotion, Becca was still sound asleep. Authia went over to her and gently shook her arm to wake her. "Becca! Becca, I need you."

As Becca stirred in her bed, Hansen, Tammy, and Nathen came into the room. Authia felt Hansen's hand on her arm as he gently pulled her away from Becca. Authia turned to face him and was met with an expression of fear and anger. She tried to hold back her emotions but failed. With tears streaming down her face, her expression pleading, and her voice halting with sobs, she spoke. "Please, I need Becca to find Joshawa."

Nathen approached Authia, who could not control her sobbing. He wrapped his arms around her and tenderly held her close. "Come with me, my love. Let's go sit by the fire." Authia slowly pulled away from Nathen's embrace and allowed him to guide her to the small sofa that faced the fireplace. He sat next to her, his left arm around her shoulder, keeping her close to him. Authia placed her head against his chest and listened to the rhythmic sound of his heartbeat. She breathed in his scent and felt his warmth, which would normally calm her, but not this time.

Hansen moved the wooden rocking chair so he could sit facing the sofa. Tammy knelt in front of Authia and placed her hands on Authia's knees. That distracted Authia, and through eyes that were blurred with her tears, she gazed about the room.

Hansen and Tammy were staring at her, and their expressions spoke volumes. She could tell Tammy was frightened, and she had every right to be. Hansen appeared upset, and if he berated her, well, she deserved it. Authia knew she was upsetting everyone because she couldn't control her emotions. But it was when Becca approached her that Authia finally found her strength.

Becca walked over to the sofa, and Nathen immediately

stood up, offering his seat to her. Becca sat down, quickly scanned the room, and then focused her attention on Authia. "Aunty, what's going on? Did you find Joshawa?"

Authia smiled at Becca, then turned to Tammy. "A cup of coffee would be really good right now. Would you mind?"

Tammy stood up and returned Authia's smile. "Of course not."

Tammy headed to the kitchen as Hansen grabbed a couple of kitchen chairs and placed them by the sofa. Authia gently placed her hand on Becca's knee. "Joshawa is still missing."

Becca's eyes went wide, and the color drained from her face.

Authia could hear Tammy gasp from the kitchen, and when she glanced up, she met Hansen's gaze, who now appeared more frightened than angry. Authia then returned her focus to Becca.

Becca looked as if she'd been punched in the stomach. "What do you mean he's still missing? I thought he just wanted to be alone. Didn't Uncle Nathen find him?" Becca glanced over to Nathen. "You went to find him. Why didn't you find him?"

Nathen slowly shook his head. "I can't sense him. And when I could, it was faint. He's either unconscious, or he's—"

Authia snapped at Nathen. "Don't you dare finish that sentence! He's hurt, that's all. And we're going to find him."

Tammy carried over a tray containing four coffees and a small glass of warm milk. She passed the tray to everyone, placed the empty tray on the hearth, and then sat in one of the kitchen chairs. She waited while Authia took a sip of her coffee before she spoke. "Authia, you know that Hansen and I are behind you one hundred percent." Tammy looked over to Hansen for support.

"Of course, Authia. We'll help find him. But if Nathen can't sense him, and as far as I know, no one here knows where his secret place is. So where do we start?"

Authia smiled at Becca. "We start with you."

"Me? I don't know where his secret place is."

"Maybe not consciously, but I think you may have an idea subconsciously." Everyone, including Nathen, looked at Authia as if she had grown horns. She sighed and returned her attention to Becca. "When you gave me the vision of the cave, it was of Joshawa in a place you've never been."

"Okay, I remember. But what has that got to do with finding Joshawa?"

"You and Joshawa have a special connection, and I think it goes deeper than either of you realize. I think that Joshawa's love for you has enabled him to imprint on you." From everyone's expression in the room, Authia knew that no one understood what she was saying.

Tammy was the first to speak up. "Imprinting? Isn't that what wolves do?"

"They might, but from what I understand, people who have gifts like myself can imprint when their gift senses a soul mate. When my mother and I lived out here, she told me a story of her imprinting on her soul mate. At the time, I had no idea it was my father. She tried to explain the feeling to me. She said it was like getting punched in the stomach but in a good way. At the time, she didn't understand the feeling. All she knew was that she had to be with my father. Nothing else made sense. Unfortunately, he was so engrossed in building Burwood, my mother felt that he had no time for her, so she walked away."

Becca's eyes started to tear, and Authia could feel her anguish. "So, you're saying that Joshawa loves me, but like Burwood kept your father from your mother, Africa might keep us apart."

Authia gently cupped Becca's chin as she tenderly placed

a lock of Becca's hair behind her ear. "I honestly believe that Joshawa loves you with a passion, and that passion is what is keeping him here. Serena is doing her best to connect with him, to convince him that Africa needs him. I think you are the reason Serena is failing. I need to meld with you, Becca, and see what's hidden deep inside your mind. You gave me the vision of the cave. I'm hoping that I can see much more."

Becca squared her shoulders and took Authia's hands in hers. "I'm ready. Let's do this."

Authia gently squeezed Becca's hands as she slowly shook her head. "I'm afraid it's not as easy as that."

Becca appeared puzzled. "I don't understand. It was easy before."

"Yes. Because you weren't expecting it. I need your mind to be free, which means I need you to be totally relaxed and unaware of what I'm doing." Authia let go of Becca's hands and turned to face Tammy. "I need your help."

"My help? What exactly do you want me to do?" Before Authia could speak, Tammy's eyes went wide, and she appeared shocked. "You want me to drug my daughter?"

"No, not drug. Just relax her. I need her to be unaware of me rattling around in her subconscious."

Tammy was quick to correct Authia. "Authia, that's the same thing."

"Please, Tammy. I have to find my son, and Becca is my only chance."

"Mom, I want to do this. It's okay."

Authia could only guess what turmoil was eating at Tammy. She didn't take her focus off her daughter for several seconds. Then finally, she turned to face Hansen. "So, are you okay with me drugging our daughter?"

Hansen got up, went into their bedroom, and came out carrying Tammy's medical bag. "If it was our daughter that was lost, Authia and Nathen would do it for us." He handed

Tammy her bag, tenderly kissed her forehead, then turned to face Becca. He extended his right hand to her. "Come with me. If we're going to sedate you, you might as well be comfortable." Hansen led his daughter to her bedroom, followed by Authia. After she laid down, he sat next to her on the bed. With his right hand, he lovingly cupped the left side of her face. "You're going to be fine. Your mom will calm your mind, and between you and Authia, we'll find Joshawa."

"I hope so, Dad. I don't know what I would do if he was lost forever."

Authia stood at the end of the bed, her determination stern, aware her body language was shouting anger. "He is not lost to us. And if you want to find him, you had better have a more positive outlook."

The fear etched across Becca's face didn't go unnoticed by Authia. When she glanced over to Hansen, his emotion of concern and protection of his daughter hit her like a brick wall. Authia closed her eyes and slowly shook her head. She knew that she'd gone too far. When she opened her eyes, she went to sit on the other side of the bed. She took Becca's hand in hers, and with her right hand, she delicately brushed away the tears that were running down Becca's cheeks. "I'm so sorry." Authia glanced up to Hansen, then back to Becca. "I was out of line, and I apologize to both of you. But you have to understand I need everyone, including myself, to be strong. To believe that Joshawa is alive and that he needs our help. That's the only way this meld will be successful."

Becca smiled up at Authia. "I'll be strong. I *will* help you find Joshawa. And when we do, I'm going to tell him that I love him and that I don't want him to go to Africa!"


Serena sat at the very edge of the Realm and observed the interaction between Authia and Becca. She was displeased, because she believed that Lord Chike would also be aware of the interaction. As if he'd read her mind, Lord Chike walked up behind her. "I thought you were watching our Lord?"

Serena stood up, slightly bowed her head, then smiled at Lord Chike. "I was, as you instructed. I placed a block in his mind. He should not be able to hear his parents or feel their presence."

Lord Chike walked to the edge of the Realm and peered down to see what Serena saw. He observed for several seconds, then returned his focus to Serena. "If the block is in place, then why watch these outsiders?"

Serena was going to correct him but thought better of it. What did interest her was that he didn't appear upset about Becca's revelation. Serena smiled to herself. *He did not hear it.* "I am watching to make sure that my block is strong. It does have to withstand the probing of an extremely powerful Priestess."

Serena took pleasure in the blank expression on Lord Chike's face. "What Priestess?"

"You may not like her, but Mistress Authia is a strong Priestess. Her melds are strong. I thought it would be in your best interest if I made sure she did not succeed."

Lord Chike glanced down at the outsider and then back up at Serena. "Your faith in that outsider's strength is misguided. Or are you telling me that she is a stronger, more powerful Priestess than you?"

"Of course not, my Lord. But it does not hurt to be sure."

"Do what you have to do." Lord Chike moved closer to Serena, so close that he was able to whisper in her ear. "You fail me, and I will not only destroy you but everyone you hold close, including your pet outsiders."

Serena watched as Lord Chike disappeared into the jungle. She turned her back to the jungle and smiled down at her Mistress. "We have an opening, my Mistress, and I fully intend to take advantage."


Amy remained on the ground, not moving a muscle. She focused her attention in the direction she thought the noise was coming from—a futile attempt, because in the dense forest, the noise could be coming from any direction. Minutes later, Amy could tell that the animal was no longer walking. It had most likely picked up her scent and was now crashing through the forest. Amy's breathing became rapid, almost to the point of hyperventilating. She glanced up at the cottonwood tree in the hopes of climbing it, but she knew that the branches would not hold her weight.

As the crashing came louder and louder, she curled up into a ball on the ground, bent her head down toward her chest, and covered it with her arms. The crashing stopped, and Amy could hear the animal approach her. He stood so close to her that she could feel his breath on her body. The animal gently nudged her with his snout, which caused Amy's fear to dissipate. Reason replaced fear, and Amy knew what animal stood over her. Slowly Amy drew her arms away just enough that she could look up. Standing over her was nine hundred pounds of grizzly.

Amy's arms drooped down as she heaved a heavy sigh. She rolled onto her back, trying to regain her composure. Once she realized she wasn't in any danger, her anger built up inside her, ready to explode. She stood up, pointed her right index finger at him, and yelled as loud as she could. "What are you doing? You nearly scared me to death! You're supposed to be watching Joshawa. Why are you here?"

Her breathing was labored, and she tried to compose herself. Even after the scolding, Alex only looked up at the sky. Amy followed his gaze then looked back at him. It took her a second, but she realized why he was there. "It's getting dark, and you were worried about me." She wrapped her arms around his neck as best she could and held him tight. "I'm so sorry for yelling at you." She let go then stood so she could face him. "I need the roots and branches from this tree." She pointed to the black cottonwood that stood behind her. "We don't have much time. Can you help me?"

As if Alex understood every word she said, he ambled over to the exposed roots and started tearing at them with his massive claws. In five minutes, he tore up more roots than she could have in an hour. As he clawed at the roots, she gathered as many buds as she could. The last item on the list was the branches.

Alex stood up and clawed at the tree, tearing several branches from its limbs. Amy filled the second bucket with the roots and buds. Then she layered the branches across Alex's back. When she had everything that she needed, Amy picked up the buckets and headed for the cave with Alex close behind. As she made her way back, she glanced up at the evening sky. If she hurried, she could be back at the cave before the sun completely disappeared.

Authia sat with Becca while Hansen left to let Tammy know it was time. She held Becca's hand within both of hers. Authia could sense Becca's fear and trepidation, but it wasn't for herself. It was for Joshawa. "We'll find him, Becca. I have every confidence that you are the answer."

"And what if I'm not?"

Authia smiled at Becca as she gently squeezed her hands. "I've been doing this for a very long time. Trust me." Behind her smile, Authia had her reservations. She had great expectations of a successful meld only because of a slight glimpse into Joshawa's future that she'd previously seen through Becca. Her special gift was not an exact science. There were a lot of variables. But hopefully, the love Joshawa had for Becca would be the thread that connected them. If he had imprinted on Becca, Becca would see what Joshawa saw, and through the meld, Authia would see it as well.

Tammy returned to the room, pulling an I.V. pole with her. Hanging from the pole was a saline bag and the lines that would be inserted into Becca's arm. Authia was slightly alarmed at the sight of the I.V. pole. "What are you doing? I just need her to be sedated."

Tammy placed the pole at the edge of the bed just behind Becca's head. She inserted one end of the line into the saline bag and laid the other end on the bed. "You want her unaware of you rattling around in her head. You also want her reasonably responsive."

"Yes. But don't you have something you can give her? Like a pill or a mild injection?"

"Yes, but I would have to go to Burwood for that, and I'm assuming that we don't have that kind of time."

"You're right. We don't."

"Okay. All I have on hand is propofol, which I need to administer through an I.V. It's used to sedate patients for surgery, and it helps to slow down the brain. However, if I administer a very small dose, then she'll be sleepy and somewhat unaware of her surroundings. But she should have enough cognitive ability to interact with you. For the record, I'm not happy doing this. Propofol is not a drug to mess around with, so you'd better take real good care of my daughter."

Authia understood that Tammy was requesting, not issuing a threat. "I will take care of her, I promise you. If the meld is going down a road I can't control, I won't hesitate to pull both of us out."

"Are you sure? If Joshawa is at the end of that road, will you still leave the meld, leave him?"

"I can't help Joshawa if I'm trapped in the meld, so yes, I'll leave the meld. Knowing that I can reach him means that he's alive, and I can work with that."

Tammy smiled at Authia, then leaned over and kissed Becca on her forehead. "Well then, let's make this happen." Tammy sat at the edge of the bed, rolled up Becca's sleeve, and exposed the inside of her arm. She then placed a surgical pad under Becca's arm and cut four strips of surgical tape. Tammy lay the I.V. needle on the pad, then tied a band around Becca's bicep.

As she gently slapped at a vein that appeared promising, she asked Becca to pump her hand. "Okay, this is going to sting a bit." Before Becca could comment, Tammy had inserted the I.V. needle into the vein. She placed the tape across the line and stint to secure it in place. "When I administer the drug, it's going to act fast." Tammy glanced over to Authia. "How long did you want her under?"

Authia hadn't even thought of that. She had no idea how much time she would need. "What would be a safe amount of time?"

"I can keep her under for quite some time, but I'd rather not have her under any longer than an hour. Would that work?"

"An hour is perfect." Authia focused her attention on Becca. "Please give me your hands." Becca extended her hands, which Authia took into hers. "Now, I want you to focus on Joshawa and think of all the happy memories you shared with him. I want you to listen to my voice. I will guide you through the meld."

Authia glanced over to Tammy, who already had the syringe filled with the appropriate amount of propofol. Authia nodded to Tammy, who injected the drug into the shunt, located just under the saline bag.

Authia returned her attention to Becca to find that her eyes were closed and her body relaxed. Authia closed her eyes and sought out Becca.

At first, Authia felt as if she were in a bubble of light, yet she could see nothing. *Seek me out, Becca. Hear my voice. Look around and show me what you see.* The bubble started to expand. Then ribbons of color whirled around Authia's mind, forming objects that she recognized as pieces of Becca's bedroom furniture. She was seeing Becca's room through Becca's eyes.

*Good, Becca. I see what you see. Now I want you to think of Joshawa. Picture Joshawa. Picture a memory of the two of you.*

The bedroom swirled around her, the colors bleeding into each other. Then Authia could smell the woods, and she could feel the dampness in the air. Becca was sitting on a large rock at the edge of the river that flowed past their cabins. But Authia could only see Becca, not Joshawa.

*Focus harder, Becca. We have to find Joshawa. Search deep inside your memories. Find Joshawa.* Authia's mind was flooded with memories, but none were of Joshawa. They were all of Becca. Then Authia remembered something Serena had said to her. *You are not as clever as you used to be.* Authia needed to look closer at what she was seeing. *What are you showing me, Becca? Are you showing me Joshawa?*

At that very moment, it hit her — imprinting. She'd asked Becca to find Joshawa. What if that was precisely what she'd done? Authia delved deeper into Becca's subconscious. She cleared her mind, creating a blank canvas ready for any impression Becca could give her. However, all she was given was darkness, void of scent, emotion, or memory. She reached out to Becca, but Becca was no longer the dominant mind in the meld.

The room began to take shape, and Authia found herself in the forest, but not a place she was familiar with. The sun was just above the horizon, so Authia assumed it was mid to late morning. She could see the Rocky Mountains that towered before her. She slowly scanned the area, trying to find some sign of where she was. Judging from how close she was to the mountain range, she guessed she was in the northern section of the forest. She needed more. She needed to find out whose eyes she was looking through.

*Hello? Who's there? I want to speak with you.* Authia scanned the area again, but there was no response. *I'm looking for my son. His name is Joshawa. Have you seen him?* Immediately Authia could feel herself being lifted high into the trees until she settled on a large branch of a redwood tree. Her entire being was encased in fear, fear of discovery.

*What are you showing me? Who are you?* There was a faint noise coming from below. Authia peered down to discover a man dressed in camouflage. He was looking up, and now the fear that consumed Authia was so intense it made her feel as though she was going to throw up.

*I don't understand. Who are you? What are you showing me?* The man was gone, and for only a minute, Authia felt at peace. But it was fleeting, for no sooner had the fear left her than another emotion far stronger than the fear hit her as if she'd been struck with a brick. She saw the bear charging the tree, she felt the tree shaking, and as Authia fell toward the ground, she heard a voice.

*Mother, help me!*

# CHAPTER FOURTEEN

Amy had reached the cave just as the sun's rays disappeared behind the mountains that towered high above her cave. As she stood at its entrance, she could hear the howling of the wolves that stalked their prey in the cover of darkness.

She glanced over at Alex, who had already settled in his usual spot, only this time, he was facing inside the cave. Puzzled by his action, she approached him, placed the buckets down, then sat on the ground cross-legged facing him. She ran her right hand along his snout up to the top of his head.

"Why are you facing this way? You can't see if danger is coming if you are looking inside the cave." Alex didn't budge. He just lay there with his gaze fixed on her. Amy shrugged her shoulders, stood up, grabbed the buckets, and turned to head over to the firepit. She had only taken a couple of steps, then decided to turn around and see if Alex had moved. His vigil remained fixed on the inside of the cave. "All right, face that way, but if I get eaten by wolves, it's going to be all your fault." She was frustrated with Alex, somewhat like a child would be with a parent.

Amy went over to the firepit and took one last look in Alex's direction. She rolled her eyes, then placed the buckets down and started a fire that would be hot enough to boil the water. She went back to the entrance, bundled up all the leafy branches, and took them over to the firepit. Using her hatchet, she cut up the branches so they would fit in the pot of water.

Then she retrieved the moss, placed it in a tin bowl, and,

using a rock, started to grind the moss down to a paste. Now she needed something to wrap around the wound and for his elbow and leg. She rummaged through her trunk and found an old sheet, stained and thin from years of use. She tore the sheet into long strips, then placed one of the strips in the water that was being heated over the fire. She glanced over to Joshawa and sighed.

"This is going to hurt. I'm so sorry." Using one of the cotton strips, she made a temporary sling to immobilize his elbow. Then she carefully rolled Joshawa onto his uninjured side so she could clearly see his head injury. As she did, Joshawa quietly moaned in pain, though he remained unconscious. Satisfied that he would remain on his side, Amy took the cotton strip out of the water and squeezed it over the open wound. She repeated the action several times until the wound was clean. Then Amy delicately packed it with the moss she'd made into a paste. She took a couple of the cotton strips and wrapped Joshawa's head so that the moss would stay in place.

As gently as she could, she rolled him back over, then placed her hand on his forehead to check if he had a fever.

Amy stared at her stranger, who now had a name, though she couldn't remember when she'd learned it. After she checked his forehead, she ran her fingers down the bridge of his nose, over his cheekbones, then finally allowed her fingers to rest on his lips. She had always wondered what he was, and now she knew.

"You have a fever and a bad gash on the back of your head. I packed it with moss that will stop the bleeding and help with your fever. When it starts to heal, I will add a salve to the mixture that will help heal the wound." Amy cocked her head to one side. "I don't know if you can hear me. I'm going to heal you."

Amy glanced down at Joshawa's elbow and his leg. Then she returned her gaze to Joshawa's face. "I'm sorry, Joshawa, but I have to hurt you to heal you. But when I'm finished, I have something that will help with the pain. I'll fix your leg first; it will hurt less, but I'm afraid the elbow won't be good."

Amy went to the back of the cave and retrieved two branches that were about three feet long and about six inches in diameter. They weren't perfectly straight, but they would do. She placed a branch on either side of Joshawa's broken leg then sat on the ground with his foot between her legs.

With her knife, Amy cut open a three-inch slit at the bottom of his pant leg. She grabbed the edges of the slit and ripped his pant leg right up to the middle of his thigh. As tenderly as she could, she ran her hands from his ankle upwards toward his knee until she found where the break was. It was a clean break. The bone was slightly out of place. With one hand, she applied pressure to the break. With her other hand, she grabbed his ankle and then pulled. She smiled as she felt the bone slip into place, and thankfully it didn't appear to cause Joshawa much pain.

"There, that wasn't so bad." Amy fastened the branches to Joshawa's leg using the cotton strips. After she was finished, she had just enough strips left for his elbow.

By this time, the water was boiling, and Amy started feeding the leafy branches she had previously cut up into the pot. When all the branches were submerged in the water, she glanced around the cave, looking for something she could drape over the steaming pot and Joshawa. If she could get him to inhale the steam, it would help reduce his pain.

Again, Amy returned to the back of the cave, rummaging through her supply of firewood. She had everything from the size of kindling to huge branches that Alex had dragged to the cave for her.

An hour later, she'd managed to rig up something similar to a teepee made with old blankets and towels. There wasn't a lot of room, but it would suffice for what she needed. Now she had to take care of the injury she wasn't looking forward to doing.

She crawled into the teepee and sat next to Joshawa's dislocated elbow. Gently she removed the temporary sling and gingerly placed his arm across his chest. She then placed her hand on his stomach and watched him as he slept.

"You look so peaceful. I'm really, really sorry for what I have to do. It's going to hurt . . . a lot. But if I don't fix it now, it will be even worse later." As skillfully as if she'd done this procedure a hundred times before, Amy grabbed his wrist with her right hand, placed his elbow in her left hand, and then she twisted his wrist as she brought his wrist up to his shoulder. The standard pop you would hear when the elbow went into place was drowned out by Joshawa's screams of agony.

And now, he was no longer asleep. Brown eyes that were as dark as night stared at Amy, and within the darkness of his eyes, Amy could see all his fear, pain, and confusion.

Joshawa felt as if his mind was swimming in a fog of uncertainty. His entire body hurt as if he had been chopping firewood for hours on end. He tried to open his eyes, but they wouldn't cooperate. So he lay there as he listened to his surroundings. A strange scent seemed to envelop him, and he could hear a woman's voice. She was speaking to him, called him by name, though he didn't recognize her voice.

He tried to remember where he was and how he got to this place. This was not home—he was sure of that. The ground he was lying on was cold and hard. He searched his mind for answers, but his thoughts were incoherent. He tried to focus his mind so he could reach out and get help. And that was when she came to him—a voice he knew that he had to remember.

*You know my name.*

*Yes, whispers in the wind.*

*Good, Joshawa, whispers in the wind. Can you hear the whispers?*

*Yes, I hear the whispers.*

*Good. Who do you seek?*

*Serena.*

*No. Who do you seek?*

*Whispers in the wind.*

*Yes. Now, what do you have to say to them?*

Joshawa was so confused. His mind was not his own. He needed to say something to the whispers. But they were only whispers. They were nothing more than the sounds of the wind.

*Speak, Joshawa, speak to the whispers. What do you want, Joshawa? Speak to the whispers.*

There was only one thing Joshawa wanted. *I want my mother.*

*Good, Joshawa. Speak to the whispers in the wind, for they will travel far.*

From within his mind, Joshawa could see a soft blue light. As he thought of the whispers, the light grew in intensity. Then suddenly, Joshawa knew precisely what he had to say to the whispers.

*Mother, help me!*

Nathen quietly sat in one of the kitchen chairs. His arms were folded across his chest, his eyes were closed, and his mind was focused on Authia. She hadn't invited him to join the meld, so he would respect that. However, she said nothing of monitoring her emotions. At first, the emotions were chaotic, as if several people were screaming at him. He had to zone in on Authia and feel only her emotions.

He reached out and allowed these sensations to connect with him. One was child-like, and it was frightened. Nathen believed that one belonged to Becca, so he blocked that emotion and went in search of Authia. Normally Authia's feelings would come to him easily, but not this time. It was as if Authia's feelings were not her own. He could sense her confusion and fear, but those were secondary to someone else's. These other emotions were much stronger than Authia's. There was something familiar about the third set, but no matter how hard Nathen tried to concentrate, he couldn't make out whose they were.

These unfamiliar emotions were scared, and they were so strong that Nathen could actually feel the fear as if it were his own. This fear continued to build until it climaxed, and then all the sensations attached to this third person disappeared.

Now he was left with only Authia's emotions, which were full of fear, anger, and a tragic sense of loss. Nathen opened his eyes and glanced around the room to find Hansen sitting on the couch, staring at him. Authia's feelings were too much for Nathen to handle. He got out of the chair and headed for Becca's room, Hansen right behind him.

When Nathen entered the room, he found Authia sitting on the floor, her back resting against the bed, her arms wrapped around her legs that she had pulled tight against her chest. Tammy was sitting next to her, and Authia had her head resting on Tammy's shoulder. Tammy had her arms wrapped around Authia in an obvious attempt to comfort her. Authia looked up at Nathen, tears running down her cheeks, her eyes red from crying. Nathen went and sat by her side, then he gathered her in his arms, holding her close against his body. He glanced over to Tammy. "What happened?"

Hansen extended his hand to help Tammy to her feet. She stood in front of Nathen and shook her head as she shrugged her shoulders. "I don't know. One minute she was holding Becca's hands, totally immersed in the meld, and then her eyes flew open, and she just kept saying *no*, over and over again. I had to pry her hands away from Becca's, and then one second Authia was standing, and then the next thing I knew, she was on the floor."

Nathen could see how troubled and upset Tammy was. He looked over to Becca, who remained sleeping peacefully on the bed. "How's Becca?"

Tammy glanced over to Becca, then returned her focus to Nathen. "She's fine. It's Authia I'm worried about."

Nathen gently pulled Authia away from him so he could see her face. Tenderly he cupped her chin and lifted her face so that she could look into his eyes. "What happened, my love? What has upset you so much."


Authia could see Nathen, and she knew that he was holding her, but she couldn't hear him. All she could hear was the plea, *Mother, help me.* It played over and over in her head. For the first time in her life, Authia felt helpless. She didn't even have the strength to communicate her thoughts to Nathen. Her son needed her to be strong, and he needed her to find him.

However, she couldn't even contain her composure long enough to understand what she'd experienced in the meld. She closed her eyes and laid her head back against Nathen's chest. He immediately wrapped his arms around her, which provided her some semblance of peace. Authia thought if she could remain still that maybe, just maybe, she could compose herself.

Then she heard it—a voice reaching out to her from deep within herself. It was not just in her mind. The voice felt as if it were a part of her.

*Clues . . . left you clues. You're not as clever. Hear me, my Mistress . . .*

Authia's eyes flew open as she pulled away from Nathen's embrace. She wiped the tears from her face as she concentrated on the voice.

*Is that you, Serena?*

*Whispers in the wind.*

That was not the same voice. Authia was sure the first comments were Serena's, but the last comment was made by someone very different. Authia gazed over to Nathen and saw the fear in his eyes. Not for himself but for her. She slowly shook her head and thought to herself. *What are you doing? Pull yourself together, girl!* Authia had to find her strength, and not just for Joshawa. She had to be strong for Nathen as well.

She placed her hand on the side of his face, and even though she couldn't muster up a smile, she knew that her emotions would comfort him. "I'm so sorry, Nathen. I lost it, big time."

Nathen took her hand in his, brought her fingertips to his lips, and softly kissed them. Then he took both her hands in his and smiled in a way that she knew she was going to be okay. "Can you tell me what happened in the meld?"

Authia took a deep breath and allowed the fear that she felt in the meld to build up inside of her. Only this time, she knew it wasn't her fear—it was Joshawa's. If she was going to help him, she had to separate the two. Authia had to allow Joshawa to take over. "Our son is alive, but he's hurt, and if we don't find him soon, we may not be able to save him. He's scared and confused, and the pain is so bad that it's completely encompassing his mind, and I think that's why you can't find him."

"So you were able to meld with him?"

"Not really. Nathen, Joshawa has imprinted on Becca. What I saw, I saw through his eyes. I felt what he felt. Problem is, I'm not totally sure where he is."

"He couldn't tell you? You couldn't ask him?"

"I couldn't communicate with him. I could only see what he saw. I think he's north of here, closer to the mountain range. He was in a tree, a large redwood tree. And there was a man."

"A man?"

"Yes. Dressed in camouflage. He looked like a hunter, and he was holding a GPS. He looked up at Joshawa, but I don't think he saw him." Authia stopped as the sadness washed over her. "Nathen, Joshawa fell from the tree. Before he hit the ground, he said, *Mother, help me*, and then there was nothing."

"He's unconscious. That's the only explanation."

Authia was quiet for a moment. Something wasn't sitting right with her. "How did he know to call out to me? He didn't know I was there. I wasn't there when it happened. So why ask me to help him?" Authia let go of Nathen's hands and stood up. She was missing something — something important. Nathen stood up and smiled at her as he shook his head.

Authia was puzzled, almost put off by his smirk. "What? What's with the look?"

"You're yourself again. Now let's figure this out."

Authia smiled back at Nathen, and then it hit her. "I'm not as clever as I used to be."

Nathen looked at Authia with a puzzled expression. "Sure you are."

Authia waited for just a second, then Nathen's eyes lit up. "Serena! Serena said that *you aren't as clever as you used to be.*"

"Exactly! She said more. When I was on the floor feeling sorry for myself, she said she'd left me clues. She said *hear me, my Mistress.* I heard another voice that said *whispers in the wind.*"

Tammy had removed the I.V. from Becca's arm and was pulling the covers over her daughter's shoulders. She looked back at Authia. "Another voice? How many voices do you have rattling around in that brain of yours?"

"Too many. But right now, I want to focus on Serena. Okay, I'm not as clever. So what am I missing?"

Tammy closed her medical bag and walked over to Authia. She placed her hand on Authia's arm and smiled as if she was reassuring Authia that everything would be okay. "Why don't we go into the living room and let Becca sleep? I'll make some more coffee." Tammy and Hansen started to head for the door, but Tammy stopped and turned to face Authia. "Didn't she say that before? When you melded with her? That you weren't as clever as you were before. She said that when you were interpreting the vision you had with Becca."

It was as if a light went off in Authia's head. "You're absolutely right. She did say that." Authia glanced over to Nathen. "In my vision, I heard a noise. I asked Serena if it was the falls. I thought for sure it was the roar of the falls. But obviously, I was wrong."

Nathen reached for Authia's hand and started to leave the bedroom. "Then what could it be? What would make a roaring sound?"

Authia stopped dead in her tracks. "That's it!"

Nathen let go of Authia's hand and turned to face her. "I don't follow."

"In my first vision, I saw Joshawa in a cave, and I heard a roar. Naturally, I thought it was the cave behind the falls." Authia was almost giddy at the realization that she'd figured it out. "Nathen, Joshawa fell from the tree because a huge grizzly charged the tree. It's the bear. The bear is in the cave. The bear made the roaring sound."

"So it's not the cave by the falls?"

"No. It's a cave right here in BC, which means we still have time to save him, not only from his injuries but also from whatever is going on with Serena."

Serena watched and listened from the edge of the Realm. She smiled at her Mistress. "You are as clever as you were before. Good luck, my Mistress." Serena glanced over her shoulder toward the jungle. Satisfied she was alone, she returned her focus on her Mistress. "Show him just how powerful a Priestess you are."

Jax woke early, long before Dameon. It was four in the morning, and he wanted to be prepared for the journey to find the cabin. Jax sat at the edge of his bunk, dressed only in his underwear. He held his flashlight in his right hand and quietly listened to the rhythmic sounds of Dameon sleeping. Satisfied that Dameon was deep in sleep, Jax turned on his flashlight.

He faced it toward the back wall of the bunk so it wouldn't light up the entire room. Jax moved his pillow to the side, which revealed the journal and his *357 Ruger Redhawk*. Jax picked up his *Ruger* and held the stock in his right hand, the barrel in his left. He gazed upon it as if it were an extension of himself, which, to him, it was.

He closed his eyes and softly whispered, "Please, don't force me to use this on you." He glanced up at Dameon's bunk, then back down to the *Ruger*. He placed the gun on the bed and reached over and picked up the journal. A sinister smile crossed his face, for he knew that this would be the day that they would find the cabin, which would put them one step closer to the creature.

Jax opened the journal to reveal two folded pages of lined, letter-size paper. These pages represented hours of work. He hated making maps, deciphering where they needed to be by landmarks, especially when the landmarks were over twenty years old. That was Dameon's thing. However, it was all worth it if it meant keeping Dameon away from the journal. Jax wasn't stupid. He knew that Dameon wanted his hands on the journal. So, going forward, the journal would never be in the open. He would hide it from Dameon, and that would give Jax one less reason to kill him.

Jax turned around in the bunk so that he was facing the

back wall. He maneuvered the flashlight so he could read the journal and his notes. Then for the next two hours, Jax made sure he had copied every mention, every notation of where to find the cabin. Just before six in the morning, he had finished, and he was confident that he hadn't missed anything crucial.

He shut off the flashlight. Then he listened to make sure Dameon was still asleep. Confident that he was, Jax quietly slipped out of bed and sat on the floor next to his bunk. He skillfully ran his hand along the floorboards positioned slightly under the bunk. He felt the indent that he'd carved earlier with his hunting knife and then carefully lifted the board and set it aside. From underneath the board, he pulled out a small canvas bag. Jax placed the journal into the bag and then returned the bag to its hiding place. As he replaced the board, he felt giddy, for this was his secret treasure, and Dameon was not going to deprive him of it.

Dameon awoke to the sounds of Jax making coffee. He lay there as he glanced around the room. The only light source came from the lantern that was on the kitchen table. It lit up the table and the kitchen area, but everything else was in shadows.

The first thing Dameon noticed was that the journal was nowhere in sight. He rolled his eyes, climbed out of his sleeping bag, then jumped down from his bunk. Jax, who was already dressed, looked over as Dameon pulled on his camo pants.

"Good morning, Princess. Have a good sleep?"

Dameon pulled a t-shirt over his head and tucked it into his pants. "Princess, my ass." He smiled as he glanced down at his watch to check the time. It was fifteen minutes after six. "Fifteen minutes is hardly Princess material. I'm going to the ladies' room. It's your turn to make breakfast."

When Dameon returned, the cabin door was propped open, and the scent of bacon and eggs wafted throughout the cabin. "Smells good." Dameon sat at the table where a steaming cup of coffee was waiting for him. However, besides a couple of pieces of paper, the journal was still nowhere to be seen. "So, are we still heading out to find the cabin?" Dameon took a sip of his coffee without taking his focus off Jax.

Jax placed a plate of bacon and eggs in front of Dameon, as well as a plate in front of his seat. He sat down, picked up the folded pieces of paper, and handed them over to Dameon. "You bet we are. We're leaving right after we eat."

Dameon took the papers from Jax and looked at him questionably. "What are these?"

"I did your work for you. On those sheets is every mention of the cabin, in date order. We shouldn't have any problem finding it." Jax stuffed a forkful of eggs in his mouth and appeared to be waiting for Dameon's response.

Dameon glanced at the papers, then back at Jax. Jax was playing games, and he was being evasive. *Okay,* Dameon thought to himself. *I'll play along.* Dameon put the papers on the table and started to eat his breakfast.

Jax placed his fork on his plate and picked up a piece of bacon with his fingers. "You're not going to check out my work?"

"Not right now. I'm going to eat my breakfast. Besides, I'm sure you have everything I need on these papers." Dameon pointed at the papers with his fork and then ate his breakfast in silence.

# CHAPTER FIFTEEN

Nathen woke to the sound of birds singing in the treetops and to the sunlight streaming through his bedroom window. Usually, Nathen loved the serenity and the feeling of peace that the birds and the sunlight brought to him every morning. But now, it was just a reminder that it was a new day, and his son was still out there, alone, frightened, and hurt.

He rolled onto his right side to check on Authia, but she wasn't there, and judging from the coolness of the sheets, she hadn't been in bed for a while. Nathen got up, pulled on a pair of jeans, and went to find her. She was in the living room, curled up in her favorite chair, a fire roaring in the fireplace. The drapes were open, allowing the morning sun to brighten the room, and the aroma of coffee filled the cabin.

When Nathen entered the room, Authia glanced up from the notebook she had resting on her lap. She smiled at Nathen and motioned toward the kitchen. "I just made a fresh pot of coffee."

At first glance, Authia appeared to be in better spirits. However, Nathen knew that Authia was battling her emotions in her attempt to keep them from him, at least the ones that would cause him to be concerned. Her appearance of being in a better place was only a façade. Nathen knew only too well that Authia was putting on a brave face so he would concentrate on Joshawa and not her as well.

Not that it mattered. Authia was on a mission to find Joshawa, and nothing in this world, or the Spirit World for that matter, would stop her. Nathen poured himself a cup of coffee and went to sit on the loveseat, but not before he kissed Authia tenderly on the top of her head. "Did you get much sleep?"

"Not really. I wanted to write down everything I remembered from the vision I received through Becca and the meld we performed last night." Authia held up a notepad that had several pages filled with notes.

"Looks like you've been up for quite a while."

"Two coffee pots' worth. You know me when I get started on something." She smiled as she offered Nathen her coffee mug. "Would you mind?"

"Of course not." Nathen took the mug and went to fill it. "You seem to be a little more relaxed, and your emotions aren't screaming at me anymore." He smiled as he handed the mug back to Authia, and then he sat down on the loveseat.

"I am more relaxed. I'm certain that Joshawa is alive. I wouldn't have been able to see what happened to him through his eyes if he were dead. And now, just knowing that the cave from my vision is in BC and not Africa, well, that's changed everything for the better. I feel that the odds are finally on our side. I just need to figure out how to find him and why he called out to me." Authia started to flip through her notes and stopped on one of the last pages. "I also wrote down everything I remember Serena saying to me. The obvious was that I wasn't as clever as I used to be. She also said to remember the past. I'm thinking that she didn't mean just what happened in general, but rather how I dealt with her, with Casandra, with all the obstacles that we encountered."

"Okay, that makes sense. But if Serena wants you to remember the past, do you think that she's referring to her past? To only our interactions with her?"

Authia stared into the fire, allowing memories of her interactions with Serena to fill her mind. There were so many memories, good ones, bad ones, and some that were nothing less than ugly. She glanced down at her notes, and one word jumped out at her. *Communicate.* She looked over at Nathen. "If I remember correctly, the majority of our communications with Serena were through melds. Whether she was a spirit or alive, that was how we privately communicated."

"Mostly. But the melds weren't always private."

"Yes, I know. But they were when we designed them to be. Serena said that my tattoo was the only way we could communicate, because it afforded us privacy."

"Privacy from who?"

Authia covered her tattoo with her right hand. "I don't know, but let's see if we can find out." Authia closed her eyes and started to run her fingertips along the edges of the tattoo. As before, it began to burn under her touch. The pain intensified with each pass, but Authia didn't allow that to discourage her. She focused on Nathen and then reached out to Serena.

*Can you hear me?*

There was no response.

*I know you're there, Serena. I can feel your presence. I need your help. I need to know if we're on the right path.*

Authia could hear something, but it was faint as if it were coming from a great distance.

*Is that you, Serena? I can barely make you out.*

*Whispers in the wind. I can hear whispers in the wind.*

The connection was gone. Authia opened her eyes to find Nathen kneeling in front of her. He was holding her left hand, and he seemed very concerned. "Are you all right, my love?"

"Yes. Did you hear that?"

"I only heard you. Did Serena say something?"

"No, it wasn't Serena. The voice said *whispers in the wind. I can hear whispers in the wind.* It was the same voice that I heard when I melded with Becca."

"Did you recognize the voice?"

Authia felt confused. It was as if the answer was at the very tip of her consciousness but still out of reach. "The voice was too weak. I couldn't make it out. I know it wasn't Serena, and I also know that the voice is familiar. Maybe Serena is not the only one reaching out to us to help find Joshawa."

Nathen stood up and offered his hand to Authia. "We need to figure out what that phrase means to us. But first, let's have some breakfast, and then—"

Before Nathen could finish his sentence, Authia interrupted. "I'm not hungry, and I don't have time to eat. I have to figure this out."

Nathen knelt in front of Authia and took her hands in his. "You're not sleeping, and if you don't eat, you won't have the strength to find Joshawa. You and I are going to have something to eat. And while we're eating, we'll go over your notes. We'll figure this out. We'll find Joshawa." Nathen leaned forward and wrapped his arms around Authia. He would support the woman he loved, but Nathen had his reservations. He was not as confident as Authia that they would find Joshawa alive.

Serena smiled as she observed her Mistress and Lord. Lord Nathen was skeptical, but she had no doubt that Mistress Authia would keep him on track. Her plan was in place, and Serena was confident that her Mistress would figure it out.

*You are as clever as you used to be. Prove me right.*

Serena started to head over to the area where she could watch Joshawa. Halfway there, she was confronted by Lord Chike. She bowed respectfully. "Good day, my Lord. What brings you to my little world of the Realm?"

Lord Chike moved closer to Serena until he stood only two feet away. "How is our Lord doing?"

Serena really wanted to refer to Lord Nathen, but she knew that it would only infuriate Lord Chike, which would not end well for her. "He is doing well. The girl that tends to him is skilled and is helping him heal."

"When will you be able to continue your invasion of his mind and convince him to come home?"

"Is that what you think I do? Invade the mind?"

"That is exactly what you are doing. What you have always done, and you are well aware of that fact. So do not try to tell me it is anything else."

Serena was troubled by Lord Chike's choice of words. Did she invade people's minds? Of course she did. But to call it an invasion, as he put it, didn't ring true. She needed to learn more about Lord Chike, and the sooner, the better. "My apologies." Serena bowed slightly to Lord Chike. "His mind is very fragile right now. His mind needs to be strong in order to survive the transfer."

"That does not answer my question."

Serena was about to respond when Lord Adeeowale came up behind Lord Chike. "Priestess Serena, it pleases me to finally see you. I thought you would have arrived in the Realm much sooner." Lord Adeeowale turned to face Lord Chike. "And what question do you have for Priestess Serena?"

Serena watched the interaction between the two Lords. She could sense that Lord Chike was doing everything he could to control his anger. To Serena, it was apparent that Lord Adeeowale knew nothing of her obligation. She had to play this right, for deep down, she knew there was more to Lord Chike than he was letting on. "Lord Chike was just inquiring about my welfare, that I am comfortable here in the Realm. He has honored me with the obligation to watch over certain members of our tribe." Serena averted her attention to Lord

Chike. "To answer your question, my Lord, I am well and happy to serve as a guardian to the people of our valley."

Lord Chike observed Serena with caution. What was she up to? "I am glad to hear that." He turned his focus onto Lord Adeeowale. "Shall we join Imani?" He motioned for Lord Adeeowale to walk ahead of him, which he did for a couple of steps. Then Lord Adeeowale stopped and turned to face Serena.

"Priestess Serena, will you not join us?"

Lord Chike positioned himself so that Lord Adeeowale could not witness his anger toward Serena. He glared at her, daring her to say anything against him.

Serena bowed to the Lords. "Thank you, my Lord. But I would like to finish my vigil. Perhaps I can join you later."

Serena focused on Lord Adeeowale, knowing full well that Lord Chike was not appeased. "That would please us. Come, Lord Chike, let us join Imani." Lord Adeeowale turned around and headed toward the jungle, with Lord Chike following close behind.

Serena knew if she was going to make a move, she had to do it now. She focused all her attention onto Lord Adeeowale in the hopes that her meld would only be heard by him.

*Things are not as they appear, my Lord.*

Without hesitation, Lord Adeeowale responded. *We are aware.*

Dameon had finished his breakfast and was now pouring over the two pages of notes Jax gave him. He had a map drawn from the page Jax had torn from the journal, and with the two, he was able to input coordinates into the GPS.

Dameon couldn't be sure how accurate his coordinates were without the journal, and honestly, he didn't care. In truth, he hoped that the GPS would lead them to the middle of nothing. Maybe if they didn't find anything, it would work in Dameon's favor. Jax was so desperate to find his creature that perhaps he'd allow Dameon a peek at the journal.

Dameon turned the GPS off and placed it on the kitchen table. He looked over to Jax, who was packing his backpack with essentials for the hike. It appeared that the only weapon Jax was bringing was his semi-automatic *Ruger*, which in itself could cause serious damage.

Dameon stood up from the table, grabbed his backpack, and started packing additional batteries for the GPS, water, and ammo, not just for his *Glock,* but also for the 50 caliber *Barrett* rifle he was planning to bring. Dameon went over to where the rifles were stored and started to reach for the *Barrett.*

"What are you doing?"

Dameon turned to face Jax. Jax had his backpack on, his skull cap pulled down over his ears, and he looked upon Dameon with a gaze that was nothing more than narrow slits. Dameon couldn't tell if Jax was upset or just plain angry. "After my last encounter with our bear, I'm going to be prepared this time." Dameon turned and again reached for the *Barrett* only to have Jax pull his arm back. Dameon glanced down at Jax's hand, then he averted his attention and looked Jax square in the eyes. "What the hell do you think you're doing?"

Jax removed his hand and took a couple of steps back as he held his hands up at shoulder height as if he were surrendering. "Hey, I'm sorry. But if you shoot our bear with that rifle, it will kill him. He's worth a lot to us, or have you forgotten that?"

"I haven't forgotten. But the money is worth nothing if I'm dead."

Jax lowered his hands and took a step closer to Dameon. "You're being ridiculous. We're not going to run into our bear. We can see where he is on the GPS. We'll just avoid him."

"Our bear is roaming out of his comfort zone. There's no guarantee where he'll be. If he's between us and the cabin, are you willing to forgo the cabin?"

"Look, I may not be able to read maps like you do or figure out places by landmarks that are twenty years old. What I do know is that our bear is way further north of us than the cabin is. We're not going to run into him."

"What if we run into your creature?"

"I don't want to kill it either. Look, how about we take the *Pak* rifle? If we run into our bear, you can tranquilize him. If we run into the creature, you can tranquilize it so that we can have time to figure out what it is."

Dameon had a gut feeling that this hunt for bigfoot wasn't going to end well. But until he could figure out precisely what Jax was up to, he was going to have to play along. Dameon grabbed the *Pak 22* tranquilizer rifle and rested it against the bunk beds. He then strapped the case of tranquilizer darts onto his backpack, put his arms through the straps, and buckled the waist strap tight to ensure the backpack would remain in place. He holstered his *Glock*, pulled his skull cap over his blond hair, grabbed the rifle then motioned toward the door. "After you."

Jax smiled at Dameon. "Good. Let's find that cabin."

Dameon picked up the GPS off the table, closed the cabin door, and then stood for a second as he watched Jax head into the forest. There were two different doses of tranquilizer darts in the case, and Dameon was seriously considering loading the rifle with the dosage that would safely take Jax down.

Imani was in her usual spot, sitting in front of a roaring fire as she marveled at its beauty. She glanced up as Lord Adeeowale and Lord Chike entered the clearing. At first, she smiled at her companions, but something about Lord Adeeowale told her to be cautious. "Lord Chike, Lord Adeeowale, it pleases me to see you. How has your morning been?"

Lord Adeeowale sat next to Imani while Lord Chike sat across the firepit from them. Lord Adeeowale returned Imani's smile. "It was rewarding. Priestess Serena has finally joined us."

Imani appeared to be delighted, but she knew as well as Lord Adeeowale that Priestess Serena had been in the Realm for quite some time. "This is good news. Where is she?"

Lord Chike provided what Imani knew to be his version of the truth. "She is tending to our people. Serena is taking her obligation very seriously. But I am sure she will join us later."

"Well, I will be pleased to finally meet her. I have heard many stories of her gallantry." Imani placed her hand on Lord Adeeowale's knee. "As I have heard many stories of yours." Imani gazed into Lord Adeeowale's eyes. There was so much that she wanted to say, and she wanted to say it out loud for everyone to hear. But that was not her place, so she removed her hand from his knee and placed it in her lap as she gazed over to Lord Chike. "I have heard stories of you as well. However, I do not know how long you have been an Ancestor. I imagine it has been a very long time, even longer than Lord Adeeowale."

Lord Chike was losing patience with this woman who pretended to be a Priestess. To him, she didn't possess the intelligence or nobility that a true Priestess would have. When Lord Joshawa was in his rightful place, Lord Chike would see to Imani's destruction. It would give him great pleasure. In the meantime, he would play this game knowing that when judgment day came, he would stand above them all. "My Priestess, I became an Ancestor when our tribe was very young. I am among the first of our Ancestors." He watched the expression of his companions and reveled in the knowledge that they would never know exactly how or why he became an Ancestor. "But the time is late, and I must attend to my obligation." Lord Chike stood and respectively bowed his head to his companions. "I take my leave. When I return, I will be certain to have Priestess Serena at my side." Lord Chike left without waiting for a response. He could care less what they had to say.

Lord Adeeowale watched as Lord Chike disappeared into the jungle. "The news of his betrayal is disheartening."

"Let us not jump to conclusions. It is but rumors that we have heard from the Land of the Spirits."

"This is true. But he has known that Priestess Serena was here and neglected to tell us." Lord Adeeowale turned to face Imani, making his concern clearly evident. "She melded with me."

Imani's eyes grew wide. "She did? And Lord Chike did not hear her?"

Lord Adeeowale slowly shook his head. "I do not believe so."

"Her reputation is well earned. What did she say?"

"Things are not as they appear."

Imani stared out into the jungle. "No, they are not."

Authia was finishing the breakfast dishes when there was a knock on the door. Tammy opened the door only slightly, then peeked in. "Everyone decent?" Tammy once had the misfortune of catching Authia and Nathen making good use of the rug in front of the fireplace. They'd had a good laugh over the incident. However, since that day, her standard greeting was *everyone decent?*

Authia still had her hands in the soapy water. "Yes. Come on in." She glanced over her shoulder to see not only Tammy but Becca and Hansen as well. "Good morning. I'm almost finished. Hansen, Nathen is out back if you want to join him."

"Good idea." Hansen left as Becca went over to the kitchen sink, grabbed a dish towel, and started helping with the dishes.

Authia smiled lovingly as she glanced over to Becca. "How are you? Did you sleep well?"

Becca returned Authia's smile. "Yes, Aunty, very well. Did our meld help? Mother won't say anything." Becca and Authia turned to face Tammy, who was sitting at the kitchen table.

Tammy rolled her eyes at them. "How would I know? I wasn't in the meld. Now, if you were to ask what happened after the meld, then I could help you."

Becca refocused her attention on Authia. "So, did it help."

Authia drained the sink, dried her hands on Becca's dish towel, and then joined Tammy at the table. "Come sit with us, Becca. Those dishes can air dry." Becca did as she was told and joined Authia and her mother at the table. "I can make one observation with absolute certainty. Joshawa has definitely imprinted on you."

"Really!" Becca's eyes went wide. "So you're saying that he loves me."

Tammy chuckled. "You don't need a meld to tell you that."

"Mother!"

"I'm just saying that it's as plain as the nose on your face that he loves you."

Becca turned to face Authia. "So, Aunty, is there a

difference between what my mother sees and him imprinting on me?"

"A big difference. To be in love is wonderful. However, it could be fleeting. When you imprint on someone, that person becomes one with you. Your soulmate. And the love that you feel runs so deep that it will never go away. You can't even explain it."

"Did Uncle Nathen imprint on you?"

"Yes, and I on him. You know that Serena is trying to convince Joshawa to leave here and go to Africa."

Becca's happy demeanor changed to that of sadness. "Yes. And I'm so afraid that he will choose Africa over me."

Authia reached over and placed her hand on Becca's. She smiled at her as she gave Becca's hand a slight squeeze. "Serena is a very powerful Priestess, and believe me, if Joshawa hadn't imprinted on you, he would probably be dead by now. And his spirit would have been whisked away to Africa."

"So you're saying that because he's imprinted on me, he can't leave me?"

"It's the last thing he would want to do. Every fiber of his body and soul is telling him that he needs to stay close to you."

Authia smiled as she watched Becca's face light up. "To answer your question, yes, the meld helped. I know Joshawa is alive, I know he is hurt, but unfortunately, I still don't know where he is. However, I think you do."

"Me?"

"Yes, the meld we did was a shallow one. I just skimmed the surface of your subconscious. I believe that if I do a deeper meld, then I might just reach the core of Joshawa's imprinting."

Tammy raised her hand, palm facing out, several inches from the table as if asking permission to speak. However, she didn't wait to be called on. "What do you mean a deeper meld? You said you needed Becca to be somewhat alert to perform the meld."

"Yes, I did, for the initial meld. But now that I've connected with Joshawa, I need Becca to be unaware of my presence, or Joshawa's, for that matter. This probably isn't the best way to put it, but Becca will only be a vessel. One that holds Joshawa's memories."

"A vessel? No, that's not a good way to put it. For her to be a *vessel*, as you put it, that would mean putting her completely under. I'm not sure I'm happy with that."

Becca shot her mom a disapproving glare. "How could you say that? If putting me under will save Joshawa, then that's what we have to do."

Tammy pointed at Becca. "Listen, young lady —"

Tammy's sentence was cut short by Authia. "Okay, you two." Authia focused her attention on Tammy. "Yes, I need her under, but before we do that, we have to get a handle on what Serena is up to. If I can figure that out, then maybe we would have the last piece of the puzzle for finding Joshawa. Tammy, you said to write everything down, and that's exactly what I did." Authia pushed the notepad toward Tammy. "Somewhere in there are the answers. And I think it has to do with communicating."

Tammy started to flip through the pages. "Communicating?" Tammy glanced back up at Authia. "Like through a meld?"

"Well, yes, but we communicated other ways. Like my tattoo, for instance, and then there was communication through touch, or through an object."

Authia was cut short when Nathen and Hansen entered the cabin, each carrying an armful of firewood. They placed the firewood in a metal stand that was located next to the fireplace. Then they came to join the girls at the table.

Hansen turned his chair around so that the back was facing him. He straddled the chair, then rested his arms on the back of the chair, which was a little lower than his chest. "So, what are you girls up to?"

Tammy continued to flip through the pages as she answered Hansen. "We're trying to figure Serena out." She glanced up at Authia, and from the look Tammy gave her, Authia knew she wasn't pleased. "And Authia wants me to sedate our daughter as if she was being prepped for surgery."

Hansen also glanced over to Authia, only his expression was more of confusion. "You want to drug Becca again?"

"Yes, she does, Dad. And I'm totally fine with that."

Tammy shot Becca a warning glance. "You have no say in this decision."

"But, Mom."

"No buts, this is a decision that your dad and I will make." Tammy turned her attention to Hansen. "So, do you want me to drug our daughter again, only this time with more drugs?"

Authia felt for Hansen. He was trapped between the two women he loved, and each was looking at him to choose a side. Authia decided Hansen needed a little help. "Let's put the *drugging your daughter* to the side for now. Serena is giving me clues, and she's trying to help with whatever is going on. We need to figure that out. I need everyone to think back to when we were in Africa and how Serena influenced the outcome. Now, she has said to me that I'm not as clever as I used to be, that she has left me clues, that I need to hear her. And someone else is saying *whispers in the wind . . . I hear whispers in the wind.* Everything I just spoke of means something. We just have to figure it out."

Hansen seemed to be miles away, and he was grinning like the cat that ate the canary.

Tammy reached across the table and gave his shoulder a little shove. "Earth to Hansen. What are you thinking about?

You're grinning like a schoolgirl."

Hansen went red as if he'd been caught doing something he shouldn't be. "Sorry, but when you said the word *whispers*, I couldn't help but think of Serena in that rather skimpy blue dress and how she could turn into a wisp, whispering in everyone's ear."

Authia's eyes went wide. "And how she would enter Casandra and speak through Casandra."

Authia searched her mind, and her first thoughts were of Travis and how he heard whispers. Whispers in the wind.

# CHAPTER SIXTEEN

Jax had been following Dameon for what seemed like hours. They first headed south of their cabin, then deviated southwest. Dameon was continually stopping, checking the GPS and the notes Jax had made. Jax's patience was running thin, and he was beginning to think of Dameon as an obstacle rather than a lifelong friend and hunting partner.

As Jax trudged through the forest, dodging low-hanging branches and stepping over exposed roots and deadfall, an unhealthy dose of distrust was festering inside of him.

*Is Dameon taking me on a wild goose chase just because I wouldn't give him the journal?*

Finally, after two hours of hiking in silence, Jax had had enough. "Are we even close to this cabin? It didn't seem that far from the notes I gave you."

Dameon turned to face Jax and started to hand him the GPS. "Do you want to do this? Because apparently, you're better at this than I am." Dameon stood his ground, his right arm extended.

At that moment, Jax realized he had to be more careful and keep his thoughts to himself. He needed Dameon, at least until they found the creature. After that, Dameon would be expendable, especially if he tried to interfere with Jax's plans for the creature.

Jax approached Dameon and gently pushed the hand holding the GPS back toward him. "You know very well you're the best at this. I'm sorry, really, I am. I guess I'm just anxious to find the cabin, and I have no idea where we are or where that GPS is guiding you." Jax smiled at Dameon, and for just a second, the Jax of long ago surfaced, if only to appease Dameon. "We're a team, and sometimes I forget that. But you haven't said a word since we left the cabin, and usually, I can't shut you up." Jax wanted to say more in his attempt to placate Dameon, but he could see that Dameon was digesting what he'd already said, so he figured that less was better and kept quiet.

After what felt like minutes but in fact was only seconds, Dameon sighed, his expression solemn. "Yeah, I guess I've been a bit of a jerk. I've been feeling like we're on different paths with different objectives for some time now."

Jax approached Dameon and placed his right hand on Dameon's left shoulder. "This is tough for both of us. I'm still having a hard time getting used to the idea that this bear is our last hunt as a team. But if that's what you want, who am I to stop you? I should be grateful that you're indulging me with this bigfoot hunt."

"Yeah, you should be."

Jax could tell that Dameon was letting his guard down.

Dameon went to stand next to Jax and showed him the GPS. "Our bear is here, way north of the direction of the cabin, so we should be safe as far as encountering him goes. See this line?" Dameon ran his finger along a blue line that ran the entire length of the screen. "This is the river that runs by our cabin. It looks like it winds its way from the top of the mountain all the way to the very bottom. According to your notes, it also runs close to the cabin we're looking for. I plan to intersect it here." Again, Dameon pointed to the screen. "It should be less than thirty minutes from where we are now. Then we just follow the river to the cabin. The river is really the only constant in your notes, so we follow the river."

Jax slapped Dameon on his arm. "Now that's the Dameon I know. After you." Jax continued to follow Dameon single file through the dense, unforgiving forest. When they finally reached the river, Jax was ecstatic. He was ready to burst inside, because he believed that the cabin was the answer to finding the creature. He continued to follow Dameon, who was so focused on the GPS that he apparently didn't hear when Jax unsnapped the safety strap on his holster that covered the grip of the *Ruger*.

Amy woke early, just as the sun was rising. There wasn't room for her in the teepee she'd made for Joshawa, so to stay warm, she'd spent the night curled up next to Alex. She took a deep breath as the scent of the mountain air filled the cave.

Amy could feel Alex rousing behind her, so she got up and went to sit in front of him. Amy placed her arms on either side of his neck and rested her head against his. "Good morning, Alex. Thank you for keeping me warm last night."

Amy stood up and glanced over to the teepee. "I'm going to check on Joshawa, and then maybe we could get some fish for breakfast. I'm sure Joshawa will be hungry." Alex didn't move. He just raised his head and glanced over toward the teepee. Amy interpreted that to mean that Alex approved of her suggestion. She made her way over to the teepee and pulled back two of the towels to let in as much light as she could. Then she crawled in through the opening she'd made and sat next to Joshawa.

Joshawa was lying on his back with his head turned toward the firepit. His elbow was still secured to his chest, which led Amy to believe that he hadn't moved too much in the night. His breathing had improved, and when he did move ever so slightly, he didn't appear to be in too much pain. This pleased her, for it verified that the cottonwood branches were doing their job.

The firepit still had a few embers burning, which kept the

teepee warm during the night and into the morning. Amy checked the pot, and as she suspected, it had almost boiled dry. She placed the palm of her hand on his forehead and was relieved that his fever was almost gone. Amy would have to change the dressing on the back of his head one more time with the paste before Joshawa would be free of the fever.

She would also need more cottonwood branches to lessen Joshawa's pain. Amy stared at Joshawa, nibbling on her lower lip as she did. "I know you can't hear me, but maybe you can." She drew a deep breath and slowly released it. "I know that I have to save you, but I'm not sure why I know that. Alex knows, but he says it's a secret." Amy shrugged her shoulders. "Maybe he will tell me later. He's such a silly bear." Amy delicately placed her hand on Joshawa's chest. "I guess it really doesn't matter. I'm happy to heal you." She smiled, leaned forward, and gently kissed Joshawa on his forehead. "You still have a fever, but it's getting better."

Amy crawled out of the teepee and pulled the towels back into place. She then placed her hatchet in one of the empty buckets and went over to her trunk. It was a chilly morning, and she needed warmer clothes. She found a pair of worn jeans and a zippered sweater. At the bottom of the trunk, she found a pair of sneakers.

She pulled on the jeans and rolled up the bottoms so they wouldn't drag on the ground. Next she zipped up the sweater, rolled up the sleeves, and then slipped her feet into the sneakers. As she headed toward the entrance to the cave, she grabbed the handles of the two buckets in one hand, and with her other hand, pulled back a towel to take one last peek at Joshawa. Amy felt confident to leave him alone, mostly because he couldn't go far with his injuries.

Alex was standing just inside the cave, facing toward the forest. He glanced over his shoulder as Amy approached him. She stopped a couple of feet away from him and frowned.

"Why are you upset?" Alex turned and ambled toward Amy. He gazed up at her, and as he did, he slowly shook his head from side to side.

"You're being silly. It was just a little kiss to see how hot his forehead was. Come on, Alex. We have to make one stop before we get breakfast." Amy didn't question how Alex knew that she'd kissed Joshawa. To her, it was just something a person did. She walked around Alex and headed out of the cave, with Alex dutifully following her.

Serena smiled as she witnessed the interaction between Amy and Joshawa. He would survive his injuries, but sadly he would never heal one hundred percent. She was planning to change into a wisp and revisit Joshawa. Serena wanted to make sure the seed she'd planted was strong enough to send a message to her Mistress.

But before she could step off the edge of the Realm, she heard movement coming from behind her. Serena turned to discover Lord Chike emerging from the jungle. *This cannot be good.* She respectfully bowed as Lord Chike approached her. "What can I do for you, my Lord?"

"Shall we start by you answering my question?"

"And what question would you like answered?" Serena could see the rage in Lord Chike's eyes. Though she couldn't see his hands, she knew they were balled into fists, and Serena braced herself for the blow she thought would be inflicted.

"When will Lord Joshawa be ready to make his final journey?"

Serena was stunned, though she tried not to show it. She was sure he was going to hit her. "He is mending, my Lord. When his mind is his own, then he will be ready to make his final journey."

"You are still avoiding my question."

"My Lord, I cannot say how long it will take. The mind is delicate and requires time to heal. However, I will inform you the minute his mind is strong enough to make the transfer."

"And how will you know when that time will be?"

"I will know, my Lord."

Lord Chike stood motionless, and his stare was so intense that even Serena was intimidated. "Need I remind you that if you fail me, I will see to your destruction and watch as you serve an eternity in darkness."

"I am very much aware, my Lord."

"My soul knows no patience. Do not press me." Lord Chike stood a breath away from Serena. "You are not the only Priestess that owes me her life." Lord Chike turned and disappeared into the jungle.

His comment puzzled Serena, for she had no idea which Priestess he would be referring to. It would have had to be a Priestess that lived long before Serena's time, or else she would have known about her. Besides herself, in the past two hundred years, there was only Imani who owed her existence to the generosity of the Ancestors. And as far as Serena knew, it was only herself that owed her existence directly to Lord Chike.

Serena searched her mind for any inference that there had been another honorary Ancestor, but nothing came to light. She needed to learn more about the tribe's history, and the only way to obtain that knowledge was to have access to the scrolls of her people. Those scrolls dated back to the very beginning of the Jelani Tribe, and contained within them would be the answers she needed.

There were two sets of scrolls. One set was in the Land of Spirits, and the other was in Africa with the Jelani Tribe. The scrolls that were with the Jelani Tribe had always been with the family of the High Priestesses who sat at the side of the ruling Lord. They were hers to protect, hers to learn from, and hers to hand down when the new High Priestess took her place.

When Serena was High Priestess, she'd seen no benefit in reading parchments that contained the history of the tribe. Her sole interest was focused on the spells and potions.

The new Mistress of the Jelani Tribe was the High Priestess Tamara. She was, and always would be, loyal to Lord Nathen and Mistress Authia. The problem was that Serena, on her own, even as powerful as she was, could not communicate directly with Tamara. The scrolls that were in the Land of Spirits could only be accessed by a true Ancestor. Like Imani, Serena was only an honorary Ancestor, and neither of them would have access to the scrolls.

Serena walked over to the edge of the jungle and stared deep into its depths. She smiled as an idea formulated in her mind. Serena was not alone, and somehow, she would find a way to communicate with Tamara unnoticed by Lord Chike. A smug look of satisfaction graced her delicate features, for she knew that redemption would be hers, and once again, she would save her Mistress and her Mistress's family.

Joshawa's head began to clear, and for the first time in what felt like forever, he could actually make out his surroundings. He was lying on the ground, and even though the air felt warm, the ground was cold, almost bone-chilling. Without moving his head, he allowed his gaze to roam the small room he was in. It appeared to be a makeshift shelter, with blankets and towels being used as walls.

He tried to move his head to the left, but the sudden pain and throbbing that encompassed his entire head convinced him to lie still. He was sure there was a firepit to his left, because his left side was warm, whereas his right side was slightly cooler.

Joshawa glanced down to his chest and discovered that his left arm was bandaged and lying across his chest. He tried to move it, but once again, the sudden shot of pain that radiated from his elbow to his shoulder convinced him not to. He attempted to move his legs with little success. His right leg wanted to cooperate, but his left leg wouldn't.

After the pain he'd experienced up to that point, he had no desire to push it. He tried to recall how he'd been injured and how he got to wherever this place was, but his memory was a blur. He closed his eyes and reached out to the two people he knew could help him. As he called out to his mother and father, a blue light filled his mind. It was bright, but at the same time, it appeared to be as dense as the thickest fog he had ever experienced. Joshawa could feel himself drifting away, drifting away from the fog, drifting away from reality, and within minutes he fell into a deep, painless sleep.


Amy had been gone longer than she would have liked. However, her time away was rewarded with a bucket full of fish and enough cottonwood branches to last several days. She could only bring back one bucket of water for the pot, which meant another trip to the river. Amy planned to take apart the tepee and feed Joshawa. After he finished, she would tend to his injuries, and then she would rebuild the tepee. Joshawa needed to spend his time in the tepee, which allowed the steam from the cottonwood branches to ease his pain.

Amy carefully dismantled the tepee so that Joshawa would be more accessible. Once she had cleared away the shelter, she went about building a fire on which to cook the fish. As the fire came to life, she poured the bucket of water into the pot that hung over the fire, then dumped the fish from the second bucket onto the ground. Amy glanced back at Joshawa to confirm that he was still asleep, then she grabbed the two buckets and ran down to the river.

When Amy returned, she found Alex lying at the entrance of the cave, and as before, he faced inside the cave. His massive head rested on his front paws, and his focus was fixed on Joshawa. Amy maneuvered around Alex, trying not to spill any water as she did. When she finally succeeded, she turned and frowned at him. "You could have moved, you know. Even a little bit."

Alex glanced up at Amy, then returned his focus to Joshawa. Amy rolled her eyes at Alex, muttering, "Silly bear," under her breath, then went over to the firepit. She filled the pot with one of the buckets of water and kept the second one for drinking. Amy skillfully filleted the fish and then skewered them so they would be ready for cooking. She leaned the skewers against the small rocks that encircled the firepit.

Amy glanced over to Joshawa and sighed. She had to figure some way to sit him up so she could feed him, but at the same time, she didn't want to cause him any further pain. She scanned the cave until her gaze fell on Alex. She smiled at him. "You will do."

Amy walked over to Alex and knelt on the ground so she could look directly at him. She placed her hands on either side of his snout. "I need a favor, Alex. I have to sit Joshawa up, but only slightly. You are all I have to do that. I need you to lie behind him so I can rest his back on you. Would that be all right?"

Amy remained quiet as she stared into Alex's eyes.

Alex averted his attention from Amy to Joshawa and then returned his gaze to her.

"Yes, Alex, I need you to help me with Joshawa. Will you do that for me? Please?"

As if he understood her, Alex got up and ambled over to Joshawa.

Amy was so excited. She ran up to Alex and hugged him

as best as she could. "Thank you, Alex. This means so much to me."

Amy stood back from Alex and pondered her last comment. Why did it mean so much to her? She glanced down at Joshawa and immediately forgot what she was questioning. Amy stood over Joshawa, one leg on either side of him at chest level.

"Okay, Alex, I'm going to lift him, and I need you to lie behind him. But you have to be quick about it." Alex moved closer to Joshawa so that his length ran horizontal to Joshawa's back. "Good, Alex. On the count of three, lie down as close as you can get." Amy reached down and grabbed Joshawa's shirt at either side of his collar. "Sorry, Joshawa, this is going to hurt." She looked back up at Alex. "Okay . . . one . . . two . . . three." Amy used every bit of strength she had to pull Joshawa up. As she did, Alex lay down behind Joshawa and moved his body as close to Joshawa as possible. Amy lowered Joshawa as gently as she could, but still, Joshawa cried out in pain. As Amy glanced down at him, Joshawa's eyes flew open.

Dameon kept glancing down at the GPS as he maneuvered his way through the dense forest. They were getting close, and every fiber of his body warned him not to go any further. He knew deep down that this hunt for Jax's bigfoot was not going to end well. The GPS started beeping louder with every step they took, and then when Dameon knew that they were only a few minutes from their destination, he stopped and turned the GPS off.

He turned to face Jax, who had been on his heels ever since the river. "The cabin is ahead of us, less than ten minutes away." Dameon took his backpack off and placed the GPS inside while he watched for Jax's reaction. Dameon wasn't happy with what he saw. His expression was no different than when he had his prey in sight and was ready to pull the trigger. "Jax, are you prepared for what we might find?"

Jax appeared puzzled by Dameon's query. "What do you mean?"

"I mean, if we find the creature, are you prepared to tranquilize him, then decide what we're going to do? Or are you going to shoot first, ask questions later?"

Jax looked at Dameon as if he'd just asked the dumbest question he could possibly ask. "Tranquilize him, of course. He's no good to us dead. Dameon, if this creature still exists, it will be worth its weight in gold! So get your tranquilizer gun ready, and let's see what we can find."

Dameon watched as Jax started heading in the direction of the cabin. Sadness filled his heart, because he knew Jax would exploit whatever they found, which went against everything Dameon stood for. Sure, he hunted endangered animals, but never to kill. As far as Dameon was concerned, the animals he caught were living a pampered life in private zoos or as pets for the wealthy. Dameon shook his head as he knelt on his knees, placed the rifle on the ground next to his backpack, and retrieved the case of tranquilizer darts.

Who was he kidding? In many ways, he was no better than Jax. Dameon peered over his shoulder in Jax's direction. Memories of Jax murdering the park ranger filled his mind. Softly he said to himself, "I may hunt illegally, but I am not a murderer."

Dameon opened the case, placed it on his backpack, and studied the darts. He had six, of which four would take down his bear, and two would take down a two-to-two-hundred-fifty-pound man. Jax didn't know about those tranquilizers. Dameon had included them for leverage. He hesitated as he reached for the more powerful tranquilizer, his hand hovering over the case. What was he more afraid of? Jax, or whatever creature they would come across? He had no way of knowing if the creature existed, or if he did, whether he could be reasoned with Jax could, to a point.

"What's taking you so long?"

Dameon didn't hear Jax come up behind him and was so startled that he knocked the case on the ground. "What the hell, Jax?" Dameon picked up the case and placed it back on his backpack.

"How long does it take to load the rifle?"

Dameon remained kneeling on the ground as Jax moved in front of him. He glanced up at Jax, hoping that his startled expression wouldn't give him away. "What's your hurry? I was doing the math on the strength of the darts."

"And?"

"These darts are meant for our bear. If your creature is the size of a man, then the tranquilizer could kill him."

Jax's attitude was pure condescension. "And you care? The creature is worth a lot to me alive, but if it's dangerous, then better it than us. And maybe you should be referring to the creature as *it* rather than *him*. It will be easier on your conscience if you don't humanize it."

Dameon just stared at Jax in disbelief. He truly believed the creature was real and still roaming the forest. If that was true and the creature did exist, then the best thing Dameon could do for the creature was to make sure he wasn't a threat to Jax. Dameon selected a dart under Jax's scrutiny, loaded the tranquilizer gun, then strapped the case of darts to his backpack. He got up, put on his backpack, and slung the rifle over his left shoulder. Dameon continued the trek through the forest in silence, with Jax close behind.


Authia sat at the table in silence as the rest of the group recounted memories of Serena when she was a wisp. Authia replayed her last adventure in Africa as she listened to the stories of when Serena entered Thomas's mind and convinced him that he was whole. Or of when she entered Travis's mind so that he and his men could find the Jelani Tribe.

And now, almost two decades later, Serena was back. She was speaking to Joshawa, showing him images of the tribe. She was speaking to Authia, but not freely, as though she had to be careful of what she said. Authia smiled to herself—as if Serena ever kept her tongue in check. Nathen placed his hand on Authia, which brought her focus back to the present.

"What do you find so funny, my love?"

"Memories of Serena. She's being so careful when she speaks to me, as if she's being watched. But when she speaks to Joshawa, she speaks more freely."

Tammy stood up from the table and gathered the empty coffee mugs. "Maybe she's meant to speak to Joshawa but not you." Tammy placed the empty cups in the sink then headed for the door. "Okay, family of mine, we have chores to do."

Authia stood, intending to walk over to the door, but something Tammy had said had her mind reeling. "You're absolutely right, Tammy. She's supposed to be speaking to Joshawa. She's trying to convince him to go to Africa. But Serena is not one to tread lightly—unless she's being forced to. Her encounters with me have been cryptic. Maybe she's trying to tell me something, but somehow, she's being censored."

Tammy interrupted Authia when she peered out the window. "We've got company. And they're not from Burwood."

Hansen was immediately at Tammy's side. He cautiously looked out the window. "It's two men, and from the way they're dressed, I'd say they're hunters." Hansen glanced back to Nathen. "And they're armed."

Nathen went to head for the door, but Authia held him back. "Go to the bedroom, sweetheart, and draw the drapes. We have no idea what these men want, and I don't think it would be a good idea for them to see you."

Nathen hesitated. "It's my job to protect you."

Authia gave Nathen an exasperated look. "Really? Well, it's also my job to protect you."

"You died in Africa trying to protect me and our people."

"Okay, I'll give you that one. But these men are not a threat, and if they become one, then you can be my knight in shining armor. Until then, please go hide in the bedroom."

Authia watched as Nathen reluctantly did as he was told. "Becca and Tammy, you wait here. Hansen, you're with me." Authia didn't wait for a rebuttal — she just opened the door and headed out into the yard with Hansen close on her heels.

She found two men, both dressed in camouflage. Both were wearing sidearms, and one of the men was carrying a rifle. The man who carried the rifle had his back to her. He appeared to be checking out Hansen's cabin. As they approached the men, Hansen quickened his pace and put himself between Authia and them. She was a little annoyed with his gallantry, but she didn't react. It was only when they stood directly in front of the men that she stood off to the side so she could see the strangers.

Hansen held out his hand to the man that was facing them. "Hi. Name's Hansen. What brings you out to our neck of the woods?"

The man accepted Hansen's hand and appeared friendly enough. "I'm Jax. We're hunting in the area and just happened to come across your cabins."

Authia watched as the second man moved closer to Hansen's cabin. She returned her focus to Jax. "What are you hunting?"

Jax didn't answer right away. It was as if he was sizing her up. "A rather large black bear. Was tracking him when we found your cabin."

Authia glanced over to Hansen, who had been watching

the second hunter. He looked back at Jax. "You expecting trouble?" Authia followed Hansen's gaze to Jax's sidearm. "Your sidearm isn't locked in its holster. And if you're hunting bears, you're not going to get it off the mountain if all you're carrying is that tranquilizer gun." Hansen motioned toward the second man.

At that moment, the second man turned and faced Authia.

Her heart almost stopped dead when she saw his face. Authia gasped as her eyes widened. Hansen lightly put his hand on her arm. "What's wrong, Authia?"

Authia's mind raced out of control. This was the man she'd seen when she melded with Becca. He knew where Joshawa was. She could hear Nathen's meld, and she knew if she didn't control her emotions, Nathen would risk everything and leave the safety of the cabin. Authia calmed her breathing as the man approached her.

*Stay where you are, sweetheart. I've got this.*

She glanced over to Jax and realized that he knew something was wrong. Authia smiled at Jax, then turned her attention to the second man. "I'm so sorry. But you are the spitting image of my late husband." Authia offered her hand to the second man. "My name is Authia."

"I'm Dameon."

As soon as Damien took hold of hers, Authia's mind went back to the place she'd seen Joshawa fall. He knew where it was, and he wasn't hunting black bears—he was planning to capture a grizzly. Authia's mind emptied, and then the next second, she was in his cabin. Authia let go of his hand and tried to hide her horror, for in the cabin was a book lying open on a table, and on that open page was a drawing of Nathen.

# CHAPTER SEVENTEEN

Joshawa felt as though his entire body was screaming at him. All he wanted to do was succumb to the darkness so that he wouldn't have to endure the pain that played havoc with his body. He slowed his breathing and was about to allow the darkness of unconsciousness to engulf him when he felt someone grab the collar of his shirt. He heard a voice. Then he felt the pain as it intensified throughout his body. The pain ravaged his head then continued its journey to his chest, arm, and leg. He felt as though none of his body was immune to the pain.

Joshawa's eyes flew open, and as the fog dissipated, he could see her. She was young with long blonde hair, and she was so tiny. Even though Joshawa knew his mind wasn't as clear as it could be, he was confident that he didn't know her. She stared at him with a look of concern and uncertainty. When the fog completely cleared and Joshawa had some semblance of control over his mind, he realized that he was no longer lying on a cold floor but instead on something that was soft and warm.

He watched her as she sat beside the firepit and placed something into the fire. She glanced over to him and smiled as a child would smile upon a parent. Oddly enough, the smile comforted him, and at that moment, he felt safe.

She placed her hand on his forehead, then on the side of his face. "Your fever is going down, Joshawa, but I'll still have to replace the medicine from your wound. How are you feeling?"

The only thing that registered with Joshawa was her calling him by his name. How did she know his name? "Do I know you?"

Amy smiled as she rolled her eyes. "Of course you do, silly. I'm Amy. And your pillow is Alex."

Amy returned her attention to what she was cooking in the fire. Joshawa moved his head slightly to the right. His heart nearly stopped when he locked gazes with the grizzly that had caused his injuries. Joshawa started to panic, and his breathing became more rapid as flashbacks from his accident flooded his mind. His first reaction was to get out, but the pain that ensued when he tried to move made that reaction a moot point.

Suddenly Amy appeared between him and the bear. She placed her hands on Joshawa's shoulders. "You mustn't move." Amy applied just enough pressure so that he would have no choice but to lie back against Alex. "Alex will not hurt you. He's my friend." Amy reached over to Alex and affectionately stroked his snout.

"Your friend? Your friend tried to kill me. I remember. He was attacking the tree I was in. He forced me to fall."

Amy became solemn as she chewed at her lower lip. She glanced over to Alex then back at Joshawa. "I know, and I'm so sorry. He thought he was protecting me. Alex didn't mean to hurt you. He didn't know who you were. But I told him, and he knows we're friends, so now he'll protect both of us."

"We're friends?"

Amy giggled as she moved over to the fire pit and pulled the fish from the hot embers. Using her fork, she removed the fillets from the skewer and placed them onto a tin plate. "Of course we are." Amy turned to face Joshawa. "You need to eat. And I have fresh water for you, too."

"Where am I?

"In my home. Where else would you be? Well, actually, it's

Alex's and my home." Amy sat cross-legged at Joshawa's side and fed him the fish.

"How long have I been here?"

"Not long. One night. Now eat. You need your strength."

Joshawa allowed Amy to feed him the fish and the water. She acted as though she knew him, but he had no memory of her. Joshawa glanced over his right shoulder toward Alex.

*You, I remember.*

When Amy left to clean up the remains of the fish, Joshawa closed his eyes and sought out his parents.

*Mother, Father, I need you. I'm north of our home, and I think I might be in a cave. Please find me. Father, please help me.*

Serena witnessed the interaction between Joshawa and Amy. "Do not worry, my young Lord. Your mother will find you. Now there is something that I need to do."

Serena walked over to the edge of the jungle. Lord Chike had forbidden her to enter the jungle. However, he'd said nothing of her alter ego. Serena smiled as she continued to stare at the lush foliage that lay before her. She closed her eyes and sought out the presence of Lord Chike and discovered he was with Lord Adeeowale and Imani.

*Good, you are distracted. I will find out what and who you are. I promise you.*

Serena morphed into a blue wisp and headed toward the Ancestors.

Authia wasn't doing a very good job hiding the fear she felt. Everyone was focused on her, as if she had grown horns. And to make matters worse, Nathen was no longer content to stay in the cabin. Authia turned to face Hansen so their visitors couldn't see her face. "Could you check on Becca and see how's she's feeling?" Then she quickly mouthed the words *keep Nathen in the cabin.* Hansen understood, and Authia sighed a breath of relief when Hansen disappeared into the cabin before Nathen could make an appearance. Jax's inquiry brought her attention back to the problem.

"Are you okay?"

She smiled at Dameon and Jax as she attempted to play down her reaction. "I'm fine. I'm so sorry, where are my manners. Would you gentlemen like some water?"

Jax was quick to answer. "Actually, that would be nice. You know we haven't seen another human being for weeks. Wouldn't mind sitting down and chatting, that is, if you're not busy."

Authia was pleased, because that was precisely what she wanted. She needed more information on these two, especially Dameon. She smiled at Jax, hoping she didn't appear too excited as she accepted his proposal. "I would love that. We don't get much company up here."

Jax started to head for Authia's cabin, only to have Authia quickly block his path. She motioned toward Hansen's cabin. "Let's sit on that porch. My niece is not well, and she should be asleep on my love seat. I don't want to disturb her." Authia headed for Hansen's porch, and just as Dameon and Jax were getting settled, Hansen joined them. Authia prayed that Hansen would know to follow her lead. "How is she?"

"Stubborn, but I think she'll stay put."

Authia knew he was referring to Nathen. "Good. I explained to Jax and Dameon that she wasn't well and that I didn't want to disturb her. I was just going to fetch some water. Would you like some?"

Hansen grabbed one of the wicker chairs and sat facing the two men. "Would love some."


Hansen sat in silence for a couple of minutes as he sized up his visitors. Authia had obviously seen something when she shook Dameon's hand. That would be the only reason she would keep them around. He glanced over to the *Pax* rifle that was leaning against the porch railing, then back to the two men. "So, you say you're hunting a black bear?"

Jax spoke up right away. "Yeah, a pretty big one. Trophy bear for sure. We've been tracking him for some time now."

"So, you guys are avid hunters?"

Again, Jax continued the conversation. "We've been hunting since we were old enough to hold a rifle. We're from Manitoba, and we usually hunt in that area, but decided to treat ourselves this year and came out here."

Hansen was going to continue his questioning, but Authia emerged from the cabin carrying a tray with four glasses of water and a plate of cookies. "I thought you might want something to nibble on."

Dameon smiled at Authia as he accepted a glass of water. "Thank you. You're very kind."

Hansen had always been good at reading people and what he gleaned from Dameon was sincerity. Jax, on the other hand, Hansen wouldn't trust as far as he could throw him. Hansen waited till Authia was settled before he continued his questioning. "So, how big is this bear of yours?"

Jax took a bite of his cookie, and at the same time, he shot Dameon a look that Hansen translated to *I'm doing all the talking*. "It has to be pushing six hundred pounds. We'll know for sure once we bag him."

"Are you going to release him?"

"Not to offend you, but we'll be doing a full mount with this guy."

"No offense taken. We hunt all the time. That's how we feed ourselves. I'm curious, though. If you're planning on killing the bear, why would you hunt with a *Pax* rifle?" Hansen could tell that his comment angered Jax. However, Dameon appeared more like the child caught with his hand in the cookie jar.

Jax finished his cookie and continued, "The *Pax* is for protection. There are a lot of grizzlies in the area. If we come across one, we'll just tranq it. They are amazing creatures. We don't want to kill them."

"Not to mention that they're protected and illegal to hunt." Hansen knew that he'd hit a nerve immediately. It took everything he had not to reveal the satisfaction he felt with Jax's uneasiness. "So, you say you've been here a while. Where have you been hanging out?"

Dameon glanced over to Jax and knew he was going to a place that wouldn't be good for either of them. Dameon decided that now was a good time to jump into the conversation. "Actually, we were camping northeast of here, but while tracking our bear, we came across an old homestead. It looks like it's been abandoned for decades. How long have you guys been here?"

Hansen glanced over to Authia, who took up the conversation. "Pretty much all my life. Hansen's my brother-in-law. He moved here when Nathen, his brother, and I married."

Dameon could see the excitement in Jax's expression, and before he could say anything, Jax butted in. "All your life? You wouldn't happen to know who owned the homestead that we're staying at?"

Authia shook her head as she responded. "To be honest, no, I don't. We don't travel very far north of here. We pretty much keep to the south, toward Gainsbourgh. And, as you can guess, we don't get much company. Have you two encountered anyone else while you've been here?"

Dameon glanced over to Jax, then back to Authia. The only encounter he'd experienced was when he was confronted by their bear. "No, no one. But as you know, it's pretty isolated up here. So you guys are happy living in the middle of nowhere with no human interaction other than yourselves?"

Dameon observed Authia as she responded to the question. She smiled at him, and in that smile, he saw contentment and honesty. "We love it here. I don't know how to explain it, but there's something about this place. It's so peaceful, the seasons are amazing, and if we're craving human contact, we just have to head into town."

Dameon finished his water and was about to suggest that they head out when Jax locked onto Authia, his expression sinister. "When we were in town, we heard a story of a creature that roams these woods. Part man, part animal. Have you ever heard those stories or maybe seen something in the woods?"

Hansen laughed. "Sounds like you're talking about bigfoot."

Dameon wasn't laughing—he was watching Authia, and she looked as though she'd seen a ghost. He was sure she knew something, so he decided to take it one step further. "Actually, at this cabin we're staying at, we found a journal." Dameon ignored what he was sure would be Jax's scowl of disapproval. "And the interesting thing is that the author spoke a lot about a creature that walked like a man. Apparently, this creature roamed these very woods twenty years ago."

Authia felt like her heart was going to explode from her chest. She could feel the color draining from her face, and by the obvious expression on both Dameon's and Jax's face, she knew she wasn't hiding it very well. The grizzly wasn't the only thing they were hunting. They were looking for Nathen, and possibly Joshawa as well.

Hansen placed his hand on Authia's knee, which distracted her from her thoughts and brought her back to the present. She could see that Hansen was concerned, and she knew it wasn't so much for her as it was for Nathen. She had to think fast and come up with a plausible explanation for her dire reaction.

"I'm so sorry." Authia didn't have to force herself to produce tears. They were genuine, and she hoped the tears would convince Dameon and Jax to accept her explanation. "My late husband was a big man, well over six feet tall, and he had a deformity. That's why we lived out here. To hide from the cruelties of man. A little over ten years ago, some hunters came across him just north of here. They shot him thinking that he was this bigfoot you're looking for. He died in that cabin." Authia motioned toward her cabin. "The hunters followed his blood trail, and when they got here, we told them that something ran through our yard. They believed us and disappeared into the woods. We never saw them again. Hansen went to get a doctor, but my husband died before he could get back. There is no bigfoot. There was only a man who wanted to live a normal life, and that privilege was taken from him."

Dameon looked ill at ease, whereas Jax acted as though Authia had taken his prize away from him, and he wasn't the least bit happy about it. Dameon was the first to stand. He grabbed the rifle and slung it over his shoulder.

"I'm so sorry for the intrusion. We meant no harm. We'll leave now." Dameon glanced over to Jax, and Authia could tell that Jax was reluctant to leave.

Authia stood, and as she did, Hansen was at her side. He put his arm around her shoulders, which Authia interpreted as a sign of protection. "Yes, it's probably best that you leave."

Authia watched as Jax reluctantly stood, and then the two men walked through the yard and disappeared into the woods. She closed her eyes and sighed a breath of relief. Hansen just shook his head at her. "Wow! How did you come up with that?"

"It's very close to the truth. Please go make sure Nathen stays in the cabin. There's something I need to do."

"You're not planning to follow them, are you?"

As Authia glanced over to the chair Dameon was sitting in, she slowly shook her head, indicating that her plan was not to follow them. When Authia turned to face Hansen, she could tell that he was concerned. "I'm fine, really. And I'm not going to do anything stupid. Between you and Nathen, I wouldn't have a chance."

"You saw something when you shook that guy's hand, didn't you?"

"Yes, and I'm hoping that he sat long enough to transfer his energy to this chair. Please, just go sit with Nathen." Hansen smiled at Authia and quietly left the porch. There was a reason Authia wanted Hansen to sit with Nathen.

She closed her eyes and melded with him. *Thank you for staying in the cabin, sweetheart.*

*It wasn't easy. What happened? You were so scared, almost terrified.*

*I had reason to be, but now I need your help.*

*Of course, I'll be right there.*

*No, I need you to stay in the cabin and meld with me.*

*Is that why Hansen just planted himself in front of me?*

*Yes. Nathen, when I shook Dameon's hand, I saw things. Most importantly, I believe he knows where Joshawa is.*

*What!*

*When I melded with Becca and was seeing what Joshawa saw, he saw Dameon. However, I don't believe Dameon saw him. But if Dameon was there, maybe I could find the place through him. I want to sit in the chair he sat in and see if I can see anything else. I need you to meld with me, but only meld with me. You can't try to protect me or come out to me. I need to stay in the meld no matter what I see or hear. That's your job. Keep me in the meld.*

*This isn't going to be good, is it?*

*Possibly not. You may see things about yourself that will upset you, but you have to be strong for me as well as for Joshawa. Don't react to what you see. If you feel that I'm frightened or want to leave the meld, you have to convince me to stay.*

*Okay, then let's do this.*

Authia walked over to the chair that Dameon had occupied, took a deep breath, then sat down. She pressed her back into the chair and rested her arms on the armrests. It had been a very long time since she'd used this one particular gift. It was a form of telepathy, a gift she shared with her mother. Not only could she touch someone and see into that person's thoughts, but she could also touch something that belonged to them and see into their past. Authia hoped that Dameon's brief stay in this chair would be enough for her to see the truth.

She closed her eyes and calmed her mind. She sought out whatever energy Dameon had left behind. At first, it was as if she was staring at a blank canvas. Her mind was void of color, depth, and perception. Then she felt Nathen as he joined her in the meld. She could feel his strength, and she could hear his words.

*I am here, my love. Seek out his energy. Find Dameon.*

Authia searched her mind for any sign of Dameon. She could sense his energy, though it felt miles away.

*Come on, Dameon, show me what you were thinking. Show me the journal. Show me where you were when you saw my son.*

Nathen quietly interjected. *Authia, focus on one thing. Focus on the recent events. What was he thinking when he was sitting in the chair?*

Authia nodded her head, and then she focused on the memory of Dameon sitting in the chair. The canvas started to take shape, and she could see Dameon as he listened to Jax speaking to Hansen. She could tell that he was very uncomfortable. Through Dameon's eyes, she could see Jax, and she could see Hansen, but not herself.

*Right, I was getting water. What upset you, Dameon?*

Dameon was looking at Jax, and he was thinking of a bear, but not a black bear. It was the grizzly.

*You're uncomfortable lying.*

Authia smiled to herself. Dameon was the perfect candidate, because he actually had morals, something Authia believed was missing in his friend.

*Okay, show me the bear you're really hunting, the one that occupies your every thought.*

A massive grizzly filled Authia's mind. She knew this grizzly, because it was the one she'd seen through Joshawa's eyes. Dameon was there, the grizzly was there, and that was her connection to Joshawa.

*Authia, calm yourself. Dameon is our connection, but we have to know where to find him. Focus on Dameon, focus on the homestead, and we'll find Joshawa.*

Authia returned her focus to the conversation. Dameon was speaking of the homestead they were staying at. Visions of the homestead filled Dameon's mind, and Authia could see them as clearly as if she were standing right next to Dameon.

There were two buildings and an outhouse. The smaller building scared Dameon so much that Authia thought it would be best not to press that particular memory. The other building was very old with basic amenities. Obviously, the homestead had been there for quite some time, but unfortunately, she didn't recognize it. The impression Authia received was that Dameon was uneasy. He felt that what they were doing was wrong.

A memory started to materialize in his mind, but it faded when he heard the word bigfoot. His thoughts went to a journal that was sitting on what looked like a small square table with four chairs. The journal was open to the same page she'd seen before. It was the drawing of Nathen. She wanted to see more, but Dameon's focus was now on her.

She was telling a story of the death of a man she claimed to be her husband. Dameon was almost sick to his stomach. He felt shame and hated what he and his friend were doing. Dameon's energy was fading, and Authia panicked.

*No! Dameon! You have to stay with me. You were somewhere with your bear. Just you and the bear. You had your GPS out. Where were you?*

Dameon's energy was spent, and there was nothing more she could see. Authia covered her face with the palms of her hands and burst out crying.

Nathen sat on the couch in his cabin, his eyes closed, his mind focused on strengthening the meld. He was puzzled, because he couldn't feel her emotions even though he was with Authia. It was as if they were not her own. He also couldn't see anything, as if he were encased in darkness.

However, he could hear Authia as if she were speaking directly to him. He knew when he had to calm her, and he knew she heard him. There was something Authia was saying to Dameon. Even though Authia was losing the meld, she continued to press Dameon. She asked him about the grizzly, about where he was, and about the GPS.

The meld was gone, and Nathen's eyes flew open. He ran out of the cabin and straight to Authia. He found her sitting in the chair with her elbows resting on her knees. She had her face buried in the palms of her hands, and she was sobbing uncontrollably. Between the sobs, Nathen heard her say Joshawa's name over and over again. Nathen scooped her up in his arms, then sat in the chair with her on his lap. He wrapped his arms around her, pulling her close to him. "My love, there is no need to cry."

Authia sat up as she wiped the tears from her face. "How can you say that? We didn't learn anything from that meld."

Nathen smiled at Authia as he reached with his right hand and gently cupped her chin. "Not true. You said that when Joshawa got hurt, Dameon and the bear were there."

"Yes, but we don't know where that is."

"Maybe not us, but the GPS will."

Authia's eyes grew as big as saucers. "The GPS?"

"When you melded with Becca, through Joshawa's eyes, you saw the GPS. You said it was on, because you heard the beeping. I'm sure the GPS these guys have is the best money can buy, and wherever it has been, there will be a record of it."

"Okay, say you're right. How do we get it? We don't know where they are, and even if we found them, I don't think they're going to hand it over to us."

"Well, first things first, we have to find them. I couldn't see anything in your meld, so I couldn't see the homestead. I've lived here all my life. I must have come across it at some point. Describe it to me."

Authia appeared as if she was looking off into the distance. "It was old. The yard was overgrown with trees and grass. I was standing in the middle of the yard. To my left was an old cabin, small, with no windows, and Dameon was really scared of it. To the right of that, and set back a bit, was an outhouse. To the right of the outhouse was a larger cabin. Again, I'm not sensing any windows, just a door. There was a square table in the middle of the cabin, and a book was sitting on the table." Authia paused for a second. "I think there were bunk beds in the cabin."

Nathen listened to Authia's description, and something about it was familiar, though he couldn't put his finger on it. He knew he'd seen or heard about that layout before. Small cabin, outhouse, larger cabin. No windows. And then it hit him with a force that caused his stomach to churn. He glanced up to Authia. "I know that cabin. I've seen it in Billy's drawings."

Authia looked completely bewildered. "Billy?"

"Billy Jenkins." Nathen watched as the color drained from Authia's face. "It's the Jenkins homestead."

# CHAPTER EIGHTEEN

Serena rested on a branch of a very old kapok tree that stood at the edge of the Ancestor's campsite. In the form of a wisp, she could easily conceal herself in among the foliage of the giant tree that stood over two hundred feet tall. Another advantage of being a wisp was that the Ancestors could not sense her presence.

She observed the interaction between the three Ancestors. Lord Chike, whose back was facing her, sat across the firepit from Lord Adeeowale and Imani. Serena could sense that this was not a choice but rather a tactical position for Lord Chike. Serena needed to get closer to hear them, but more importantly, she needed to access Lord Chike. If she could enter his body, become one with his mind, then she could discover what he was up to. The only problem was that she had to figure out how to do that without his knowledge. Not an easy feat, even for her.

Serena flew to the ground using the girth of the kapok tree to conceal her descent. Once she was back on the ground, she used the massive buttress root system to conceal her further. From her hiding place, she heard the conversation between the Ancestors, and she could sense the contempt Lord Chike had for his companions.

She couldn't see his face, but she didn't have to. His tone weighed heavy with anger, and as she closed her eyes, his face filled her mind. His eyes were narrowed, his face flushed, and his teeth were clenched. Serena suddenly realized that what she sensed was not only anger but also pure, raw hatred, not just for his companions, but for others as well.

Serena closed her eyes and allowed Lord Chike's facial features to fill her mind. She didn't understand why his companions couldn't sense what she could so easily see. Serena opened her eyes and flew to the very upper edge of the buttress root. From there, she watched the interaction between the Ancestors. Lord Adeeowale and Imani didn't appear distressed. Could they not tell that Lord Chike despised them? Could they not sense his hatred?

Serena had to find herself a better vantage point. She flew back to the top of the trees and made her way to another large kapok tree. The tree Serena chose was located directly behind Lord Adeeowale and Imani. She flew to the ground, keeping the tree between her and the Ancestors. The buttress roots of this tree were not as immense as the last tree she'd hidden in. Serena had to be careful, or else she could risk being discovered.

Slowly she inched upwards until she had a clear line of sight to Lord Chike. Serena was shocked by what she saw. Lord Chike appeared utterly amicable. But that made no sense, which compounded her confusion of the situation. This wasn't the expression of a man filled with hatred. Serena stared at Lord Chike with her focus trained on his eyes. There was contempt, but where was the hatred? Serena blocked every sensation, every sound so that all that was left was Lord Chike and his emotions.

She closed her eyes, and once again, Lord Chike's face revealed his hatred and his anger. When Serena opened her eyes, she saw the face of contempt, but that was all. Serena's eyes widened as she realized what she was experiencing. It was not the emotions of one man, but rather two men trapped in one body. Some distant memory told her that she knew what this was, but she didn't have the energy to bring the memory forward.

Jax and Dameon made their way back to the homestead in silence. Jax's mind was reeling with the information he'd gleaned from his visit. He knew for sure that Authia and Hansen were hiding something. When the subject of the creature came up, Authia went white. She bounced back quite effectively, but her initial reaction gave her away. Authia knew of the creature, and it had nothing to do with her dead husband.

Jax smirked to himself. *That's if you actually have a husband who's dead.* The way Hansen had protected Authia and his obvious concern for her led Jax to believe that Hansen was her husband. Jax decided to set up surveillance at the couple's homestead, and maybe he would even set up a few cameras. Jax glanced over his shoulder to Dameon, who followed close behind him.

Would Dameon be on board? Somehow, he doubted it, but he would give Dameon a chance. One chance and one chance only to help capture this creature. Jax stopped and placed his backpack on the ground. He retrieved his canteen of water and offered it to Dameon.

"Let's take a break." Dameon placed his backpack next to Jax's, then rested the *Pax* rifle against a nearby tree. Jax watched as Dameon accepted the canteen, unscrewed the cap, and took a couple of gulps of the water. As far as Jax was concerned, there was no better time like the present to find out if Dameon was on board. "So, what's your take on our friends back there?"

Dameon passed the canteen back to Jax. "Friends? I didn't get the impression that you cared for them."

"I don't. But you seemed to be chummy. I think they're hiding something."

"Or maybe we just made them uncomfortable. They wouldn't get much company living so far north of the main road."

"True, but did you see her reaction to the mention of the creature?"

"Yeah, what of it? She told you that the creature was her husband. There's no bigfoot."

Jax hesitated — he had to be very careful about how he approached Dameon. Capturing this creature would be easier with Dameon's help, but when it came down to it, he could manage on his own. He took a large gulp of the water, screwed the cap in place, then smiled at Dameon. "Yes, she did, but I don't believe her. She's hiding something."

"Yeah, probably the fact that you made her uncomfortable." Dameon retrieved his backpack, placed his arms through the straps, and then buckled the strap that secured the backpack to his waist.

Jax followed suit, putting his backpack on. "No, she's not uncomfortable. I'm sure she's hiding something. We could go back at night and set up a couple of cameras."

Dameon's expression spoke volumes, and Jax knew he disapproved. "You want to spy on them?" He retrieved the *Pax* rifle and slung it over his right shoulder.

"Not spy . . . recon. We do it all the time."

"With animals. Not human beings. We have no right to invade their privacy."

Jax placed his hands on the backpack's straps that covered his chest. He stared at Dameon and wondered just how far he could push him. "Look, we could argue about this till the cows come home, or you could prove me wrong." Jax watched Dameon's reaction to his comment. He was actually thinking about it.

"And how do I prove you wrong?"

"We put up a couple of cameras. Retrieve them in two maybe three days, and if there's no sighting of bigfoot, then I'll concede and drop the whole thing."

"Really? You'll back off and not mention the creature or the journal ever again."

Jax smiled at Dameon. "Well, at least not in your presence."

Dameon extended his right hand to Jax, who readily accepted it. "Okay, Jax, you're on. But you're placing and retrieving the cameras."

Jax watched as Dameon passed by him, taking the lead. He smiled as he shook his head. He was going to find that creature, of that he was certain.

Nathen knew precisely what he had to do, and he also knew he didn't have much time. Joshawa had been missing for two days, and from what little information Nathen had, there was no doubt that Joshawa's injuries were severe — so severe that it could be too late if Nathen didn't find him soon. Nathen walked over to the front door and grabbed his jacket that was hanging on the wall next to the door. As he was putting the jacket on, Authia approached him.

"Where are you going?"

"Burwood. I have to see Billy."

"I'm coming, too." Authia went to reach for her jacket, but Nathen stopped her.

He gently placed his hands on either side of her face. "No, you're not."

Authia stepped back, clearly put off by his comment. "And why the hell not?"

Nathen smiled at Authia. "I can get to Burwood a lot faster on my own. You know that. I'll bring Billy back here, and then we'll go from there." Nathen could tell by Authia's expression that she knew he was right. He also knew she wasn't happy about it.

"All right. Go. But let me know when you get there."

Nathen placed his arms around Authia and drew her close

to his body. "I will." Slowly he pulled her away so he could see her face. "Billy is the answer. We'll find Joshawa." Nathen kissed Authia with so much tenderness that she started to cry. He wiped the tears from her cheeks, kissed her on her forehead, then left for Burwood.

Joshawa opened his eyes and tried to focus on his surroundings. His head felt heavy, and his mind felt as if it was surrounded by a dense fog. The air felt moist and had a strange odor that Joshawa couldn't quite make out. It took a few moments before he realized that he was in the makeshift tent, and the odor was coming from the pot hanging over the firepit.

He also realized that he was no longer resting against the bear. Joshawa tried to sit up, but as soon as he lifted his head off the cold ground, the intense throbbing forced him to remain still. Joshawa tried moving other parts of his body and discovered that the pain that had held his body captive seemed to have lessened, and for that, he was grateful.

Joshawa closed his eyes and thought of his parents. Why haven't they found him? Why had he not heard from them? He felt exhausted, and all he wanted to do was sleep. Before he surrendered his mind to the calm and emptiness of a dreamless sleep, he reached out to an unlikely ally. *Serena, I hear you. Whispers in the wind. Help my father find me.*

Nathen made good time of the four-mile hike to Burwood and arrived there in less than twenty minutes. When he walked past the gates, he was greeted by Edward, who was on his way to the medical building. Edward was carrying a small wooden crate filled with medical supplies. Nathen reached out to take the crate from him. "Here, let me carry this."

Edward willingly passed the crate to Nathen. "Thanks.

What brings you to Burwood?"

"Actually, I'm looking for Billy."

"Billy? He's in our cabin." Edward and Billy had shared a cabin ever since Billy arrived at Burwood. Billy felt safe with Edward, and Edward had an endless supply of patience when it came to Billy. "Why are you looking for Billy?"

"I'll fill you in when I see him."

"Okay, the supplies can wait. Let's head over to my cabin." Edward's cabin was only twenty feet from the medical building, so he didn't have far to go.

"How's Charles?"

"He's good. Worried about Authia. I think he would be happier if all of you moved to Burwood."

"Well, that's not going to happen. Authia loves that cabin, and it's all she has left of her mother."

When they arrived at the cabin, Edward held the door open for Nathen. "I know, and that's why Charles will never bring the subject up. Just put the crate on the table." Edward motioned to the small, round kitchen table. Billy was sitting in a rocking chair with a child's picture book opened in his lap. He was wearing a pair of blue jean overalls and a long-sleeve red-checkered flannel shirt.

"Billy, Nathen's come to visit you."

Billy glanced up, and when he saw Nathen, he jumped up, his book dropping to the floor. Billy ran over to Nathen and wrapped his massive arms around Nathen's stomach. He pressed the side of his face tight against Nathen's chest and held on as if he never wanted to let go. Nathen gently pulled Billy's arms away and gazed down at the child trapped in a man's body. Billy looked up at Nathen and rewarded him with a smile that revealed how much he loved Nathen.

"Billy happy to see Nathen. Nathen stay with Billy?"

"Yes, Billy, I've come to visit you. I need to ask a favor of you."

Billy took Nathen's hand in his and led him to the fireplace. Then he sat cross-legged on the floor and glanced up at Nathen. "Sit with Billy?"

Nathen removed his jacket, placed it on the back of one of the kitchen chairs, and then joined Billy on the floor. There was a small fire in the fireplace, which captivated Billy's attention. "That's a nice fire, Billy."

Billy smiled as he turned to face Nathen. "It's pretty." Billy folded his hands in his lap and just stared at Nathen as if he were waiting for some special news.

"Like I said, Billy, I need your help."

Billy nodded his head excitedly. "Billy help. Billy help Nathen."

"Thank you, Billy. Do you remember where you lived before you came to Burwood?"

Billy was no longer smiling. He lowered his head slightly so that he didn't have direct eye contact with Nathen. Then he started softly rocking back and forth as he held his hands tight together. "Yes. Billy remember. Not a nice place."

Edward had been sitting at the kitchen table, but when Nathen asked his question, Edward came to sit in the rocking chair next to Billy. "What are you doing, Nathen?"

"Trust me, Edward. I have to ask this." Nathen returned his attention to Billy. He reached out and tenderly placed his right hand on top of Billy's. That caused Billy to stop rocking and make eye contact with Nathen. "If I took you back to my cabin, would you be able to find your old home from there?"

"Billy don't want to. Bad place."

"I know, Billy. It's a very bad place. But I need to find it. Billy, Joshawa is missing, and he's hurt."

Before Nathen could continue, Edward spoke up. "What? When did he go missing? How's he hurt?"

Nathen glanced over to Edward. "I'll explain everything, but in the meantime, maybe you should go get Charles. I'll tell you together." As Edward left, Nathen refocused on Billy. "Your old homestead has the answers. I need to find it, Billy, but I can't do it without you."

"Joshawa at my home?" Billy started shaking his head from side to side. "Not good. He will die." Billy then wrapped his arms around himself and started rocking back and forth as he shook his head. "Not good. He will die. Not good. He will die."

Nathen gently placed his hands on Billy's shoulders to stop him from rocking. "Billy." Billy kept his eyes focused on the floor. "Billy, look at me." Slowly Billy raised his head. "Thank you, Billy. Joshawa is not going to die, because we're going to save him. He's not at your home. But there's someone there who knows where he is."

Billy's eyes lit up. "Is she pretty? Amelia is pretty."

Nathen was confused, because there was never any mention of a woman being at the Jenkins home. "I don't believe there's a woman there. Just two men."

"Not good. Two men. She's dead."

Nathen had no idea what Billy was referring to, and unfortunately, he didn't have time to figure it out. "Billy, the two men know where Joshawa is. I have to find him fast, or he may die. Can you show me where you used to live?"

"Billy no go." Once again, Billy started shaking his head from side to side. "Billy not go back."

"You don't have to go inside the cabin or even in the yard. Just get me close, Billy, and then you can come back home to Burwood. Billy, please, I have to save my son."

Billy looked at Nathen as if he were trying to recall something. "I can save again?"

Nathen wasn't sure what Billy meant, but he decided to play along. "Yes, Billy, you can save again. You can save Joshawa."

"Billy wants to save. But no tell Dext. Shhhh." Billy placed a single finger in front of his lips, then whispered, "Our secret. No tell Dext."

Nathen was relieved though confused about the mention of Dext. Billy knew Dext had been killed, and that was how Billy came to be at Burwood. But Nathen didn't have time to play word games with Billy. He needed to find the Jenkins homestead, and he needed to do it now. Nathen stood up and pulled Billy to his feet just as Charles and Edward burst into the cabin.

Billy excitedly ran up to Edward. "Billy get to save again."

Edward placed his right hand on Billy's shoulder. "That's great, Billy. Good for you."

Charles walked over to Nathen. "What's going on? What happened to Joshawa?"

"Joshawa went for a walk and never came back. I can't connect with him, and I have no idea where he is. He's alive, but he's hurt, possibly unconscious. That's the only explanation to why I can't feel his emotions or find him."

"What does Billy have to do with finding Joshawa?"

"I'm sorry, Charles, but I don't have a lot of time for explanations. Joshawa's out there somewhere, and I have to find him. Call Authia on the radio, and she'll fill you in. Edward, can you get Billy dressed for a long walk? I'll be right back." Nathen didn't wait for a response. He left the cabin in search of Adrian.

Nathen knew that Billy wouldn't find his way back to Burwood on his own. Adrian and Joshawa might have been bitter rivals, but Adrian knew the woods better than anyone. He could bring Billy home safely after they found the Jenkins homestead. Nathen didn't have to go far to find him.

Adrian had just returned to Burwood after spending the morning hunting rabbits. He wore a jean jacket over his black hoodie. The jacket was open, and one couldn't miss his *Ruger Single Six*, which was holstered in his gun belt. He had a large burlap bag slung over his left shoulder, and by the bulge of the bag, Nathen assumed he had a successful morning.

Adrian stopped just inside the gates and glanced over in Nathen's direction. Nathen continued to approach Adrian. From Adrian's stance and the glare he was shooting Nathen's way, it appeared as if Adrian was preparing for a confrontation.

Adrian started in on Nathen before he could even utter one word. "Look, I'm sorry. I didn't mean to startle or hurt Becca."

Nathen was confused by Adrian's comment. "What are you talking about?"

Adrian shifted his weight from one foot to another. "The night of the dance. I'm sure Hansen told you all about it."

"No, he didn't, and we will continue this conversation later. But for now, I have a favor to ask of you."

Adrian had a look of complete puzzlement. "You want a favor from me?"

"Yes, I do. Joshawa's missing, and has been for two days."

Adrian placed the sack he was carrying on the ground. He looked at Nathen as if he'd lost his mind. "You want me to help you find Joshawa? Are you kidding me? Your son hates me, and the feeling's mutual. Why would I want to help him?"

Adrian bent down, picked up his sack, and tried to leave, but Nathen blocked his path. Nathen had no time for childish bickering, which was evident by the glare he shot Adrian. "I don't care about your feelings or lack thereof for Joshawa." Nathen took a step forward, which left little space between them. "I need you to come with me so that you can help Billy find his way back to Burwood."

"What? You're not making sense. What does Billy have to do with Joshawa?"

Nathen grabbed the sack of rabbits out of Adrian's hand. "I'll explain on the way. I want you to stay here. I'll be back with Billy."

As Nathen walked away, Adrian shouted at him, "What about my rabbits?" Nathen didn't respond. He just made his way back to Edward's cabin.

Authia slowly rocked the porch swing back and forth as she waited for Nathen's return. She had no idea how long he'd been gone. She was focused on the forest, praying that Joshawa would walk into the yard and everything would be okay. She closed her eyes, rested her hands in her lap, and reached out to her son.

*Joshawa, please answer me. Please help us find you.*

No matter how much she pleaded, there was no response. Authia placed her right hand over her tattoo and was about to try to connect with Serena when she heard something that came from deep within her mind. It was faint, only a whisper, and that was when it hit her. A bright blue light encompassed her entire being, and in the distance, she heard the words, *whispers in the wind . . . I hear whispers in the wind.*

# CHAPTER NINETEEN

A my had taken down the makeshift tent, and once again, she had Joshawa resting against Alex. While Joshawa was in an upright position, Amy attended to his injuries. She knelt to one side of him and gently unwrapped the bandage from around his head. Carefully, she placed the wrapping in the boiling water, then turned to face Joshawa. In the process of removing his bandages, Joshawa had woken up, and Amy greeted him with a smile. She was thrilled when he smiled back at her. "I'm going to clean your wound. It may hurt some."

"I trust you."

If Amy had any doubts about Joshawa's origins, they were now a moot point. When she gazed into his eyes, she saw tenderness, pain, fear, and trust. She didn't understand why, but she knew that these were the eyes of a kind and gentle man.

Amy moved to the other side of Alex so she could have easy access to his head wound. First she removed the old salve from the wound and threw it in the fire. Beside her was one of the buckets of water she'd brought from the stream. She submerged an old cloth in the water, and then she gently ran the soaked cloth through Joshawa's hair.

At first, the water ran red, but after twenty minutes and a lot of patience, his hair and the gash on the back of his head were clean. Amy smiled to herself as she applied the fresh salve to the wound.

Her mind was preoccupied with only one thought, and that was to save Joshawa. However, deep in her subconscience was a voice that was no louder than a whisper. This voice questioned her new abilities and who Joshawa was. Amy paid no attention to the subtle whispers because she chose not to. Amy was happy to have the company and even more delighted that she could heal him.

When she'd finished applying the salve, Amy wrapped Joshawa's head with the damp, warm bandage that she retrieved from the pot of water hanging over the fire. She knew that the warmth from the bandage would help the salve penetrate the wound.

"Where did you learn to take care of people?"

Amy finished tying the knot in the bandage and then sat in front of Joshawa. She started to unwrap the sling to inspect his elbow. "How are you feeling?"

"My head is still pounding, and my chest and leg really hurt. Though not as bad as yesterday. And I can't believe how exhausted I am."

Amy gently moved Joshawa's arm and tried to straighten it. She focused on Joshawa's face to watch for any indication of pain. "You are hurt, really bad. Being tired is your body healing. I think we can leave the sling off. Your elbow seems to be doing very well."

"So, where did you learn to do this?"

Amy had moved over to Joshawa's leg. She gazed up at him trying to understand the question. "I don't know. I think I've always known." Amy returned her attention to Joshawa's leg. The bruising was quite bad, but the swelling had receded. "Your leg is getting better. But I think it'll be a while before you can walk on it." Amy sat cross-legged on the ground, rested her hands on her knees, and just stared at Joshawa. "Where do you come from?"

"I live not far from here. Not too sure where I am now, but I'm thinking you brought me north, closer to the mountain range."

"Do you live alone in your cave?"

"No, I don't, and I live in a cabin."

Some memory that was buried deep inside of Amy tried to surface. She was afraid, though she wasn't really sure why. "Cabins are not safe. You should leave. Caves are safe."

Joshawa could see the fear in Amy's eyes at the mere mention of a cabin. He glanced around at his surroundings until his gaze fell back on Amy. "How long have you lived here?"

Amy shrugged her shoulders. "A long time. I was little when I came here."

"Where are your parents?"

"Parents?"

"Your mother and your father."

Amy looked as if she was searching her mind for the answer.

A sense of sadness washed over Joshawa as he realized that she might not know who her parents were. "How did you find this cave?"

Amy smiled, her eyes brightened, and to Joshawa, she looked like a child who was happy because she knew the answer to the question. "He brought me here because it is safe. I'm safe here."

"Who is he?"

Once again, Amy appeared as if she was searching for the answer. "I don't remember. It was a long time ago."

Her gaze met Joshawa's, and he knew she wanted to say something, but she appeared frightened to do so. "Did you want to ask me something?"

"Yes, I do." Amy hesitated as she glanced down on the ground, then slowly looked back up at Joshawa. "Will you hurt me if you don't like the question?"

Joshawa was taken aback. "Of course not. Why would I

hurt you?"

Amy shrugged her shoulders. "I don't know. It just happens."

"Amy, first of all, I'm in no condition to hurt you, and even if I was, I would never harm you."

Amy studied Joshawa, averted her gaze to Alex, then back to Joshawa. She straightened her back, and her demeanor was that of a child who had the soccer ball and dared anyone to try to take it. "Good. Because if you try to hurt me, Alex will hurt you."

Joshawa glanced over to his right to find Alex staring at him. It was uncanny how the bear seemed to understand everything she said. Joshawa returned his focus to Amy. "I don't doubt that for a moment. I won't hurt you, Amy. What's your question?"

Amy smiled as she leaned in ever so slightly. In almost a whisper, she asked her question. "Why do you look like you do? You look more like my friends, not me."

Joshawa wasn't surprised by the question. However, he was surprised that the question didn't upset him. Normally he would be offended and ready to confront anyone who would dare to question his origins. But Amy was different. Her child-like innocence warmed his heart. Joshawa smiled at her as he answered her question. "I look like I do because I look like my father. What do you mean by your friends?"

"The animals of the forest are my friends. They take care of me, and I take care of them."

Joshawa smiled as he gently shook his head. "I'm very much like you. But I'm also different. I belong to a tribe of people who live very far from here."

"What's a tribe?"

"It's a family, a very large one. We all look alike."

"What's a family?"

Joshawa was shocked by the question. Had she been alone

for so long that even something as simple as understanding family was lost to her? "Family are people that take care of you. They protect you, and they love you no matter what. Family are the people that you can always count on."

"And you don't live with them?"

Joshawa sighed. "No, I don't." Joshawa thought of what he'd just said, and the reality of the true meaning of family hit him like a two-by-four upside his head. His father had always told him that family is not *what* you are, but rather *who* you are. "I take that back, Amy. I don't live with the people that look like me, but I do live with my family. Have you not had anyone to love and protect you?"

"Alex protects me, and I love him. He's my family."

Serena had made it back to her post in time to witness the interaction between Joshawa and Amy. She sat at the edge of the Realm and smiled down at the young Lord. He was starting to discover what his father had been trying to teach him all his life. Her joy was quickly overshadowed when Lord Chike walked up behind her.

"You seem pleased with yourself. Is Lord Joshawa ready for the transfer?"

Serena stood and slowly turned to face Lord Chike. She had to choose her words carefully if she was going to continue to have the upper hand. She showed her respect and bowed to Lord Chike. When their eyes met, she smiled, "Lord Chike, it is good to see you. Lord Joshawa is healing nicely, and the block I placed in his mind is very effective. He cannot hear his parents, and they cannot hear him."

"You have done well. But you still have not answered my question."

"He requires a little more time."

Lord Chike took a step closer to Serena. Through clenched

teeth, he asked his question. "How much time?"

Serena didn't budge. She placed her hands in front of her, linking her fingers together. "To perform the transfer, the condition of his body is unimportant. However, the condition of his mind is extremely important. At this point, his mind is not strong enough to endure the transfer. If you try now, you risk losing all that is Lord Joshawa."

"I ask again, how long?"

"As I said before, the mind heals at its own rate. A lot depends on Joshawa and his willingness to survive. To answer your question, I would have to guess."

"Then guess."

Serena took a deep breath and gave an answer she was certain Lord Chike would disapprove of. "At least one week."

Serena braced herself for the backlash she was sure to receive. Lord Chike stepped so close to Serena that she could feel his breath on her face. He grabbed the front of her neck with his right hand and squeezed. Again, she felt the pain, but she would not give him the satisfaction. She kept eye contact with him and showed no facial expression.

"You have one week." Lord Chike pushed her away as he let go of her neck. "One week, Serena. Then I'm taking him whether he is ready or not."

Nathen, Billy, and Adrian headed out into the forest. Nathen wanted Billy to lead the group down the path so he could keep an eye on him. As far as Adrian was concerned, Nathen had him at the rear. Nathen didn't want Adrian's foul mood or sarcastic tongue to upset Billy.

Billy had not left Burwood since his arrival twenty years ago. Nathen smiled as he watched Billy renew his acquaintance with the forest and its inhabitants. He had an uncanny way of interacting with the animals. They weren't afraid of him, and he stopped to greet each and every one of them. Nathen knew that Billy's ritual of stopping to greet each animal was impeding their goal to be back at the cabin with plenty of daylight left. But he also knew that Billy was scared, and if these animals calmed him, then it was worth the diversion.

On the other hand, Adrian wasn't happy being on this quest to find Joshawa, which was clearly evident from his foul mood. Nathen tried to ignore him, but after an hour of Adrian's sarcastic comments and brooding, Nathen had had enough. He stopped short and almost caused Adrian to slam into the back of him.

"What the hell, Nathen!"

Nathen checked on Billy, who was preoccupied with a squirrel, and he didn't appear to have heard Adrian. Nathen turned to face Adrian, and he made sure that Adrian knew that he wasn't impressed. "Change your attitude, or I will change it for you."

Adrian looked as if he was considering challenging Nathen. "Since when do you threaten people? I thought you were this high and mighty protector of the people."

Nathen's patience for Adrian was running thin. He had to shut Adrian down, and the only way to do that was to intimidate him. "I don't have time for this right now. If you know what's good for you, you'll shut your mouth. You and I will address this when we get to my cabin. Do I make myself clear?"

Adrian glared at Nathen, then sadistically smiled at him. "Perfectly, sir." Adrian's words dripped with sarcasm, but Nathen didn't care. All he wanted was for him to be quiet.

The remainder of the trip was relatively uneventful, but unfortunately, they didn't arrive back at the cabin till five. Authia was sitting on the porch swing, and when Nathen entered the yard, he could feel the relief of his arrival wash over her.

Authia was overjoyed to see Nathen enter the yard, and most importantly, Billy was with him. She hurried down the stairs, ran up to Nathen, and threw her arms around his neck, hugging him as tight as she could. "You brought him. He actually came." Authia let go of Nathen just as Adrian entered the yard. She was surprised to see Adrian and was about to comment on that fact when Billy rushed up to her. He wrapped his arms around her, pinning them to her side. Then he buried the side of his face into her chest.

"Billy happy to see Authia!"

Billy's grip was tightening, which caused Authia to experience difficulty breathing. "Gentle, Billy."

Billy lessened his grip and looked up at Authia. She could tell by his expression that he was upset. "Billy bad. Billy hurt Authia."

Authia managed to free her arms from Billy's grip. She wrapped her left arm around Billy and placed her right hand on the back of his head. She held his head against her chest, and even though he couldn't see her face, she smiled so tenderly. "You didn't hurt me, Billy. I'm happy to see you, too." Authia let go of Billy so that she could see his face. She took his hands and hers, and in a soft, gentle voice, she calmed him. "You have so much love in you, Billy. You just have to remember how strong you are."

Billy smiled at Authia. "Billy very strong." Billy had always been proud of the fact that his strength was almost equal to that of Nathen's.

"Billy, why don't you go to my cabin. Hansen is there. I want to speak with Nathen for a moment."

Billy excitedly nodded his head in agreement and almost ran to the cabin door. Adrian tried to follow, but Authia placed the palm of her hand on his chest. "Not so fast." She lowered her hand then focused her attention on Nathen. "Why is he here?"

Adrian rolled his eyes, which did not go unnoticed by Authia. She stepped in front of him and pocked his chest with her index finger. "I don't know why you're here, but while you are, you will show respect for my family, Hansen's family, and especially Joshawa. You put one toe out of place, roll your eyes one more time, and Nathen's wrath will be the least of your worries. Do you understand?"

Adrian nodded his head that he did.

"Good, now go sit on the swing." Authia pointed in the direction of the swing and watched as Adrian walked past her. He muttered a comment under his breath, which Authia clearly heard but chose to ignore. She then turned her focus on Nathen. "What's he doing here?"

Nathen kept his focus on him as he walked away. "What did he say?"

Authia sighed. "He said I'm not a child. So what's he doing here?"

"I need Billy to find his old home. Problem is that he's scared, and he doesn't want to go anywhere near the place. I've promised him that if he can get me close, then he can go home. I don't know if he can find his way back to Burwood, so I've asked Adrian to make sure he gets home safely. I know he's not our favorite person, but he knows the woods, and he's young enough and strong enough to make the trek and keep Billy safe."

"You're right. But it must be killing Adrian that he's helping to save Joshawa."

"It does, and I need to have a conversation with him. His attitude needs to be taken down a peg or two."

Authia glanced up at the sky and back to Nathen. "When do you plan to go?"

"I would love to leave right now, but it's going to be dark

soon. On my own, I wouldn't care. I can take care of myself. My problem is that I'll have Billy and Adrian in tow. Billy's scared to death about making this trek to his home, and I don't think the dark is going to help matters. We'll leave at first light."

Authia's heart sank. Joshawa would have to endure whatever he was going through for another day. He'll have to spend another night cold, hurt, and alone. She looked up at Nathen, tears forming in her eyes. "I'm so scared for Joshawa."

Nathen gathered Authia in his arms and held her close. "My love, we'll find him."

Authia closed her eyes and found comfort in Nathen's warmth and the sound of his heartbeat. As she stood safe in Nathen's embrace, she allowed her mind to reach out to whoever could hear her.

*We'll find you, Joshawa. I promise. Stay strong. We will find you.*

Authia then reached out to the only person that could help.

*I know you can hear me, Serena. Please help us! Help us find Joshawa!*


Jax had laid out his video surveillance equipment on the kitchen table. Dameon had gone to the stream to catch dinner, leaving Jax to pack what he deemed necessary for the surveillance of the cabin. He replaced the batteries in all four cameras and made sure the lenses were clean and that the cameras were operational. He had everything he needed to secure them in place, and the thought of catching the creature on camera thrilled him to his very core.

He grabbed his backpack off his bed then proceeded to pack it for the trip back to the cabin. He was zipping the backpack closed when Dameon returned with a bucket of fish, gutted and ready for the fire. Jax looked over at Dameon, who seemed uninterested in what he was doing. "Looks like you were successful."

Dameon placed the bucket on the kitchen counter and turned to face Jax. "Looks like you're packed. When are you planning to set up the cameras?"

"Later tonight. I figured we'd leave and get to the cabin by midnight. They should all be in bed by then, and we can install the cameras unnoticed."

Dameon leaned against the counter and folded his arms across his chest. *"We'll* install? I thought I told you that setting up the cameras is your thing."

Jax lifted the backpack off the table and set it down by his chair. He looked at Dameon and tried to figure out whether he was serious or just playing around. "I believe the agreement was that I had to climb the trees and set up the cameras, but we go there together. We don't go anywhere at night alone. You know that."

Dameon just stood there, and Jax waited until a smile graced Dameon's lips. "Okay, I'll have your back. But you're doing all the work." Dameon pushed himself away from the counter and went to sit in one of the rocking chairs that faced the fire. "And you're cooking dinner, and you're making the coffee."

"Fair enough." Jax smiled to himself—this was a small price to pay to have Dameon cooperate. He needed Dameon to watch for any animals that could be a threat to them. But mostly, he needed Dameon to warn him if the inhabitants of the cabins decided to take a moonlight stroll. Jax placed the coffee perc on the grate over the fire, then went to prepare the fish.

Serena observed the interaction between Nathen and Authia, and her heart was saddened when she heard Authia's plea and knew that she couldn't respond. Her only hope was that her Mistress would understand the clues she had set in place.

Serena returned to the edge of the Realm, where she could watch Joshawa and Amy. She was pleased and extremely grateful that the seed she planted in Amy's mind had taken root, and now Joshawa was receiving the treatment he needed to survive. Serena remained at her post and observed Amy as she filled the pot of boiling water with cottonwood branches and reconstructed the makeshift tent over Joshawa.

He would sleep now, probably till morning. Serena gazed over her shoulder and into the jungle. She had one week to figure out who Lord Chike actually was, and in order to do that, she needed help.

It was late, and she could only assume that all three Ancestors were back at the camp and would remain there for the evening. Unfortunately, they didn't require sleep as a spirit, so entering Lord Chike's mind unnoticed wouldn't be easy.

She sat there for almost an hour as she tried to come up with some way to access Lord Chike. Then it came to her. She was trying to access the wrong Lord. Serena was annoyed with herself that she hadn't thought of this sooner. Lord Adeeowale was the answer to learning more about Lord Chike. He had the privilege of leaving the Realm whenever he chose to. He would have access to the Land of Spirits and the sacred scrolls.

Serena was pleased with herself and anxious to make another trip to see the Ancestors. She walked over to the edge of the clearing and stared into the dense jungle. Serena closed her eyes and sought out Lord Chike. He was not close, so Serena felt confident in what she had to do. She changed into a wisp and went in search of Lord Adeeowale.

# CHAPTER TWENTY

Becca, Hansen, and Tammy were all in Nathen and Authia's cabin as they waited for Nathen's return. However, Becca knew the real reason was to keep Authia company and to make sure she stayed put. Becca was sitting on the floor in front of the fire. She'd placed a pillow between her back and the hearth and was engrossed in a novel. Tammy and Hansen were preparing dinner, and they were both startled when Billy burst into the room.

On the other hand, Becca was delighted to see him, because that meant if he was here, then they were one step closer to Joshawa. She got up, placed her book on the hearth, and went to greet him. As soon as Billy saw Becca, he ran up to her and threw his arms around her.

"Billy happy to see Becca."

"I'm happy to see you, too."

Billy let go of Becca and ran over to Hansen and Tammy, hugging them and giggling like the child he was. "Billy happy." Billy glanced over to the stove then back to Tammy. "Billy is hungry. We walked lots."

Hansen put his arm around Billy's shoulders. "Supper's almost ready. Do you want to sit by the fire while you wait?"

Becca smiled as she observed Billy. His eyes sparkled, and he had the biggest grin. He didn't have to say he was happy. It was clearly evident.

"Billy loves fire."

Hansen smiled at Billy. "I know. Come with me." Hansen led Billy to the rocking chair that faced the fire. Billy sat down and was immediately engrossed in the vibrant colors that danced among the logs. Hansen walked over to the front door and grabbed his jacket off the peg on the wall. "I'm going to get another pie. Do we need anything else?"

Before anyone could answer, Becca had glanced out the window and saw Adrian sitting on the swing. She was infuriated that Adrian was here, sitting on the swing as if he were a welcomed guest. "What's he doing here?" Becca grabbed her jacket and was on the porch before anyone could stop her. She was about to confront Adrian when her dad joined her.

Hansen stood next to Becca. "I'm surprised to see you here, Adrian. Care to tell us why?"

Becca turned to face her dad. "I've got this." She turned back and walked over to Adrian. "So why are you here?"

Adrian smiled at Becca. "That seems to be the million-dollar question."

"And what's the million-dollar answer?"

"I'm here at Nathen's request."

Becca glanced over her shoulder and discovered that in addition to Nathen, Authia was also on the porch. Authia's arms were wrapped around Nathen's left bicep, and the disapproving glare directed toward Adrian indicated that she was just as upset as Becca was. Becca focused her attention on Nathen. "Why did you bring him here? You know he hates Joshawa."

Hansen interrupted. "Becca, you're being disrespectful."

Nathen approached Becca and calmly interjected. "No, she's not. Becca, we need him. Billy needs him."

"I don't understand."

"I'll explain everything over dinner. Why don't we go inside and get out of the cold?"

Becca looked over at Adrian, who was standing now, and then returned her focus to the others. "All right. But I'd like to have a few moments alone with Adrian first." Becca knew her dad would be worried about leaving her alone with

Adrian, so she decided to reassure him. "I'll be fine, Dad. Adrian isn't going to try anything stupid." Becca looked over her shoulder at Adrian. "Right?"

Adrian sat down, and he appeared highly annoyed at what was transpiring. "Of course not."

Becca had to hide her amusement when her dad scowled at Adrian, which was his way of sending a clear warning. Hansen left the porch to get the extra pie. At the same time, Nathen and Authia went into their cabin, leaving Becca alone with Adrian.

Adrian moved over to the corner of the swing and rested his arm on the back of the seat. "Well, you have me all to yourself. What did you want to talk about?"

Becca sat as far away from Adrien as she could. "You know very well, so don't play dumb with me. Why are you here?"

"I told you. Nathen asked me to come. I have to take Billy back to Burwood after he finds the cabin he used to live in."

"And you came willingly?"

"Not a chance."

"Exactly. So why did you come? So you can revel in the fact that Joshawa is missing, that he's hurt so bad that he could die if we don't find him?" Becca's voice started to falter, and tears began to well up in her eyes.

Adrian watched as Becca tried to hold back the tears. He was shocked at her reaction, and now that he had her undivided attention, he needed answers to his own questions. "Becca, what is it about Joshawa? How can you love him?"

Becca squared her shoulders as she wiped the tears away. "How can I not? Adrian, if you would just try to see Joshawa for who he is, you wouldn't have to ask me."

"I know who he is. He's just like his father, a freak of nature."

Becca slapped Adrian's face so hard it actually made his ears ring. Adrian placed his hand on his left cheek, and he could actually feel the heat from the handprint outlined on his face. "What the hell, Becca?"

"You deserved that. What has Uncle Nathen or Joshawa ever done to you?"

Adrian sat quietly with his eyes locked on Becca's. His mind recalled every event that fueled his hatred for Nathen and Joshawa. "You really want to know? Do you think you can handle the answer?"

Becca sat back on the swing and folded her arms across her chest. "Yes, I want to know. And yes, I can handle anything you have to tell me."

Adrian heard Hansen approaching, and when Hansen climbed the stairs to the porch, pie in hand, Adrian just smiled at him.

Hansen hesitated as he reached for the doorknob. "Everything okay here?"

"Yes, Dad, we're fine." Becca smiled at her dad, but as soon as he shut the door behind him, she turned to Adrian, and she was no longer smiling. "You were saying?"

Adrian had no intention of hiding the contempt he felt for Nathen or Joshawa. "Nathen has everyone convinced that he is this gentle, caring person. That he's no different than us. But it's all a lie."

Becca looked questionably at Adrian. "What do you mean, it's a lie?"

"Do you know the story of how Billy came to be with us?"

"Yes, I do."

"Really? Nathen has been endangering Burwood for decades. He should have stayed hidden behind the walls. But he didn't. He went out into the forest and got himself seen."

"Seen by who?"

"Dext Jenkins, Billy's brother. My dad told me everything.

Dext kidnapped a young girl while she played right here, in this yard. He hoped Nathen would come to save her, and he did. But not before he ripped off Dext's arm with his bare hands. Why do you think Billy is the way he is? It's because he witnessed what Nathen did."

"Billy has always been this way. He was born with his handicap."

"That's not what my dad told me."

"Adrian, Uncle Nathen ripped off Dext's arm in self-defense. Dext had stabbed him in the back. And believe me, to this day, Uncle Nathen still hasn't forgiven himself. He saved that girl and Billy. Has your dad told you that?"

"He didn't save anyone that day. That girl was so traumatized by the event that she left Burwood."

"According to who?"

"My dad."

"So you've hated Uncle Nathen all these years because your dad hated him? What has Uncle Nathen ever done to your dad?"

Adrian didn't know if he wanted to continue this conversation. It was treading in waters that he could easily drown in. He scrutinized Becca, and all he could see was tenderness and compassion, but didn't he already know that? Wasn't that what had attracted him to her? If he continued down this road, then he might lose any chance of ever winning her over. But on the other hand, the truth could sway her in his direction. "Do you know the story of my mom's death?"

"Didn't she die in a snowstorm?"

"Yes, and that's the reason my dad is missing three fingers and all his toes. He was caught in that snowstorm as well. He nearly froze to death."

"What has Uncle Nathen got to do with that?"

"My mom and dad went to Gainsbourgh for supplies. There was a storm coming. They knew that, so Nathen was going to meet them at the old logging road and help them bring the supplies back so they could beat the storm. Nathen never showed. By the time Charles and Edward found my parents, my mother was dead, my dad barely alive. So much for the great savior."

Becca placed her hand on Adrian's knee. "I'm so sorry, Adrian. Really, I am. I never knew. Has your dad ever spoken to Uncle Nathen about it?"

"No. Why should he? Your uncle should have apologized to my dad. He never did."

"Does Uncle Nathen even know?"

"How could he not? Everyone knows how my mom died. Everyone knows it's his fault."

"Not everyone. This is the first time that I've heard this story. My mom tells me everything, and so does Edward. I think if Edward knew that Uncle Nathen was supposed to have met your parents, he would have said something."

"You're so naïve. Edward loves your uncle. He wouldn't say anything against Nathen. As a matter of fact, he would do his best to protect him."

"So you blame Uncle Nathen for your mother's death, and you hate Joshawa because he's Uncle Nathen's son?"

"Can you blame me? Nathen killed my mom. Almost killed my dad. How can I not hate him?"

"Adrian, I don't know why Uncle Nathen never showed up, but I'm sure he's got a very good explanation. Uncle Nathen would never intentionally jeopardize anyone's life."

Adrian couldn't believe what he was hearing. He told her the truth, and she was still supporting those freaks. Adrian got up and glared at Becca. "You're just like them."

"If you hate my uncle so much, why are you helping him?"

"I'm not helping him. I'm helping Billy. I could care less what happens to Joshawa." Adrian paused for just a second. "Actually, I hope he dies. Then your uncle will know what it's like to lose someone you love." Before Becca could react, Adrian left the porch and headed toward her cabin.

Nathen was setting the table when Becca entered the cabin. He glanced up at her, smiled, then realized that she was alone. "Where's Adrian?"

"He decided to hang out at my cabin."

Nathen had a feeling that Adrian would prefer Becca's cabin over Joshawa's. "Are you okay with that, Hansen?"

"Sure. But maybe Becca can spend the night here."

"We would love to have her. She can stay in Joshawa's room." Nathen finished setting the table, and as he did, he was very much aware of Becca's mood. He could sense that she was conflicted, and she was also very quiet. Whenever Nathen would glance in her direction, he would catch her staring at him. He dismissed her apparent trepidation believing that it was just her being frightened for Joshawa and wanting to go look for him sooner than later.

Nathen called everyone to the table. When the plates were full of food and the commotion died down a bit, Nathen shared his plan to retrieve the GPS. "At first light, we're going to leave to find Billy's old home." Nathen glanced over to Billy, who was sitting across from him. He was stuffing his face with mashed potatoes. "Billy." Billy's head shot up, and he smiled at Nathen as he swallowed his mouthful of food. "Will you be able to find your old home from here?"

"Yes. Dext and me come here lots. Billy knows how to go home." Billy gently stabbed a piece of chicken meat with his fork. He appeared delighted when he lifted his fork and found the piece of meat successfully skewered.

Nathen continued. "Okay. Billy, Adrian, and I are going to find the cabin—"

Hansen interrupted. "Include me in this adventure."

Nathen shook his head. "No, I need you here in case those hunters come back."

"Do you really believe that they will?"

Authia chimed in. "Definitely. Especially the one called Jax. I didn't get the impression that he completely believed my dead husband story."

Nathen raised an eyebrow. "I'm dead?"

Authia smiled. "Yes, and it was a heartwarming funeral."

Everyone at the table chuckled, except for Becca. Nathen knew something was up with her, and now he wondered if it had anything to do with Adrian. He decided to leave it alone for now, but he would definitely speak with her later if she continued to be upset. He focused his attention on Billy, who was totally preoccupied with his meal. "When Billy gets us close to his old home —"

The words barely left Nathen's lips when Billy looked up at Nathen, his eyes wide. "Billy not want to go close to cabin. Bad things happen at cabin." Billy was slowly shaking his head side to side, and his expression was dire.

Nathen reached across the table and held his hands out with the palms facing up. Billy stopped moving and stared at Nathen. Then his focus went to Nathen's hands. The table was quiet, and all eyes were on Billy. Nathen knew that Billy didn't completely understand what was happening. "Billy, take my hands."

Billy dutifully placed his hands in Nathen's. He glanced up at Nathen, his eyes full of fear. "Billy scared."

Nathen gently squeezed Billy's hands. "I know you are, Billy. But I promise you, you only have to get me close to the cabin. I will protect you. No one will get hurt."

Billy froze, his eyes wide, his mouth gaped open. Flashbacks of Dext and Nathen flooded his mind. Those words, he'd heard those words before. *No one will get hurt.* Billy let go of Nathen's hands, wrapped his arms around himself then started rocking back and forth in his chair. "You said . . . you said no hurt. You said . . . you said no hurt." Billy stopped rocking and faced Nathen. "You said no hurt. But you hurt Dext. Dext hurt me."

Billy started crying and resumed rocking back and forth so violently that he hit his head on the table every time he rocked toward it. He didn't care—he even welcomed the pain. He hoped that the pain would distract him from the pictures that were exploding inside his head. He squeezed his eyes closed as tight as he could as he attempted to block the visions of Dext whipping him with the leather belt.


Nathen felt as if he had been punched in the stomach, for he knew exactly what Billy was referring to. Nathen glanced around the table to find that everyone appeared shocked at what they had witnessed. Everyone but Authia, for she also knew what Billy was remembering.

Nathen got out of his chair, walked over to Billy, and pulled his chair away from the table. He turned the chair so that Billy would be facing him. Billy continued to rock back and forth and appeared to take no notice of Nathen. However, after a couple of seconds, Billy stopped his rocking and slowly gazed up at Nathen.

Billy's forehead was bruised, and there was a gash that ran across the middle of his forehead. The blood from the open wound trickled down his forehead and nose and onto his face. Billy still had his arms wrapped tightly around himself, and his expression was that of a lost child who didn't understand what had happened.

Nathen knelt on his knees in front of Billy so that he would be at eye level with him. Then he tenderly pulled Billy into his arms and held him tight against his chest. "I remember, Billy. And I am so sorry for how that turned out." Nathen placed his hands on Billy's arms and gently pulled him away so Billy could see his face. Billy's gaze was fixed on the floor, and he seemed not to notice the blood that dripped from his wound and onto the floor like a leaky faucet. "I didn't want anyone to get hurt. Do you remember what your brother did?"

Billy didn't look at Nathen. He kept his eyes focused on the floor as he nodded his head that he did remember. "Billy, please look at me." Billy slowly raised his head until his eyes met Nathen's. "You have to believe me that I didn't want to hurt anyone that night, especially you. And I have no excuse for what I did."

Billy tilted his head slightly to the left as if he were trying to figure something out. "Dext hurt you. You hurt Dext. Dext took me home. Dext hurt me."

Nathen's heart was about to break, for he could only imagine what Dext did to Billy. Billy's body was a roadmap of the beatings he'd endured at the hand of his brother. Nathen brought Billy close to him so that Billy's head was on Nathen's chest. Nathen didn't care about the blood that was transferring onto his shirt. He just placed his right hand on the back of Billy's head and slowly rocked Billy back and forth. "Billy, I'll give my life to protect you. No one will ever hurt you like your brother hurt you. Now, why don't we let Tammy look at your forehead?"


Becca watched the interaction between Billy and Nathen. She was overwhelmed by the raw emotions being displayed. Adrian's words played in her head, and she couldn't believe that the man who held Billy so tenderly, who spoke with so much compassion and love, could intentionally hurt anyone. Adrian had to have been mistaken. And at that moment,

Becca vowed to find the truth and prove Adrian's father wrong.

Jax was sitting at the table with the chair turned so that he would be facing the bunkbeds. His left arm was resting on the table, and he was strumming his fingers to the beat of a song that played in his head. That was something he would do subconsciously when everything was quiet and his mind was occupied by thoughts that he couldn't share. Jax had everything he needed in his backpack, which he'd placed by the door.

He continued to stare at the bunkbeds until his watch started beeping. It was his alarm telling him that it was time to leave. He walked over to the bunk beds, placed his right hand on the railing, and gave it a shake. "Rise and shine, sleeping beauty. Time to set up surveillance."

Jax was excited beyond measure. He had a gut feeling that not only was the creature still alive, but it was hanging out around that cabin. He tried to tone down his excitement, because the last thing he needed was Dameon getting upset with him and changing his mind about helping.

Jax grabbed his jacket that was hanging on the back of the kitchen chair. He zipped it up, pulled his skull cap down over his ears, then placed the night-vision goggles on his head. He glanced over at Dameon, who was finishing getting dressed. "I think we should take the *Remingtons* as well as our sidearms. There are wolves in the area, and I don't want to take any chances."

Dameon put his jacket and skull cap on. Then he retrieved the GPS from his backpack. He placed it on the table and reached across the table for his night-vision goggles. "I agree. You can watch my back while we make our way to the cabin, and then I'll watch yours while you're setting up the cameras."

"Sounds like a plan." Jax strapped his backpack on, then slung one of the *Remington* semi-automatic rifles over his shoulder. At the same time, Dameon was pulling up the directions to the cabin from the GPS's memory.

He watched as Dameon placed the strap to the GPS around his neck, and then he picked up his rifle and headed outside. Jax was right behind him, closing the door to the cabin as he left. Jax stood in the yard and waited till Dameon disappeared into the woods. He stared after Dameon with only one thought in his head . . . *I know the creature exists, and I will stop at nothing to capture it. So don't come between me and my prize, good friend. It will not go well for you.*

# CHAPTER TWENTY-ONE

Serena soared through the jungle toward the Ancestor's camp. The evening sky was alive with thousands of twinkling stars, and the full moon bathed the jungle in a soft, comforting light. The sounds of the animals that played at night echoed throughout the jungle. Serena loved to listen to them, because to her, they brought life to the darkness.

Serena knew only too well what life was like existing in the darkness with no light and no sound. She'd been released from that hellish prison by the Council of Five. However, according to Lord Chike, his voice had convinced the Council, and now Serena owed her existence to Lord Chike. Serena would do anything not to return to that place. However, what Lord Chike had demanded of her was now becoming more than she was prepared to do. Serena's intuition told her that Lord Chike had an agenda that required more than just stealing Joshawa's spirit.

The blue glow that emanated off Serena's body was more evident at night. Add in the full moon, and she could be seen from a far greater distance than she was comfortable with. She would have to be careful, and she would have to be smart if she wanted to go unseen by Lord Chike.

As soon as Serena saw the glow from the Ancestor's fire, she sought out a kapok tree and landed on one of its branches. She didn't want to risk getting any closer to the camp. Serena flew to the ground, hid behind the tree, then morphed back to human form. As a wisp, she would have to enter Lord Adeeowale's body to be heard and for their conversation to be private. In human form, she could meld with Lord Adeeowale. Unfortunately, privacy during a meld wasn't guaranteed.

Carefully she peered around the tree and scanned the area for Lord Chike. She discovered that all three Ancestors were at the camp. Serena hid behind the tree and closed her eyes as she rested her head against the tree's trunk.

With Lord Chike so close to Lord Adeeowale, Serena wouldn't be able to enter the campsite without Lord Chike seeing her. Her only other option would be to meld with Lord Adeeowale. The only downside was that she didn't know how strong a melder Lord Chike was. If she melded with Lord Adeeowale, Lord Chike might be aware of the meld, and Serena could only guess what her punishment would be. She opened her eyes and stared off into the jungle. For Joshawa's sake, she had to take the chance.

*My Lord, I must speak with you.*

*What must you tell me?*

The tension that had built up in Serena quickly washed away, for it was Lord Adeeowale's voice that responded. *What I have to say cannot be said in a meld. I must join with you, but I must do that unseen by Lord Chike.*

*I understand. Go back to where Lord Chike has secluded you, and I will come to you.*

Serena was elated. He heard her, and she was sure that he would help her uncover who and what Lord Chike was. She transformed back into a wisp and headed back to her place in the Realm.


Joshawa was once more on his back in the makeshift tent. The steam that emanated from the pot over the fire pit hung over him like a dense fog. After ten minutes of inhaling the steam, the pain that ravaged his body started to lessen, and he could relax. His breathing improved, his mind became clearer, and his thought process had become coherent enough so that he could make sense of what was rattling around in his head.

His first thoughts were focused on his father. Why couldn't he feel his pain? Why couldn't he or his mother hear his pleas? Joshawa closed his eyes and allowed his mind to fill with only thoughts of his father.

*Father, hear me. Please, Father, I'm so sorry for how I have treated you. If leaving me here is punishment, then I've learned my lesson. Please, I love you, please find me!*

Joshawa's eyes filled with tears as his mind became encased in fear at the thought that he would never be found.

*Joshawa, do not lament. You will be found. This I promise you.*

Joshawa's eyes widened, and he searched his mind for the person who was speaking to him. He knew the voice, though it wasn't his mothers.

*I hear you. When will I be found? Who will find me?*

*You must continue to reach out to your parents. You must strengthen the meld.*

*You're Serena, aren't you?*

*Yes. Now reach out, and never stop.*

*I have reached out, but my parents won't respond.*

*Will not or cannot. That is the question you should be asking yourself.*

She was gone, leaving him with a puzzle. What could possibly be stopping his parents? Was he being punished, or was something more sinister at work? Joshawa thought of all the visions Serena afforded him. She wanted him to go to Africa, to be with the Jelani Tribe. He thought of all the things Serena said to him, like how he didn't belong here. It was as if she knew how he felt and purposely fanned the contempt he held for his father.

But since the accident, she'd changed her approach. She was helping him to find his parents. Joshawa was so confused. If Serena was helping, then why hadn't his parents found him? Joshawa was distracted when Amy pulled back a blanket and entered the tent.

"How are you feeling?"

"Better. That steam seems to be helping."

Amy placed a tin mug on the ground, then carefully helped Joshawa sit up just enough so he could drink. She supported his weight with her own tiny body and reached down to pick up the mug. "Here, drink this."

Joshawa took the mug from Amy with his right hand and held it under his nose. The odor was strong, smelling something like the compost bin at home. He wrinkled his nose and offered the mug back to Amy. "I think I'll pass."

Amy frowned at him. "You have to drink it. You haven't been sleeping. This will help. Now drink it, or I'll lay you back down and make you drink it."

Amy held the mug before him, and Joshawa knew she wasn't making idle threats. She would pour it down his throat if she had to. Joshawa sighed, accepted the mug, then downed it in one gulp, grimacing as he swallowed the foul broth. In the time it took for Amy to gently lay him back down and leave the tent, he was already drifting off.

Dameon weaved his way through the forest with ease. After decades of hunting prey at night, both Dameon and Jax were proficient at seeing the forest through the night-vision goggles. He could barely hear Jax, who was following close behind him. Dameon's ears were tuned to listen for any predators that might have picked up their scent, even though he knew he had nothing to worry about. Jax was his lookout, which meant he would have his rifle aimed into the forest, ready to shoot.

Thanks to the GPS calculating a more direct route, their journey to the cabin seemed to be a lot quicker this time. It wasn't long before Dameon could see the outskirts of the open yard. He stopped and held his left arm upwards at an angle, and his fist closed into a ball, which indicated to Jax to stop. Dameon scanned the yard, which, like the cabins, was in total darkness. He lowered his arm, and Jax came to stand next to him. Dameon scanned the nearby redwood trees that lined the yard. Softly he whispered, "Do you have a preference?"

Jax scanned the area, paying particular attention to the trees that bordered the yard. He located four large redwoods that would enable him to observe the front and sides of the yard. He motioned Dameon to follow him to the first tree.

Jax easily hoisted himself onto the lowest branch, then made his way to one that would serve his purpose. Dameon stood at the tree's base facing toward the forest, his rifle loaded and ready to use.

After Jax had installed the last camera, he climbed down from that tree and picked up the remote device that was lying on his backpack. He was about to turn it on, but Dameon stopped him.

Again, he whispered, "What are you doing?"

Jax also replied in a whisper, "Making sure the cameras are working."

"If you turn that screen on, then we'll have to take the goggles off, and anyone will be able to see the light from the screen."

Jax pushed his goggles up so they could rest on his head. "Everyone's asleep. No one's going to see the light. And I'm not walking back into the bush only to find out one or more of the cameras aren't working. So take your goggles off or turn around, cause I'm doing this."

Jax impatiently waited while Dameon pushed his goggles onto his head. Then Jax immediately flipped the switch and watched as the device lit up. The screen was divided into four sections. Each section revealed what the camera saw. Jax played with each camera, making sure he could turn it on, zoom in or pan out and move side to side.

Satisfied that everything was working, he turned the cameras off, shut down the device then placed it back into his backpack. Jax pulled the goggles back over his eyes and motioned to Dameon to head out. Before he left, Jax took one last look at the yard. He would have loved to have the cameras on twenty-four-seven, but at night, someone would surely see the green light that indicated the camera was on. So he would have to be content with only daylight surveillance.

Jax smiled to himself as he surveyed the yard. He was absolutely sure that he was going to catch the creature, something the writer of the journal had failed to do time and time again.

Jax turned and quietly caught up with Dameon. While they hiked back to the cabin, all Jax could think about was whether or not he should sell the creature. He also considered performing the experiments he'd read about in the journal.

A wicked smile graced his lips as he envisioned the creature strapped down on a table. His belly would be cut open, and there would be blood oozing from every wound Jax inflected. But the best part would be that the creature would still be alive while Jax inflicted every torture that was outlined in the journal.


Adrian was given the couch to sleep on, even though Becca's bed was empty. He lay on the couch, his hands behind his head, his fingers linked together. Hansen had given him a pillow off Becca's bed and her comforter. Adrian smiled as he recalled Hansen's reaction when he suggested that he sleep in Becca's bed. That wasn't happening, and to be honest, Adrian knew that Hansen was worried that he would slip out in the middle of the night and pay Becca a visit. Of course, he would never do that. However, he did enjoy inferring that he might, for no other reason than to upset Hansen. Deep down, Adrian had great respect for Becca and would never hurt her. However, she chose Joshawa over him, which did not sit well with Adrian. It only fueled the hatred he had for both Joshawa and Nathen.

Even though pajamas were offered, Adrian had remained dressed for his night on the couch. The temperature had dropped significantly after sundown, and he figured he would need the extra warmth. Adrian sighed as he slowly scanned the room. Everyone had gone to bed hours ago, but he couldn't sleep. The memories of his mother's death weighed heavy on him. He would love to march right up to Nathen and call him out for what he did. But his dad had warned him about Nathen's temper, and an altercation would not end well for Adrian.

Again, he sighed, only this time he threw the comforter off him and went to add a couple of logs to the fire that was now just red-hot embers. As he walked past the window, something caught his eye. His curiosity was piqued, so he took a step back and glanced out the window. He could see a small light where the forest met the yard, but as soon as it was there, it was gone. Adrian continued to scan the yard, but he saw nothing. He shrugged his shoulders, assumed he was seeing things, then returned to the job of breathing life into the fire.


Serena had returned in time to witness Joshawa pleading with his father to save him. Her heart went out to him, and after she reassured him, Serena felt like she was doing him more harm than good. Unless Authia learned what the clues were and what they meant, Joshawa might never be found in time.

She glanced back over in the direction of Authia and Nathen. There was only one thing left that she could do to save Joshawa, and that was to discover the truth behind Lord Chike.

Becca lay in Joshawa's bed, unable to sleep. She could smell his scent on his pillow, and when she closed her eyes, she could see him as clearly as if he were sitting next to her. So many things were rattling around in her brain. She now knew with all certainty that Joshawa loved her and that he was her soul mate. But this knowledge came at a time when she could very well lose him. His parents didn't know how severe his injuries were. What they did know was that if they didn't get to him soon, his injuries could kill him.

Tears began to form in the corners of her eyes. Why hadn't she spoken up and told Joshawa that she loved him? Maybe then he would have taken her to his secret place, and she would know where to start looking for him. Authia wanted to place her under heavy sedation in the hope of finding Joshawa. Of course, she would do it, but her mother disagreed.

And to make matters worse, her mother was trying to get her dad to side with her. Going under heavy sedation could save Joshawa. Why didn't her mother see that? And then there was Nathen and the accusation that he'd caused Adrian's mother's death. There was way too much on her plate. Becca threw the covers off and headed for the kitchen.

Nathen struggled to sleep with no success. He kept reaching out to Joshawa in the hope that by some miracle, Joshawa would respond. But there was nothing, and Nathen had no sense of Joshawa's emotions. It was as if he didn't even exist.

At one point, Nathen thought he heard something that sounded like whispers. But they were so faint he couldn't tell if they were from a person or if he only heard the wind.

Nathen turned to his side so he could face Authia. She slept peacefully, and if she found out that Nathen had added a sedative to her hot chocolate, well, that slap he'd received earlier would be the least of his problems. Nathen was about to close his eyes and try once more to sleep when he heard someone in the kitchen.

Nathen was concerned that Billy might be up, so he got out of bed, pulled on his jeans, and went to check it out. He discovered that Billy was still asleep, and it was Becca that was roaming around. She was cooking something on the woodstove, and from the aroma, Nathen knew it was hot chocolate. "Is there enough for two?"

Becca quickly turned around, obviously startled. When she saw Nathen, she quietly whispered, "Uncle Nathen, you nearly scared me to death." She went back to stirring the hot chocolate. "Yes, more than enough."

Nathen sat at the kitchen table while Becca filled two mugs with the steaming hot chocolate. She placed one cup in front of Nathen, then sat across from him. Again, she whispered, "Why are you up?"

Nathen smiled. "You don't have to whisper. Billy will sleep through pretty much anything."

Becca glanced over to the loveseat where Billy was sleeping. "Really? Lucky guy." Becca placed her hands on either side of her mug, brought it up to her mouth, then gently blew on it in an attempt to cool it.

Nathen wrapped his hands around his mug, glanced over at Billy, then back to Becca. "I gather you can't sleep either."

Becca placed her cup back on the table and just sighed. "No, I have so much rattling around in my head. I feel so helpless, Uncle Nathen. The only way I can help Joshawa is to sedate myself so Aunty Authia can look for him in my subconscious mind. But my mom says no. So I can't help. And I'm responsible for him being lost."

Nathen was puzzled by her comment. "How are you in any way responsible?"

"If I had told him I loved him, then maybe he would have shown me his secret place. Or maybe he wouldn't need to go there anymore. Because of me, nobody knows where the place is."

Nathen gently shook his head, indicating that he disagreed. "You can't know that, Becca. There's a right time to say I love you. If you haven't said it yet, then you haven't found the right time."

"Well, the way things are going, I may never have the right time to tell him."

"Don't think like that. We'll find Joshawa." Nathen smiled at Becca as he leaned back in his chair. "And just a heads-up. If you say that in front of your aunt, you will suffer her wrath."

Becca's eyes met Nathen's, and in those eyes, she found love and compassion. She smiled at Nathen. "Well, I wouldn't want to do that."

Nathen took a sip of his hot chocolate. "We're going to find him. The GPS is a map straight to him."

"What if they delete the memory every day?"

"Somehow, I don't think they do that. But if they do, then we know that the one called Dameon was there."

"Okay. If they delete the memory, how is my dad going to convince Dameon to show him the way?"

"It won't be your dad. I'll do the convincing."

Becca was suddenly very much afraid, not only for Joshawa but also for Nathen. "But then they'll see you. What if they try to shoot you? Mother said they were looking for you."

Nathen smiled at Becca in an obvious attempt to lighten the mood. "Actually, they're looking for bigfoot."

"It's not funny, Uncle Nathen. They could hurt you."

"And I could hurt them. Becca, if I have to cross that bridge, I'll figure it out then."

Becca didn't hear anything Nathen had to say after the words *I could hurt them*. She thought of Billy's brother and of Adrian's parents. She was staring at her mug, and when she looked up, the expression on Nathen's face broke her heart. "Are you okay, Uncle Nathen?"

"Yes. But you do know that I would never hurt anyone unless I had to defend myself or the people I love, which includes you."

"I know, Uncle Nathen."

"Then what's bothering you? You've been quiet since dinner, and the look you just had on your face clearly says that something's on your mind. Do you want to talk about it?"

Becca wanted the truth, but she was afraid she might not like the answer. However, if she didn't talk about it, it would fester inside of her until she did. Becca took a deep breath, looked Nathen square in the eyes, and asked her question. "Will you tell me the truth no matter what?"

Nathen appeared shocked by the question. "Of course. I would never lie, Becca. It's not my way."

"Okay. Do you know Adrian's parents?"

"Yes, I do, but his mother has been dead a long time now."

"Do you know how she died?"

"Yes, I do." Becca could sense that Nathen wondered where this was going, and he did not disappoint her. "Has this got something to do with your talk with Adrian?"

"Yes, and I want to hear your side of the story."

"My side? There are no sides, just the truth."

"Then tell me the truth as you know it."

Nathen leaned forward but kept his hands wrapped

around his mug. "It happened the winter before Joshawa was born. Your aunt was pregnant and very sick. Adrian's parents were going into town for supplies and a present for Adrian's birthday party."

"He must have been really young."

"If I remember, he was turning two. It was early in the morning, and they were all set to go out when we heard that a winter storm was coming, and it was going to be a bad one. Charles canceled the trip to town, but Adrian's father was insistent. He asked for my help, but I had to turn him down. Authia and I were fighting Serena. She had taken control of Authia's body and was trying to kill her. I couldn't leave your aunt. I had to stay and protect her from Serena. I told his father that I would help him another day, that it wasn't a good idea to risk getting caught in the storm.

"I remember he was upset. He really wanted to get the present he'd purchased and have a party for his son on his birthday. It wasn't till late in the day when Charles discovered they went anyway. The storm had hit, and we had to wait till it calmed down before we could go looking for them. His mother died in that storm. I carried her body back to Burwood. As you know, his father lived, but he lost all his toes and a couple of fingers to frostbite."

Becca was overrun with emotion. If she had to believe one story, Nathen's made the most sense. "That's not exactly how Adrian's dad tells the story."

"Somehow, I'm getting the feeling that he blames me for his wife's death."

"He told Adrian that you were supposed to meet them and help them back so they could be in Burwood before the storm hit. He said you never showed."

Nathen just shook his head. "I never knew he blamed me. We were never close, but I never thought for one moment that anyone blamed me for what happened."

"Uncle Nathen, Burwood is a small community. So you're saying that there were no rumors of how he felt?"

"You have to understand, Becca, it was wintertime and a particularly bad one. People kept to their cabins, and I was nursing Authia back to health. When the spring came, we got married and left for Africa. I wasn't around very much."

"I believe you, Uncle Nathen. And first thing in the morning, I'm going to set Adrian right."

"No, leave it be."

Becca was surprised by Nathen's comment. "Leave it be? But he hates you and Joshawa because of the lies his father told."

"Yes, and that's fine. Becca, Adrian's father obviously couldn't live with the fact that his insistence to go to town caused his wife's death. So he blamed me, and that's fine with me. I know firsthand what it's like to have your son hate you. I wouldn't wish that on anyone. If blaming me saves his relationship with his son, then so be it." Nathen smiled at Becca. "Besides, the people who know me and love me know the truth. They know the kind of person I am."

Becca went over to Nathen and threw her arms around his neck. "I love you, Uncle Nathen."

Nathen returned her hug. "I know, and I love you, too." Gently he pulled Becca away from him so he could see her face. "I've always loved you as if you were my daughter, and I would be honored to have you as a daughter-in-law."

"You're going to make me cry."

Nathen stood up and gave Becca a proper hug. "Now, let's get to bed. It's going to be a long day tomorrow."

Becca was heading toward Joshawa's room when she remembered the story of the little girl that was kidnapped. She stopped in her tracks, almost causing Nathen to run into her back.

"What's wrong, Becca?"

Becca turned to face Nathen. "Do you know what happened to that little girl you saved?"

"Tracy?"

"Yes."

"Well, she had an aptitude for the sciences. She applied to a university with a strong science program and got in. I think it was in Toronto. Why do you ask?"

Becca made a sour look. "Adrian's father said she had to leave because she was so traumatized by what you did to Billy's brother."

Nathen turned Becca around and guided her to Joshawa's bedroom. "And that's another story that will be left alone. Now go to bed."

Becca closed the door to Joshawa's bedroom and climbed into bed. Her conversation with her uncle had lifted a huge weight off her shoulders. And as she was lying in bed, she scolded herself for believing for one moment that Nathen would intentionally do anything to harm another individual.

Becca closed her eyes, and her thoughts immediately went to the two hunters. She prayed they would cooperate, because if it meant finding his son, Becca had a bad feeling that Nathen would revive the beast he'd buried so many years ago.

# Chapter Twenty-two

It was early in the morning, and Nathen stood at the window, coffee mug in hand, staring out into the yard. The moonlight cast a soft glow, leaving most of the yard in shadows. It would probably be another couple of hours before the sun would even begin to touch the morning sky.

Nathen took a long sip of his coffee as he recalled his conversation with Becca. Even though he portrayed himself as being completely confident with his plan, the truth was he had no idea what he would do if he couldn't steal the GPS from the hunters. What if they saw him, or even worse, caught him in the act? According to Authia, Dameon could be reasoned with. However, Jax was another story.

Nathen was about to take another sip of his coffee when he heard Billy moving about. Nathen turned around to find Billy sitting up, staring at the fire that Nathen had started earlier. He was still wearing his socks, jeans, and red-checkered flannel shirt, buttoned at the neck and wrists. When Nathen had offered him pajamas, Billy refused them, muttering something about a quick escape. Nathen had learned long ago not to question Billy. He spent much of his time in a world that only existed in his mind.

"Good morning, Billy." Nathen walked over to the rocking chair and turned it around to face Billy. He sat down and quietly waited for Billy to acknowledge him.

It took a few minutes before Billy noticed Nathen, and when he did, he gave Nathen the biggest smile.

"Did you sleep well, Billy?"

Billy smiled as he nodded his head in agreement. "Billy slept good. We leave now?"

"The sun isn't up yet. We'll leave soon."

Billy stood and walked over to the window. He gazed out into the yard as if he were considering something important. "No, we leave now. Lots of light."

"Only moonlight. We can wait."

Billy turned around to face Nathen and shook his head from side to side. "No. Leave now." He had a look about him that puzzled Nathen. It was as if he understood something that was foreign to Nathen. "We can sneak in the dark. We are safe in the dark. Cabin can't hurt us if it can't see us."

Billy turned back to the window and started to slowly rock back and forth. "Safe in the dark." Nathen joined Billy at the window and gazed out into the darkness.

"It will be light soon. Wouldn't you rather travel in the sunlight?"

"No. Safe in the dark." Billy glanced up at Nathen. "We go now."

Nathen watched in astonishment as Billy retrieved his coat from the hook by the door. The tan-colored winter coat covered him to mid-thigh and had an attached hood. Billy slipped the coat on, then pulled his boots on. The boots were winterized rubber boots that came halfway up his calf, and Billy took great care at making sure his jeans were securely tucked inside them.

When he was done, he went to the fridge and stuffed the deep coat pockets with some leftover chicken. There was bottled water in the fridge, which Billy also took. He quietly closed the fridge door, zipped up his coat, and left the cabin.

Nathen kept watch over Billy from the window. He walked to the edge of the yard, sat down, and stared out into the forest. Nathen shook his head and took one last gulp of his coffee. He whispered, "I guess we're leaving now." Then he went to the kitchen and put his mug in the sink. He left a note for Authia and then grabbed his jacket and headed out into the yard.

Billy sat on the ground, waiting for Nathen. But in his head, it wasn't Nathen he was waiting for. Billy glanced around and smiled, for he knew the darkness would keep them safe. Usually, the darkness meant pain and suffering, but he'd learned that it could also keep them safe from the evil that lived at the cabin. They would head to the mountains, where they would be safe.

Billy smiled and closed his eyes. He saw the mountains, he felt the cold, and it made him happy. Billy was distracted from his thoughts when he heard someone approach him. He opened his eyes, and when he glanced to his right, he found Nathen crouching beside him. Billy's first reaction was that of sadness, because it wasn't who he wanted it to be. But when Nathen spoke, all Billy's memories faded, and he was back in the present.

"Billy, I'm going to get Adrian. Can you wait for me?"

"Yes, Billy wait." He smiled at Nathen, then continued to stare into the forest."

Nathen stood up, but he didn't leave to get Adrian. Instead, he watched Billy and wondered what was going on in his head. Billy had always hated the dark, but now, for some reason, he felt safe. Nathen glanced around the yard and imagined Billy hiding in the forest with his brother, watching and waiting for Nathen so that his brother could capture him.

Being here, in this yard, in the dark, must have triggered some distant memory. Nathen looked up to the sky and could see the faint glow of the sunrise. If leaving in the dark comforted Billy, then that was what they would do.

Nathen walked over to Hansen's cabin and quietly opened the door. The cabin was engulfed in darkness, with the exception of the warm glow coming off the fireplace. The darkness didn't deter Nathen, for his vision was quite adapted to the dark. He grabbed Adrian's jacket off the back of a kitchen chair and walked over to the couch. Nathen nudged Adrian's arm and softly called out his name. After the third nudge, Adrian woke up. He opened his eyes, and Nathen watched as his expression went from mild curiosity to pure contempt.

"What do you want?"

Nathen whispered, "Quiet. Everyone's sleeping." He threw Adrian's jacket on the couch. "Get dressed. We're leaving."

Adrian sat up and looked around the room. Softly he whispered, "Now? It's still dark."

Nathen placed a note for Hansen on the kitchen table then focused his attention on Adrian. "Billy is waiting for us. Let's go."

Adrian threw his comforter off, stood up, and reached for his jacket. "I'm one step ahead of you."

Nathen glanced over to Adrian to find him already dressed. He chuckled to himself because he knew Adrian's state of dress would have annoyed Hansen. Nathen was sure that Hansen would have wanted to hide Adrian's clothes, leaving him with only his underwear to sleep in. That way, he wouldn't try to take a short stroll in the middle of the night. "I'm surprised he didn't chain you to the couch."

"I'm sure he thought about it." Adrian put his jacket on, zipped it up then glanced over to the kitchen. "No coffee?"

"We're on Billy's schedule, which doesn't include coffee." Nathen opened the door, waited for Adrian to lace up his boots, then quietly closed the door behind them.

Jax propped open the door to the cabin then went to sit at the kitchen table. He had the remote to the cameras on the table in front of him. Jax had chosen to face the door so that he could watch as the sun rose above the horizon. It wasn't for the purpose of enjoying the beauty of the sunrise, but rather an indicator that he could turn the cameras on. He didn't think to start a fire, and even as the cold invaded the cabin, he remained at the table and continued to stare out into the darkness.

After one hour of patiently waiting, he was rewarded as the sun's rays reached up into the morning sky. Jax smiled as he placed his right index finger on the switch. He was ready to turn on the cameras the second the sun's brilliant light overtook the darkness.

Dameon shivered from the cold and unconsciously pulled his sleeping bag up around his chin. A few minutes later, the cold won out, and Dameon woke up. He rolled onto his left side and discovered that the cabin door was propped open. He saw Jax at the table, and he also noticed that the fire had either died out or was never started.

"What are you doing? It's freezing in here." Dameon jumped down from his bunk, pulled on his jeans, threw on a sweatshirt, and went to retrieve his boots that were by the door.

Without taking his focus off the yard, Jax replied to Dameon. "What does it look like I'm doing?"

"It looks like you're obsessed with the creature. How long have you been sitting there? And why didn't you start a fire?"

Jax glanced over to Dameon. "You sound like an old woman. If you want a fire, then start one." Jax returned his focus to the yard.

Dameon stood next to the door and watched in disbelief. Jax was obsessed, and nothing was going to deter him from finding the creature. Dameon was fooling himself if he believed anything else. "I'm going to the ladies' room. Start the damn fire."

Jax didn't take his eyes off the yard. "The sun is almost up, and I'm not losing one second of camera time. I'll start the fire as soon as I turn the cameras on."

Dameon shook his head, grabbed the flashlight that was next to the door, and left the cabin.


Amy spent another night curled up close to Alex. She'd covered herself with an old tattered comforter, and other than the ground being slightly cool, she was very content. She woke up as the sun's rays made their way into the mouth of the cave.

Amy sat up, stretched her arms over her head, then glanced over in Joshawa's direction. No sound came from the tent, so she assumed he was still asleep. Amy remained fixated on the tent. And for the first time since Joshawa had arrived, she wondered when he'd first come into her life. She felt as though she had known him for a very long time, but she couldn't recall any memories before the accident. There was just this gut feeling that she knew him and had to save him. Amy shrugged her shoulders, stood up, grabbed both empty buckets, and headed for the river.


Authia felt chilled and tried to move closer to Nathen. But as she reached out to touch him, she quickly discovered that he was no longer in bed. Authia threw the blankets off her, put on her housecoat, and went to find him. When Authia entered the living room, both Billy and Nathen were nowhere to be seen. She went to Joshawa's room and found Becca in bed, fast asleep. As she quietly closed the bedroom door, she melded with Nathen.

*Good morning. Where are you?*

*Good morning, my love. We're already on our way to the Jenkin's homestead.*

*You left early.*

*Something got into Billy, and he wanted to travel in the dark.*

*In the dark? He hates the dark.*

*I know. Just one more mystery to add to the pile. I'll let you know when we get there.*

*Okay, sweetheart. Please be careful.*

*I will.*

Nathen was gone, and Authia headed for the stove to make herself some coffee. To her delight, she discovered that the stove was still hot, and the coffee pot was half full. She filled her mug and went to sit in front of the fire. There was only one log left in the fireplace, and it was on the verge of crumbling to embers. Authia added two more logs to the fire then curled up in her chair, tucking her feet underneath her.

She held her mug with both hands and rested it on her knee. She watched as the heat from the embers quickly ignited the new logs, and within minutes the fireplace was alive with colorful flames that playfully licked at the stone walls.

As Authia watched the fire, her thoughts diverted to Nathen, and she couldn't help but be nervous about him trying to obtain the GPS. She didn't believe it would be as easy as walking up to the cabin and taking it, at least not if Jax was there. Dameon could be reasoned with, and deep down, Authia knew that Dameon wouldn't harm Nathen.

Authia continued to stare into the fire as her thoughts migrated to Joshawa. She wondered if he was safe, if he was warm, and if he had something to eat and drink. Was he suffering in pain with no one to hold him, to take care of him? Tears ran down Authia's cheeks as she closed her eyes and tried to reach out to her son.

*Joshawa, can you hear me? Please reach out to me. Speak to me. Your father is looking for you, and he will find you. I promise, he will find you. Can you hear me, Joshawa? Can you tell me where you are?*

Authia focused on the tree Joshawa had fallen out of. She focused on the surroundings that she'd seen through his eyes.

*I'm here, Joshawa. Can you hear me? I'm by the tree you fell out of. I'm here. Reach out to me.*

*Whispers in the wind.*

Authia's eyes flew open.

*Joshawa, is that you? I can barely hear you.*

*Whispers in the wind. I hear whispers in the wind.*

This time the voice was clearer, stronger, and Authia knew without a doubt that it was Joshawa.

*I hear you, Joshawa! Can you hear me? You're not alone. Speak to me. Tell me where you are.*

*I hear whispers in the wind.*

*They're not whispers. Joshawa, it's my voice you're hearing. Listen harder. Try to hear my voice.*

Instead of her son's voice, a brilliant blue light exploded within Authia's mind, and just as quickly as it came, it was gone. Authia jumped out of her chair, accidentally dropping her mug on the floor. It smashed, sending shards of ceramic in all directions, but Authia didn't notice. She just stared at the fireplace seeing nothing but the blue light.

*Oh my God, I understand now. These are your clues.*


Serena could sense that Lord Adeeowale was on his way and was about to transform into a wisp when she heard Joshawa's voice repeating the words *whispers in the wind*. She walked over to the edge and peered down to see who was trying to meld with Joshawa.

Serena was delighted when she discovered that it was

Authia, and the best part was that Joshawa was answering her.

Serena closed her eyes and melded with Joshawa.

*You must be stronger if you want your pleas to be heard. Focus, Joshawa. Focus on the whispers. Focus on the blue light.*

Serena opened her eyes and continued to observe Authia. She smiled as she watched Authia jump up from her chair, for she knew that Authia had finally figured out her clues.

*You do not disappoint my Mistress.*

Serena's expression became a little more ominous. She spoke to her Mistress even though she knew that Authia couldn't hear her.

*But it is not over yet. You and I both have a daunting hurdle to overcome. I promise you, my Mistress, I will do everything in my power to handle mine. I am afraid you are on your own for yours.*

"You cannot help her?"

Serena turned to find Lord Adeeowale standing behind her. "Are we safe to speak, my Lord? Is Lord Chike occupied?"

"Yes, on both counts. You need not transform."

"You are not concerned that Lord Chike will chance upon us?"

"I sent him to the Land of Spirits on the pretense of discovering why we have four Ancestors in the Realm instead of three."

"You sent him to seek an audience with the Council?"

"I inferred."

"Nothing good can come from him meeting with the Council."

"I know you have history with the Council, and I am very much aware that your meeting was, shall we say, less than pleasant. Lord Chike considers himself of greater worth than the Council. He will go to the Land of Spirits. However, I very much doubt that he will seek an audience with them."

Serena did not hear one word Lord Adeeowale spoke after

he referred to her meeting with the Council. Her mind went to the time when she'd been killed by Lord Nathen and his father. Her spirit had been ushered to the Land of Spirits, and once there, she was called before the Council. As Lord Adee-owale had so elegantly put it, the memory was far from pleasant.

The Council consisted of five members, and according to the parchments, they were the ones that had given birth to the Jelani Tribe. The parchments spoke of them as if they were nothing more than a myth, a bedtime story for children. But Serena knew the truth. She knew they existed. Perhaps not as spirits or living beings, but they did exist.

She remembered that they wore long hooded robes that completely covered them from head to toe, and their hoods extended past their face. She couldn't tell if they were men or women, and they never spoke. Their only method of communication was telepathy, with no sense of gender or voice inflections. Their thoughts appeared in her mind as if they were words written on parchment.

When Serena was called before them, she'd been led to the Gathering hut in the Land of Spirits. Inside, she found the Council sitting on the raised platform located at the back of the hut. At first, Serena was shocked at what she saw, and she quickly learned that the bedtime story she'd heard as a child had turned into her nightmare.

When she approached them, it had appeared as if they were sitting cross-legged on the platform, their arms rested in their laps, and their sleeves extended past what Serena thought would be their hands. They sat side by side, and when she gazed upon their faces, she saw only darkness. They were void of emotion, of a sense of being. But that did not hinder them from punishing Serena for her indiscretions.

The punishment was unbearable. The pain they inflicted was horrific. They were the ones that had imprisoned her, and they were the ones that set her free. They were the ones that controlled the Ancestors.

Serena realized that Lord Adeeowale was speaking to her. She cleared her mind and came back to the present. "I am so sorry, Lord Adeeowale, I was distracted. Are you certain that he will not seek out the Council?"

"I am. He does not suspect that we are questioning his intentions, and his arrogance will be his downfall. What have you to say to me?"

"My Lord, there is more to Lord Chike than either of us suspect. I went to your camp as a wisp with the intent of finding out who Lord Chike actually was. What I found was very disturbing. He is not one person. There are two entities in his body."

"Two? How is that possible?"

"I asked myself the same question. Then I remembered what Lord Chike said to me in anger. He said he would see to my destruction. He also said he would destroy me."

"He used those exact words?"

"Yes, my Lord. Words that are forbidden both here and in the Land of Spirits."

"Do you understand what you are saying, Serena?"

"Only too well, my Lord. I believe that Lord Chike is a vessel for the destroyer."

Authia's excitement did not go unnoticed by Nathen, and before Authia could take another breath, he melded with her.

*Your emotions are screaming at me again. Are you all right?*

*Nathen, I couldn't be better. I figured out the clue! Serena is watching over Joshawa. She's protecting him.*

*I don't understand. She's been trying to convince him to go to Africa. What makes you think she's helping him.*

*Do you remember what Travis said about Serena playing with his mind?*

*Are you referring to when she entered his mind as a wisp?*

*Yes. He said all he could think of was whispers in the wind. I reached out to Joshawa, and he answered me.*

*Are you sure it was Joshawa?*

*It was Joshawa. I know it was him, and he said whispers in the wind. Then a bright blue light flooded my mind. For whatever reason, Serena can't directly communicate with us. So she left us clues. Things that have happened in our past so that we would know it was her. We know that Joshawa is in a cave, and we know that the roaring sound I heard was the grizzly that attacked the tree Joshawa was in. I'm certain Joshawa is in a cave north of here, and Serena is watching over him.*

The excitement Jax felt when he switched the remote on and watched the cameras come alive was more intense than when he'd killed the park ranger. He moved the cameras so he could see every angle of the yard. If he were being honest, he'd have to admit that he was a little disappointed that his bigfoot wasn't there to be caught on camera.

Jax took a deep breath and slowly released it. He was in for the long haul, and he had no issue with staying in the cabin for as long as it would take. Jax turned on the record button, then decided to appease Dameon and started a fire. He also placed the coffee perk on the grate that was over the fire.

When Dameon returned to the cabin, he was obviously put off by Jax's earlier mood. Jax observed Dameon as he dragged one of the rocking chairs closer to the fire, sat down, and placed his stocking feet on the hearth. The fact that he didn't acknowledge Jax spoke volumes. Jax was going to have to play nice, even though it was the last thing he wanted to do.

"Do you want some coffee?"

"Sure." Dameon didn't avert his gaze. He just continued to stare at the fire.

Jax grabbed the two coffee mugs that were on the kitchen

table and set them down on the hearth. Then he retrieved the coffee pot and filled the two cups. Jax passed a mug to Dameon, who accepted without taking his focus off the fire.

"Okay. I apologize. I was acting like a complete ass earlier. And you're right. I am obsessed with this creature."

Dameon glanced over to Jax. "If you're going to continue to be an ass, as you put it, count me out. I don't need this bull-shit." Dameon returned his focus to the fire as he took a sip of his coffee.

Jax had a decision to make. Did he really need Dameon? The problem was Jax didn't know the answer. He didn't know what he was up against, and that was reason enough to suck up to Dameon. "You're right. Let me make it up to you. We need supplies from town. Let's go right now, and I'll buy you a steak for lunch."

"It's going to take us all day to get to town and back. Can you go that long without looking at the cameras?"

"Yes, and I'm going to prove it." Jax stood up and walked over to the kitchen table. He placed his mug next to the re-mote, turned the screen off, then closed the lid on the remote. The screen might be off, but the cameras would still be on, and they would be recording to the memory stick Jax placed in each camera.

Jax picked up the remote, walked over to the bunkbeds, knelt on one knee, and placed the remote on the floor under his bed. He stood, grabbed his backpack, and turned to face Dameon.

"Out of sight, out of mind. I'm going to wait for you out-side." Jax started to leave the cabin then something came to mind. "Don't forget to grab the GPS."

Dameon appeared confused. "Why do we need the GPS?"

"Because we've never found the main road from here. Only from our camp, and I sure in hell don't want to walk all the way back to our camp before we start heading south. You're the map genius. Find a route to the road from here."

"That actually makes sense. First time for everything." Dameon laughed as he downed the last of his coffee then went to get ready for their hike to the main road.

# CHAPTER TWENTY-THREE

L ord Chike stood at the Gateway to the Land of Spirits. It was located at the furthest northern edge of the Realm of the Ancestors. The jungle encroached to the very edge of the Gateway with the exception of an area that was five feet wide and eight feet tall. Through Nature's doorway, a thick fog shimmered in colors much like a prism. There was a certain beauty in this fog, but there was also death. One could not pass to either land without the permission of the Gatekeeper. He alone could stand in the fog and remain unharmed. Lord Chike raised his voice so that he would be heard through the dense fog. "Gatekeeper, I request safe passage to the Land of the Spirits."

Lord Chike waited while the Gatekeeper approached him. The Gatekeeper was a warrior from when the tribe was young. He was over seven feet tall, his flaming red hair cascaded down to the middle of his back, his strength evident in his massive biceps, his rippled abdomen, and muscular thighs. His high cheekbones accented his emerald eyes, and the clef in his upper lip was more pronounced than the warriors that lived today.

He only wore a loincloth that covered him from his waist to mid-thigh. He carried an ornate spear in his right hand, which measured over eight feet long. It was said that the carvings on his spear spoke of his conquests from battles that occurred hundreds of years in the past. A dagger with an eighteen-inch blade that curved inward was strapped to the left side of his waist.

He approached Lord Chike but stopped when he reached the edge of the fog. Even though he was safe inside the toxic cloud, to step on the ground of either the Realm of the Ancestors or the Land of Spirits meant certain death to the Gatekeeper. It was how the Council could maintain control over him.

"What is your business in the Land of Spirits, Lord Chike?"

"I wish to seek audience with the Council of Five." The question was a mere formality. Lord Chike knew that being an Ancestor afforded him the right to pass between the lands.

"Permission Granted." The Gatekeeper stood to one side and extended the entire length of his spear outwards. He kept it five feet from the ground, and then slowly, he maneuvered his spear through the fog as if he were parting a drape. As soon as the spear was at his side and horizontal to the ground, it was safe to pass. The fog had cleared, and a lush, green carpet of ferns and grasses lay before Lord Chike.

Lord Chike entered the Gateway and walked past the Gatekeeper as if he didn't exist.

As far as Lord Chike was concerned, the Gatekeeper had no importance and therefore didn't deserve Lord Chike's time.


Joshawa slowly woke up, and as he waited for his eyes to adjust to the dimly lit cave, he was reminded that he wasn't dreaming. The cave was real, and he was living his mother's vision.

He glanced over to his left and found Amy sitting cross-legged on the ground by the firepit. She wore a black zippered sweater that hung loosely on her frame and an old pair of faded and ragged jeans. She'd rolled up the cuffs to the pants, exposing her bare feet. Amy had started a fire and was filleting the half dozen fish that laid on the ground next to her.

The tent had obviously been cleared away, and Joshawa was now covered with a thin blanket. He raised his head ever so slightly and was relieved that there was very little pain. He searched the cave for Alex and discovered him lying at the entrance to the cave. Alex had positioned himself to face the inside. His head was raised, and his focus was riveted on Joshawa. Joshawa laid his head back down on the cold ground and stared at the ceiling. "Why does your bear watch me so intensely? It's not like I can do anything."

"You're awake!" There was excitement in Amy's voice, as if she hadn't expected him to wake up.

Joshawa watched Amy put down the stick that she was going to skewer the fish with. Then she moved closer to him and gently placed the palm of her hand on his forehead. She appeared delighted as she straightened out his left arm. "Your fever is gone, and it looks like your arm is better, too."

"Thanks to you."

"You're welcome." Amy stood and straddled Joshawa placing her feet on either side of his hips. The second she did that, Alex got up and ambled toward them.

Joshawa realized what was coming next, and what he really wanted was to try to sit up on his own. He knew his ribs were broken, though he didn't know how many. However, if he wanted to get well enough to leave the cave, he would have to start moving without Amy's help.

Before Amy could grab his shirt, he placed his arms down at his side and tried to use his elbows and stomach muscles to lift himself off the ground. He was able to lift himself a couple of inches before the pain consumed him, and he was forced to lie back down.

Amy now stood over him, hands on her hips, and she appeared very upset. "What are you doing? You can't sit up on your own. You're so silly. Now let me help you." Amy reached for Joshawa's shirt when he interrupted her.

"Please, Amy. I have to try this."

Amy hesitated, and to Joshawa, it looked like she was trying to understand what he wanted. "You want to sit up with no help, even if it hurts?"

"I have to at least try."

Amy thought for a second, then nodded her head in agreement. "You can try, but I don't want you in any pain. I'm going to hold your shirt. If you want me to help, I will."

Joshawa smiled at Amy. "Thank you." Joshawa placed his elbows back on the ground. He took a shallow breath then started to lift himself up. The pain came quickly and encompassed his entire chest.

"Now, Amy!"

Amy pulled him upright by his shirt. At the same time, Joshawa could feel Alex as he positioned himself tight against Joshawa's back. When Amy let go, Joshawa was sitting upright, and the pain slowly subsided. At that point, Joshawa realized that he couldn't lie down again. If he remained sitting up, he would be that much closer to getting out of the cave and going home.

But to do that, he needed not only Amy's help but Alex's, as well. Joshawa pondered his predicament, and to him, it appeared almost hopeless. For whatever reason, his parents hadn't contacted him, and his father hadn't found him. Maybe it had something to do with the cave—the cave his mother made him promise never to enter.

It was unfortunate that his mother's vision didn't foresee that he entered a cave but not of his own free will. So was it fate or karma that had brought him here? Or was it simply arrogance on his part? No matter what or who played a part that led him here, the bottom line was that he was on his own. He had to find his own way out of the cave and down the mountain.

Joshawa examined the cave and calculated the distance

between where he sat and the cave wall closest to him. It was maybe ten feet away, a distance he was confident that he could make if he could only do something about his ribs. He observed Amy as she skillfully cooked the fish over the hot embers. "Amy, do you know how many broken ribs I have?"

Amy reached over, placed four fish on a tin plate, and handed it to Joshawa. "More than one."

Joshawa placed the plate on his lap. He looked over to Amy and smiled. "I figured that much. But you know a lot about my injuries. Do you know how many?"

"Of course I do, silly." Amy sat closer to Joshawa and tenderly touched three places on his chest with her right index finger—two on his left side and one on his right.

"I was thinking, what if you bound them? Would I have more movement?"

"Why would you want to move? Can't you just let them heal?"

"Amy, I don't want to be lying down all the time. I want to sit up. I was thinking. Maybe you could prop me up against the cave wall." Joshawa nodded his head in the direction of the cave wall that was closest to him.

"But you would be sitting up all the time."

"That's fine. I'm not in that much pain when I'm sitting. Would you help me?"

Amy glanced from Joshawa to the wall and back again. Then she glanced over to Alex then back to Joshawa. "Alex likes holding you up. He likes you." She returned her gaze to Alex and smiled. "Don't you, Alex." To Joshawa, she was stating a fact, not asking a question.

"I know, and I appreciate that. But he'd probably be happier if he were free to move about."

"Maybe." Amy hesitated before she continued. She frowned at Joshawa, and to him, she looked as if she were being asked to do something that was terribly wrong. "You're heavy. I had a hard time dragging you to the fire."

"If you bind my ribs, then maybe I could move mostly on my own. You would just have to give me a little help."

Amy frowned at Joshawa. "You can't move on your own. You can't even walk! You're being silly."

Joshawa could tell that Amy was getting frustrated with him. He had to find another way to approach her. "I appreciate everything you've done for me. You saved my life. I just want to make it easier for you and for Alex."

Amy scrunched up her face as if she were giving his suggestion a lot of thought. "If I help you and I really hurt you, you'll get mad at me."

Joshawa was puzzled by Amy's comment. He was never angry with her, and he never blamed her or Alex for his pain. So why would she think that he would? "No, I won't. Trust me. I want to do this."

Amy sighed and was quiet for a moment. "Okay. We'll eat first. Then I'll help move you. But you can't be mad at me."

"I won't. I promise." Joshawa eagerly took a bite of his fish. As he chewed, he glanced over to Alex, who was, as always, watching him.

*I hope you do like me, because I'm going to need your help to get off this mountain.*

Nathen was impressed with Billy's ability to find his way through the forest with only the moonlight to guide him. He never faltered, he never stumbled, and unlike the journey from Burwood, Billy did not stop for anything. He was on a mission that didn't appear to be fueled by fear. Otherwise, he would have waited for the sun to come up before they left.

He had a purpose, and deep down, Nathen knew it had nothing to do with saving Joshawa. Billy had mentioned the name Amelia, and from his reaction, Nathen guessed that this person was important to Billy. Maybe she was a sister or his mother? It was something else to add to the pile of mysteries that Nathan wanted answers to.

Nathen made sure that Adrian followed close behind him and kept his flashlight pointed to the ground. It was evident to Nathen that Adrian didn't want to be on this trek to save Joshawa. Still, Adrian kept his comments to himself, for which Nathen was ever so grateful. He had a lot on his mind, and he didn't want to have to deal with Adrian's foul mood or sarcastic comments.

They'd been traveling in a westerly direction for at least an hour. Even though Nathen didn't have a compass on him, he was reasonably confident that Billy was also diverting them slightly north.

The trio remained quiet until the sun started to rise, and the moonlight slowly surrendered itself to the brightness of the sun's rays. At that point, Billy suddenly stopped. He remained perfectly still as if he were being watched, and any movement would give away his position.

Nathen turned to Adrian and placed his index finger over his lips to indicate to Adrian to be quiet. He gave Billy a couple of minutes, then went to stand next to him. Billy's gaze was fixed straight ahead, and he didn't blink. Nathen could tell that he was terrified by the expression on his face. Nathen leaned closer to Billy and softly whispered, "Is everything okay, Billy?"

Billy didn't respond, so Nathen tried again. "Is the cabin close?"

Slowly Billy raised his arm and pointed straight ahead. Nathen scanned the area that Billy pointed to, and in the distance, he could just make out the roofline of a cabin. "I see it, Billy. Is that where you used to live?"

Billy didn't divert his gaze as he replied to Nathen. "Yes."

"Okay, Billy. Thank you. You can go home with Adrian now."

Nathen watched as Billy's expression went from fear to determination. "No. Must help. Must save Amelia." Billy scanned the area then pointed to his left. "We go this way. This way safe."

Adrian walked up to Nathen while Billy quietly made his way through the forest. "What's going on? I thought I was taking him back to Burwood."

Nathen didn't take his focus off Billy. "You are, just not right now. Something's going on with Billy. He must be reliving some event from his past." Nathen turned to face Adrian. "I'm going to let him continue, as long as it doesn't endanger him in any way."

"Endanger him! What about us?"

Nathen glanced down at Adrian's *Ruger*. "Keep that holstered. We won't be in any danger as long as you do exactly as I say and keep quiet." Nathen didn't wait for a response. He was confident that Adrian would follow him, so he turned and headed in the direction that Billy went.


Lord Chike entered the Land of Spirits, and as he crossed that mythical line, he glanced over his shoulder. He watched as the fog engulfed the Gatekeeper and the passageway. Now all that remained was the glistening fog and the ominous threat of death. Lord Chike snickered as he focused his attention on the village and the tribesmen that went about their duties.

The village was similar to that of the village that lay hidden deep within the jungles of Africa. Only this one was on a much grander scale. It was home to most of the spirits that once resided in the land of the living since the dawn of the Jelani Tribe. The huts these spirits called home went on as far as the eye could see. However, unlike their living counterparts, some spirits also chose to live in the trees. These tree huts soared high above the village, resting on the massive branches of the kapok trees.

When a tribesman died, if they had proved their worthiness while they were alive, they would then reside as a spirit in the Land of Spirits. They lived for an eternity, enjoying much of the same pleasures as they had when they were alive. Pleasures of food, of the flesh, of love, and most importantly, the pleasure of company.

They held that pleasure above all others, because the alternative was an eternity of darkness, despair, and loneliness. That was where the spirits who required punishment would go. Lord Chike possessed intimate knowledge of the Realm of Despair, for he had placed many a spirit there, including Priestess Serena. One day soon, he would reveal his part in her punishment and have great pleasure in putting her back into that dark place she hated so much.

Lord Chike scanned the village until his gaze fell on the Gathering hut. That was where the Council resided. Lord Adeeowale had sent him to the Council to discover why there were four Ancestors instead of the usual three.

Lord Chike chuckled as he shook his head. What a fool Lord Adeeowale was to send him, of all people, to the Council. Lord Chike didn't answer to the Council. He answered to no one. But since he was here, he would make use of his time and check on his prisoner—a very special prisoner who held the key to Lord Chike's very existence.


Becca's mother and father joined her at Authia's cabin for breakfast. The news that Joshawa was alive thrilled her to her very core. As soon as Uncle Nathen got possession of the GPS, then they could find Joshawa and bring him home. Becca swore an oath to herself that the minute she saw Joshawa, she would tell him that she loved him, no matter what the outcome.

Her parents and Authia sat at the kitchen table while discussing their options for finding Joshawa. Becca was confused by their conversation. Wasn't the GPS the only option? She tried to join the conversation, but they were so focused on what they were discussing that they didn't seem to notice her. Finally, Becca had enough. She placed her hands, palms facing down, on the table and raised her voice high enough to be heard, "Hello! I'm sitting right here."

Hansen turned to face his daughter. "Becca. You're being rude, again."

"No, I'm not. You three are ignoring me. I have a right to be a part of this conversation."

Authia smiled at Becca. "I'm so sorry, Becca. And you're right. You should be a part of this conversation."

Becca leaned back into her chair and folded her arms across her chest. "I don't understand. The way you're talking, it sounds like there's more than one way to find Joshawa. Is there?"

Hansen glanced over to Becca, and to her, it appeared as if he were giving serious thought to what he wanted to say. "The GPS will help us locate where Joshawa fell. If he's in a cave—"

Authia interrupted Hansen. "Not if. He's definitely in a cave."

"Okay, for whatever reason, he's in a cave. The GPS can't tell us where that is, because, as far as we know, it hasn't been there. So we have to come up with other options to find the cave."

There was a moment of silence then Becca spoke up. "How do we know it hasn't been there? These hunters are hunting a bear, and we know there's a bear in the cave. If these hunters want this bear, then wouldn't it make sense that they know where the cave is?"

The table was quiet for a moment, then Authia spoke up.

"She's right. They're after a bear, and it's a grizzly. From what I saw through Joshawa and Dameon, this grizzly is huge. So I am confident that his roar is what I heard in my vision. I also know through Dameon that they're not hunting it. They're watching it. They're waiting for something. I saw Dameon at the tree Joshawa fell from. So the question is, was that a coincidence, or was he there because of the grizzly?"

Hansen spoke up. "These guys are professionals. If they're watching the grizzly, then they've taken steps not to lose it. I bet you any money they've tagged it, and that tag is linked to their GPS. If that's the case, then Dameon was at the tree because the grizzly was there."

Becca couldn't contain her excitement. "That's great! Then the GPS *will* lead us to Joshawa."

Hansen continued. "Not necessarily. It will lead us to a grizzly. There's no guarantee that this grizzly is in the same cave Joshawa is in."

Becca knew that her dad was right. There was no guarantee. However, they did have an option to ensure that they were on the right track. "There's a way we could be sure." All eyes were on Becca. "Aunty Authia, would you be able to see the cave and the grizzly through Joshawa's eyes?"

Becca watched as her mom's eyes went wide and her mouth gaped open. Becca had no doubt that her mother knew what she wanted to suggest, and she was obviously not impressed.

"There's no way I'm putting you under such heavy sedation."

"Mom, I want to do this. It could be the only way we find Joshawa."

"It's too dangerous!" Tammy turned her attention to Authia. "Can you promise me that if we do this, we'll find Joshawa?"

"No, I can't. I don't know if the grizzly will be there, and I don't know if Joshawa is even conscious. Also, Serena is playing around in his mind. I have no idea if that will affect my ability to see what Joshawa sees. But if he's conscious, and I can see through his eyes, then there might be a chance. I might see something that will help Nathen find him."

Everyone was focused on Tammy, but at that point, Becca didn't care what her mother's response would be. If her mother didn't help, then she would find another way. "Mom, I understand your reservations. But this is Joshawa we're talking about. We have to do whatever it takes to find him." Becca reached out and tenderly touched her mother's upper arm with her hand. Gently she stroked her mom's bicep with her thumb. "I know this is hard for you, Mom. You want to protect both me and Joshawa. Mom, I trust you, and I know that I'll be all right."

Tammy folded her arms on the table, her attention directed solely on Becca. "It's dangerous, Becca. Putting you under such a heavy sedation and keeping you there is dangerous. Yes, I want to protect both of you. But at what cost?"

Becca understood her mom's heartache, and she felt bad for her. But no matter how bad anyone felt, all that mattered was finding Joshawa. There had to be a way to help him, and at the same time, keep her mom at ease. Then Becca remembered something her mom had said the last time she was sedated. "Mom, what if we went to Burwood and did this in the medical building? Would that be better?"

"Yes, of course it would. I could monitor you there. I'd have Edward to help, and if something went wrong, I'd have the means to save you." Tammy glanced over to Authia. "Do we have that kind of time? If we're going to sedate Becca, can we do it at Burwood?"

"Of course. Tammy, I want you to be comfortable with this decision, and I need you focused on Becca's vitals, not worried if she is safe."

Hansen stood up and pushed his chair away. "Okay, then it's settled. Authia, we'll meet you in the yard in five minutes."

"That sounds good. I'll radio Edward and get him to prep the room."


Nathen, Billy, and Adrian had reached the homestead and were hiding in the forest just at the edge of the yard. Billy and Adrian were sitting cross-legged on the ground hiding behind some overgrown bushes and tall grasses. Next to them stood a large redwood tree with a girth that easily concealed Nathen. The door to the cabin was open, and Nathen could see the glow that was emanating from a fire. However, he couldn't detect any movement.

He glanced down at Billy, who appeared completely oblivious to what he was looking at. Nathen was having difficulty understanding what was going on in Billy's head. One minute he was scared to death, not wanting anything to do with the cabin, which was understandable. Nathen knew that Billy had been beaten on numerous occasions in the cabin that was his home, which should have been his safe haven.

But then it was like a switch went off in his head, and suddenly he was determined to save someone called Amelia at any cost. Now he was staring at the cabin as if it meant nothing to him. Nathen felt for Billy and was concerned that this mission could cause serious mental damage on top of what Billy already suffered from.

Nathen knelt on the ground and whispered to Adrian, "I think Billy has come far enough. It's time for you to take him home."

"Gladly." Adrian was about to stand up when someone came out of the outhouse. Nathen placed his right hand on Adrian's left shoulder to make sure he stayed down. Then he watched as the one called Dameon left the outhouse and went into the cabin. Nathen glanced over to Billy, who was still staring blankly at the cabin. He continued to stare ahead and showed no indication that he saw the man. Nathen then returned his focus to the cabin.

"Let's stay put and see what they're up to."

"What if they find us here?"

Nathen glanced over to Adrian. "If they discover us, I want you to get Billy out of here. I'll deal with the hunters."

Adrian was shocked by Nathen's response. "If they discover us, you can easily outrun them."

"I could if I were alone. But I'm not. My priority is Billy and you. If they find us, grab Billy, and run as fast as you can. I'll keep them busy."

"I have a pretty good idea of what they want with you. If they capture you, it won't be pleasant."

Nathen smiled at Adrian. "Let me worry about that. You take care of Billy."

Adrian watched in disbelief as Nathen stood up and hid behind the redwood tree. What was his deal? The Nathen he knew wouldn't care about Billy or him. He would leave them behind to save his own skin. Maybe he was just pretending that he would protect them to throw Adrian off guard.

Adrian returned his focus to the cabin, but he couldn't help thinking something was off. Nathen sounded sincere about his concern for their safety, and his actions were not that of a man looking out for only himself.

From where Adrian sat, he could hear faint voices coming from the cabin. He strained to listen to the conversation, but he was too far away.

About ten minutes later, the two men emerged from the cabin. Adrian couldn't believe it when he saw that one of the men had the GPS around his neck. He glanced over to Nathen and whispered, "That guy has the GPS."

The color drained from Nathen's face. And for just a moment, Adrian actually felt sorry for him.

"I can see that." Nathen turned and rested his back against the tree and then slowly sank to the ground.

# Chapter Twenty-Four

Serena and Lord Adeeowale wasted no time as they made their way to the Ancestor's campsite. They had no idea how long Lord Chike would remain in the Land of Spirits. If he returned before their plan was set in motion, they risked the chance that he would discover what they were up to. Serena had hoped to use Imani as a conduit so that Lord Adeeowale and she could channel their minds through Imani and become as one. By doing so, they could not only block Lord Chike from detecting them, but they might also be able to see past his façade.

Serena was first to enter the campsite, only to find Imani absent from her usual place. Her fire had been well tended and was in full blaze, which could only mean that she hadn't been gone for long. Serena's first thoughts were that Lord Chike had discovered what they were up to, and now Imani was his prisoner. She turned to face Lord Adeeowale and melded with him.

*Imani is not here, and I cannot sense her. Do you think that Lord Chike has her?*

Lord Adeeowale methodically scanned the area then slowly shook his head.

*I do not believe so.* Lord Adeeowale turned to face Serena. *However, it is clever of you to continue our conversation by melding. Lord Chike troubles me. If he is indeed a vessel for the destroyer, then we must be very cautious. Trust nothing, he says. Now, shall we put your unique talents to work?*

Lord Adeeowale moved to one side as he motioned toward

the firepit.

Serena knew what he referred to, and she was more than delighted to assist. She walked over to the firepit, stared into the flames, and then opened her mind to become one with Imani. Serena slowly circled the pit, not taking her focus off the vibrant colors that danced among the logs.

*Imani, we are worried. You are not where you should be. Are you safe?*

Serena could feel her presence, but it was faint, only an echo in the furthest recesses of Serena's mind. She stopped, closed her eyes, and crooked her head ever so slightly to the left as if she were trying to understand what she was hearing.

*I know you can hear me. Seek me out, Imani. Lord Adeeowale is with me, and he wishes to find you.*

At the mere mention of Lord Adeeowale, Imani's presence entered Serena's mind and flittered around like a butterfly. Serena opened her eyes and allowed Imani's presence to join with her mind. At that very moment, Serena knew where she had to go, though something told her she wouldn't find Imani, at least not the essence that was her soul.

Lord Adeeowale observed Serena with curiosity. She was definitely in tune with someone or something, and Lord Adeeowale prayed that it was Imani and that she was safe. He quietly moved closer to the firepit so he could monitor Serena. He had no intention of interrupting her or making any unnecessary noise. His only thought was that the closer he was to Serena, the closer he was to Imani.

Lord Adeeowale knew that Serena possessed powers stronger than any Priestess that had preceded her, including her mother. Since Serena's death, only High Priestess Tamara rivaled Serena's ability and knowledge. Lord Adeeowale smiled to himself as he thought of Mistress Authia, an outsider who gave Serena a true challenge.

Lord Adeeowale was brought back to the present when Serena turned away from the fire pit and started to walk toward the jungle. She was headed in the direction of where he kept his vigil over the Jelani Tribe. Lord Adeeowale followed Serena but kept his distance so he wouldn't disturb what he hoped was her connection with Imani. When he emerged from the jungle, he found Imani sitting cross-legged on the ground at the very edge of the Realm. Kneeling directly behind her was Serena.

Lord Adeeowale walked over to the edge and peered down upon the village. He was alarmed to discover that the village was in turmoil, and it was all centered around the Priestess's hut. Lord Adeeowale returned his attention to Imani, who was focused on the vast emptiness that lay before her. Her hands rested on her knees, she sat perfectly straight, and there was no expression on her face. Whatever was transpiring in the village didn't seem to affect her.

Serena could see over Imani's head, and she also stared into the darkness. Her eyes revealed nothing, as if her mind were empty. She had her hands placed on either side of Imani's head, and her lips were moving, though no sound came forth.

Lord Adeeowale knelt on the ground beside Imani. As he was about to place his hand on hers, he hesitated. He glanced over to Serena and then slowly withdrew his hand. He realized that Serena and Imani were connected and that any touch could disrupt that connection. Lord Adeeowale decided to sit next to Imani in silence, and while he sat there, he prayed that Serena could save his beloved Imani.

Authia leaned against the door frame of the surgery room with her hands tucked in the front pockets of her jeans. She observed quietly as Edward and Tammy prepared Becca to be sedated. Becca lay on the surgery table with a pillow under her head. She was covered with a red-checkered blanket from her neck to her feet. Edward had placed another blanket underneath her so she wouldn't have to lay on the cold table.

The surgery table was nothing more than a hospital bed that had the mattress removed. In its place was a wooden box completely wrapped in stainless-steel. The box, which was the same depth and length as the mattress, had been made slightly wider to accommodate the larger patients. It had been secured to the bed frame, and the bed itself could be lowered and raised, which made it easier to move a patient on and off the table.

The room was small, being only ten feet by ten feet. An eight-foot-long stainless-steel counter ran along the wall opposite the door. At the end of the counter was a built-in stainless-steel sink. To avoid having to haul buckets of water, a hand pump had been installed next to the sink, a luxury that was only afforded to the medical cabin and the main cabin. The ceiling contained fluorescent lights that were powered by the generator located just outside the building. The generator also powered a small fridge containing several types of medications and an autoclave used to sterilize surgical equipment.

Authia walked over to the right side of the bed and was about to say something when Nathen's thoughts exploded in her mind. She could see the forest, she could feel the cold, and she could sense his defeat.

*Nathen, what's going on? Are you all right?*

*The GPS just headed south into the forest.*

*I'm assuming not on its own. I can sense that you're upset. Please tell me you're not giving up.*

Nathen was silent, and Authia knew that he was conflicted.

*If it wasn't Joshawa that was lost . . . if it were another child from Burwood, what would you do?*

*I know where you're going with this. The problem with that scenario is that it is Joshawa that's lost, not someone else's child.*

*Humor me. What would be your next course of action?*

Authia could hear Nathen sigh. He was listening, but he wasn't prepared to participate.

*Sweetheart, you can't check out on me right now. I need you, but most importantly, Joshawa needs you. He needs you to be the person you are. And that person wouldn't give up. He would keep trying. He would have a plan.*

Again, Nathen sighed. *What did I do to deserve such a smart and beautiful wife?*

*Just lucky, I guess. We're sedating Becca, and I'm going to try to join with Joshawa. If I succeed, then maybe I can help you.*

*Tammy's okay with sedating Becca?*

*We're at Burwood with Edward in the surgery room, and yes, under these conditions, she's okay with it. Now, what's your plan?*

*Not sure yet. But I promise you, my love, I'll come up with one.*


Serena knelt behind Imani, placed her hands on either side of her head, and joined her mind with Imani's.

*Your body is empty. Your mind has joined with another.*

*Yes, I am with High Priestess Tamara, and things are not as they should be.*

*How so?*

*Our young Dava is ill, and even with all our knowledge, we cannot heal him.*

Serena was saddened by this news, for she knew all too well what was transpiring. *Forgive me, I know why he is ill, and I am at fault.*

*You? What are you not telling me?*

*Are you with us, High Priestess Tamara?*

*Yes, I am. What is happening to my son?*

*Imani must return. I will require her strength as well as Lord Adeeowale's to conquer the evil that threatens our very existence. You must take great care of your son. He is under a curse that will rid him of who he is.*

*For what purpose?*
*To become a vessel for Lord Joshawa.*

Nathen rested his head against the massive redwood, his eyes closed, his thoughts on Authia. She was right—he wasn't thinking clearly. Nathen was brought back to reality when Adrian knelt in front of him. His voice was raised but still just above a whisper, and he was pointing in the direction of the cabin.

"Go after them! You can take them!"

Nathen glanced in the direction of the cabin, then returned his focus on Adrian. "Going after them will not solve our problem. It will only add to it."

"I don't understand. You need the GPS to find Joshawa. Why not just take it?"

"There's no way I can just take it without the possibility of one or both of them getting hurt. We need to find another way to obtain the GPS. Take Billy home. This is my problem now."

"You surprise me, Nathen. You could easily just kill those two men and take what you want. Nobody would be the wiser."

Nathen was disappointed that Adrian thought killing those men would be an option. "That's not who I am." Nathen looked back toward the cabin, and from what he could see, Jax and Dameon were long gone. He stood and walked to the edge of the clearing, staying just inside the tree line.

Adrian stood by the redwood tree staring at Nathen in disbelief. He could have easily torn those men apart and recovered the GPS. Nathen had the opportunity to find Joshawa, but instead, he did nothing. Was he waiting for Adrian and Billy to leave before he revealed his true self?

Adrian observed Nathen as he looked over his shoulder at

Billy. Nathen's expression was not of anger, but rather concern and maybe even fear. The man Adrian thought he knew was not the man he was traveling with. Adrian was conflicted — so much was going through his mind. Was Nathen cleverly disguising the monster that he truly was so that he could trick Adrian into trusting him? Or was Becca right, and Nathen was the kind and gentle man she claimed him to be?

Time would tell. But until he knew for sure, Adrian would continue to keep his guard up and expect the monster.

Authia had brought an old wooden chair from Edward's office and placed it next to the surgery table. The table had been lowered so that when Authia sat next to it, she could easily rest her arms close to Becca. She held Becca's right hand within both of hers and waited for the propofol to take effect.

"You are so brave, Becca. I can't even begin to describe how much this means to Nathen and me."

Becca moved her head slightly to the side and smiled at Authia. "I would do anything for Joshawa." Authia could see that Becca could barely keep her eyes open. "I love him so . . ." Becca's voice trailed off as her head drooped against her pillow.

Authia glanced over to Tammy. "Is she ready?"

"Yes, she's ready. Take care of her while you're rattling around in there."

"I will." Authia closed her eyes as she gently squeezed Becca's hand. Her mind became one with Becca's. Only this time, she delved even deeper than she had before. Authia hoped that if she dug deep enough, she would be able to separate Joshawa from Becca and see only what Joshawa saw.

*I'm here, Joshawa. I'm with Becca. Show me what you see.*

Authia tried to focus on what Joshawa had shown her before. She searched for an image of the tree he'd fallen from and for the bear that charged the tree. But all she found was darkness.

*Please, Joshawa, hear me. Your father and I are trying to find you, but we need your help.*

The darkness started to lift, and Authia could see Nathen. He was behind the cabin, chopping wood.

*That's good, Joshawa. I see your father chopping wood. Can you show me where you are now?*

The vision of Nathen chopping wood swirled around her, and within seconds it cleared, and she could see Dameon staring up at her.

*Yes. This is where you fell. What did you see next?*

Once again, the vision swirled around her. Only this time it didn't completely clear. One minute she could see the ground, it was a couple of feet beneath her, and it was moving as if she were floating above it. The next minute the vision went dark. There was no swirling effect, only darkness. Authia could sense that Joshawa was confused, as if his mind were not a part of him.

Then the darkness cleared, and again she saw the ground.

*I'm not understanding what you're showing me. Joshawa, you have to focus. Focus on the present. Show me where you are right now. Becca loves you and wants you to come home, help her find you.*

The darkness cleared and a blue light, soft and shimmering, filled Authia's mind.

*Serena, you're with my son, aren't you? You're protecting him. But why are you protecting him from us? Help us find him.*

Authia focused on the blue light, trying to see past it. Trying to see what Serena was hiding.

*Whispers. Whispers in the wind. I hear whispers in the wind.*

Authia gasped. She heard him. She knew it had to be Joshawa.

*I hear you, Joshawa, but it's not whispers you're hearing. It's me. It's your mother. Show me where you are. Show me something so your father can find you.*

The blue light swirled around Authia's mind, spinning faster and faster. Blended into the blue light was a glimpse of something dark.

*Slow down, Joshawa. Your mind is racing. Calm yourself, so I can see what you're trying to show me.*

As if Joshawa understood what was being asked of him, the blue light started to slow, and the brown blur began to take shape. After a few more passes, Authia knew what Joshawa was showing her.

*Thank you, Serena. I know you've taken part in this. Joshawa, I understand what you've shown me. Stay safe. Your father is coming for you.*

Lord Chike purposely avoided the tribe members and headed toward the outskirts of the village. He didn't want to interact with any of them or the Council, for that matter. To Lord Chike, they were beneath him, therefore they were a waste of his time. There was only one tribe member that he cared to visit, and that was only because he could torment him, make him suffer, hear him plead for death and never grant it.

A sinister smile crossed his lips as he thought of the tribe member, his prisoner for eternity. This prisoner was his revenge on the Lord who had not only scared his face, but on that same day, almost vanquished him. Lord Chike vowed that he would never again allow his life to be exposed to the darkness of death.

Jax followed Dameon down the mountain toward the main road. It was an arduous trek with nothing to mark the way. Usually they would use colored tape to mark the trees, but Dameon decided he didn't need the tape. That proved troublesome for Jax, because he wasn't as familiar with the GPS as Dameon was. Jax had to make sure that the trek to the main road was being recorded to the GPS memory, so he decided it was time for a break.

"Dameon, wait up. I need some water." Jax took off his backpack and straddled an old tree that had fallen to the ground. He watched as Dameon turned to face him.

"Getting old? We've only been hiking for half an hour."

"Yeah, well, it's not like we're following a well-traveled path. Are you sure that this is the most direct path to the road?"

Dameon's expression went from mildly annoyed to pissed off. Jax held his tongue, hoping if he remained silent, Dameon would calm down and play right into his hand. Which was exactly what Dameon did.

"No, it's not."

Jax was actually surprised by Dameon's answer. It wasn't what he was expecting. However, he was right about keeping silent. Dameon took the bait and laughed at Jax as he joined him on the tree.

"What the hell is so funny? And what do you mean that we aren't taking a direct route?" Jax reached for his canteen and placed it in front of him.

"Sorry." Dameon smiled at Jax as he let go of the GPS, which allowed it to hang from the strap around his neck. "I'm not taking us to the road. I'm taking us to our vehicle."

Jax took a gulp of water then offered the canteen to Dameon. "Isn't that the same thing?"

Dameon passed on the offer of water. "Not really. If we head straight to the main road, then we'll have to walk at least two miles down the road to get to our vehicle. That exposes us to somebody stopping and asking questions we don't want to answer."

Jax felt like an idiot. He was so wrapped up in wanting to find a way to the road from the cabin that he forgot about the vehicle. If he kept making stupid mistakes like that, Dameon would catch on to what Jax was doing. Jax shook his head as he smiled at Dameon. "Wow. I can't believe that I missed that. I guess that's why you have the GPS."

"You got that right. So if you're rested enough, how about we continue. We still have at least another hour or two before we get to the vehicle." Dameon smiled at Jax as he stood up. "Even longer if you have to take a break every half-hour."

Jax picked up his backpack and started to put it back on. "I was thinking . . ."

Dameon laughed. "Well, that's a first."

Jax tried to appear very serious. "This is important. You didn't want to tape the trees because you have the GPS."

"So?"

"What if something happened to you. How the hell am I going to find my way back?"

"Nothing's going to happen to me."

"And what if it does? I'm damn good at what I do, but even the best trackers can get lost in the woods."

"Jax, you're not going to get lost. If anything happens to me, you have the GPS."

"That only works if you're saving this hike from hell to the memory."

Dameon shook his head at Jax. "What the hell is wrong with you? You know I save everything to the memory." Dameon turned, muttered something under his breath, and continued making his way down the mountain.

Jax snapped the buckle that secured the backpack to his waist. Everything was falling into place. He'd already decided that he wasn't going to sell the creature, and he definitely wasn't going to release him. He'd find the creature and bring him back to the small cabin. Then he could take his time with it, dissecting and torturing him. When he was done, he would use the GPS to guide him off the mountain.

Jax picked up the pace to close the gap between him and

Dameon. Dameon was a liability, but he was also Jax's best friend. He wouldn't let Dameon suffer. Jax decided the best way to neutralize Dameon was a bullet to his head. Then he would bury him under the pit that was filled with bones. Jax was giddy with the anticipation of finally acting out what he had spent years dreaming of.

Billy remained sitting on the ground hiding behind the bushes. He took no notice of the fact that Adrian was no longer beside him. Billy was focused on something much more important. He watched as the two men left the cabin and entered the woods. Billy cautiously observed the cabin, for he believed that the evil that resided within would come out and chase after the two men. But nothing happened.

He watched as the two men disappeared into the woods. Memories from the cabin that he used to call home flooded his mind, which caused tears to run down his cheeks. However, he would endure a lifetime of nightmares if it meant he would never have to enter the cabin where pain, suffering, and death made their home.

Billy glanced in the direction of the smaller cabin, and even though it had been vacant for many years, he could still hear the screams, both animal and human. He could smell the blood, and he could hear his brother's laughter.

Billy closed his eyes and thought of the girl that was so kind to him. She could always take the pain away. She could save him from his nightmares. Now it was his turn to save Amelia. Billy opened his eyes and focused on the cabin that the two men came from.

He had to be brave for Amelia, but most importantly, he had to save her from the evil. Billy decided that the cabin was safe, at least for now, and if he hurried, he could be gone before the evil returned. Billy stood, not taking his focus off the cabin door. He knew what he had to do, so he left the safety of the forest and started to walk toward the cabin.

Joshawa had remained on the cold floor of the cave for what seemed like hours. For reasons he didn't understand, Amy was reluctant to help him become more mobile. He stared at the ceiling and wondered why his parents hadn't found him. How long had he been here? How long before he was strong enough to walk down the mountain?

Joshawa had given up the idea of using Alex to get off the mountain. Alex protected Amy, so there was no way he would leave her, and Joshawa doubted that Amy would venture past her comfort zone. Joshawa was beginning to believe that the bitter taste of reality was that he would never leave this cave. He closed his eyes and started to cry. His mother's vision had become a reality, and this cave would be his tomb.

To Be Continued . . .

# ABOUT THE AUTHOR

Christine Frances was born July 29, 1958, in Halifax, Nova Scotia, Canada. She was born to a military family, her father being in the Royal Canadian Navy. Her passion for writing started at an early age with her seventh-grade teacher, Sister Lambert, playing an influential part in developing Christine's love for short stories. After a period in Christine's life when she put down her pen to run her own business, raise two boys and become a grandmother, the desire to write once again took over and the series Lord of His People was born.

Manufactured by Amazon.ca
Bolton, ON